'Excuse me. Where will I find Weight Watchers?'

'*You* want the Weight Watchers meeting?' The Sumoette behind the church office counter licked bits of glaze from her fingers and scanned me suspiciously. A Dunkin' Donuts box sat open on the desk behind her.

'Yes, please.' And maybe just the tiniest bite of donut.

'End of the hall,' she said, air-drying her fingers as she waved me out of her office, 'and down the stairs.'

I fell in behind a moving line of assorted-sized women. Aunts at a picnic. Hey, what's in the basket? Pistachio-studded duck pâté, a crusty french baguette, a creamy wheel of brie, a bottle of slightly fruity white, bunches of red seedless. Food. Lately, it was all I thought about – when I wasn't thinking of cigarettes. Twenty-five-year-old, three-pack-a-day habits are a bitch to break.

The Dieter

Susan Sussman

HEADLINE

Copyright © 1989 Susan Sussman

First published in Great Britain in 1989
by HEADLINE BOOK PUBLISHING PLC

First published in paperback in 1989
by HEADLINE BOOK PUBLISHING PLC

10 9 8 7 6 5 4 3 2

Published by arrangement with POCKET BOOKS,
a division of Simon & Schuster Inc

ISBN 0 7472 3315 2

Typeset in 10/12½ pt English Times by
Colset Private Limited, Singapore

Printed and bound in Great Britain by
Collins, Glasgow

HEADLINE BOOK PUBLISHING PLC
Headline House
79 Great Titchfield Street
London W1P 7FN

For Barry

ACKNOWLEDGEMENTS

For my friends, anorexic to obese, who fight the losing fight and who, over a two-year period, generously shared highly personal and often poignant stories of their struggles.

Special thanks to Attorney Arthur Rissman, Private Detective Joe Mahr, Francess Dincin, MSW, Sandra Hochman, Karen Lee, and field researchers Susi Goldstein and Sharon Bland for supplying professional and technical data. I am grateful to author Mary Shura Craig, literary agent Jane Jordan Browne and editor Jane Chelius for their insightful suggestions, and, as always, I am indebted to Barry Sussman, my brilliant and enthusiastic first reader.

FEBRUARY

105

ONE

I froze the way I did every morning, my hand gripping the metal door handle to room 235, my eyes fixed on the temporary name plate: Patient: QUINLIN, SARAJANE. Need a cigarette. Have to wait. Barely eight o'clock in the morning and the taste of my sixth Benson and Hedges – sucked to the filter while waiting for the hospital elevator – was fading to a stale memory.

All right body, front and center. Hup two, three, four. Hey, gang, it's time to Exorcise with Barbara. Hup two, three, four. Fear, Anguish, Hate – over there. Hup two – Hey, Anger, line up with the others. Nice demons. Don't move. I'll pick you up on my way out. Don't I always?

The dark room reeked of death. I held my breath, tiptoeing past Sarajane's bed to the windows, cracking them open to a thin stream of frigid February air. Only three cones of incense left in the box I'd hidden behind the curtain. I'd need to buy another box. Please God. I set one cone on the window ledge and held a shaking match to the tip. It glowed red in the icy wind and I pulled the sweet musk smoke deep into my lungs.

The shadow of her voice crept up behind me. 'You are going . . . to get us both kicked . . . out of here.'

'You still in bed?'

'I had a big . . . date last night.' Her eyes closed from the effort of two complete sentences. I walked to the bundle of flesh-coated sticks and stroked her feverish forehead.

'Robert Redford?' I asked. She shook her head. Limp strings stuck out of her scalp where thick red curls should have been. 'No? Who then? Selleck? Reynolds? Arnold Schwartzendooglehauffernager?'

Her sunken eyes fluttered open. They sparkled. She was still fighting. Her words crinkled like dead leaves. 'Woody Allen.'

'You are so warped.' I reached for the soft baby brush on her nightstand. Had to keep busy. Hard for pain to hit a moving target. Serpentine. Serpentine.

'You know beauty bo-ahs me,' she said, the edges of her words laced with threads from a Louisiana childhood.

'Thanks a lot.' I stroked the brush gently over her wisps of hair.

'Don't get uppity. I knew your nose when it hooked over your chin.'

'Then you will also please remember,' I sniffed haughtily, giving her my best profile, 'this emergency rhinoplasty was necessary to correct a deviated septum.'

'Lotta big words.'

'It was a lotta big nose.'

Old joke. Old friends. She drew thin lips into what

had become her smile. It broke my heart. 'All right, Insurance Breath,' she said, 'let's just say *male* beauty bores me.'

'I'm going to tell Stanford you said that.'

'Gotta find him first. Man's very busy.'

Her eyes closed again. My three minutes were up. Please deposit another . . . another what? I needed more time. Please. I was glad she could rest but jealous of the time it stole from us.

Quietly setting the brush on her nightstand, I began my morning ritual. If I straightened the room *exactly* the way I had the morning before, Sarajane would live one more day. Set the maribou-edged mule slippers – open toes bowing toward Bloomingdales – one inch out from the bed. Triple fold the Christian Dior satin robe lengthwise and lay it across the foot of her bed. Nothing had been moved since the day before but I straightened the room anyway. Franklin called me compulsive. I called me neat. Through the years, I'd tried not to clean while he was home. Sarajane didn't mind if I cleaned, even when she was well enough to notice.

I checked her nightstand drawer for supplies. Unspent money for newspapers she couldn't hold, television she didn't notice. An unopened carton of Camels. The need to suck smoke shook me like a death rattle. Hey, Pavlov, it works. I'd been off the weed for fifteen whole minutes, give or take a millennium. I could survive a little longer without a cigarette. I think I can I think I can. Under the carton were four clippings of my 'Ask Barbara' columns, one for each week she'd been here. She was the only person besides me who'd read every word I'd published. And then there was one.

'It looks like a blue ribbon day,' I said, taking out the shoebox filled with bits and pieces I'd brought over the past month. Offerings to appease the god of Lung Cancer. Ribbons for her hair. *Please don't take my friend.* Rosy beige foundation to cover the gray. *I've never asked for anything before.* Silly jewelry to gladden the soul. *She is the only true friend I've ever had.*

I dug through the box for Dick Tracy badges and pinned one on each of us.

'O.K. Crime Stoppers,' I said, pulling out two yellow strips of thin satin ribbon. 'Let's disguise ourselves.'

'You said a blue ribbon day.'

'These are blue.'

'Those are yellow.'

'My god, you're eyes are going! Call the healers. Get a colorectomy team in here. Stat!' I waved the ribbons under her nose. 'Smell.' She sniffed.

'You're right,' she said. 'Blue.'

'Never trust your eyes, Sarajane. Life is all illusion.'

Thin-veined eyelids fluttered like moth wings against the light. 'There's some culture,' she rasped, 'where a person who is dying changes clothes with someone who is healthy. That way,' she paused for breath, 'when Death comes collecting, he doesn't recognize the dying person. Passes right by, slick as snot.'

THE DIETER

I ran a few strands of her hair through my fingers. 'Why doesn't Death take the friend?'

'Can't. The friend's healthy. Death figures he made a mistake and takes a hike.'

The ribbon blurred as I braided it into her hair.

'Sarajane Quinlin, I *knew* this whole hospital routine was a con.' I tugged the thin braid gently. 'You're after my new suit. You expect me to swap my first Ungaro for a used hospital gown.' I began another braid. 'You are so perverse.'

She rolled her head toward Amelia Bearhart. The stuffed bear hung goggled and scarved, flying for her life from the bedside IV. 'First time in thirty years I can fit into my best friend's clothes,' Sarajane whispered to Amelia. 'You'd think the woman would share.'

Amelia swayed sympathetically.

I clasped my hands together, pleading. 'Take my husband. My children. My recipe for Oriental Chicken Salad. Name it. It's yours.'

'The suit.'

'God's punishing me for paying retail.'

'The suit.'

'You always were pushy.'

That smile again. Colorless lips stretched over beautiful teeth.

'Imagine *me* being able to fit more than my left thigh into one of *your* skirts . . .' Voice cracking like a dry river bed, '. . . well, I always said I'd absolutely *die* for cheekbones . . .' Her eyes closed. Tomorrow I'd bring the Ungaro.

She made a soft, smacking sound. I dipped my fingers into her water glass and slid them along her parchment lips. She hadn't vomited yet. That would come. I settled into the chair next to her and slipped my hand under hers, waiting.

'And now, class, we have two new students to meet today. Barbara, Sarajane, please come to the front of the room.'

I slid out of my seat graceful as a cat and affected a West Side Story chic, as if my world weren't spinning, as if my head weren't about to fly off. I felt the stares of my new fourth-grade classmates as I sauntered to the front of the room in one of my father's old shirts and skin-tight jeans. I'd give these midwest hicks a lesson in cool.

Two rows over, the other new girl bumped against desks, knocking off papers and pencils on her way to the front. White and formless as the Pillsbury dough boy, she'd been stuffed into a blue satin puffy-sleeved dress. A sash designed to tie around her waist inched up in front, hiking the hem enough to expose a white lace slip. Her thick red hair, tortured into hundreds of ringlets, sagged and drooped in the humid spring air. It was one of those rare times I didn't mind being motherless. Not that any mother of mine would ever do to me what this girl's mother had done to her. I hooked my thumbs through my jean loops and stood off to one side so my new classmates wouldn't associate me with this great blue whale.

'Barbara Marlow is from New York,' said the teacher. I shifted my weight to one leg, trying to look

8

casually worldly as she read what I'd written on my Student Information Sheet. 'Barbara says she likes writing, playing sports, shopping at Bloomies, and watching experimental films. She lists her favorite hobby as dodging muggers.' I smiled. No one smiled back. I shrank, my cheeks burning. 'Dodging muggers' had seemed so sophisticated when I'd filled out the information sheet in New York. The line sure as hell didn't play in Peoria.

'And, Sarajane Thomson is from New Orleans where . . .'

My head snapped around. What about my father! What about the part where I wrote my father is the new editor-in-chief of your daily rag? Hey. Wait. How's anybody supposed to know who I am?!

Walking home, I discovered Sarajane and I were Astor Street neighbors. I'd find out what time she left for school so I could beat it by a good ten minutes.

'I liked that bit about dodging muggahs,' she said. 'Wish I'd thought of writing down something interesting.'

Well, maybe I'd walk with her the first week. Until I decided what crowd to hang with. We'd bonded like epoxy, prowling the city, discovering boys, sharing our first cigarette at fourteen. In college we declared both cigarettes and sex overrated, and found only one addictive. At twenty-five, we each married and settled two blocks apart in lakefront mini-mansions on Chicago's North Shore. We talked every day, did lunch at least three days a week, and went to California twice a year for our spa fix.

*Over the years I forgave Sarajane her Southern
softness and she forgave me my Eastern arrogance. We
were as unlikely and as perfect as s'mores, losing the
shape of who we were BC, Before Chicago, as we
melded into each other.*

Sarajane moaned. Her hand on mine was without
substance, the bent stick fingers weightless as a daddy
long-legs. Too shrunken to support Sarajane's jewel-
encrusted rings, the naked hand was an abstract of blue
veins, clear tubes, yellow skin, old IV marks. Her eyes
opened slightly.

'You still here?'

Stanford called at midnight.

I'd been standing in my closet, crying, trying to find
a garment bag for the suit. In the room behind me,
Letterman's 'Stupid Pet Tricks' mixed with Franklin's
post-sex snoring. I'd knocked him out with the quality
of sex usually reserved for birthdays, anniversaries and
gifts received. Franklin wouldn't understand what I
intended to do with the silk suit whose price he still
managed to drop into conversations. 'Well, I just paid
this month's rent on Ungaro's villa.' Ha ha. 'We'd love
to meet you for dinner. How about Burger King? My
wife just bought a new Ungaro.' Hee hee.

'Barbara?' Stanford's nauseating nasal voice
squeezed through the receiver. 'The hospital just
called.' Pause, two, three. Sigh, two, three. A ham
actor doing grief and stoicism. 'Sarajane's gone.'

'Where?'

'What?'

'Nothing.' A joke, son. Shame on me. I lit up. A no-no in the bedroom. Sorry Franklin. 'What can I do to help?'

'Well, first . . .' Never a doubt he'd have a list, neatly typed, alphabetical order. I copied everything down, mashing the pen's felt tip, the splayed fibers leaving tails on the nearly illegible words.

I spent the night in the living room staring out the huge picture window, a tumbler of J&B in one hand, cigarette in the other. A ridge of jagged ice edged Lake Michigan like a crumpled Cristo. Endless moon-tipped waves washed in over the ice. I willed them to stop. Just once. A small sign that Sarajane had passed this way. They kept coming.

'Stop, damn you!' The waves moved in and in and in.

Death dug in its claws and pulled out a chunk of me. The pain was beyond bearing. Her passage through this world, through my life, could not go unmarked. I pulled a cigarette from the pack and picked up the heavy Ronson from the table. Sarajane's death demanded a tribute as dynamic as our friendship. My hands shook. I pushed down on the Ronson once, twice. Spark. Spark. No fire.

'Come on, come on.' Cigarette clenched between my teeth, body tensed with anticipation. 'Come. Fucking. On.' Spark. Spark. Shazaam! I brought the flame toward the cigarette. And I knew. I didn't want to, but I knew what the gesture would be. Had to be. It was the one gesture in the world powerful enough to say how much I loved her.

I clicked off the lighter, snapped the cigarette in two, and poured scotch into the rest of the pack. With shaking hands, I drowned the butts that overflowed the ashtray. Staggering to the kitchen, I grabbed the two full cartons from the pantry and one half-empty pack out of the cutlery drawer.

The back door opened to a punch of cold air. Clutching the cartons to my breast, I slid across the children's makeshift ice rink, clamboring up its low bank toward the lake. My slippers skidded on the ice. Bitter night air reached under my nightgown freezing my skin in its grip. No going back. No stopping. I had the big mo. Gotta be now or never. I slipped, cracked my knees on the ice, forced myself up and slipped again. Feet numb, knees throbbing, fingers not working, I reached the border of ice. Screaming, I hurled the first carton at the lake.

'I HOPE YOU'RE HAPPY SARAJANE QUINLIN.' The words skipped along the water and disappeared. The carton hit the waves and floated.

'WHAT THE HELL AM I SUPPOSED TO DO FOR THE *NEXT* THIRTY YEARS?' The second carton caught the brink of the ice and teetered. A wave lapped over the edge and floated the carton away. I ripped open the half-pack, shredding strands of tobacco onto the ice.

'Ashes to ashes,' I said between sobs, tears freezing on my face. 'And dust to dust.' I crumpled the empty package and hurled it at the water. 'Sarajane Quinlin, you goddamn friend-leaving fink, I commend your sweet Southern soul to the sea.' My body jerked in uncontrollable spasms. Partly from the cold, but mostly from the anguish and terror of losing my two best friends in one night. How would I face the morning without them?

I watched the cartons bob on the waves. Not so far out that I couldn't reach them. The packs inside would still be dry. I might have to lay spread eagle on the ice and stretch way out. I took two steps toward them then forced myself to turn away and walk back toward the house.

MARCH

115–130

TWO

'Back already?' Franklin stood towel-wrapped and dripping in front of the wall of steamed mirrors. I sucked in the muggy bathroom air. It was like breathing oatmeal. Brown sugar, milk, a sprinkle of raisins. I will not think about food. I will not think. I will not. The chill of the March morning melted from my clothes. Ice cube in chicken soup. Ritz crackers on the side. I will not think. I peeled off my mittens and hat. Franklin flicked on the hair blower and neatly defogged a hole over the sink. His face, on the craggy side of handsome, still gave me pause. I slithered up behind him, slipping my arms around his firm waist. 'Hey.' He jerked away, shivering. 'You're cold and sweaty.'

'Am not,' I said, needing to hold him. I stripped off my barely damp warm-ups, my long johns, my walking bra, my Calvin jocks, and pressed my body against his back, molding myself to him.

'Come on, Barbara.' He massaged mousse into his hair.

'Kids are off to school.' I blew a warm stream of air along his neck.

'Hon, I've got a breakfast strategy meeting.'

He combed and picked his hair. A thick blond forest grew from last year's transplants. I set my chin on his spine and butterflied my body down his, lightly, slowly, my hands untying the towel at his waist.

'Bwabwa!' He brushed and spat. Water Pik, unwaxed floss, Pearl Drops, Crest. The man had feelings about his teeth. I circled the tip of my tongue gently in the dimple at the base of his spine. He tasted faintly of soap. In front, my hands stroked, tickled, fondled. Nothing. Not his fault. Franklin was not a morning person.

He turned, lifting me by the elbows. His warm hands pressed against my cold cheeks as he kissed me quickly and not unkindly on the lips. 'Hold that thought,' he said.

Seduced and abandoned. Well, one outta two. Franklin entered the shaving, deodorant phase. I sat on the edge of the tub and turned the gilded wings that sent water spewing out the swan's mouth. Franklin had reached mid-lather. Barring nicks, I had two minutes of his undivided attention.

'I'm going to quit my morning walk,' I said quietly.

'Ummmm?'

'It's boring.'

'Sure that's not a cop-out?' He snapped the orange top off a Bic disposable. The sterling silver Elsa Peretti sat plastic-wrapped against tarnish in his Gucci dop kit on the top shelf of his closet. There were items he kept 'for good' and items he used every day. Hereditary. The beaded cashmere sweater I'd given his mother in honor of our wedding sat plastic wrapped on the top shelf of her closet. She'd worn it seventeen times in as many years, when she served us our specially ordered from the butcher prime rib Mott's applesauce twice baked potato sourdough rolls from my own starter Klaussin dill pickle Grandma Aver's secret recipe double chocolate cheese cake I've been on my feet all day in a hot kitchen and you two pick at your food like a couple of birds anniversary meal.

'It's not a cop-out,' I said. 'The walk's not the same without Sarajane.'

'Unnnggghhh.' His eyebrows bowed sympathetically as he de-fuzzed his Adam's apple.

'There's no magic. You know those two old housebreakers Sarajane spotted, the ones who use their morning walk as a cover while they case houses? I saw them today.' I flicked my fingers through the stream of water. It was just this side of scalding. The pain was comforting. 'Without Sarajane, they looked like two old people out for a walk.' His left eyebrow arched compassionately.

New bath steam merged with the old. I heard my hair kink. Franklin's mirror fogged over his half-shaven face. Ghosts of electric bills past haunted his eyes as he switched on the exhaust fan and heat lamp. I stretched out on the thick white carpet, staring at myself in the de-misting mirrored ceiling. The ten new pounds had distributed themselves evenly over my body and the weight barely showed. That didn't stop the hysteria I felt each morning as the scale's needle inched up and up and up. Except for pregnancies, I'd never let myself gain more than two pounds. As soon as that needle hit 107, I cut out wine with dinner or dinner with wine until my weight was back to normal. I had to do something before Franklin noticed. He had unbridled contempt for fat women like his mother and sisters. Franklin never understood how I could love Sarajane.

I stretched my arms enticingly over my head, arching my hip bones heavenward. A scene from a high-class porno flick. Lush body in a lush setting. Franklin scraped the hairs off his right cheek. Oh, for a masked man in gartered black socks and a director yelling 'Action'. I criss-crossed my hands on my chest, bent my knees, and started my fifty sit-ups.

'The worst part about walking without Sarajane . . . is it's taking me . . . twice as long to . . . walk half as far.'

'You're doing those too fast,' said Franklin, turning off my half-filled tub. I slowed down.

'This morning I cut across lawns . . . crossed streets on the diagonal.'

'That hardly makes sense.' He scraped his left cheek. 'You're walking for exercise, not to make good time.'

'Sarajane's . . . not there to tell me not to.'

He shook aftershave into his palm and slapped his face gingerly. 'How about finding someone else to walk with?'

'How about you?'

'Barb, you know I don't have that kind of time.'

Never had it, never will. He ran his pinky around the inside of his ear, wiping out a speck of shaving cream. 'The Fitzpatrick case is up for trial. Between that and my campaign, I'm lucky if I can put in an hour at the gym at lunch. What about joining some of those women I see walking up and down Sheridan Road every morning. Lydia Collins, she's always walking her dog.'

'I've seen horses . . . smaller than that Doberman.' My abdomen ached from hauling the ten new pounds off the floor. 'Besides, I'm not about to spend an hour a day with a woman who's . . . cornered the market in black leather. You know, Sarajane had some intriguing ideas about Lydia and that dog.'

'Sarajane had intriguing ideas about a lot of things.' Death had not softened his contempt. No hypocrite, he. Franklin sucked in his non-existent gut, posed like a Greek discus thrower, and turned slowly, scrutinizing his athlete's body from all angles. 'All right, then, what about Rita Frantz?'

'She walk-runs. Does a four-minute mile . . . Woman has an ego problem. I'm not training for the Olympics.'

Franklin faced me dead on, hands on slender hips, the family jewels dangling just out of grabbing range. 'Betsy Gollub?'

'Slooooowwwwww. She stroooools.'

He knelt between my legs, and I kissed him briefly at the top of a sit-up. 'Barbara, I know it's hard for you without Sarajane.' A knot tightened in my chest. 'But you can't stop your life. That's the last thing

Sarajane would have wanted. Don't give up your walk.' He rested a hand on my inner thigh. Before I could get excited, he pinched an inch. 'It's your only exercise.'

I slipped my arms around his neck, pulling him down on me. 'Not my *only* exercise.' I licked after-shave off his left earlobe, needing the feel of his weight on me, anchoring me.

'Barb . . .'

'Mmmmm?'

'I don't . . .'

'Won't take long.' It didn't.

Later, floating in the tub, I tried to plan my day. My thoughts wouldn't focus. Needed a cigarette. I nudged the left swan's wing with my toes, starting a trickle of steaming water around my feet. Pain, I'd found, was distracting. I leaned my head back, watching my fragmented body in the ceiling tiles. The night he'd proposed over a Pump Room dinner, Franklin had removed a folded magazine page from his wallet.

'When you're the oldest of ten kids in a one-bathroom apartment, you have certain dreams,' he'd said, tenderly unfolding the worn photo.

I expected to see a mansion, fancy car, exotic honeymoon suite. What I got was a double-page spread of Louis Armstrong's bathroom. Satchmo's smiling face reflected off hundreds of mirrored strips which covered every square inch of the room. I sensed Franklin and the tinseled toilet were a two-fer. No problem. I'd dated men obsessed with expensive cars, slobbering family hounds, exotic stocks, obscure

operas, manipulative mothers, three-on-three basketball games, wine cellars, fox-hunting, art films, slo-
pitch softball, tournament bridge, body-building,
sailing, skeet-shooting, self-awareness groups, and
Bach fugues. I'd dated handsomer men, men with
greater humor, sensitivity, and wealth. But what
Franklin Avers had, the rare trait I'd seen in four,
maybe five people in my life, was power. Franklin
exuded power. It rushed from him like a tidal wave,
pushing aside everything and anything in his path. He
was an up and comer, a mover and shaker, and I
found power sexy as hell. If a totally mirrored bathroom was part of the Franklin Avers package, so be it.
I'd patted his hand reassuringly, said I Do, and
bought stock in Windex.

Franklin, nearly dressed and trailing the scent of
Gianfranco Ferre, reentered the bathroom for our
morning conference.

'I miss the Old Spice,' I said.

'I haven't used that since high school,' he said,
handing me my notebook and pencil. 'It's too
old-fashioned.'

'Not for me.'

'You're not my campaign advisors.' He set his
check list on the sink and began tying his tie. For years
this moment had been one of my daily light-up cues. I
pushed the pencil into the paper, bracing against a
wave of withdrawal.

'My new suit and pants should be ready at Bixby's,'
he said. 'I put two shirts on the bed for the laundry to
do over. They left spots on the striped and pressed a

crease into the front of the blue.' As he rattled off his list, he made a small neat check-mark next to each item to indicate he was finished with it. 'Make June, July, and August reservations in Springfield. Round-trip air, rooms. I have the dates and hotels here.' Check.

'The kids will be in camp July and August,' I said. 'Maybe I'll go to Springfield with you.'

'Fundraising is a madhouse. I'll be running around from group to group. There's nothing there for you to do. You'd go crazy. Then you'd drive me crazy.'

I sucked on the pencil and inhaled. 'You're going alone?'

'Of course I'm not going alone.' He fumbled the knot and ripped the tie off. 'I'll have the p.r. crew with me. They'll be shooting footage for commercials.' He flipped the tie over his head and began again.

I puffed the pencil. No kick. 'What if the hotels want a deposit? Do you want it charged to your business account or –'

'There.' Hands busy knotting, he jutted his chin toward three checks on the sink. 'Use those to open an account at the Highland Bank under "Avers for Senator". Have them print the campaign headquarters address and phone number on the checks.'

'Wouldn't it be more convenient to use Stone Federal?'

'Their new computer system's a joke. They're averaging one error per statement. I can't risk them mixing my business and campaign accounts. That's all I need is a scandal over misuse of funds.'

I checked over my notes for loose ends. The page was filled with curls and lines, a throwback to my years at the *Globe*. 'Only hacks leave themselves at the mercy of dead tape recorder batteries and steno pools,' warned my father. He didn't hire hacks, even if they were his daughter. Especially if they were. I spent my college summers juggling an internship at the paper with steno school.

Franklin wiggled the knot side to side, pushing it snugly against his charcoal gray collar. Seventeen years of pale shirts and dark ties had been banished in the blink of a p.r. director's eye. He scanned his list. 'That should do it,' he said.

'Here.' I handed him my notebook and pencil which he put next to the three checks on the sink. His body was still in the room but I could feel his thoughts moving on into his day. 'Franklin?' I called him back. 'You won't forget Rikki's play tonight?'

He winced. 'Tonight?'

'Eight o'clock.'

'Damn. I'll have to meet you at the high school. I have a dinner meeting with Sam Rosenthal and the p.r. people to go over the layouts for the posters and flyers.'

'The tickets are on my dresser, you'd better take yours with you.' Franklin and I rarely arrived at functions together. My fault for being attracted to a high-powered overachiever. Sarajane said we all marry our fathers. Why didn't I remember mine was never home?

Franklin left for work and my gut lurched for a cigarette. My hand reflexed tubside. Not there. Not anywhere in the house. I slid under the water, releasing bubbles of air slowly through my nose. Not one puff since the night Sarajane died and not one second that I didn't miss it. I was not having a good time.

I came down to the kitchen later than usual. Sophia had cleaned the children's breakfast dishes and left to do the shopping. All right, Chubs, you've got to cut out the chocolate marshmallow cookie breakfasts. Seems like they're a tad more fattening than six cigarettes and half a pot of black coffee. If I was going to get a handle on my weight, I'd have to eat healthy. I chopped green pepper and onion in the *Cuisinart*, skittered margarine across a Teflon skillet, then dumped in the fixings while I started the coffee. Oh the smell of brewing coffee and sautéeing onion. Saliva poured like sweat down the sides of my tongue and I took a bite of bagel to tide me over. When the veggies browned, I beat two eggs into submission and cut in cubes of sharp Cheddar. The instant the mixture hit the pan, the phone rang.

'Mrs Avers?' The webby voice took forever to form the words. 'This is George Payne.' The pan billowed smoke. I stretched the coil of phone cord to the stove and shut off the flame.

'Yes?'

'I'm sorry to bother you at home,' switch the pan to a cool burner, take another bite of bagel, ease a

26

spatula under the eggs so they don't burn, 'but I can't seem to get hold of Mr Avers.' George Payne. The name clicked. 'Old George Payne-in-the-glass,' Franklin called him. His wife, Franklin's client, was dying from twenty years of inhaling some chemical on an assembly line. The company owners, it seemed, knew the stuff was toxic but failed to mention it to the employees.

'Oh, yepf, Mr Payne.' Swallow the bagel. 'Franklin has told me so much about you. He has been very busy lately. Running for State Senator, you know.' He didn't. 'Would you like to leave a message?' He would.

I sat at my kitchen desk, pushed aside the unopened 'Ask Barbara' letters, and took his message. Words poured from him like cold honey. Too slow for shorthand. Hell, too slow for longhand. I doodled elaborately around the words. 'Sorry to be late repaying loan. Wife suffered setback. Hope to put a few dollars down on what I owe real soon.' I knew his wife's case, knew the pain in his voice was real. I also knew the man was lonely and, according to Franklin, would stay on the phone for hours if I let him. I tried to comfort without encouraging conversation. The pencil point broke in mid-doodle and I took out a new one. That point broke. It defied every law of nature to try and carry on a telephone conversation without smoking a cigarette.

By the time I returned to the pan, the eggs had curled away from the edges and congealed around the limp vegetables. Half-melted cubes of cheese dotted the surface. It looked like fake vomit. I flipped the omelet bottom side up onto a plate, poured my coffee, and turned on Oprah. Cake mix commercial. I hunched over the plate, taking teeny bites, chewing each one twenty-seven times, ala the ashram. Sarajane and I would get hysterical trying to mimic the solemn faithful who seemed able to make brown rice and soybean curd *last* twenty-seven chews. We did much better after hours with the pizzas we sneaked in and washed down with bottles of rotgut red. The 'Inn of the Twenty-Seven Chews' was one of several health spas we were asked to leave over the years.

The television cake was mixed, baked, iced, and eaten. Yea for Mommy, she loves us. The scene dissolved to a commercial for frozen dinners. Yea for our working Mommy, she loves us. I chewed faster. Funny thing about that call from Mr Payne. I assumed the case had been settled. Franklin used to complain about Old Payne-in-the-glass constantly, but I hadn't heard the name in weeks. I'd have to remember to ask. Anyway, I was pleased Franklin had loaned poor Mr Payne money to help until the case was closed. I sometimes worried that years of handling personal injury cases had hardened Franklin. He could be brutally caustic when describing some of his clients.

Small bites or no, I'd finished breakfast in two minutes. Oprah came back as I tossed my dishes into the sink. Pretty lady. Energetic. Next to the newly slim Oprah and half her audience, I was positively svelte.

Today's topic was You and Your Mother. Oprah
raced up and down the aisles milking the audience for
stories. Didn't apply to me. I flicked off the set and
grabbed a chocolate marshmallow cookie on my way
out. One for the road. Try and plug up that mid-gut,
post-meal pothole I used to fill with smoke.

The bank's copier was working for a change and I
took out the three checks Franklin had given me to
open his new account. All three were from insurance
companies and had Franklin's little check-mark in the
upper-right-hand corner to indicate Case Settled. The
checks were made out to Franklin with the client's
names noted on the bottom. Marcia Hoffman.
Laurence Spagnoli. Thomas Cadbury. Cadbury.
Chocolate bars at the grocery check-out. Almond,
bittersweet. I lay the checks face down on the copier.
'Smile pretty,' I said, hitting the Print button. These
copies would begin my Campaign Funds file at home.
Careful recordkeeping skills were one of the assets
I'd brought to the marriage. If Franklin found
organization and efficiency sexy, who was I to
complain?

The Personal Banker spoke in triplicate. 'Please
have your husband and anyone else besides the two of
you who will be drawing money from this account fill
out one of these cards so we can have their signature
on file. They must fill out a card. We need their signature on file. Anybody who will be drawing money
from this account.' A perfectly good ashtray sat
unused on the desk.

'Thank you so much,' I said. 'So very much. Thank you.'

My infrequent visits to the bank always ended with a quick visit with Mother. The chill of the basement seeped into my bones as I walked down the stairs. Old Mrs Whittiker, framed by the vault door's huge metal gears and bolts, shivered behind her desk in one of her hand-knit sweaters. Stitches, randomly knitted and pearled, dropped and picked up, created quirky designs. The yarn she had used to join the left sleeve to the torso was from a different dye lot. 'With loving hands from home,' Grandma would have said. Had my mother knitted? I'd never thought to ask and now I'd never know. Five years ago my father died taking with him all the answers to all my future questions about my mother. I pulled our large safety deposit box out of the vault and followed Mrs Whittiker to one of the tiny rooms.

'Now, you call me, dear, if you need anything,' she said.

'I could do with a lasagna on rye, extra pickles.'

She smiled and nodded. 'That's right, dear. You just call.'

The door clicked shut and the overhead lights blinked on. The room smelled of stale air and cigarettes. No old butts in the ashtray. Waste basket empty. Must commend the bank on Mrs Whittiker's efficiency. Damn. Pulling up a chair, I set the unopened box on the table and stared at it for a long while.

'Sarajane's dead,' I said, running my fingers along

the cold metal. I opened the latch, eased back the hinged top, and lifted out Franklin's haphazard jumble of stock certificates, insurance policies, envelopes of all sizes, colors, and thickness. He was in and out of the box constantly, always at a run. I reached the bottom layer of red velvet cases and lifted them gently, lining them in front of me according to size. One by one I opened their tops.

'You're looking well,' I said. The diamonds, rubies, sapphires, and emeralds sparkled. I laid a couple of bracelets across my wrist. 'I'm afraid I've put on a bit of weight since you saw me. Can you tell? Do you mind? Dad said you never gained an ounce. Until I came along, of course.' Soft footsteps creaked the floor outside the door. Mrs Whittiker could never figure out who I talked to. 'Takes a worried man, to sing a worried song,' I sang. Her Red Cross oxfords padded away.

'I know I said I was going to give a part of you to Rikki on her sixteenth birthday. Maybe a ring, or a bracelet. I couldn't do it. She's too young. Maybe when she's eighteen. Girls today don't wear fancy jewelry. Maybe twenty-one. Or when she has her first child.' I was crying. I always cried. This was the part where I usually lit up. I dug in my coat pocket for a tissue.

'You should be proud of me. I quit smoking. Me. Cold turkey. Sort of my farewell tribute to Sarajane. I mean, there's no one else around who seems to care that she's gone. I couldn't *not* do anything. Who knows, might add a year or two to my life. Not that life seems –' I blew my nose noisily, ' – all that worth living without Sarajane and cigarettes.' Gently, I replaced the jewels in their satin-lined boxes. 'I promise to give some of you to Rikki when she's ready. When I'm ready.

'Aside from that,' I began arranging the boxes neatly into the deposit box, 'things are going along just great. Rikki's playing Amanda in *The Glass Menagerie* at school tonight. She's also taking driver's ed. Franklin won't let her practice driving his car and, since he doesn't like riding in mine, it's up to me to take her. I was all right until I stopped smoking. Now I jam my foot down on an imaginary brake, and jump when she gets too close to the cars on my side. She says I make her nervous. Last time I drank a shot of scotch before we left and Rikki said I seemed much calmer. Let's see. I'm still keeping a hand in, writing that weekly column for the *Globe*. Daddy warned me about getting newspaper ink in my veins.'

I closed the lid to the box and hugged it to me. I didn't want to leave her.

'Your grandson's been a little nervous lately. His big tough macho gang took a vote and decided that from now on it's all right for them to talk to girls. Jason was happier when girls were The Enemy. Poor kid's terrified that talking will lead to kissing. I don't have the heart to tell him what comes after *that*.

'Franklin's campaign is shaping up and I'm sure I'll wind up working for him nearly full-time. In a way, it will be a blessing to be busy. Since Sarajane died and I gave up smoking, I haven't been able to string two words together in a coherent way. You'd think after all those years at the *Globe* I could manage a few hundred lousy words a week. I mean, I can manage a few hundred lousy words. It's the good words I'm having trouble finding.'

Tears rolled off my cheeks onto the metal and I smeared them into designs with my finger. 'I think I understand a little of how Daddy felt when you died. It's like being – oh, I don't know – stranded. Or cast adrift. I'm feeling a little lonely.' I smeared the tears into a series of connected hearts along the border of the box.

'Actually, I'm feeling a lot lonely. And it doesn't seem to be getting any better. And I don't know what the hell I'm going to do about it.'

THREE

'Excuse me. Where will I find Weight Watchers?'

'*You* want the Weight Watchers meeting?' The Sumoette behind the church office counter licked bits of glaze from her fingers and scanned me suspiciously. A Dunkin' Donuts box sat open on the desk behind her.

'Yes, please.' And maybe just the tiniest bite of donut.

'End of the hall,' she said, air-drying her fingers as she waved me out of her office, 'and down the stairs.'

I fell in behind a moving line of assorted-sized women. Aunts at a picnic. Hey, what's in the basket? Pistachio-studded duck pâté, a crusty french baguette, a creamy wheel of brie, a bottle of slightly fruity white, bunches of red seedless. Food. Lately, it was all I thought about – when I wasn't thinking of cigarettes. Twenty-five-year-old, three-pack-a-day habits are a bitch to break.

I tried to catch the mood of the women as I followed them down the stairs. Excited? Fearful? Enthusiastic? Depressed? I couldn't read them.

Come on, ladies. You've seen this show before. Give me a clue. Should I pays me money and buys me ticket or turn my ever-widening tail toward home and a good book? The impassive line moved slowly. I followed it down a narrow spiral staircase.

'I feel like Orpheus descending,' I said to the woman ahead of me. She turned, smiling blankly. Come on, it wasn't *that* obscure. I ached for Sarajane.

'Funny,' said a beautiful bell-like voice behind me.

I turned. She was a shock. A multi-chinned mountain of a woman, she nearly spanned the two-person-wide stairwell. Swathed in a flowing paisley challis cape thrown over and around, she looked like a statue awaiting unveiling.

She swayed her weight side to side down the stairs. I'd walked like that for two pregnancies. It had to be hell living life forever in the ninth month. She paused for breath. I felt the impatience of the group stuck on the stairs behind her.

'Think Orpheus was on his way to Weight Watchers?' I asked.

'Doesn't matter,' she said, swaying her body to a start. 'I figure one descent into hell is pretty much the same as another.'

She paused again at the bottom and I lost her as I followed the others through the winding corridor. Eau de wet cement permeated the dank air. Rusty water dripped from gigantic pipes criss-crossing the low ceiling. Wedged above them, a round neon tube flickered from a dangling socket casting harsh erratic shadows on our procession. I shuddered, trying to shake off premonition. I wasn't going to make it out alive.

Why hadn't I left a farewell note – perhaps 'I died for my chins' – etched in the chocolate frosting of Jason's birthday cake? Trouble was, I'd eaten the frosting. Not that I'd meant to. I'd made the '12' uneven so I scraped off the numbers and ate them, squeezing a new '12' from the icing bag. Something deep in my gut cried out for more. I'd already licked the frosting bowl and beaters so I ran the merest tip of my thumbnail around the rich chocolate at the base of the cake plate. Then, up one side, down another, take a little off the top until there wasn't enough frosting left to scrape over the cake's bare spots. I wouldn't have time to make a new batch before dinner. I'd have to remember to buy a can of frosting on the way home. If I lived.

The line wound into a huge room. Up in front, a frazzled fiftyish woman watched the unending line, frantically opening more and more folding chairs into tidy rows. A long table spanned one side of the room. Behind it, a plump young woman took checks, pulled cards from a file, licked stamps to put into small booklets, weighed each person and duly recorded the weight in little stamped books.

The woman in front of me turned, speaking conspiratorially out of the side of her mouth. 'Isn't this the most depressing Weight Watchers you've ever been to?'

'Gawd, yes.' I sighed, pressing the back of my

hand to my forehead. 'I'm on the verge of leaving. I don't think I can take much more of this.'

'I'm Florence.' She extended her hand and I shook it. Dry handshake. Firm without feminist rancor. A friendly gesture, I reckoned. 'From Kenosha. I usually try and be home on weigh-in days but my daughter's getting married and I needed to buy fabric for her dress and they have the *perfect* lace at Vogue Fabrics in Evanston so I drove in and . . .'

I smiled and nodded and tuned her out. She'd never know. My grandmother, a marathon talker, had never caught on all those years she raised me, and she was one sharp cookie. Famous Amos chocolate chip. Matt's oatmeal with raisins. The line inched forward. Many women stopped to chat with the weigher-inner. Personal bits and pieces. Weddings, Bar Mitzvahs, restaurants they'd gone to and had or hadn't been 'good' at. The weigh-in table was a verbal dump site. It wasn't too late for me to leave.

Florence stopped. I sensed she'd left a question hanging in the air for me to answer. Time for a delaying tactic. I doubled up, grabbing at my left eye.

She gasped. 'What's the matter!'

'Something in my eye.' I threw my head back, blinking crazily. I began to feel the imaginary speck.

'Wait. Let me look.' She ripped a Kleenex from a small packet and twisted one end to a point. Like the martini and the hiccup, everyone had a recipe for something in the eye. I let her poke around for a while. 'I can't see a thing,' she apologized.

'I know.' Blink, blink. 'This light's crummy.'

'Here, pull your upper lid out and down over the eyeball.' At some point in her day, Florence had eaten onions. 'That's it. Now, hold the lid down and blink fast. That's it. That's it.' I finally dared to release the lid. I blinked and looked around. The ex-cripple at Lourdes.

'It's gone,' I said. 'Florence, you're amazing.'

'Oh, it's nothing. Really. My family calls me Florence Nightingale. Why, just last week . . .'

One cigarette. Just to get me straight. One drag. I couldn't do this any more. I scanned the room for smokers. 'Thank you for not smoking' signs were everywhere. Not a rebel in the room. I'd have to go around sniffing people for tell-tale staleness, then beg shamelessly.

'Yes?' I felt the word aimed at me. The woman behind the table waited, smiling expectantly. 'Are you new?'

No, previously owned. 'Yes, this is my first time.'

'Here with a friend?' She nodded smilingly at Florence who was stripping off bracelets, rings, skirt, shoes, setting anything detachable on the table in front of the scale.

'No,' I said. 'Just me.'

'Oh, well, welcome.' She pointed to the price list. 'Please make out your check to Weight Watchers. This top fee is your first-time fee. The weekly fees are smaller. Unless, of course, you miss a week in which case you must pay for the missed meeting in addition to the current meeting.' She wrinkled her nose in what I guessed she guessed was a cute bunny-rabbit smile. 'It's our little incentive to keep you coming each week.'

I left everything on during my weigh-in. It would make the next week's weight loss more dramatic. I'd show this group what a little self-control could accomplish. She noted my height, a smidgen under five feet four inches. I weighed in at 124. After the frosting fiasco, I'd eaten a hearty last meal at the local I-Hop. A pot of coffee, large orange juice, one egg over easy, rye toast with butter and jelly, sausage links. It hadn't been enough. I tried to fill the empty after-the-meal-cigarette space with a heated pecan roll smothered with butter. It didn't even come close.

An animated group of women occupied the front row. They wore variations on a theme of Fila sportswear and none of them looked more than mildly overweight. I slid into the row behind them, listening.

'Lunch at Lyles?'

'Their salad bar stinks.'

'Chicken's good.'

My stomach lurched. Every mention of food triggered the need to smoke which triggered the need to eat. I tuned the women out, studying the literature I'd been given. Weight Watchers figured something called my 'Range Weight' to be between 114 to 135. Anything within that was acceptable. I tried to picture myself at 135. Acceptable to whom? I'd written my Goal Weight as 114. I'd get back to 105 on my own.

I scanned the booklet which listed foods I could eat

the first week. A few of my favorites were missing. Dry white wine. Crisp toasted bialys. Milk chocolate Dove bars. I'd have to make substitutions. The booklet contained some kind of diabolically complicated food exchange system. I tried to decode it. If two ounces of chicken equaled one protein exchange and I was allowed six protein exchanges a day, how many acrobats could stir a '59 Buick in May? Intricate bookkeeping loomed large on my horizon. Flipping through the booklet, I wondered if Franklin had been right after all. He'd asked what the hell I needed Weight Watchers for when a little self-control on my part would take the weight off just as fast.

The caped paisley whisked down my row in a swirl of fabric, a rattle of bracelets, and a hearty dose of Joy. Her face – full though it was with no hint of cheekbones – held promise. Translucent skin, clear blue eyes, thick black lashes. Her striking features were framed by a wild black mane. She had the carriage and attitude of a woman who knew she was beautiful. Hey lady, whatcha got under the cape? I felt an unaccountable joy that she'd decided to come to Weight Watchers and make her body as beautiful as her face.

Settling into the chair next to me, she adjusted and readjusted, liberated an oversized woven handbag from the folds of her cape, set it down, picked it up, dug around inside for a pen, Binaca breath spray, small spiral notebook, then reset the bag on the floor, kicked it under her chair, finally hanging it on the back of the chair next to her.

I was exhausted.

She turned abruptly, catching me open-mouthed and staring. Her smile was instantaneous and warm. 'Takes me a while to settle in. I'm Kathlyn.'

'Barbara,' I said.

'This your first meeting?'

'It shows?'

She pointed to the Week One booklet on my lap. 'Lousy plot. I don't figure anyone would read it twice voluntarily.'

'Have you been coming long?'

Her eyes glazed. 'A few months.'

'And?'

She shrugged, her eyes drifting away from mine. None of my business. I'd gone too far.

'Good morning.' The fiftyish chair setter-upper called us to attention.

'Good morning,' we chorused.

'You're all looking wonderful and beautiful today.' She opened a worn three-ring notebook. Scraps of magazine articles and recipes stuck out from all sides. Finding the page she wanted, she stood the open notebook on the front table. I stared at the 8x10 glossy of a heavy woman. 'For those of you who are new, this was me forty pounds ago.' Hearty round of applause. 'I've been this weight,' she rotated slowly in front of us, 'for nine years, nine months, twenty days.' Another round of applause. 'The program *does* work. I'm living proof.'

I listened attentively, taking careful notes. Good time to lose weight. Summer ahead of us. Bathing suit weather. Good motivation. Fat is hot. Kathlyn sat pen poised, notebook open on her lap, head tilted to one side. I filled up one page, two. Tips, hints, ideas. I felt first-day-of-school enthusiasm coursing through me. I was ready. I had never had to diet before but I could do this. I was *up* for it. Why had I worried so much about a few lousy pounds?

'All right,' our leader clapped her hands together happily, 'let's turn to the person next to us and discuss what type of exercise we would like to do . . . we are *going* to do.'

I turned. 'What kind of . . .' Kathlyn's eyes were closed. Her cape rose and fell under deep even breaths. I looked around the room for another partner. No luck. The class was two by two. I looked at her again. So peaceful. Still, she wasn't going to lose weight sleeping.

I stood and moved past her, roughly jostling her legs as I went to the front table for a Weight Watchers pen. When I returned, she had that pop-eyed eight a.m. Biology Lecture stare. It hadn't quite come back to her where she was.

I moved to my seat, all sunshine and light. 'Do you want to go first or should I?'

'You,' she said, thickly.

'Well, let's see.' I pondered, pen on chin. 'What kind of exercise *would* I like to do?' She processed the information and was with me immediately. Bright lady. 'I guess I enjoy walking most. At least, I used to before I lost . . .' it hurt so much, '. . . I lost my walking partner.'

She yawned. 'What about aerobics?'

'Boring.'

'Jogging?'

'I have bad knees.'

'Swimming?' She'd had practice playing devil's advocate.

'I tried that,' I said. 'The swimming part wasn't so bad. But I couldn't face that split second before my nice warm body hit the cold water.'

'The YW keeps the water at eighty.'

'That's where I went.' We laughed. 'Your turn,' I said.

'Oh, I guess I hate all forms of physical activity equally.' She opened and closed her notebook, clicked her pen open and shut, tilted her head back and shook her black mane. 'I just don't see what all the fuss is about. I can't think of one form of exercise that isn't painful or boring or a waste of time or money.'

'Sex?'

Her eyebrows jumped, hitching the corners of her mouth. 'A minimum of thirty minutes, nonstop, three times a week?'

I thought of Franklin. His schedule lately was so harried and hurried he didn't *have* thirty minutes unless he could ride me and his stationary bike at the same time. I sighed. 'I see your point.'

'Two more minutes, ladies,' said our leader. 'Then we'll have discussion.'

'Quick,' I said. 'Name the one exercise you'd least hate to do.'

'You're talking hemlock or arsenic.' She chewed the inside of her cheek thoughtfully. Kathlyn's beauty intrigued me. Sarajane also had a beautiful face. If I had a face like theirs, I'd make damn sure I had a body to match. Sarajane never knew what a constant disappointment her lack of willpower had been to me. She *smoked*, for god's sake. Why did she need to eat? Kathlyn sighed, shifting and reshifting in her chair. 'I hate to be unoriginal but I guess walking wouldn't be totally devastating.'

'All right, ladies,' said our leader, 'how about some feedback. Let's start in back for a change.'

I shifted around in my chair. Except for Kathlyn, the heaviest women occupied the back rows. They looked like a gathering of Franklin's family. The set-up reminded me of grammar school where the good students sat front row center while the others tried to melt into the back of the room. Perhaps that meant Kathlyn-of-the-second-row, as heavy as she seemed to me, was a mere shadow of her former self.

The women in the back two rows laughed. 'Well, one thing we learned is that at some time we've all joined places like the Y, Nautilus, Jazzercize, or Women's Workout World and never gone once.'

'I thought I was the only one,' whispered Kathlyn.

'But you feel better for having joined?' asked the leader. 'Like you've taken the first step?' The women nodded. 'Well, you have.'

Someone snorted. 'How do we motivate ourselves to take that first step out our front door? How do we get *started*?'

There was a murmur of accord.

'Any ideas?' asked the leader. Silence. I raised my hand hesitantly.

'It used to help me when I had someone to exercise with,' I said. 'I don't seem to do it on my own.'

'Wonderful!' Our leader applauded. I beamed. 'All of you try and find someone to go with you. In fact, let's make that this week's job. Everyone take down their partner's phone number. I want you to call each other in two days to see if you've begun exercising.'

The meeting broke up, livelier and friendlier than when it began. A woman from the group in the front row turned and smiled and slipped a piece of paper into my hands. Another into Kathlyn's.

'Read it later,' she whispered. 'It's fabulous.'

Kathlyn and I exchanged phone numbers and I left to find a can of frosting for Jason's cake. Perhaps two. On the way up the stairs I glanced at the piece of paper. The 'Mayo Clinic Egg Diet' was printed across the top, followed by a daily schedule. Hadn't that made the rounds a few years back? I seemed to remember someone giving it to Sarajane. It hadn't helped. But then, nothing ever had.

Eight twenty-nine Tuesday morning I sat at my kitchen desk, staring at the cursor blinking on the empty screen. Computer on, coffee in thermos, fingers resting on keyboard, a stack of readers' letters that 'Ask Barbara' where to find the unfindable. There was a space on my desk where my cigarettes and ashtray should have been. Not so much space as black hole, sucking up whatever creative light I'd had. The clock clicked to eight-thirty. I'd been sitting there exactly one hour. Time for a break. Luckily I was in the right room.

I sliced a bialy and popped it in the toaster while I unwrapped the cream cheese. Not exactly classic Weight Watchers but I figured I'd eat the breakfast I wanted, then fast the rest of the day. The bialy I'd eaten earlier didn't really count since I was just keeping the kids company before they went to school. This wasn't a snack. More like Breakfast, Part II. The bialy popped up and I started slathering on cream cheese. The phone rang. Caught!

'That Mayo Clinic Egg Diet is bogus.'

It took me a second to connect the words to the voice. I laughed. 'And good morning to you, too, Kathlyn. What's the matter? Didn't you lose weight on it?'

'Never got that far.' Kathlyn's melodic voice barely made it over the background of ringing telephones and voices.

'Where are you?' I asked.

'Work.'

'This early?'

'Yeah. Catch more worms this way. Anyway, about that diet, I figure anything that says the QUANTITY is NOT important but that you MUST eat certain foods EXACTLY a certain way or your toenails will turn blue . . .'

'Toenails? My copy didn't say toenails. Did your copy say toenails?'

'. . . is suspicious to begin with. And how the

deuce could a medical outfit tell people to eat seven eggs in one day?'

'Kathlyn, I know we don't know each other all that well,' I licked the edges of the half-spread bialy, 'but questioning Mayo is un-American.'

'So I called the clinic.'

'You called THE Mayo Clinic? In Rochester?' I bit into the bialy, swinging the phone's mouthpiece up to my forehead while I chewed.

'They knew the diet right away. It's been around for eons. It *is* bogus. A sham. Made up. What are you eating?'

She couldn't have heard! I swallowed and lowered the mouthpiece. 'I remember a lot of women lost weight on it,' I said.

'Of course. They took in less calories so they lost weight. But it had nothing to do with gorging on eggs or hocus pocus like you MUST eat one feff after EACH gazorble.'

'But I like feff after my gazorbles.' I took a quiet bite.

'What *are* you eating? Nothing we're allowed at Weight Watchers sounds like that. Wait, hold on a sec.' She spoke to someone but it was too noisy for me to make out the conversation. She was probably an operator for one of those phone answering services or some other job where her beautiful voice mattered more than her appearance. How many clients and callers had fallen in love with her? 'Sorry,' she said. 'Mornings are chaos. Now, why aren't you out walking?'

'I'm thinking about it,' I lied.

'Oh, that's great. I've heard you burn more calories if you think about running than if you think about reading a book.'

'What if it's a book about running?'

She laughed. 'Interesting thought.'

'How about you?' I cream cheesed the rest of the bialy. 'Are you walking?'

'Only to the fridge.' I felt her waiting.

'Want to try walking together?' I asked, regretting it immediately. Never commit to more than coffee on a first date. 'Maybe just this week. See how it goes.'

'Maybe.' She was tentative, uncertain. 'Just this week.'

We made a date for the next morning at seven. I hung up and forced myself to sit back down at the computer. Had to be ready in case the muse dropped in. Putting the bialy down in the cigarette/ashtray space on my desk, I closed my eyes and pulled one of the letters from the pile.

Dear Barbara,

I am planning a 40th birthday party for my husband. He's mad about the circus so I am planning a circus theme. I want a real elephant so all the guests can have a ride.

I took a bite of bialy and dove into my files. I could do this. It might take me two days instead of four hours to write my weekly column, and my words might be disjointed and flat, but I could do this. Since I stopped smoking, the *Globe* had been doing some pretty heavy editing of my material. My facts were fine but the words stringing them together were Journalism 101. With any luck, Cameron wouldn't fire me before I got my old self back.

APRIL

130–145

FOUR

I stood at the sink rinsing a pack of raw, boneless chicken breasts. Psychologist Dr Toni Grant crackled over my kitchen radio, neatly reducing a caller to his component parts.

No, said the man, he had never auditioned for a role. No, admitted the man, he had not actually *studied* acting. That was for peons. He was a natural. He'd be a star just as soon as he chucked his demanding job as a chicken sexer.

The phone rang. It was Stanford. Reluctantly lowering the volume on Dr Toni, I cradled Stanford between shoulder and ear, gritting my teeth against his nasal whine.

'Hate to bother you, Barb.' A lie. 'But I was wondering if you'd have time this week to come over and clean out Sarajane's closet.' O.K., guys, pack up them eighteen–twenties. We got us a size four movin' in.

I ripped the skin from a slimy breast and slid my knife through the pink flesh. It parted nicely. 'Sorry, Stanford. I've been meaning to get over there . . .'

'I'd do it,' he managed a lovely catch in his throat,

'but it's still too painful for me. Besides, you'll know what to do with her clothes. I'm sure some charity can use them.'

'Oh, yes. They'll be glad for . . .'

'Be sure and send me the receipt, will you?' He had the decency not to say 'tax deduction'.

'I'll be over this week,' I promised. A lie.

'Um . . . would you call before you come? Be sure I'm home?'

'Oh, I'll probably come while you're at work. No need to get in your way.' I didn't think I could stand seeing him. 'I still have my key.'

'Which reminds me,' he said, as if he'd just thought of it, 'would you mind leaving the key on the kitchen table? The, um, cleaning girl lost hers.' Stanford didn't want me prowling around his home, walking in on him and his playmate of the month. Hardly good form for the grieving widower. As if anyone cared. Besides me.

'No problem,' I said. There was nothing in that house for me anymore.

I hung up, tossed the knife in the sink and found the cleaver from my Szechwan cooking class which had followed my Creole cooking class which had followed Nouvelle Cuisine and cake decorating and . . . The whack of the blade through the breast hacked the edge off old anger.

Stanford's infidelities had upset me more than they did Sarajane. Like the time she and I flew down to weekend at her condo in Florida. She'd found lacy *Olga* panties staticked to the dryer, a souvenir of one of Stanford's 'golf weekends with the guys'.

'No one,' she'd insisted, 'is a size four.' She pronounced it 'foe-ahhh'. Anger unleashed the South in her. 'This calls for a ceremonial panty burning.' Sarajane's jeweled fingers glittered as she unlocked the glass case containing Stanford's collection of ancient Roman glass. He'd bought the entire collection one afternoon at auction in New York, not realizing how much he overpaid until every museum he tried to donate it to turned it down. Now it was housed in Florida, exhibited in a custom display case worth more than its contents.

'Now, Sarajane . . .'

'I think I'll use this,' she said, carefully lifting out a paper-thin bowl. 'It's one of Stanford's favorite pieces. He simply *adores* things that are . . . hand-blown.' I knew that smile, knew enough to back off and shut the hell up. Picking up the panties between meaty thumb and forefinger, Sarajane dropped Olga into the bowl and placed the offering in the center of Stanford's silk prayer rug.

Lighting a page ripped from Stanford's company's annual report, Sarajane set the panties on fire, keening an incantation which sounded suspiciously like a McDonald's jingle. The panties billowed acrid black smoke, inspiring the liberal use of 'Polyester' in the final chorus. The eggshell-thin bowl cracked, spilling the flaming mass onto the floor. The panties finished melting, leaving a dark glob the shape of a burnt marshmallow welded to the center of the prayer rug.

'Happy?' I asked.

'That, my de-ah, wuz the appetizah.' She had the main course back in Chicago. A pair of Cartier's two-carat diamond stud earrings, the perfect size for shopping at the mall or at Sunset grocery on a Saturday.

Slices of chicken breast piled high on the platter. I liked the heft of the cleaver which I'd bought in mid-chop off a cook in Chinatown. My special talent was knowing how to find things. It was a by-product of the years Sarajane and I spent prowling the nooks and crannies of the city. Step right up, ladies and gents. So you say you need a rotating spaghetti fork, Kosher Chinese caterer, left-handed nail clipper, place to luxuriate after a face lift, ultrasuede dice to match your Porsche? No problem. Let Barbara Avers find it. Some talent.

Ten minutes later I called the family to dinner.

'Voilà!' I said, setting the colorful platter of stir-fried chicken and vegetables on the table with a flourish.

Nobody moved. Family in still life. Franklin side-saddle, right arm draped over back of chair, left fore-arm resting on table. Jason slouched, hands pushed deep into pockets, Clint Eastwood glower boring into zucchini slices. Rikki hunched forward, elbows on table, head resting on fists. I filled their glasses from the pitcher of ice water.

'I miss Sophia's cooking,' said Jason.

'Sit up,' I said. He struggled upright. Twelve-year-old boys lack vertebrae.

'Especially her beef tacos,' said Rikki.

Jason sighed. 'Yeah.'

I spooned vegetables on one side of his plate, carefully placing the chicken, untouching, on the other. 'Everything Sophia cooks clogs your insides,' I said. 'We ate much too much beef and cheese and fried foods.'

Rikki covered her plate with her hands. 'I'm not hungry.'

'You have to eat something,' I said, guilt welling, spoon hovering, low-sodium soy dripping. 'Just a little?'

'Don't force food on her.' Franklin turned forward, pulling his chair nearer the table. 'You sound like my mother.'

'I do not.' I did. 'I sound like my grandmother.' I slopped veggies on his plate and mounded chicken on top of them.

'Yes, well, cut it out, Barbara. A childhood of forced food is probably why you're having a weight problem now.'

There it was. He'd noticed. I thought he must have but he hadn't said anything. Every morning I eased onto the scale, wincing as the needle crept up, and prayed somehow the weight wouldn't show. As long as Franklin didn't say anything, I was safe.

'I'm not having a weight problem.' I banged the pot on the table. 'A slight weight increase is to be expected when one gives up smoking.' . . . and eats tablespoons of peanut butter, other people's leftovers, Hostess anythings . . .

'It's been two months, Barbara. How long are you going to use that as an excuse?'

'It's hardly an excuse, Franklin. It's a fact.'

'Which means what?' Where had that hard line in his voice come from? My face burned.

'Which means, I never had a weight problem in my life.' I sat, ignoring the creak of my delicate Scandinavian chair. 'Which means, this is not a problem. This is a glitch. A little blip on the old weight chart. Like pregnancy.'

'You mean,' Franklin winked at the children, 'this is going to last nine months?' He was ever so amused.

Why was he doing this in front of them? I looked to Rikki and Jason for sympathy. They watched, fascinated. When I stopped smoking and was still fairly rational, I had sat the whole family down. 'I'll probably be speaking out a bit more,' I'd warned them. 'I know I'm not a yeller but it's possible I'll need to verbalize the feelings I used to hold in by lighting up a cigarette.' For a while the kids crept around, waiting, listening, hoping. There were a few ground rumblings, some distant quakings, but no eruptions. No, Dr Toni, I've never been confrontational. No, I've never initiated friction. No, I don't know how to fight – constructively or otherwise. But I just know I'll be brilliant when the time comes.

'I got back to a hundred and five after delivering these two,' I said, 'and I'll come back after this.'

'Barbara, you were a lot younger then.'

'So nice of you to remind me. Maybe I'll need a little more time. Which means . . .' My stomach churned from having to defend myself, 'right about now – when I feel I'm being unfairly attacked,' drop the qualifiers you chicken shit, 'when I *am* being unfairly and unkindly attacked after planning, buying, cooking, and serving this nutritionally balanced, remarkably healthful, visually exciting meal,' ah, the drama of overkill, 'right now is the perfect time for a cigarette. And, since I can't light up, I think I'll eat something.' I flipped my napkin open hoping for applause.

'Mom, I know you're trying to lose weight,' Rikki had the good sense not to look at me, 'but I don't see why we have to suffer.'

Franklin patted her hand. 'Eating healthful foods is hardly punishment,' he said. I smiled thanks at his unexpected support. He smiled back. 'Although, Barbara, we might consider letting the children have some normal kid foods in the house, like pop and desserts.' And the Lord taketh away.

'None of it's good for them,' I said. 'Empty calories. Besides, you know how hard it is for me when that stuff's around.'

'Well, maybe we need to exercise a little willpower.' We all knew who 'we' was.

I eyeballed four protein exchanges and four vegetable exchanges and scooped them onto my plate. I'd forgotten to buy a food scale. Again. The portions looked skimpy. I added more of both.

'Nick Turner's mother stopped smoking,' Jason said, surgically removing his mushrooms from the rest of his food, 'and she only gained five pounds.'

'Five pounds would hardly show on someone the size of Joelle Turner,' I said, pouring my nightly goblet of white wine. It helped take the die out of diet. 'Besides, how would Nick know what his mother weighed?' Look out, Jason. Trick question. Do you know what *I* weigh?

'She keeps this chart inside the Preparation H box inside her medicine cabinet. She went from a hundred forty-five to a hundred fifty, then back again.'

'Yuck!' said Rikki, picking a water chestnut slice out of the pot, licking off the soy, and nibbling the edges. 'Why was Nick digging around in a disgusting Preparation H box?'

'Looking for ludes. His mom used to keep them there. He can't find her new stash.'

'Stop talking like a bad cop show,' said Franklin.

I chewed slowly, trying to make the portion last. I'd barely begun eating and already knew I'd leave the table hungry. 'I thought Joelle Turner weighed a lot more than one forty-five,' I said.

'Don't be catty,' said Franklin.

I bristled. 'It was an observation. If I were thin you wouldn't have called me catty. Thin people have credibility.'

'Yes,' he said, 'especially when they're discussing weight.'

We ate in silence. When I'd seen Joelle two months before, she'd been closer to one sixty-five. She was one of those women who refused to buy the next size long after the next size would have been too small. She wore tight teen-style clothes that accentuated her flab; a woman who grew out but not up. Her ruffled cotton knit tops strained over her small breasts, mashing her padded bras into unnatural shapes. She was all waist and stomach in her tight pants. If there was a full-length mirror in her home, she never looked in it. Not that I'd spent a great deal of time in front of mirrors lately. I'd begun using the tiny guest bathroom with the small medicine cabinet mirror. From the neck up I was still knockout.

Franklin unfurled his napkin with a flourish, letting it flutter down over the food on his plate.

'Something wrong?' I asked.

'Not at all.' He clicked a piece of food out of his back teeth. 'I've realized I'll eat whatever's on my plate. Small portion. Huge portion. Even when I'm not hungry.' He leaned back, slapping both hands against his firm stomach. 'I've decided to watch myself.'

My eyes teared as I blotted the sauce in the pot with a piece of Weight Watchers bread. Franklin meant well. He was trying to give me helpful ideas without seeming to give me helpful ideas. Ah, Franklin, you've been hanging around your campaign groupies too long. You've forgotten you married the one with working parts *above* the neck. I savored the sodden bread and washed it down with wine. Floating my napkin over my empty plate, I patted my ever rounder tummy. 'Anyone for a walk?' I asked.

'Ball game,' said Jason.

'Homework,' said Rikki. The phone rang and she got it before the second ring. 'It's for you,' she said, annoyed, holding the receiver to Franklin. 'Some lady.' Did Franklin walk with a little dance in his step?

'Hello? Oh, hello, Miss Pembrooke.' Oh

heloooooooo Miss Pembrooke? 'No, don't even consider the expense. That's not at issue here.' I'd never heard him tell anyone not to consider expense. As much as we had, it never seemed enough for Franklin. He loved expensive cars, and clothes, and homes, but was tighter than Scrooge with purchases that didn't show. He was proud of his wealth, but was also terrified of being poor again. This was not the sullen voice at the dinner table. 'Why, yes, I can take a look at them.' Cigarette. No cigarette. And I can't go in the other room and call Sarajane. I picked pieces of water chestnut off Jason's plate until Franklin hung up.

'Have to go to campaign headquarters for a little while,' he said.

'Oh? Who was that?'

'Ashley Pembrooke. She's the new publicity whiz Rosenthal brought in. Has some layouts for me to go over.'

'Great! I'll go with you and give you some cheap labor.'

'No, thanks. I won't be long.'

'You must have tons of envelope stuffing. Typing?'

Franklin stuck his hands on his hips and shifted his weight to one leg. 'I thought you hated politics.'

'I don't *hate* politics. I'm apolitical. But I've been thinking I need to find things to do outside the home.'

'That's not a bad idea. Maybe you should volunteer at the hospital or deliver hot meals to shut-ins. Right now I've got all the staff I can use. Besides, sitting at a desk is hardly the sort of sedentary activity you need just now.'

THE DIETER

I rang for Sophia to clear and almost immediately heard the creak of her steps from the attic apartment.

Franklin slipped on his kid jacket. The one he kept for 'good'.

'What's the occasion?' I asked.

'Occasion? Oh, you mean the jacket.' He shrugged, smiled, checked his reflection in the microwave's black glass. 'You know, I've had this thing four years and I've barely worn it. Today I asked myself what the hell I'm saving it for. And you know what?' He kissed me lightly on the forehead. 'I couldn't come up with an answer.' He headed for the door.

'Hold it,' I said. He froze. I put on my jacket and grabbed my purse. 'Drop me at the drug store.'

'I thought you were going for a walk.'

'I'll walk home. I need to pick up a few things.'

The diet pill display was in the back of the drugstore wedged between sanitary napkins and disposable douches. Pity the poor fat man. The store was deserted except for the cashier and me. I studied the packages carefully but they all seemed pretty much the same. The evening commuter train pulled in and a horde of harried commuters ran in for cigarettes, batteries, magazines. I peeked over the display. Had the entire universe become elegant, self-assured, thin? I wasn't belonging anymore. It was no fun not being at the top. Poking fun from the bottom had more whine than wit.

I waited for the crowd to leave, then slid a pack of diet pills off the rack, sandwiched them between a

Vogue and *Bazaar*, and strolled casually to the front. The glass-topped counter, chronically cracked and taped, was cluttered with displays of gum, dime mints, pens. Gone were the miniature bottles of Ipecac Syrup which we'd discovered our high-school daughters swigging to help them puke after pizza. The PTA threatened boycott if the manager didn't remove the tiny scarf and barf bottles. Death to binge and purge.

A box of Chunkys replaced the Ipecac. The manager's little joke. The silver-wrapped candy time-warped me to the Steinway Drug Store Sarajane and I passed on the way home from school. We'd each buy a Chunky to eat with our cherry Cokes. This new Chunky looked thinner. 'EVEN BETTER' promised lettering on a yellow band. 'Original Chunky.' I picked one up, hefting it in the palm of my hand. Ancient taste buds creaked to attention.

'I remember the original Original,' I said. The meaty clerk looked up from his *Penthouse*. He shifted cheeks slowly on his cashier's stool. A man of unclean habits. I displayed the Chunky between thumb and forefinger. 'The *original* Original was a flat-topped pyramid of solid chocolate.' I swallowed a surge of saliva. 'The old wrapper was heavy silver and unfolded at the bottom.' I tugged at the wrapper. It was welded shut. 'It had nuts. Raisins.' I tore the wrapper with my teeth, peeling back the lightweight foil. The Chunky was in four small sections. 'How can they call this "Original"?' I asked.

The clerk's eyes showed signs of intelligent life. He

wheezed. 'Think that's bad? They made it flat for a while, like a candy bar.' He leaned conspiratorially on the counter, an 'I could have told them so' sneer on his face. Another wheeze. 'Sales went all to hell. Like Coke. I don't know why them executives don't come out and talk to the People before making some half-assed change. Took the fins off the goddamn Caddy. Invented a puffed-up waffle that tastes like cardboard.'

I smiled, nodding, my newly un-dead taste buds screaming for the Chunky. My hand shook as I broke the candy in half. 'Want some?' I asked – Old Buddy Old Friend – embarrassed that I lacked the control to wait to eat it. The bastard took the piece, popping it between his thick fish lips like it didn't matter. I broke my half in half and eased one small piece onto my tongue. Juices swam over it. Around it. I closed my eyes. I'd forgotten the magic. Was it the same? It felt familiar. The raisins, the nuts, the chocolate. Yes. I think. I remembered. 'I haven't bought myself a candy bar in twenty years,' I said. 'Maybe more.'

'Yeah?' He scanned my body. Not *Penthouse* proportions. I tugged the tails of my overblouse. 'This be all?' I nodded. He charged me forty cents for the Chunky. The last one I'd bought cost a nickel and I got to eat the whole thing. I needed a cherry Coke to wash it down. But who would I sit with? And laugh with? And blow rude bubbles through a straw with? Only people with problems drink alone. I slipped the last piece of candy in my mouth and craved another.

He punched my purchases on the antique register.

My eyes fixed on the wall of cigarettes behind him. I smelled the tobacco through the cellophane. *This depression doesn't have to go on*. I felt the cool firm filter between my lips. *I could stop this insanity right now*. I pulled the smoke deep into my lungs. *One pack and its adios weight problems*.

'These any good?' he wheezed, waving the diet pills in my face.

I glanced around furtively, a virgin buying condoms. We were alone. 'I'll let you know.'

He packed my purchases. I stared at the cigarettes, suffocating. The bag ripped. He cursed, emptied it, took out another, repacked. Sweat ran down my underarms. My vision blurred, seeing all the brands at once. I'd started at fourteen with Sarajane, sneaking into the bathroom to share one of my grandmother's Kents. We'd followed the fads west to Marlboro country, and on to Salems, Mores. I'd ended with Benson and Hedges Menthol. She'd called them sissy candy sticks. But they'd done the job. My heartbeat chugged in my ears. Ca-thug. Ca-thug. Ca-thug.

I'd start with a pack of Camels. Yes, that's the ticket. That's the real tribute to Sarajane, switching to her brand. She wouldn't have wanted me to stop smoking. Of course not. Silly idea to begin with. Can't think what possessed me. Why, I'll just have me a mini-marathon, lighting one Camel off another. Maybe smoke two at once. Fill up that space, that hole, that void.

'Yeah, let me know about them pills.' He pushed the bag across the counter, wheezing with the effort,

and flicked his Bic on a Marlboro. Bring out the
cowboy hat and one hell of a sturdy horse. 'Been
thinking of taking off a couple or three pounds,
myself.' I clutched my bag, inhaling with him. He
coughed, dragged in air, and settled his weight on the
stool. An emphysemic Cheshire Cat. I fled. What if I
started smoking again . . . and kept on eating? The
only thing more disgusting than a fat woman was a fat
woman who stank of cigarettes. I had loved Sarajane,
anyway. But who would love me? I pushed back
uneasy thoughts of Franklin going off to a meeting
wearing his 'for good' jacket.

My walk home lasted as far as the curb. The bus,
which ran on alternate Guy Fawkes Days, pulled up in
front of me. Its doors hissed open. I fingered the
drug-store-change in my hand. Exact fare. Some signs
are too obvious to ignore. I'd wait for my morning
walk with Kathlyn. No need to become an exercise
fanatic. Besides, the ride would give me time to read
the directions on the back of the diet-pill package.

FIVE

'Have a nice evening, ma'am. Watch your step.' The doors folded open and I stepped into the thick fog rolling in off the lake. Soft-edged halos of light spread from antique street lamps like temperas splattered on wet paper. A real pea-souper. Dash of pepper, oyster crackers.

I exhaled until the bus and its fumes pulled away. When I inhaled, there was no mistaking the spicy smell trapped by the fog. I was a block and a half from home and directly downwind from Sophia's tacos. The Chunky had taken the edge off, but there was always room for more food. And more food. I'd become perpetually pre-menstrual.

If I paced myself slowly enough the tacos might be history by the time I walked in the door. I strolled toward the house, mellowed by the moist darkness. I could beat this weight thing. Had to. I was running out of clothes that cleared my hips. There was no way I was going to spend my summer at the country club in this condition. I could hear the poolside purrings. 'Have you *seen* Barbara?' 'What *happened* to her?' 'Do you *believe* how she let herself go?'

I used to stretch out on my chaise and light up. Puff, puff. And wonder how a woman could let herself go. Puff. I'd wondered it aloud. Puff. As a kindness. Puff, puff. In case the overweight hadn't noticed they were. Puff, puff. To let them know I cared and that I hoped they'd get hold of themselves soon. Puff, puff, puff. Sarajane, swathed in elegant billowy cover-ups and dramatic wide-brimmed hats sat next to me, nodding agreement, as if she were thin. She'd been thoughtful enough to shield her fat from the world. Not like Ramona Salter who let it all hang out and out and out. Ramona had been to France, don'tcha know, where 300-pound bikini-clad women played volley ball on the sands of the Riviera. Topless.

Two shadows loomed in the fog, their backs to me. I slowed. One of them staggered and the other reached out a steadying hand. Drunks? Druggies? Labored breaths hissed through the fog like air sucked through a SCUBA. I was still a block from my house. A lot could happen in a block.

They huddled in the darkness between streetlamps. I clutched my package. O.K., Mister Muggers, you can have my purse and my magazines, but make one move for my diet pills and you're dead meat! The unsteady shadow lurched forward, hobbling like a shackled bear.

My father taught me to tough it out. Stride straight ahead as if I knew where I was going, as if these fog-shrouded apparitions weren't Jack the Ripper and the Boston Strangler, as if the hobbler wasn't hunching over to notch my name on his knife. I summoned the child in me, the ballsy New Yorker who jumped over doorway drunks on her way to school. She set my shoulders back, lifted my chins, and picked up my pace.

'It's enough,' growled the bear.

His friend mumbled something I couldn't make out.

'Two minutes, two hours. What the hell's the difference? Enough's enough. I'm going back to the house!'

The bear negotiated a half turn as I passed.

'Evening,' he growled.

'Evening,' I answered without looking, catching a peripheral glimpse of Canadian crutches. A ruse. Sympathy ploy. Throw me off guard. I kept going, bracing my shoulders for the blow of a crutch on the back of my neck.

'Barbara?' said his accomplice. 'That you?'

I spun around. 'Cameron?' I laughed with relief. 'Am I ever glad it's you. You wouldn't believe what this fog does to the imagination.'

I turned toward his friend and felt an idiotic 'say cheese' grin freeze on my face. Black stitches laced a gash from his forehead to his eyebrow, ducked behind a black eyepatch, then continued down his cheek. Black curls glistened like gun-metal shavings around his pain-lined face. Indian? Italian? Thirty-five. Forty-five? Whatever had happened to this man had spared his other eye, an eye so pale it blended into the fog. It sparkled at me, held me, dared me to look away. I couldn't.

'Barbara, this is Mac Parker, an old friend.'

I realized I had been holding my breath. 'Pleased to meet you,' I said, extending my hand. He shifted his weight to one crutch, slid his hand into mine and lifted it to his lips.

'The pleasure is mine,' he said, stroking his thumb over my knuckles before kissing the back of my hand. And after. 'And you are . . .?'

I are I are I are.

'This is Barbara Avers,' said Cameron. '*Mrs* Barbara Avers. Happily married mother of two.'

Mac's eye never moved from my face. 'How nice for you,' he said.

'Behave yourself,' said Cameron. 'Come on, Barb, I'll walk you home.'

'But you have company.'

'Yes,' said Mac, 'you have company.'

'Mac was just telling me how tired he was.' Cameron slid his hand under my elbow, raising his voice as he led me down the block. 'He's too tired to walk any more. He can find his own way back to my house.'

'Really,' I whispered, 'I'll get home all right.' It wasn't like Cameron to be rude.

He squeezed my elbow gently. 'Trust me on this one, Barb.'

Mac's voice trailed after us. 'How far is this home of yours, Mrs Happily Married Avers?'

'Too far for you to walk,' said Cameron without slowing. I heard the shuffle of Mac's feet, the metallic clicks of his crutches.

'And how far might that be?'

'Not as far as the doctors want you to walk but further than you're willing to.'

'So, maybe I'm feeling a little stronger.'

We stopped at the corner to wait. Mac jerked and hauled his body toward us. It was too painful to watch. I looked away.

'Don't ask him what happened,' said Cameron. 'Don't offer to help him. And, above all, don't offer him sympathy.'

'So,' I groped for a safe topic, 'how 'bout them Bears?'

Cameron tapped my jaw with his fist. 'Right idea, Sport, wrong season.'

'Right. How's Myrna?' And what the hell happened to your friend with the sexy eye?

'Busy. Final luncheons. Dinners. All her organizations are winding down for the summer.'

'I don't know how she juggles all the things she does.' I heard Mac's steps pause a moment, then start again. 'Myrna sure seems to have more hours in a day than I do.'

'She's something, all right.' The man was in love with his lady. Sarajane had never believed it. She kept waiting for Cameron and Myrna to split in a deliciously ugly divorce. I wondered how Franklin sounded when he talked about me. Proud? Loving? *Did* he talk about me?

Mac caught up to us. I restrained myself from wiping the beads of sweat from his forehead. He struggled for air. 'So?'

'Just another half-block,' I said, walking away,

responding to the pressure of Cameron's hand under my elbow.

'*Just*,' Mac said to the sky. 'Very funny lady, this Mrs Avers.' I listened for the shuffle of his feet.

'Why do I feel like a carrot in front of a horse?'

'He's more like a mule,' said Cameron. 'Stubborn. Don't get too close, Barb. He bites.' Cameron sniffed the air. 'Mmmmmmm. What's that smell?'

'Sophia's tacos.' There was naked desire in his eyes. I knew the feeling. 'You haven't eaten?'

'Mac and I are batching it tonight. We were going to order in a pizza.'

'Well, you might as well come on in and see if anything's left. Besides, I think by the time your friend gets here he's going to need to sit down.' We walked up the path to the back door.

Zapata's army couldn't have finished the spread of food on the kitchen table. Four burners blazed as Sophia fried fresh tortillas into crisp shells and set them into taco racks. Rikki and a friend heaped taco-seasoned beef and chicken into the shells and passed them to Jason and his gang who added tomato cubes and shredded lettuce.

'Make room,' I said, banging the screen door.

Rikki looked up, guiltily. 'Oh, hi Mom. Mr Brady.'

'Hi, kids,' said Cameron, swinging his lanky leg over a chair back, settling in for the long ride ahead.

Sophia avoided my glare as I wiped down one end of the table and took out dishes and place settings for the men. She shrugged. What could she do? Rikki and Jason were like her own children. How could she not feed them when they were so obviously hungry? My new regime made no sense to her. How did people live without sugar or white flour or fried foods? Why would they want to? She was unable to cook the meals I requested. Demanded. Since I'd taken over the cooking, she'd watched my Weight Watchers meals 'the whole family will love' make the journey from table to refrigerator, to back of the refrigerator, to mold, to garbage.

I jostled Rikki on my way back to set the table.

'Mom, we were just helping Sophia –'

'Spare me the details,' I said. 'Jason, I believe you've already eaten dinner. Please pass that rack of tacos to Mr Brady. Rikki, bring a couple of cold beers up from the basement refrigerator.'

She shot me her best teen glower and was stomping past the screen door when she happened to look out. Her scream froze the kitchen action. Mac! In my angst, I'd forgotten. Rushing to the door, I witnessed the most woebegone expression I'd ever seen on a human face. This was obviously the first night Mac had taken his wounds public. Cameron should have warned me so I could have warned the kids. Rikki ducked behind me, gripping my shirt.

'May I help you, sir?' I asked. His face shifted into pure gratitude.

'Yes, please. I have just been forced to cross the Sahara on foot and could do with a taco.'

'Of course.' I threw the door open. Rikki's jaw dropped as Mac hauled his body past her into the kitchen.

'It's rude to stare,' I whispered. 'Better make that three beers.'

Jason and his friends nudged each other as Mac shuffled across the room. Their eyes hooked on his stitches. Rikki bounded up from the basement with the beers, staring as Mac eased into a chair. He uttered a small cry of pain when he landed. It was the only sound in the room besides the sizzle of tacos in oil.

'I thought you told me you had homework,' I said, taking the beers from Rikki.

'Oh, Sarna and I needed to study together for a test.'

'If you had time to make tacos, you probably had time to take a walk with me.' It's *your* fault I ate a Chunky. Martyr, martyr, martyr. If you had been with me I would have walked instead of taking the bus. Guilt, guilt, guilt.

'Sorry.' Rikki and Sarna grabbed a rack of tacos, a couple of Pepsis from Sophia's stash, and ran giggling upstairs. I was too late. Guilt had to be instilled from birth. Sarajane's came from her church. Mine was a gift from Grandma. In my struggle to be Perfect Mother, I'd forgotten to pass it on.

Jason and his friends banged out the back door to finish their game. I sat down with the men who had already started on the tacos. Mac took a huge bite and closed his eye, concentrating. A thin red line of salsa dribbled down his chin.

'This,' he said, 'this is heaven.'

I could feel Sophia beaming behind me. Biting into

a taco, I waited that split second before my taste buds exploded. Tomorrow morning I would wake up looking like Buddha. Swollen eyes. Feet. Fingers. The day I turned thirty-five my system ballooned whenever I ate MSG, salty foods, *anything* spicy. The skin crease above my eyes disappeared. Caucasian to Oriental in the flick of an Accent shaker.

We ate in comfortable silence, talking only as the edge of hunger subsided. I signaled Sophia to stop cooking.

'What have you been up to?' asked Cameron.

'Oh, same ol' same ol'. Franklin's begun his campaign for the Senate.'

'I heard. Good luck. Is it keeping you busy?'

'Not really. So far, I haven't been asked to do anything.' I hated the note of self-pity, but couldn't seem to stop it. It would be nice to feel needed. Or useful. Or *something*.

Mac smothered a new taco with hot sauce. 'And while your husband's campaigning, Mrs Avers, what do you do with your life?'

I picked up a napkin and started shredding it. What do people who don't smoke *do* with their hands? 'I write a Saturday column for Cameron.'

'Does everyone in this neighborhood write for the *Globe?*'

'He's met Francine and Ronald,' explained Cameron.

'Cameron and I were here first,' I said. 'But I think newspaper people do tend to live in groups. There's always been a lot in Evanston and Hyde Park.

Although, I'm not really a full-time journalist anymore. Cameron took pity on an old friend and let me keep a hand in.'

'Cameron is incapable of pity,' said Mac. 'I'll have to read some of your work.'

'If you do, you might want to go back a few months.' I glanced at Cameron but he didn't mention the decline and fall of my column's quality. 'I've been a little off since a friend of mine died.'

'I heard about Sarajane.' Cameron patted my hand. 'I'm sorry. She was a special lady.'

My eyes teared. Again. Still. I sniffed and wiped them away. 'And,' I pushed the confettied napkin pieces into a pile, 'I've been trying not to smoke.'

'Good for you,' said Cameron. 'They say cigarettes are harder to kick than heroin.'

'Just what I need to hear.' I pulled at my over-blouse. 'The problem is I've been eating instead of smoking.'

'*That's* what's different!' I swallowed, shifting self-consciously. 'I knew you looked terrific! I just couldn't figure out why.'

Mac's eye scanned me slowly. 'You must have been too skinny before.'

'You two have just made my day.'

I would have loved to show Mac how I *really* looked but couldn't think of a graceful way to bring the family album into the kitchen.

'I wish my daughter would put on a few pounds,' said Cameron. 'She's gone crazy with this weight business.'

'Bite your tongue,' I said. 'Michelle would have a fit if she put on weight.'

'She was supposed to go to a party last week. She called and canceled because she was up to a hundred and six and was too fat to go out in public.'

I shivered. 'How tall is Michelle?'

'Five nine.' We nodded sadly, for different reasons.

'I wouldn't worry too much about her,' I said. 'All sixteen-year-olds are compulsive about their weight.'

Mac lit up a Camel, not asking if anybody minded. I had to remember to buy 'Thank you for not smoking' signs for the house. Sophia slid an ashtray in front of him. I tried to inhale his smoke. 'Personally,' he said, 'I think a little softness is nice on a woman.'

'I wish the rest of the world felt that way.'

'Does it matter?'

'Yes.' I was not comfortable with this conversation. 'So, tell me, Mac, how do you know Cameron?'

'You mean he never talks about me? We wrote our way through Nam together.'

'You're a journalist?'

'Crime reporter for the Phoenix *Daily*.'

'Ah.' I nodded. My father had warned me away from crime reporters. Every profession has their crazies and crime reporters were the best or worst of the journalistic pack, depending on your point of view. Pole vaulters became crime reporters, he said. Sky divers, ice sailers, downhill racers. There was a self-destruct air about them my father didn't think was healthy for me to be around. 'So what brings you to Chicago?'

'A friend of mine died last month.'

'I'm sorry.'

'Me too. He was one of the beautiful people of this world. I came in for the funeral. Right after that I had a little disagreement with a truck which put me into Luthern General until yesterday.'

Cameron had draped his arm casually over the back of my chair and now squeezed my shoulder, cautioning me to stop. I did. But there were huge holes in Mac's story that needed filling. I'd call Cameron tomorrow.

'I think we'd better get going,' said Cameron. I offered to give them a lift and even Cameron didn't have the heart to force Mac to walk back home.

After dropping them off, I slipped in a Miles Davis tape and turned up the volume. Cameron and Mac had buoyed my spirits. If they could be believed, I wasn't totally disgusting to look at. I felt hopeful. Tomorrow I would begin the diet pills. They would keep me honest. They would make Weight Watchers work.

Around midnight, Franklin's Mercedes eased onto the gravel driveway. I slipped on the satin negligee he liked, the one with sheer lace over the breasts. Couldn't blame him for not being aroused by the oversized tee shirts I'd been wearing to bed lately. I dotted my wrists and cleavage with Opium. Maybe all I needed to *be* sexy was to *think* sexy. Kathlyn, with her flowing black hair and artistic clothing, was as sensual as any woman I'd known and she was a hell of a lot heavier than I was. Although, she'd already lost twice as many pounds as I'd gained on Weight Watchers. If I'd followed the diet as religiously as she had, I'd be back down to my fighting weight by now. Well, it wasn't too late to start. I dabbed Opium on my inner thighs and nipples, then turned off my light and waited.

Franklin didn't come upstairs. I heard the door to the den open and the squeak of his desk chair. My fault. I hadn't been a barrel of fun these past couple of months. And he had so many important things on his mind. I resisted an impulse to go to him. I couldn't risk going downstairs. I'd want to eat something. The kitchen was becoming my enemy. Better to avoid it as much as possible until I was in control. Again. Forever.

SIX

I white-knuckled the door handle and jammed my foot where the brake would have been had I been sitting in the driver's seat. Rikki started the turn directional a block too early, cut off an eighteen-wheeler as she crawled over to the left turn lane, and stopped to wait for a car approaching from the next time zone. I should have driven. Sarajane and I had honed our home-to-mall time down to seven-and-a-half minutes, portal to portal. The route was a precision drill down side streets, through just-red lights, and over one stretch of back road taken at sixty miles per hour.

Rikki navigated our boat-sized Pontiac station wagon into the huge mall parking lot. We'd started out twenty minutes early to give Rikki plenty of driving time and still didn't arrive until ten minutes after the mall opened. If I had driven we'd have finished half our shopping by now and gotten the hell out of there. But she was high with the power of her new driver's license and I wasn't feeling up to a confrontation. Not early on a Saturday morning. Not on my first trip back to the mall since Sarajane died and I'd quit smoking and I'd put on a couple or few pounds.

Rikki pulled the car between two yellow lines, put the car in park, turned off the ignition, and withdrew the key. Classic driver's ed.

'There,' she said, triumphantly. 'You can breathe now.' I did.

Rikki and Jason side-kicked each other toward the elegant glass and marble building. I followed, head down, shoulders hunched, the furtive Quasimodoesque movements of someone fearing recognition and ridicule. I had wanted to postpone my 'coming out' until I was back to a hundred and five. I wouldn't be at the mall now if the kids didn't need camp clothes.

IT'S CAMP was mobbed by the time we got there. In a diabolical plot, summer camps across the United States arranged to have all campers on the northshore receive their shopping lists the same day. I scanned the store for familiar faces. None. So far so good. Shoppers elbowed their way through the narrow aisles, grabbing items off laden tables before the stock was picked bare. Seasoned mothers had commandeered the few dressing stalls, ordered their children inside to strip, and tossed garments over the doors to be tried on. Our break came when one mother, whose daughter insisted on picking out her own clothing, had the girl lock the stall door from the inside then duck out the bottom opening. Jason, bored by our five minute wait, slipped in as soon as the girl left.

'Jasssse,' hissed Rikki, 'that's not ours.'

'Is now,' he said, kicking off his Nikes and stripping off his pants. 'Possession is nine-tenths of the law. Gimme some stuff to try on.'

'Mo-om,' pleaded Rikki, 'do something.'

'Never saw that kid before,' I said. 'But I like his style.'

Feeling like a co-conspirator, I quickly tossed him shorts and shirts which Jason draped over the door to establish territorial rights.

'Call me when you need me,' I said. 'I'm going to find more.'

Still no one in the store I recognized. I plunged into the melee, caught up in the frenzy of this pre-summer camp ritual. At either end of the long tables, untouched piles of petites and husky's framed the average sizes like book ends. Between them, shorts and shirts were toppled to the floor and ground underfoot before being retrieved and refolded by harried clerks. Shoppers ripped open sealed plastic packages and tore out the contents. If they liked what they saw they exchanged that merchandise for unopened packages.

Shrill voices ping-ponged across the store.

'Like this?' yelled Everymother, waving a pair of plain white shorts.

Five tables away, Everydaughter rolled her heavily mascaraed eyes heavenward. 'Mo-*ther!*'

'Just for camp. You don't have to wear it after camp.' Translation: It's under $10.00.

'You can buy it but I won't wear it.' Translation: It's under $10.00.

Outfitting Jason was easy. Color, style, price be damned – if it fit he took it. I'd clothe him first, then send him to Video Kingdom to be retrieved at feeding time. Hamburger with fries, thick chocolate shake, a Mrs Fields to go. Weight Watchers hadn't worked for me. There were too many decisions. Too much weighing and shopping. Too much kitchen time. I needed a no-brainer. Food without thinking or fussing or planning. Even though Kathlyn had lost over forty pounds with Weight Watchers, she was sympathetic. After all, it was easier to lose forty pounds when you weighed over two hundred. Way over. I checked out Nutri-Systems for both of us. We joined, embracing the freedom of prepackaged foods. I'd lost two pounds the first day. I was finally on my way.

I worked my way quickly along the first aisle.

'Hey, Rikki,' girls called from across the table, 'what camp you going to?' I averted my head, moved further away, held my breath, terrified I'd hear my name called and have to turn around. The girls squealed, talked, joked, gossiped. I brought another armload to Jason. The recently evicted mother-daughter team stood steaming outside his stall. I passed the clothes under the door and took Jason's rejects.

The mother glared, her green contacts glowing like wet bell peppers. Her leathery skin was the color of refrigerated chocolate, that muddy northshore blend of Puerto Viallarta Christmas, Boca Raton Winter, and Palm Springs Spring. Places I'd liked when I could still wear a bathing suit in public. If I didn't shape up I'd be checking out Juneau in January. 'You know, *we* had this stall first,' she said.

'Oh?' Innocent surprise. I tilted my head toward the door. 'Jason, did you take this stall from someone?'

'No, Mom. It was empty.' Nuthin' but the truth.

'Empty,' I repeated, shrugging. The woman reddened with rage and frustration, unable to admit she'd locked it to keep others from using it. There are advantages to stealing from a thief.

'Will your son be out soon?'

'My daughter's trying on, too,' I said. The woman grabbed her daughter and pushed into another line. 'How's it going, Jase?'

'Nearly done.'

'Don't come out. Let me send Rikki over so we don't lose the room.' Moments later I sent Jason off to the video games with a stash of quarters and started working with Rikki.

Standing still a moment, I scanned the room, quickly computing the fastest route to get what I needed. My heart quickened with the old excitement. The entire shopping process was neat, organized, exact. A beginning, a middle, an end. A need, a search, a find. Why couldn't everything in life be that clear cut? Sarajane was miffed by my hatred for the soaps, day and nighttime, and for any type of mini-series. My disdain for loose ends reached into every aspect of my life. I wouldn't begin reading a trilogy without all three books in hand as if I needed to be guaranteed the end before I'd risk the beginning. As far back as I could remember, I'd known I would marry a successful man and live in a real home with a mother, a father, and two children (although Rikki was a surprise since I'd always imagined the boy would be born first). Sarajane said my compulsive neatness, my obsession with order, was the curse of being a motherless child. I said it was the blessing.

I cut through the store neatly pulling out, pushing aside, digging under. Labels be damned, I could eye-ball Rikki's size no matter what the manufacturer chose to call it. Six, eight, ten, slim, regular, I piled them all on my arm, knowing they'd fit and flatter Rikki's narrow waist and blossoming hips. God, how I'd missed this. I was alive here, a predator hot with the excitement of the hunt. My nostrils flared at the scent of fresh cotton. Fingers tingled under the weave of coarse linen. Ears perked at eavesdropped conversations and the whirrings of registers. This was my arena. When would I be thin enough to come back to it? A violent wave of nostalgia hit and I clutched a pile of camouflage tank tops for support.

'Excuse me,' said a throaty smoker's voice behind me, 'but we'd like to see those, too.' Yvonne Rosin. The forty-year-old size three in my Great Books group. My neck hairs bristled.

I moved away, head turned. 'Sorry,' I mumbled. 'It's . . . it's a little close in here.'

I stumbled to Rikki's stall, tossed her the clothes and told her to hurry. The store was without air. I slumped against her door, unable to breathe. My head throbbed in time to the hard-driving rock music and shouting shoppers. I risked a glance up. Yvonne, absorbed in her shopping, hadn't recognized me.

'I'll get in the check-out line,' I told Rikki. 'Please try and hurry.'

The line went forever. I felt like an easy target, standing up front where anyone could see me. *Hang in there.* A couple of vaguely familiar women looked at me, heads tilted, debating. *Don't recognize me, please.* I turned away toward the two teen gum-cracking clerks who gossiped loudly while they teased pins and tags out of the clothing, trying not to chip their blood-red, three-inch fingernails. I felt hazy and far away. I tried to force myself to focus by extracting 'like', 'you know', and 'he goes' from the clerks' conversations but could find no words in between. 'He goes, like, y'know?' All mortar, no brick. *You can survive this.* Women who had thirty minutes in line to fill out their checks or find their charge cards waited to begin until their bills were totaled and everything was bagged. *Don't scream.* Rikki came. I pressed the charge card into her hand, left her in line, and escaped to a bench in the cool mall.

Part of the problem was I hadn't slept the night before. I'd been too nervous about this trip. This had been *my* mall. Sarajane and I made daily runs to watch it being built and drove past it every chance we got. My family, who benefited most from my love of shopping, kidded me mercilessly about my excitement over something so stupid. One night at dinner I announced, 'Sarajane just told me Stanford's company has contracted to build a domed stadium for the Chicago Bears just fifteen minutes from here.' Jason and Franklin went crazy, jumping up and down, hitting each other on the back, slapping hands across the table in high fives. I let them go for a few minutes. 'Just kidding about the stadium,' I said. 'But now maybe you understand how I feel about the mall.' They weren't amused, but they also stopped making fun of me.

For seven years I'd shopped the mall at least three times a week. I became bitchy if I didn't. I knew all the stock in all the stores that mattered. Key salespeople kept index cards listing my clothing sizes, color preference, designer preference, previous purchases, and specific items I was in the market for. Several times a week I'd get calls, 'Mrs Avers. I've got something fabulous for you.' 'Mrs Avers, that Anne Klein just went on sale. I can hold it for you until tomorrow.'

But I had been away too long, changed too much, and the prospect of returning to the mall had kept me up all night. At two in the morning, giving up on the idea of sleep, I'd eased out of bed, tiptoed downstairs, and liberated half an old deep-dish pizza from the back of the freezer. Contentedly sucking the frozen sausage slices, I watched 'The Bishop's Wife' on the late late. I truly believed David Niven was a Bishop. I happily accepted Cary Grant as an angel. What I didn't buy for a second was the circumference of Loretta Young's waist. It made me acutely aware of what the pizza was doing to mine. But I couldn't stop.

The dizziness wouldn't pass. The mall storefronts swam in and out of focus. I tried to read the headlines in the newspaper rack outside the tobacconists:

DRUG KING ARRESTED
IN COMMODITIES DEATH

Cameron *never* used type that large across the front page. I wondered how deeply Mac was involved in that story. I had seen him a few mornings on his walk around the neighborhood and invited him in for coffee. Sophia fluttered around him with coffee and sweet rolls. She liked men with strong appetites. Mac was a talker and I loved listening. He told stories about him and Cameron in Viet Nam and about characters in the Phoenix crime scene. I once asked about the friend he'd come to Chicago to bury. A commodities trader, said Mac, who had died from cocaine. It was obviously a painful subject and I didn't push it. I understood the hurt of losing a friend.

The dizziness eased. In the shop across from me, Roxanne's Boutique featured ankle-length ribbed tube-knits in soft pastels. The leggy mannequins looked like popsicles. I salivated. My colors. My style. Thirty pounds ago. Roxanne had been my favorite, putting together entire ensembles for me. She even provided a fitting-room ashtray. I didn't need the ashtray anymore. Or Roxanne's. I wasn't up to facing the brutality of her triple-mirrored dressing rooms. It was against Roxanne's ethics to buy for women with hips and thighs. She carried mostly Azzadine Alaia's, garments specially seamed to grip the body, cup the ass like a hand. 'My clothes flutter when you fart,' she'd say dragging a Chesterfield through a gold holder, curling her upper lip slightly. 'If women want to shop me, let 'em take it off and firm it up.'

I shivered. A surge of sweat poured down my neck, my underarms, my back. A vise pressed my head from both sides muffling the sounds of the mall. The Sweat Shop next to Roxanne's had a few outfits I might be able to use. I tried to focus on the full-cut mauve sweats with matching socks and headband. I needed something to wear Monday when Kathlyn and I began Nautilus. 'Wear any old thing,' the trainer had said during our free introductory session, but I couldn't fit into any *old* old things. I needed *new* old things. A thin high-pitched whine, like death on a heart monitor, blared between my ears and I bent forward, drooping my head between my legs.

'Mom?' Rikki's frightened voice came from miles away. Her cool hand rubbed my sodden back. 'You okay, Mom? Should I go for help?'

I tried to pull air into my lungs. 'I'm okay.' My tongue was thick. 'Water?'

'I'll get some. Don't move. Don't move. I'll be right back.'

Gradually, the dizziness passed and I risked sitting up. Rikki pressed a paper cone of cool water into my hands. She sat rigidly on the end of the bench as I sipped.

'I'm all right, honey. Honest. Just a little dizzy. It was too hot in there.'

'Want to go home?'

'Good idea.'

'I'll get Jason.'

92

I collapsed into the Pontiac's back seat, head back, eyes closed. It was lunch time and, at Jason's urging, Rikki swung into McDonald's drive-thru. Lately I had lost my resistance to junk food, unable to pass up anything fried, sugared, or salted. But, as I half-opened my eyes and scanned the order board, I found no appetite for anything. Maybe I had the flu. Maybe I could keep getting the flu until I lost thirty pounds.

Back home, Rikki pulled the car into the garage and the kids carried their camp clothes into the house. Bundles of Franklin's campaign posters lined the garage. FRANKLIN AVERS in blue block letters across the top. A close-up of his sincere face. FIT TO LEAD bordering the bottom.

'Fitness is going to win this for me, Barbara. Look who I'm running against. Everything about Kurtz is slovenly. The way he looks, the way he runs his office. Fitness is going to be the key to my campaign.'

Franklin stared at me from the posters. Handsome man. Getting handsomer by the year. Somewhere he had a closet with one hell of an ugly portrait. If only I could erase the sadness I saw creeping into Franklin's eyes lately when he looked at me. No, not sadness. Emptiness. Maybe he'd decided he wouldn't really look at me until I was back to my proper weight.

'I, Franklin Avers, promise I will never smoke cigars or talk in movies,' he'd said in our verbal prenuptial.

'And I, Barbara Marlow, will build you a mirrored bathroom and I'll never get fat.' So help us God. It seemed so little to promise. Puff, puff.

'Ah, Franklin,' I said to his FIT TO LEAD face, 'why couldn't you have had a fat mother you loved instead of hated?' The posters didn't answer. I cleaned out the McDonald's bags from the front seat, eating the leftover fries and sandwich scraps. With the flu and all, I'd probably be throwing it all up soon, so what the hell.

MAY

145–157

SEVEN

'I used to do that,' whispered Kathlyn, opening her purse, taking out a pen, closing the purse, opening the purse, finding her glasses, closing the purse, checking off items on the Nutri-Systems order form.

I sat next to her in the Nutri-Systems reception room, studying my food list, trying to decide if I could face yet another box of powdered tomato soup. 'You used to do what?'

'Watch that gal with the kid.'

An obese young woman with elegantly coifed blond hair and impeccable makeup approached the Nutri-Systems reception desk. A cranky toddler tugged the hem of her hand-smocked Swiss cotton tent, trying to drag her back the way they'd come.

'Brian, please,' she said sweetly, 'Mommy has to do this. Here, look.' She bent over a huge toy-filled Gucci bag, her long dress hiking in back, exposing thick Petunia Pig calves and small ankles. 'Here's your truck. You can . . .'

'Noooooo-o-o-.' The whine ended in short sputtery cries. 'Let's goooooooooo-o-o-.'

'Brian,' the woman glanced around the room apologetically, lest they be disturbing anyone.

Kathlyn elbowed me. 'I called this my St Joan routine.'

The white-smocked reedy girl behind the desk was firm. 'Mrs Rand, I told you last time we discourage our clients from bringing young children here. It's disruptive to the other . . .'

'Oh, I know.' Sweet smile, gushing apology. 'But I couldn't find a sitter and . . .'

'Let's gooooooo . . .'

Women seated in chairs around the room registered a mixture of sympathy and annoyance. My gut knotted with the remembered anxiety of this kind of situation. Rikki and Jason kicking each other under the restaurant table, fidgeting and whining while Grandma Avers dawdled over her second pre-dinner cocktail. Rikki and Jason running around the shoe store, doctor's office, dentist's office, anywhere there was an interminable wait – which was everywhere we needed to go. Luckily, when my kids were small I smoked.

'I don't understand what you mean,' I whispered to Kathlyn. 'What's she doing?'

Kathlyn flipped her glasses up on top of her head and tapped her pen on her food form. 'The trick here is to set up a martyr situation. This place has sessions from seven in the morning until nine at night.'

'So?'

'So, when does Miss Such a Pretty Face come in? Now. Nap time. Wants to be sure little Brian is good and cranky.'

'But, she said she couldn't find a sitter . . .'

'Barbara, I know the con. Look at her. She found time to get a Paul Glick haircut and buy a hand-smocked Bisoulis. That woman can *buy* a sitter. Or she could have changed her appointment time until a sitter was available. Or asked a neighbor to watch little Brian for an hour. Or waited until her hubby came home and let him watch Brian. Obviously she's done this before and has been warned before. She wants to be kicked out.'

'Kathlyn, you're such a cynic.'

'I'm a realist. I had a father who went to AA meetings to get my mom off his back. He kept drinking. I went to Overeaters Anonymous for years before my divorce to get my family off my back. I kept eating. The name of this particular game is to make it appear you're doing everything possible to get help, so your loved ones get off your back.' She shifted her low voice into a high-pitched whine. 'Its not *my* fault I had to leave Nutri-Systems today, Fenster. Lord knows I certainly tried to go. But little Brian . . .' Kathlyn sighed dramatically. 'And that, Barbara, is what this little scene is all about.'

Brian exploded into a full-blown tantrum. With an ear-splitting scream the pitch of a piping tea kettle, he threw his little body belly down on the carpet, kicking and hitting the floor.

'I'm sorry,' said his mother, calmly gathering him in her arms. 'I'll have to call for another appointment.' She smiled all the way out, a resigned 'Well, I tried' look on her face. The room became blissfully silent.

'Now,' said Kathlyn, 'she'll go home, put little Brian to bed, watch "General Hospital", and explain to her mother-husband-psychiatrist-butcher-sister-friend that she *tried*, but just can't begin to think about losing weight until little Brian is older. If she spaces her pregnancies right, she can blame her fat on her kids for another ten years.' Kathlyn lowered her glasses and scanned her food list. 'How's your gas?'

It was a challenge to keep pace with Kathlyn's abrupt topic changes. 'Pungent. The kids call it "Killer Gas". It's funny. I think they're kind of surprised to learn I have natural bodily functions. My grandmother never allowed them in our house. Proper young ladies didn't burp let alone expel gas.'

'That anything like a fart?'

'Not in my home it wasn't.'

'That explains a lot about you.'

'Thanks.' I scanned my food list. 'I thought these beef dinners might be causing it, but I changed to chicken this week and the gas is still there. The cramps have eased a little.'

'I'll bet it's all that raw broccoli and cauliflower. Amazing what healthy food'll do to you.'

'It doesn't bother you at all?'

'Nope.'

We turned in our order forms and paid for the week's food supply. I weighed in at 146. Kathlyn had continued to lose steadily since Weight Watchers and was down to 210. It was beginning to show. The leader called our discussion group and we entered the small room, taking chairs around the large table.

I loved the camaraderie of eight women banding together to fight a common enemy. I felt cushioned, loved. Most important, I felt understood. I forgave the discussion leader her thinness and youth. She shared our collective anguish and was here to lead us in battle. Opening our Nutri-Systems booklets, we laid our eating lives in front of her. She read over our carefully recorded food intake, cooing her approval, her pride in our progress.

'Pre-menstrual,' I said, explaining my two-and-a-half-pound increase. Kathlyn cleared her throat. I'd been pre-menstrual the week before, and the week before that. Luckily, I'd had different leaders but I was running out of new ones. Hopefully their memories were short. I cringed as the girl noted 'pre-menst' on my booklet in non-erasable non-forgeable green ink. I really would have to lose weight before next week's class. Although, at the rate I was going, being up only two-and-a-half pounds for an entire week was almost like losing weight.

'Today, we're going to discuss our problem eating times,' said the leader. 'What is the hardest time for you? Let's start at this end and go around the table. Birdie?'

'Coffee breaks at work,' said the gray-haired woman, absently rubbing a liver spot on the back of her hand. 'Sitting in that room with all those vending machines.'

'I just bring enough money for coffee,' someone offered, 'then take the coffee somewhere else to drink.'

'But the vending room is where everyone sits around and talks. It's my only chance to socialize. The rest of the day I'm sitting behind a computer.'

'Perhaps you can save something from your breakfast or lunch to eat on your break,' said the leader.

'Oh, I'd be embarrassed to bring in my own food.'

'Have any of you noticed,' asked the leader, 'that so many of us who are overweight seem preoccupied with what other people might say or think?' We nodded. 'We assume people are talking about us, watching us, judging us.'

'That's probably because they are,' I said. Gentle laughter.

The leader pursed her mouth. 'I'm not so sure. I wonder if that's not a bit conceited. I suspect people are concerned about their own lives and problems and don't give yours much thought. Birdie, try turning the situation around. What would you think if a friend of yours brought her own snack to the break?'

Birdie raised her thin penciled eyebrows. 'Actually,' she said, 'I have seen people bring their own food from time to time. I never really gave it much thought.'

'Exactly. Try bringing your own snacks this week and let us know next session how it went. Linda?' She turned to the frazzled young woman next to Birdie. 'What's your problem time?'

'Making the kids' lunches.' We murmured our agreement. 'Licking mayonnaise off the knife, wiping tuna fish out of the bowl with a Ritz cracker, folding a piece of American cheese into my mouth. And I can't seem to physically move leftovers from the table to the garbage. You know, those tiny ends of hot dogs, crusts of peanut butter sandwiches.' We let out a collective sigh. Peanut butter was a hands-down favorite.

'This week,' said the leader, 'I want you to shove that food down the sink or run water over it before you have time to *think* about putting it in your mouth.'

'That's so wasteful.'

'Then wrap it and save it for their next lunch.'

'They'd never touch it.'

The leader smiled. 'Right. It's not wasteful. Don't pass moral judgment on a piece of uneaten food. It's simply left. No one will ever know if you *don't* eat it. Only if you do. Have you ever seen a fat dispose-all?' We laughed. 'Me neither. Try it this week and let me know how it goes. Barbara?'

I stopped filling in the letters on the cover of my booklet. 'I don't know if there's any one time. I guess those times I used to light up a cigarette are pretty rough. Telephone calls, writing, making shopping lists, driving. I'm hungry most of the time.'

'Can you narrow it down to one time that's particularly rough?'

I ran my day through my mind at high speed. 'Late afternoon,' I said. 'Going into the kitchen to start dinner. I'm salivating before I'm through the door. I get crazy, sometimes. Most times. I'll cram all sorts of food into my mouth for about five minutes. Cookies, crackers, peanut butter on celery, carrots, leftover anything. I lean against the counter, gasping and chewing. Sometimes I kind of step outside myself and watch me eat.'

'And how do you look to you?'

'Crazed. Like someone guzzling their first drink of water after three days on the desert. I look ridiculous. But I don't stop.'

'Kitchens are rough, aren't they?' asked the leader. Murmurs of agreement hummed around the table. Mine was a universal problem. 'Can anyone in your house help you with dinner?'

'No, not really. The kids have homework and my husband, when he's home at all, comes in late. I used to have a cook but she's visiting her mother in Guatemala.'

'What about eating half your dinner before you begin handling food. Maybe your potato.'

'I'm too hungry.'

'Then try eating your entire dinner at your rough time. You can have tea while your family eats.'

'Thanks,' I said. 'I'll give it a try.' She was so hopeful, so helpful. No point mentioning I'd already done just that and wound up eating a second meal with my family.

I wasn't too concerned. This was a temporary problem. I'd leave the kitchen forever the moment Sophia returned. Although, Franklin didn't seem too eager to have her come back right away. He'd mumbled something about 'watching our pennies' until the campaign was over. 'Our pennies' meant my pennies because he sure wasn't scrimping on his campaign expenses. I'd paid catering bills to Jewel, Gapers, and The Lunch Basket for campaign staff breakfasts, lunches, and dinners. Franklin had explained that a man with a FIT TO LEAD slogan can't very well send out for pizzas. He'd made me feel guilty for bringing the matter up. When I questioned the extravagance of his campaign, he took over the campaign account, moving the check book and my records to his office.

'Nutri-Systems is perfect for the women whose family isn't sympathetic,' said our discussion leader. We all nodded. 'We don't have any decision-making here. No food preparation. It's all done for us.'

'I'd be fine,' I said, 'if I could bomb my kitchen.' The group laughed.

'I said that to my mother,' said Kathlyn, weaving the fringe of her shawl in and out her fingers. 'Just as a little joke. She lashed into me about what a lousy mother I'd become. Selfish. Only thinking of myself.' Like the rest of us, Kathlyn let her weight-guard down in the intimate sisterhood of the class. 'She pointed out that my sister, my married sister, my thin married sister who worked full time in New Jersey managed to cook and bake fabulous dishes for her family. Every night.' Derisive whispers of 'Superwoman' circled the table. Kathlyn sniffed and tossed back her hair. 'I don't know how my mother knows all that. My sister never calls or writes unless she wants something.' She pressed her lips together. Tears glistened on her thick black lashes. 'My mother calls me at work, at home, expecting me to drive her to the store, meetings, hair dresser.'

'Do you?'

'You bet.' She affected a high nasal voice. 'You only have one mother, you know. She won't be around forever.'

'I have that record,' said Linda. 'My mother gets jealous if I do anything for anyone but her.'

Kathlyn nodded. 'Years ago, before I worked, I volunteered at a senior citizens' home. My mother was furious. She said I had time for everyone in the world but my own mother. When I'm with her, all she ever talks about is how wonderful my sister is.'

'Are you ever going to be able to please her?' asked the leader.

'Not in this lifetime,' said Kathlyn.

'So?'

Kathlyn looked down, using one thumbnail to scrape the polish off the other. She sobbed a few breaths and I slid my arm around her. 'So,' tears dripped onto her lap, 'so tell me why I don't stop trying.' There wasn't a dry eye in the place. Our tough-talking, wise-cracking Kathlyn sobbed, shaking in my arms. After a full minute she looked up, laughing at the effect she'd had on us. 'I really know how to perk up a party.'

The leader patted her arm. 'You've taken the first step,' she said. She looked around the room. 'Why do we do this to ourselves? Obviously we care about being overweight or we wouldn't be here. I'd like each of you to think about that this week. What is it in you that won't let you refuse a piece of cake or pass a Baskin Robbins? Why do you reach for that 300-calorie roll and butter before dinner? How can you hate your body on the one hand and continue to feed it on the other? Let's talk about that next week. And Kathlyn, you've made a good start. I wonder what would happen if you stopped trying to please your mother quite so much, quite so hard.'

'The world would come screeching to a stop,' said Kathlyn.

'It seems a small price to pay.'

Mountainous clouds the dusty black of Necco licorice wafers roiled in from the Northwest. The first few drops of icy rain pelted us as we raced through the parking lot to Kathlyn's car. Thunder rumbled in the distance. A full-blown spring storm was heading straight for us. This was Sarajane's favorite weather.

'Drop you at home?' asked Kathlyn. I didn't want to be alone.

'I thought we could eat lunch together.'

'Can't.' She plugged in her fuzz-buster and peeled out of the lot. 'Have to go to the office.'

'On your day off?'

'Bosses don't get days off. Three of my people conned me into letting them take a FAM trip to Portland. The height of my family vacation season and I'm shorthanded. Damn!' She slammed on the brakes as the commuter train guardrail came down. I stared out my window and pouted. I had no one to play with.

Kathlyn, far from being the telephone operator I had first imagined, owned and operated Mom's Travel Agency in the new Merchantile Exchange. Her 'boys', mostly young turks high on making and losing millions, demanded and received solid gold treatment from Kathlyn. If they sniffled, she sent up chicken soup wrapped in brochures for the Bahamas. Marriage problems? She delivered roses and a red-ribboned packet of 'Ten Lovers Weekends guaranteed to rekindle the old flame'. Secretaries fed her information in exchange for travel perks. Because of Kathlyn's size, she was non-threatening, a relief to the secretaries and wives and a soft cushion for the hard problems of her young clients.

All right, so she was busy, but if she had time for Nutri-Systems she could manage a quick lunch with me. I shivered against the chill in the car, flipping up the hood to Rikki's Chicago Bears sweat shirt, grateful she'd ignored my advice and bought an extra large.

'If you're so damned busy, Kathlyn, why'd you bother coming to today's session?'

'Don't get bitchy, Barbara. It would be real easy for me not to make time for the sessions. All my life I've been finding reasons why I couldn't do something I should have done. I had to take care of my mother, my kids, my ex, my schooling, my work. But not this time.' Kathlyn screeched into my driveway and threw the car into neutral. 'I don't think there's any way to lose weight unless I start putting myself first. And if that means a one-day delay in booking the Fitzwilliger family to Disney World, well, it can't be helped. And if it means your nose gets bent out of joint because I have to earn a living, so be it. I'm not going to apologize for taking care of myself, least of all to you.'

A crack of thunder shook the car. 'I'd better go,' I said, throwing open the door and racing into the house. I headed straight for the kitchen. Hot chocolate with marshmallows in front of the fireplace, a good book. It was that sort of day. Sarajane had understood this weather. I knew Kathlyn was right but that didn't keep me from being pissed at her. I banged around the cabinets, poured milk into a cup, stirred in Nestle's, topped it with marshmallows, and set it in the microwave for three minutes. Maybe later I'd make a bowl of hot-air popcorn with just a touch of melted low-cal margarine and wash it down with a cold can of Diet Chocolate Fudge. The red light blinked on the telephone answering machine. I hit the play button.

'I forgot to tell you this morning to pick up my shoes at –'

'Hello to you, too, Franklin. Yes, I'm fine. So nice to hear your voice.' I jammed my finger on the fast forward.

'Oh.' Silence. 'Well, um . . .' A slow creaky voice not used to speaking to a machine. 'I see. Well, um, this is George Payne.' Old Payne-in-the-glass. My finger hovered over the fast forward. The machine would keep recording as long as someone spoke and from all Franklin had said, Payne went on and on ad nauseum. 'I was hoping to speak to Mr or Mrs Avers. Um, to be sure my check reached Mr Avers. I don't know when I can make the next payment. Mrs Payne, my wife, isn't doing all that well and – um – I can't seem to reach Mr Avers at his office and his secretary said she'd give him the message but that was a week ago and I didn't want him to think his loan wasn't heavy on my mind. Well, um, I guess you can call me if you have any questions.' He gave his number and I jotted it on the note pad. He repeated it to make sure. 'And that's about all I wanted to say.' He had not hung up right away. I pressed the receiver to my ear, listening to him breathe, feeling his need to talk. While I was out agonizing over a few extra pounds, this poor man was trying to keep his whole damned life from falling apart. I'd check with Franklin. Find out if he got the money. I'd set aside a half-hour and call Payne myself. Ask about his wife. Let him talk it out a bit. Maybe touching someone with real problems would help me put mine in proper perspective. George finally hung up and the answering machine whirred to the next call.

'Barbara, this is Cameron. I need you. It's an emergency. Call me the second you get in.' I jotted down the number to his direct line. The microwave dinged. I opened the door to the heavenly smell of chocolate but the cup handle burned my fingers. I'd let it cool while I called Cameron.

'Brady here.'

'Hi, Cameron, it's me.'

'Barb! Thank God. Now, before you say no –'

'What a great build-up.'

'I need to borrow you. Just for a few weeks.'

'For what?'

'Sydney Kreiger jumped ship to the *Sun-Times*.' I whistled softly. Kreiger's irreverent column dominated page two of the *Globe* for years.

'What happened?'

'They upped his salary and sweetened the pot by sponsoring him in a weekly half-hour TV show. I want you to fill in –'

'No.'

'Listen a minute. I've got a couple of other people here who will feed me a few columns. Just help me out a couple of weeks until I find a replacement.'

'No.' Cigarette. I swallowed against the need.

'I told you not to say that.'

'That's not what I write.'

'It's what you used to write. And I can trust you to meet a deadline. And I've read enough of your op ed freelance articles over the years to know you haven't lost the touch.'

'You know how I feel about staying at home, Cameron. At least until Jason is in high school. A daily column is a full-time job.'

'I'm not asking daily, Barbara. Did I say daily? I'll find someone to take Kreiger's place. I just don't have him yet. I need fill in, two maybe four weeks. I'll split the load between a few writers. I don't want our readers to get out of the habit of looking for a column in that space.' I heard another voice behind his and the phone being juggled around.

'Barb?'

'Hello?'

'This is Mac.' Surge of warm fuzzies. He hadn't

stopped by for breakfast since Sophia went back to Guatemala. Sophia the chaperone, he'd teased her. Maybe he hadn't been joking. 'My friend here is too polite to tell you he needs you to save his bony ass. He's already tried five different people and none of them is heavyweight enough to go up against Sydney.' I wasn't crazy about his choice of words. 'This group column idea is all he has. I'll write a few if you will.'

'It's very flattering, Mac, but I can't.'

'Listen, you can write the damned things at home and I'll pick them up.' If he came over on business it would be all right. Right?

'I've got to get my kids ready for camp.'

'I'll sew on their goddamned name tags.'

'My husband's campaign is gearing up.'

'I thought you said he doesn't need you right now.'

'You have a good memory.'

'Steel trap. Cameron needs you, Barbara. This man is a mess.'

My grip on the phone turned clammy. Kathlyn was right. You could always find excuses if you wanted them. Hadn't Franklin told me to find something to do? 'I could work at home?'

'Thanks, Barb.' Cameron had recaptured the phone. 'You won't regret this.'

'Cameron! I didn't say yes.'

'Look, Sydney has to give me two more weeks of articles. Get your life in order and then get me three or four columns say, next Friday.' He clicked off.

It was a dumb idea. My features writing was rusty. Cameron might take one look at my work and say thanks but no thanks. I didn't know if I was up for any more rejection in my life just now. I dimly remembered the agony of blank paper and impending deadlines, the way I could almost recall the pain of childbirth. It always seems so manageable from a distance. My 'Ask Barbara' column was a relatively easy matter of finding specific answers to specific questions. Even during my first cigaretteless weeks there was little blood on the computer keys. I'd have to open a much bigger vein to produce the kind of writing Cameron was talking about. I took three files marked 'IDEAS' out of my desk. They bulged with clippings, jotted notes, photocopied articles. There had to be the seeds for some good columns in there, enough to help Cameron out for a couple of weeks. It might be fun to go down to the *Globe* after all these years. I hadn't been back since my father's death.

The marshmallows swelled and I poked them with my finger, turning them over to soften all the sides. There was the problem of how to approach Franklin. He didn't mind if I volunteered a thousand hours a week but he'd hate me working a real job.

'Poor women work!' he'd yelled years before when I'd casually mentioned taking some sort of job. I'd enrolled Jason in kindergarten and suddenly had too many hours in my days. 'My mother had to work and I had to raise nine brothers and sisters. Is that what you want? You want to rob your children of their childhood? You want people to think I can't support this family? Then go to work!' He slammed out of the house and didn't come home until the next day. I never mentioned working again. I realized that my mother, had she lived, would have happily given up her career to stay home with me.

The hot chocolate burned my lips. I stirred the marshmallows into the liquid. It had been years since I mentioned working. No one now could question Franklin's success. Wives of the most prominent politicians in the country held jobs, a fact the men proudly alluded to when courting the women's vote. As for neglecting the children, would Franklin still object to my working once Rikki and Jason were away at camp? I had never knowingly set our marriage on a collision course and I didn't want to start now. Over the years our friends' marriages heaved, hurled, and broke apart, but Franklin and I remained comfortably compatible, wonderfully in sync, superbly attuned. Puff, puff. Wasn't that what made a good marriage? The give and take? Puff puff. The compromise?

I thought Cameron's offer over from every possible angle. Even after playing devil's advocate I couldn't find a single thing Franklin might object to. The children would be away. I wasn't needed at home. Franklin's campaign didn't need me. And, if he should need me, I could bend my hours around his erratic schedule. Best of all, work would keep my mind off food.

I wrapped my sweat shirt around the burning cup of hot chocolate, took another cup from the cupboard and poured the hot chocolate back and forth over the sink, cooling the creamy liquid, savoring the smell that transported me back to Sarajane's after-school kitchen. Sarajane. Damn. I still hadn't cleaned out her closet. I'd better do it now before I started working on the columns. No dessert until I finished my mashed potatoes.

Sheets of rain pelted the window. The sky turned the sickly gray-green of citrus mold. Lightning ignited the sky. Thunder exploded, rattling the windows and shaking the house.

'All right, all right, I hear you.' I dumped the thick marshmallow chocolate mixture down the drain. Thunder boomed again. 'I said, all right. I'm coming.' Five minutes later I was driving through hailstones on my way to Sarajane's house.

EIGHT

I couldn't do it. Sarajane's key waited unturned in the ornately carved teak door. There was no way I could go inside. A tiny Buddah next to my knuckles preached to a gathering of monks. I ran my fingers along the carved figures. There must be hundreds of scenes on that door I'd never noticed. Maybe I could study them now, stay close without going inside.

The raging stormfront had boiled over into Indiana leaving behind a steady rain. I shook out my umbrella in the shelter of the pagoda roof. This outside entrance was classic Sarajane. On a trip to Japan she'd fallen in love with a formal Japanese garden and imported it whole, complete with stones, ornaments, benches, and tiled overhang. Self-denial rarely figured in her life except for her yearly Lenten agony, forty days without candy. I turned to set my open umbrella to drain in the entry yard.

'Shit,' I said softly. The garden of tiny gray pebbles she'd lovingly raked into formal Japanese designs had been gouged into a giant tic-tac-toe. Two warped pool cues, their varnish mottled by moisture, lay abandoned on the game. I covered the desecration with my umbrella. Gray rain on gray stones makes a gray sound. Music to cry by. The courtyard reverberated with distant thunder.

'All right, all right, I hear you.' The garden air was thick with the perfume of the two junipers I had given Sarajane to guard the door. We had planted them together, some chemical in their branches raising itchy red bumps over our arms which we treated with massive doses of Benedril (on the scratch), and Benedictine (down the hatch). The plants, once trim and tidy, had grown ragged and wild without her care. Shaggy branches brushed the door and I tugged off a tip, rolling it between my fingers, pressing it to my nose. I thought my grief had healed but it was only scabbed over, thin as a flake crust.

'You will turn the key,' I said. I turned the key. 'You will enter the house. One. Two. Three.' I pushed open the door. BZZZZZZZZZZZZZZZZZ. The burglar alarm! I leapt into the foyer, jamming my finger into the panel of numbers. The buzzer was insistent. I had thirty-five seconds to disarm the alarm before a signal would sound at the police department. I couldn't remember the damned sequence. Stanford's birthday. When the hell was it? April. April is the cruelest month. Tax day. Seconds ticked down. I punched the code, cracking my nail. Done! I slumped against the credenza, gasping for breath in the wonderful silence. Sweat rolled off my face. My clammy clothes stuck to my skin.

The credenza mirror was brutal. An eerie glow

through the foyer skylight pushed down on my face, deepening the lines, furrowing the brows. I put my fingertips on the sides of my cheeks and lifted, smoothing the crescent-shaped line running from nostril to mouth. The corners of my eyes lifted exotically. I could last about one more year. Two at the outside if I never went any place brighter than a five-star restaurant. Maybe I'd have an eye job first, a little nip and tuck warm-up for the main event. The one good thing about gaining weight was my face didn't look as haggard as when I was thin. I'd once seen romance writer Barbara Cartland interviewed. 'Women have two choices as they age,' she'd said, diamond tiara glittering, taffeta gown crinkling, pet Pekinese panting, 'they can be thin . . . or they can look good. I have chosen the latter. All it really requires is that when one enters a room one sits down as quickly as possible.' Sarajane and I had a good laugh. We both knew what *we'd* choose. Puff, puff.

'You're a big girl,' I said to my uplifted face. 'You cannot write one single word for the *Globe* until you go in and clean out your friend's closet. You will not fall apart. You are doing this for yourself and Sarajane, not for Stanford. You will do this with love and joy in your breaking little heart.'

The house felt wrong. The air on my cheek was warmer than Sarajane would have liked. She'd always been too warm. I'd never been warm enough. Although, lately, I hadn't felt as chilled as often. And my hands weren't cold all the time. Which was just as well since Franklin wasn't home very often to warm them. Amazing, the changes caused by a little layer of fat. The smells of the house were wrong, too. The melange that created Sarajane's scents of identity – foods, detergent, shampoo, perfume, cigarettes, body powder, floor polish – had changed.

Stanford's gold putter leaned against the thick glass coffee table at one end of the living room. Old Neiman Marcus balls spilled from the ultrasuede shag bag onto the antique oriental. Sarajane hated that rug, one of Stanford's auction 'finds'. The man couldn't keep his hand down. The rug had to be cleaned, 'deloused' she'd said, and re-fringed. Over half the color came out in the cleaning, color the owner or auctioneer had painted to camouflage a century of foot paths. Her cancer had been diagnosed around that time. Throughout therapy Sarajane spent hours on the living-room floor, armed with a portable TV and pack of felt-tip pens. For weeks, from 'Oprah' through 'Wheel of Fortune', she sat dabbing color back into the pale threads, lying back on pillows when she tired, then resuming her work as if, when she finished, something would be changed. Hours of her life wasted, hours she didn't have to give. One small patch under the coffee table remained undone, left colorless by her death. And now the rug had shifted from sacred surface to putting green in the flick of a coffin lid.

One of Stanford's chewed cigar stubs sat in an ashtray alongside a pink lipsticked clove cigarette. Dried moisture rings from the two highball glasses marked the glass top. A pizza box lay open on the end of the sofa. I walked over and sat down next to the uneaten crusts and leftover pieces. I could just picture last night's scene, the size four curled on the sofa wearing something pink and angora, ooaahing and aahing as Stanford played with his stick, squealing as he said, 'Ain't how you drive, honey-baby-cutie-sweetie, it's how you arrive.' His hand wasn't the only thing Stanford couldn't keep down. I spilled the remains of a highball on the glass top, using the pile of pizza napkins to wipe off the marks.

'And just what the hell do you think you're doing?' I asked.

'Cleaning my friend's house,' I said, resenting the question.

'Your friend is dead, Barbara. This is not her house.'

The napkins circled toward the ashtray whose butts included a whole half of an unsmoked cigarette. Not too much lipstick on the tip. No one had trench mouth any more. Herpes? Aids? I could break off the filter. A match book from Georges was on the table, the trendy sort of place Stanford hated in those days before oriental rugs became putting greens. My tongue itched as my left hand reached for the cigarette. Before I could touch it my right hand squeezed the sodden wad of napkins onto it.

'Dammit,' I said, 'what the hell'd you do that for? Half a cigarette isn't going to kill me.'

'No, only the four hundred thousand that would follow.'

I dumped the napkins into the ashtray, slouched

back on the sofa, and ripped off a jagged piece of pizza. The cold cheese topping slid off like a sheet of dental wax. I lifted it back on. 'It's all right,' I said, 'I forgot to have lunch. I'll just have this one slice.' None of us believed that. I curled up and chewed and stared at the room. Sarajane wouldn't have minded Franklin's other woman nearly as much as the mess.

'Mother says it doesn't matter where the man goes during the day as long as he comes home at night. And Daddy always came home at night.'

'That's shit, Sarajane. When I have a home it's going to be a real one, where people stay married their whole lives and never need anyone else.'

'There's no such marriage,' she said.

'If my mother had lived, that's the sort of home we would have had.' I'd always known everything about 'real' homes. The advantage, Sarajane claimed, of not growing up in one.

'Why don't you just confront Stanford?' I'd once asked.

'What the hell do you think I'm doing?' Sarajane adjusted the emerald brooch, moving back from the counter mirror, trying to decide. The Tiffany clerk stood a discreet distance away.

'Not like this. I mean verbally.'

'Oh, Sugah.' She took my hands in hers. 'Now where's the fun in that?'

Stanford never made the connection between Sarajane's jewelry purchases and his affairs. Smug bastard. It never occurred to him she knew, had known from the beginning when his first secretary, whose bird legs started at her neck, called to tell Sarajane to give Stanford up. Sarajane said 'shonuff, honey buns', deposited a basket of his dirty laundry with the secretary's doorman along with the kids' car-pool schedules, daily routines, food preferences, and allergies. Stanford had paced for days after that, wringing his hands, muttering about ungrateful secretaries quitting without notice, oblivious of his affair's tie to Sarajane's new diamond ring framed by two emerald baguettes.

The dregs of the other drink tasted like cheap perfume but helped push down the pizza. I had to restrain myself from cleaning up but the house was obviously under new management. I guessed the mess was meant to wait until tomorrow for old Selma. I was glad this was her day off. I needed to be alone with my friend one last time. Tiptoeing down the hall to Sarajane's bedroom – why tiptoe? – I eased open the children's bedroom doors. Unmade beds. Clothing everywhere. Dressers buried under the detritus of adolescence. The rooms smelled ripely of molding apple cores and black banana skins. No, Sarajane sure as hell didn't live here anymore. How did her kids feel about Miss Pink Angora? Hell, what could be bad about a size four who ate pizza in the living room and smoked clove cigarettes?

Sarajane's closet dwarfed some hotel rooms I'd stayed in. Four metal poles ran the length of the ten-foot-long space, each crammed with clothing neatly organized according to sizes, seasons, and styles.

Shoes lined the racks below, accessories the ones above. Taking the box of plastic garbage bags from my purse, I started packing the size sixteens. I'd work my way up.

Two hours later I had twenty bags stuffed and labeled. I hauled the ladder up from the basement to reach items off the top shelf. I found the large manila envelope hidden in a plastic box between two moth-balled sweaters. Sitting on top of the ladder, out of breath and sweaty, I flipped open the envelope and slid the contents onto my lap.

There was a sheaf of neatly typed reports on heavy bond paper. I ran my fingers over the raised letter head. HALSEY INVESTIGATIONS. The reports, each addressed Dear Mrs Quinlin, dated back fifteen years.

'Pursuant to your request to do surveillance on August 23, your husband was observed . . .'

'Here are the photos we obtained during surveillance of your husband on November 11 taken at the Sybaris Inn by operative Lou Sobel.'

'Where he was seen entering Rogie's Lounge, 305 W.
Adams St . . . At 4:05 he was met by a Eurasian woman, approximately 23 years of age, with waist-length black hair. They proceeded to hold hands, drinking until 5:15 at which time they left together and were followed to . . .'

'Leaving the convention, your husband and the woman (later determined to be a call girl regularly working Las Vegas casinos) entered room 610 of the hotel.'

'Left his foursome at the first hole pleading a sciatica attack and drove to the Lake Forest Oasis where he picked up a woman who had been waiting for him. They proceeded to . . .'
'. . . returning in time to join his golf group as they completed the round.'

There were more. Many more. The closet heat pressed in on me. Clutching the letters and the envelope, I climbed shakily down the ladder, and sank onto Stanford's unmade bed. Shuddered. Bounced back up and sat on the floor. The second manila folder was crammed with photos of Stanford and:

– a Las Vegas hooker at the craps table. The two of them coming out of his hotel room.

– a western-garbed girl at a Texas two-step bar. The two of them coming out of a trailer.

– Kippy Laughlin, assistant manager of our club's golf shop, exiting behind him from a room at the Knight Out motel on Lincoln Avenue.

The back of each photo was tagged with an identification label. Written in bold black ink were the date, time, place, and name of operative. Next to each label was another later date penned in Sarajane's flowery style. The first date was the detective's notation, the second was the date of Sarajane's retaliation. Antique ruby brooch set in white gold. Two-carat diamond studs. Five tennis bracelets, with fifteen diamonds each. The first eight years detailed jewelry purchases which became increasingly more expensive. I sometimes wondered if she wasn't upping the ante, hoping he'd confront her with her extravagance so she could retaliate with his affairs. It never happened. I had known about the jewelry. What I hadn't known about was the men.

It took a few moments for me to realize what I was looking at. I didn't want to believe it. The first affair dated back seven years. It was penned on the back of the Kippy photo:

9/14 PB – Waiter at Munich Club.

I knew the place but not the initials. I remembered Sarajane dragging me there for a few weeks claiming a craving for oxtail soup. Evidently that wasn't the tail she had a taste for. I vaguely remembered an arrogant young waiter. PB no doubt:

12/3 FR – Conventioneer – Palmer House

2/7 GS – Mim's Dance Club

She was picking up strangers. 'Oh, Sarajane, Sarajane, why didn't you tell me?' How could I not have known? When didn't I know where she was and what she was doing? Had she been so afraid to tell me? Yes, obviously. And I knew why. We'd had the conversation over and over through the years. It never changed much.

'Affairs are how civilized adults survive marriage,' she'd insisted, both before and after we'd married and had children. 'Which is why I hold such little hope for yours.' Her parents had separate bedrooms connected by a narrow passageway. When I slept over, Sarajane and I snuck into the passageway after dinner, running our hands over the carpet nap to stand it up on end so we would be able to detect footprints in the passage. In all those years there never were any.

'You think Ozzie Nelson and Bill Cosby had affairs?' I'd ask. 'Not on your Nielsens.'

'Television families are not real life.'

'You're so cynical.'

'I've got to be, for both of us.'

I thought she'd been baiting me. Now I realized she'd been trying to tell me about PB the waiter, and FR, and GS. Was I so righteous my best friend was afraid of offending me? Of losing me?

I returned the photos to the shelf, the ladder to the basement, and dragged the clothing bags to the front stoop for a Salvation Army pickup. Setting the key on the kitchen table, I looked around one last time. No, I didn't belong here anymore. I wished I could see Stanford finding the photos of himself. Surprise! Sarajane *knew* and had her revenge, you pompous prick.

That vision was instantly replaced by a more vivid one of Stanford and his girlfriend in bed, pouring over the photos and reports, her pert pink nipples jiggling as she laughed. I went down to the basement, brought up the ladder, and took the envelope with me. Stopping briefly in the stale cigar stink of Stanford's closet, I scented his clothing with a deposit of killer gas and shut the door firmly behind me. Coals to Newcastle. Cookies to Mrs Fields. The piles of garbage bags stacked outside the front door pleaded not to be left behind. 'All right, all right, I'm not going to leave you.' I loaded Sarajane's clothing into my car and took her home with me.

The kitchen table groaned under the piles of material from my 'IDEAS' files. The junk I'd accumulated! Articles ripped from newspapers and magazines, photocopies of book pages, notes jotted on restaurant napkins, spiral notepads, matchbooks, Jewel receipts. Half the material now seemed stupid and the other half made no sense at all. Why the photo of a barber holding up an envelope containing $25 and an anonymous note from a man who robbed him fifteen years before and never overcame his guilt? Or the Boy Scout in front of the stop lights he petitioned to have installed at a dangerous school crossing? Or the migration of monarch butterflies to Mexico.

A large clump of information on Sumo wrestling was stapled to articles about American women wrestlers. I couldn't begin to remember what I'd intended. Maybe I could do an article about the way weight was venerated in some countries. Maybe I could move to

Japan and become the first female Sumo wrestler. Barbara-San. Had a certain ring to it. Weight around the world. Wasn't there something in *Mondo Cane* about a ruler who received a yearly salary equal to his two wives' weight in gold? The two young women were shown being fattened for the weigh-in. *Mondo Cane.* God, I hadn't seen that since it played at the Esquire when I was a kid. Maybe an article on 'Do you remember . . .' I jotted the idea down under others that filled a sheet of yellow legal paper. Even if nothing useable turned up in the files they might trigger new ideas.

I tried to arrange the files into some sort of order. It was impossible. For someone capable of keeping meticulous financial and household records, there was no excuse for this mess. Except, in the grand scheme of the perfect household, my writing had never really mattered. It was the vestige of a previous incarnation, reborn into my married life as a bit of silly putty to cram into odd cracks of time between my wifely, motherly, household jobs. As long as I didn't ever look into my 'IDEAS' files, I could sustain the illusion there were real stories waiting to happen.

The stove timer buzzed me back to the real world. Time to turn the chicken. The phone rang. I grabbed it and turned off the buzzer.

'Hello?'

'Barb?'

'Hi, Franklin.' I shouldered the phone against my ear and basted the bird with bar-B-que sauce.

'I've been trying to get hold of you.'

'Oh, I was at Sarajane's house . . .'

'Going to be a little late tonight. Emergency strategy committee meeting. Can you get someone else to go to the play with you?'

'Well, I suppose . . .'

'I'm sure sorry about this.' He'd had a pre-dinner drink or two. Not like Franklin.

'You sound a little sloshed.'

'Me?' He dropped the phone and fumbled around to retrieve it. 'Must be a bad connection. Gotta go. See you later.' He made a couple of smacking sounds into the receiver. 'Kisses to the kids.'

I slammed the chickens back into the oven and reset the timer. When had the telephone Franklin become so different from the personal appearance Franklin? His voice was more tender, his words more caring when traveling through miles of fiber optics. I wondered if he was playing his doting father, concerned husband act to an audience on the other end.

The phone call killed my enthusiasm for sorting the mess on the table. It also gave me the resolve to write Cameron's articles. I shoveled the stuff back in the folders. Tomorrow I would devote the entire day to setting up my workspace. I would make neat lists of ideas, set in the supplies I'd need, warn the kids to leave Mommy alone unless they were bleeding in a life-threatening manner, not pick up the phone no matter what. I would set aside daily writing time and would brook no interruption. If I didn't take myself seriously it was a sure bet no one else would.

While the chicken finished cooking, I lugged the bags of Sarajane's clothes to the attic and stashed them in the back of the cedar closet. I slipped the Halsey Investigations envelopes behind the bags. A quick call to Kathlyn and I had my date for the night. Neither Rikki nor Jason wanted the chicken.

'I'm growing pin feathers,' said Rikki.

'Are you going out again?' said Jason.

Frick and Frack. They had the routine down pat. Daddy had to be out, he had important business. I wanted to be out, I was deserting them. I wasn't feeling guilty enough to cancel the theater, just to freeze the chicken and leave them pizza money. Everyone made out, except the chicken.

One of 'The Art of Dining's' two main characters cooked all the way through the play, the other one ate. The air was redolent with sautéed garlic, frying fish, spicy orange, and cinnamon. Even theater wasn't safe any more. Everyone on stage ate except the cook. Fiction. Luckily, Kathlyn had read the reviews and came fortified with two baggies filled with tart Granny Smith slices. I crunched a couple before the lady in front of me turned and glowered. After that I quietly broke off pieces and held them waferlike in my mouth. I'd forgotten what kind of sin it was to swallow. Mortal or venial? Come on, Sarajane, what did you tell me? I strained and reached and grabbed and clawed, but the memory wouldn't come. The other hand wasn't clapping.

'Do these seats seem a little snug to you?' I asked Kathlyn during intermission.

'No. But then, everything is beginning to feel roomier to me. Another fifty pounds and I won't have nightmares about being stuck in airplane toilets.'

On the ride home, I nearly told Kathlyn about Sarajane's affairs. My feelings and thoughts were hopelessly confused – my shock of discovering her affairs, the betrayal I felt at Sarajane's secrecy, my guilt for not being a friend she could confide in, sadness that she bore the weight alone – and I thought talking to Kathlyn would help me. In the end, I couldn't. Sarajane hadn't wanted me, her best friend, to know. How could I betray her confidence to a stranger?

Maybe Franklin would be home. I needed to touch him and be touched. I'd been so miserable since Sarajane's death, so caught up in my own life that I'd been ignoring his. On most days our only contact was in the bathroom, going over his morning list. I wondered if he needed me to hold him as much as I needed to be held. It was nearly midnight when Kathlyn dropped me off. Franklin wasn't home. I undressed slowly, soaked in a hot tub, rubbed Opium cream over my body, dressed in a lacy negligee, and waited reading in bed.

At one o'clock I went downstairs and brought up a double scotch and a jar of Planter's dry roasted nuts. Much healthier than the oily kind. By one-thirty, the room was swimming nicely. Was Franklin fooling around? Does the sun rise in the east? Did I really want to know? Should I have him followed? I shuddered at the slimy thoughts oozing up from the murk. Jason cried out in his sleep. I staggered into his room and re-covered him with the kicked-off bedclothes. 'Night,' I said, kissing his forehead. Had I been neglecting the children as well? Tomorrow I would begin fresh. I would get my life in order. Renewed, I staggered back down the hall to my room.

Another fifteen minutes passed with my book lying open and unread on my lap. I licked my finger, ran it around the salty remains of the empty nut jar, and drained the last of the scotch. On the other hand, what if Franklin *wasn't* fooling around, and here I was suspecting him unfairly? Poor Franklin. Poor dear Franklin. All those pressures from work and the campaign and here I was just waiting to heap more stress on him. I *owed* it to him, to us, to the children, to God, Country, and the American Way to clear my doubts.

I staggered to the attic, tripped on the nightgown, and crashed into the rough wood stairs. A thick splinter dug into the flesh around my knee and snapped from the stair. Gritting my teeth to stop a scream, I grabbed the jagged end and yanked the bloody thing out. A sign, Sarajane would have said. A sign, sure as anything. But a sign of what? To turn back or to go ahead? Dealer's choice. My knee burned and throbbed. Warm blood dripped down my leg staining my gown. I continued up to the closet, dug under Sarajane's clothes bags for the Halsey Investigations envelope and tore the detective's letterhead off a report. Back downstairs I cleaned my wound which was already turning an ugly purplish black, and anointed it with Bactine. Snuggling down into the sheets, I slipped the detective's name under the pile of lo-cal cook books on my nightstand. I fell asleep immediately, feeling unaccountably safer, as if I'd put a gun nearby.

NINE

Metal wheels on metal rails. I'd forgotten the train's primal rhythm. The blurred landscape out my dirt-streaked window shifted from suburb to city. I felt I was riding a graffitied time shuttle reconnecting who I was with who I used to be. Cradling my briefcase on my lap, I leaned back and enjoyed the sensual vibrations.

How many years since I'd ridden the El to the Loop? Twelve? No, thirteen. The exact day had became one of life's little nightmares that sometimes shattered the fragile moments before sleep. God, what a snob I must have seemed. 'Suburbs or no suburbs,' preached St Barbara of The City to her Sheltered Suburban Sisters, 'Rikki is three years old and it's time she knows what it means to ride public transportation.' For a week before 'our adventure' I'd primed Rikki, telling her over and over about our wonderful train ride. On The Day, I fed her a hearty breakfast so she wouldn't have motion sickness, bundled her up in strippable layers, and packed a variety of traveling foods and games. Frontier families crossed a continent with less. We boarded the train and traveled three stops before Rikki started throwing up. I'd thought I'd been preparing her. I'd been scaring her to death. Thirteen years.

The train entered my favorite stretch where blocks of apartment buildings bordered the track. Framed by curtainless windows, lives flashed like flip-cards. Sarajane and I used to make up stories about the people for our soap opera 'The El and I'. She created torrid love affairs with brutal men and bawdy women, all willful and in control. My characters were old people and small children, despairing and on death's door, victims all.

I'd been jittery all morning about this trip. Strange, really, since it wasn't as if I never went into the city. Franklin and I subscribed to the opera, ballet, theater. I'd drive downtown after rush hour and pick Franklin up at his health club. We'd meet friends for dinner or eat at our private dining club. We were regulars at the constant round of charitable affairs – black tie at the Shedd Aquarium for Muscular Dystrophy, late-night dinner and scavenger hunt at Neiman's for Juvenile Diabetes – events orchestrated by women like Sarajane and myself who were fabulous organizers and loved excuses to play dress up. Naturally, all that had stopped temporarily. Until Franklin's campaign was over. Until I looked good in clothes again. I'd been returning invitations with our regrets and generous checks. Franklin complained a few times about the amounts I was donating. Something about the new tax laws and charitable deductions. Silly, really, since I saved twice the donated amount by not having to buy new gowns. Poor Franklin was so on edge lately. I suspected campaign contributions were not as plentiful nor as generous as he had anticipated. Although, when I asked, he said everything was fine. Now that he'd moved his records to his campaign office I had no way of keeping track.

A thick coat of dust layered my throat by the time I got off at the Merchandise Mart. I stopped at the lunch counter for a Diet Pepsi. The Milky Way was an afterthought, a little pick-me-up between breakfast and lunch to help replenish the drain of the train ride. Besides, the walk to the *Globe* would work off the calories. It was a perfect spring day and I strolled east, savoring the chocolate-covered stringy caramel, swinging my briefcase. The five articles inside didn't weigh much. They would have fit easily in a manila envelope. But I liked dusting off the old briefcase, rubbing the cordovan leather with saddlesoap. It had been a gift from my father on my eighteenth birthday when I declared my interest in journalism. It was the only present I'd ever received from him that hadn't been picked out by my grandmother.

As I neared the *Globe*, a wind shift carried the smell of meat sizzling at Billy Goat's. Cheeseburger, grilled onions, potato chips. Dad's favorite food combination with the possible exception of a Fluky's hot dog with the works. I'd sit next to my father at lunch, picking at my fried egg sandwich, smoking, stealing chips off his plate, listening to him and his buddies talk about the Cubs, White Sox, Bears, 16″ slow-pitch tournaments, judges, aldermen. Bubbles of conversation floated like foam on beer. Being newsmen was the one thing that mattered most in their lives and the one topic I never heard them talk about. Only cubs and hacks told people what they did. Real newsmen recognized each other in the gut way cops and crooks and alcoholics knew their own kind. Still half an hour until my appointment. Plenty of time for a sentimental bag of chips. The wind shifted again, swapping grilled hamburger for truck exhaust. I'd eat after my meeting.

The *Globe* squatted at the south end of the Magnificent Mile, dwarfed in both size and circulation by the *Sun-Times* and *Tribune*. Chicago's three major papers stood like sentinels guarding the bridges which reached like thick fingers across the Chicago River into the Loop. Should I go up to Cameron's office? This isn't a blind date, Barbara. Afraid Cameron won't like your stuff? He'll love it. It's good. Not quite what he ordered, but you never were predictable.

My stomach geared up for a case of the runs. Why had I eaten the Milky Way? Hell, why had I eaten breakfast? I should have stopped after the half grapefruit, but the sour citrus begged for a sweet chaser. Just the tiniest slice of a Dinkels Black Forest torte I'd stored in the freezer for unexpected company. And what kind of masochist could stop after one slice? The cake occupied the freezer space abandoned by a five-pound bag of mixed nuts and two-pound box of assorted chocolates. I couldn't have eaten all of them. Rikki and Jason must have had some, too. But they didn't eat nuts. And I'd wrapped the candy in freezer paper marked 'Liver'. The wrapper had been untouched each time I opened it for another one or three pieces.

I leaned against the railing overlooking the Chicago River, trying to quiet my insides. Warm winds gusted, blowing my bright fringed shawl over and around my gauze tent. I prayed I looked more artistic than fat. Writing at my kitchen desk had turned out to be hell. The last time I worked for the *Globe* I was in the newsroom lighting one cigarette off another. This time when I had a writing problem I took a trip to the fridge. I'd averaged a pound per column.

Michigan Avenue stretched out behind me, running downhill from the river to The Drake Hotel. There were actually two Chicago 'downtowns'. For my northshore neighbors, downtown was a euphemism for this stretch of north Michigan Avenue whose exclusive stores were so dimly lit that customers wandered around clutching merchandise in search of a light source. This Magnificent Mile was a beige lady, quiet and proper and boring.

In front of me, pulsing and undulating across the dark river, was the real downtown Chicago, a bawdy, earthy, gutsy babe with clashing colors and rude manners. Habitués of the Magnificent Mile knew better than to cross over wearing the furs and jewels so de rigueur when shopping Neiman's and Bloomies. Their designer clothing flashed like neon 'fair game' signs to street kids prowling the State Street Mall, kids who were equal opportunity terrorists. A group of them, walking four abreast, bumped my frail grandmother who hadn't moved out of their way fast enough. Her hip snapped like balsa against a lamppost and the hospital stay led to a pneumonia which killed her and left me motherless, again, at sixteen. A pigeon flew down, landing on the railing near me. I glanced at my watch. Five minutes to my appointment. 'Show time,' I said. It nodded.

In the lobby I had to enter my name in the registry while the guard called upstairs to verify my appointment with Cameron. Will the Mystery Guest sign in please? The receptionist on the third floor motioned to the plush sofa where I was to wait until Cameron came to fetch me. I realized, halfway down, the sofa was too low. Somehow I kept forgetting to seek out the hard-backed high-seated chairs my grandmother used to favor. Once I passed a hundred fifty pounds, I understood the attraction of a chair I could get out of with dignity. I struggled up awkwardly, preferring to stand rather than have Cameron see me trying to hoist my fat ass off the fake suede.

'Welcome home!' He emerged from a corridor I didn't remember and embraced me warmly. 'Well?' he said, leading me to the newsroom, 'how does it feel to be home?'

The scene was strange and familiar at the same time. Cameron led me through the maze of desks whose clean metal lines replaced the old dark oak. 'No splinter,' I said, running my hand along a desk edge. 'And I'll bet the drawers don't swell shut in the summer.'

'You remember,' he patted my hand. 'You're making me nostalgic for the old days.'

'Me too.' Gone was the cigar and cigarette smoke that hung like a blue cloud over the newsroom. 'Has everyone here stopped smoking or is the exhaust system better?'

'A little of both,' he said.

'And it's a hell of a lot quieter than I remember.' A sea of silent computer screens sat patiently, cursors blinking, awaiting commands. The only typewriter in the room, an ancient black Royal, sprouted ivy from where the platen once was. Pleasant dinging sounds replaced the old shrill phone bells. Except for a couple of familiar faces at the rewrite desk, the staff was new and unrelentingly young.

'And, of course, you remember this,' said Cameron, opening the door to an office partitioned by glass walls from the rest of the newsroom. I hadn't prepared myself for this moment. In my mind this was still my father's office, his wall of photos showing him with all the presidents from Ike through Carter, entertainers who'd come to town, crooks, foreign dignitaries, sports personalities. He'd had a few letters, too, personal ones from Nelson Algren and Saul Bellow and a few he'd bought which had been written by Walt Whitman and Carl Sandburg. I'd packed all of it in boxes after his death and stored them in my basement. Still, when I thought of his office, all those things were in place. But the wall I was looking at held Cameron's life. Somewhere inside of me a door to my past slammed shut.

141

'Brought you a present,' I said, flipping my brief-case onto his desk, snapping the clasps smartly, neatly extracting the manila envelope containing the columns. Smooth. So smooth. As if each page wasn't drenched with sweat, as if each sentence printed wasn't born of a hundred miscarriages, as if I were used to slicing myself open and bleeding onto paper eight hours a day; more, if I counted the early morning hours when I couldn't sleep. If I worked like that every day the writing would come faster, like a muscle being strengthened. But it would never ever come easy. Cameron opened the envelope.

'Have a seat,' he said.

'You're not going to read them now!'

He dangled the thin envelope between thumb and forefinger. 'This isn't *War and Peace*, Barbara. Don't be so nervous. Have some coffee.' He nodded to the pot in the corner, propped his feet on his desk, and started reading.

'Who's taking political p.r.?' I asked, trying to keep the walls from closing in. 'I've got some of Franklin's stuff to give him.'

'Last desk, second row. Name's Spears.' He went back to the articles. I slid Franklin's packet from the briefcase and left Cameron to his reading. Butterflies beat their wings inside my stomach. What the hell made me think I could still write after seventeen years? Editing school newspapers for Rikki and Jason or freelancing a handful of articles hardly counted as journalism. My 'Ask Barbara' column was straight reportage, clean investigative work. Sydney Kreiger's columns looked at the world and commented on it with wit and insight and irreverence *daily*. Even his off days were brilliant. I had to be crazy to think I could do it.

Spears turned out to be Sonia Spears, a tall leggy redhead with a Brenda Starr face. Sarajane and I once worked out an intelligence formula for people like Sonia Spears. It came out something like: IQ = Weight – Height + age. A one hundred nine pound, 72-inch, twenty-one-year-old would have an IQ of 58. My current IQ figured out to 132, and was increasing by leaps and pounds. The system wasn't infallible but it was pretty damned close. I'd speak slowly to Spears, choosing simple words to be certain she understood.

'Hi,' I said, brightly, 'I'm –'

'Casey Marlow's daughter.' She jumped up from her desk, extending a long-fingered hand. 'Yes, I know. Cameron said you'd be coming in so I was looking out for you.' Her cool grip made me aware how hot and damp my hands were. 'Please, please sit down.' We sat. 'I'm so glad to get a chance to meet you. Your dad's a legend around here. The old guard sure talk about him enough. They have some stories about him even I'm not allowed to hear.' Words tumbled out of her. 'One of these days I'm going to bug the bar at Riccardo's, learn the "untold story" and all that. And I'm pleased as punch you're taking over Sydney's column.' She paused long enough to light a cigarette. I checked for smoke direction and shifted downwind.

'I'm not taking over –'

'I always thought he was a royal pain in the ass. Always preaching from the Mount. A couple of us once ran a help wanted ad for a sculptor to Boswell him around and chisel Sydney's words in stone. He was not amused. Anyway, Cameron was a basket case until you agreed to take the job.'

'I'm just one of –'

'I know I'm jumping the gun. But he really wants you back. I tried writing a couple of columns for him – hell we all did – but everything I touch turns to politics.'

'Which reminds me . . .' I handed her Franklin's public relations packet. 'As long as I was coming in to see Cameron, I thought I'd save postage and bring these straight to you.' Franklin had insisted I do it. She scanned the material. The exhaust system sucked up most of her cigarette's smoke before it got to me. She dragged deeply and exhaled. I got some before it disappeared. Had the soft lines of her face tensed slightly?

'I've covered your husband's activities, of course. I finally met him a few weeks ago at that open house he threw at his campaign headquarters. Funny, I don't remember seeing you there.'

'I wasn't able to make it that evening,' I said, wondering which evening it was. Franklin had neglected to mention an open house. No matter. I'd probably had a hot date with a frozen pizza.

'Your husband is a very – intense person. He must be exhausting to live with. I just met him that once and it wiped me out.' Just once does not an affair make. Strange thought, Barbara. Where was this jealousy coming from? 'That p.r. gal of his is a real tiger,' she said. I nodded. I hadn't met the p.r. team yet. 'What's her name?'

'All those p.r. people look alike.' We laughed. Despite her good looks and bubbly personality I was beginning to like Spears.

'I'll bet your husband's happy to see you back at the *Globe*.'

'Oh, yes.' He'd hated it. Why couldn't I volunteer at high-visibility charitable places like soup kitchens and meals for shut-ins where he could benefit from the publicity? Although he didn't hesitate for a second to use my *Globe* connections to help his campaign along.

'I'll look this stuff over,' she said, 'and plug it in where I can.'

'Thanks.'

Cameron was not in his office but Mac was there, dwarfing the chair I had sat in earlier, engrossed in the day's sports page. A midnight-blue, three-piece suit replaced the rumpled clothing he'd worn on his morning walks around our neighborhood. It had been a couple of weeks since I'd seen him. He'd been to a good hair stylist, someone who'd trimmed without trying to tame. There was a constrained wildness about Mac, like a jungle cat in captivity, that I found both frightening and exciting. His unpatched eye looked up and caught me staring. 'Ah, the phantom of the fog. Perfect timing. We're just off to celebrate. The grand jury's come in with indictments against the goons who did this to me.'

'I thought you were hit by a truck.'

'A carefully aimed, expertly driven truck. Some people weren't happy that I was investigating my friend's death.'

'You're pulling my leg.'

'Enticing idea. Come to lunch and I will tell all.'

'I can't leave.' I sat in a chair across from him. 'I have to talk to Cameron about something.'

'Your columns?'

I groaned. 'Does everyone in this place know about them?'

'Let's see. He read excerpts to me, the elevator operator, the cleaning staff, catering cart, and, yes, I'd say to just about everyone he could find. First time I've seen him smile since Kreiger left the *Globe*.' Strip me bare, Cameron, and put me on display. I'd forgotten the casual intimacy of the newsroom. The good news was Cameron liked the articles. 'You look surprised,' said Mac.

'I wasn't sure, you know, that they – the articles I mean – were any good. It's been a while.' He narrowed his eye, as if trying to decide if I was being coy. I wasn't.

'You used to be a hell of a good writer. That doesn't go away.'

'Just because Cameron says I was good –'

'*I* say you were good.' He cleared his throat. 'I, ah, I had the research department photocopy all your articles for me.' I groaned. 'There's not a lot to do at Cameron's house at night and I haven't exactly been in any shape to go dancing. I thought I'd see what you were like before you became taco queen to the northshore. I read myself to sleep on your stuff for a few nights running. Some of those "Ask Barbara" columns gave me heartburn but the rest of it was pretty good. A little dated, maybe –'

Mac rolled to one side, pushed up from the chair and balanced on a thick cane. No crutches. The man was healing. He leaned across Cameron's desk, grabbed a black marker and scrawled a message on a legal pad. A few black curls wound down over his shirt collar. His broad shoulders strained the back seam of his jacket. The suit hem hiked up and my eyes followed the curve of his buttocks down his thighs. For some reason, I found the image of Mac stretched out in bed reading my work suffocatingly intimate. He finished the note and held it up for my approval: Have kidnapped Barbara. Mac.

'Come on, Ace.' He pulled me out of my chair and slipped his arm around my shoulder, resting just enough of his considerable weight on me to make me feel needed. His touch did strange things to my respiration.

'Where are we going?'

'To celebrate your columns and my indictments.'

'What about Cameron?'

'Unfortunately, he'll find us.'

'I have to leave by one-thirty.' I slowed to Mac's pace as we walked to the elevators. 'I have a two o'clock appointment.' I prayed he wouldn't ask with whom. I didn't think I could say 'hypnotist'.

He glanced at his watch. 'Then we'll have to drink fast.'

*　　*　　*

We stood inside Riccardo's door, waiting for our eyes to adjust to the dark. I heard someone yell 'Hey, there's Mac.' Then many voices. 'Way to go, Mac.' 'You showed those bastards.' He laughed.

'Looks like word's out on the street.' The crowd swarmed, sweeping Mac toward the bar. I backed off. It was his time with his newspaper buddies and I didn't really belong. Not any more. Not yet. Mac's big hand reached out through the mob and grabbed me, pulling me along as he limped toward one of the oversized booths. Leaning heavily on me and the cane, Mac lowered himself and slid back to the wall and waved me in next to him. Two more people squeezed in next to me and five more across from us. Others crowded around talking, laughing, questioning.

The room throbbed with rich sensory textures that triggered forgotten memories; smells of stale beer and fresh cigarettes, garlic bread and grated cheese, seeds of magical conversations that beanstalked crazily, the energy of the inert crowd that created an illusion of motion. I had stopped coming here when I got engaged. Franklin was never comfortable around these people who weren't turned on by his kind of power. It was frustrating for Franklin to talk about his newest car with a guy proud of the original paint job on a '58 Chevy. Franklin was box seat and my buddies at the *Globe* were bleacher. It was impossible to explain one to the other.

'I sat front row center where Whitney and Marquart could have a good look at me,' Mac was saying. 'I want them to remember whose testimony got the indictment. Who's going to put them away.'

The crowd fed him questions. A low-voltage current tingled my skin where Mac's arm draped around my shoulders, where his thigh pressed against mine. I hadn't felt that particular sort of buzz since fifth grade when Daniel Greenberg kissed me on the cheek in the darkness of the Esquire theater. I had been embarrassed and confused by the way my body had responded then and I wasn't doing a whole hell of a lot better now.

'When will you go back to Phoenix?' someone asked.

'I'll wait and see this thing through,' said Mac, gently squeezing my shoulder. What thing was that, Mac? A round of drinks came and somehow my chablis order had been translated into a double scotch. The waiter spun an antipasta tray onto the middle of the table, compliments of the house. I thought I was too nervous to eat but I was wrong. The spicy sausages, burning peppers, creamy cheeses mingled nicely with the scotch. Another round of drinks came and went. Then a third. I hadn't had so much to drink since the night Sarajane died. That time I threw my cigarettes in the lake. God keep me from doing anything as dumb this time.

The crowd dwindled with the food supply and the room settled into a post lunch lull. As the people left our booth I started to move away from Mac to give him more room but he held me against him, stroking my hair, describing the courtroom scene that morning,

the players, the drama. My body relaxed against his.
I'd forgotten how good it felt to be held. Such a
simple thing, really, a hug.

Comforted by the warmth of Mac's body and three
double scotches, I must have entered the twilight
before sleep because his voice drifted in from far
away.

'Funny thing about nearly getting killed,' he was
saying, his voice soft and husky. 'It tends to
reorganize your priorities. Makes you reach out and
grab hold of things you might have let pass before.'

'Like?'

'Like you. That first night I saw you, I thought you
were one of the most beautiful women I'd ever seen.'

'Sure,' I said, dreamily, 'I was surrounded by fog.
It's my best side.'

'Don't you ever let up on yourself?'

'What'd I do?'

'What do you say when a man tells you you're
beautiful?' Dunno. It had been a while.

'Is this multiple choice?'

He pressed his lips to my forehead. 'You say
"Thank you very much, Mac, for your wonderful
taste in women". '

'Mac Parker, you're flirting with me.' I struggled
to sit up. 'M'gosh. What time is it?'

'Relax. You're already half an hour late for your
appointment.'

I moaned. Kathlyn was gonna kill me for blowing
the appointment with her hypnotist. Mac poked the
ice cubes down into his drink then licked the scotch

from his finger. The small gesture did big things to my body.

'You married?' I asked. Now where did that come from?

'Was. Cameron and Myrna fixed me up. Nice woman. Traditional. I tried to tell her what life with a crime reporter would be like but that's like trying to describe blue to a blind person. She figured our life would be like Myrna's and Cameron's. Well, crime reporters are different.'

'So I've heard. What happened?'

'I'd get phone calls from strange people at odd hours and have to go out. I'd come home and she'd be crying. Anyway, one night I got a call from a cop that they'd found two bodies in a water tower. He thought it might be murder. I went out at four in the morning to cover the story. Turned out to be two missing kids who'd gotten good and drunk, climbed up the tower, and fallen in. They'd been in the tank a while. The meat was falling off their bones. I got home around seven that morning, sick, sad, mad at the world. My wife accused me of being out with another woman.'

He pressed my hand against his cheek. It was burning.

'You have a fever,' I said but he didn't seem to hear.

'I would have given anything if it could have been another woman instead of seeing those two dead kids. I never cheated on my wife. I would have liked my marriage to have worked. But it was wrong from the start.'

Mac picked up his drink. A few drops spilled on his

tie and I wiped them off. He cupped my hand in his and methodically kissed the tips of my fingers. I pretended not to notice, as if the hand being kissed was not mine, as if the nerve endings weren't wired directly to my crotch. And just what did I think I was doing here?

I was the happily married mother of two, after all.
Whose husband forgot to invite her to the ball.
Or was it an Open House?
The louse.

I was drunk. I yanked my hand away from Mac. 'I need some air,' I said, sliding out of the booth and fleeing the restaurant.

Halfway up the stairs to Michigan Avenue I reversed course and ran back down, escaping underneath to the cool darkness of lower Michigan Avenue. I paced up and back, up and back. Had to get my head clear. Up and back along the sidewalk strewn with litter blown down from Michigan Avenue or wind-whipped from the lane of loading docks. There had to be a way to reason out what I was feeling, what was happening, but the rational parts of my brain were out of order.

'Barb!' Mac's voice echoed through the underground. Buses and cars rumbled the street overhead, metal loading dock doors clanged open and shut. He walked toward me, leaning on his cane, dragging one leg behind, the painful effort contorting his face. I didn't run away, but I didn't go to him, either. It took a while for him to reach me, and a longer while for him to catch his breath. 'I'm not going to apologize, Barbara.'

I held up a hand to stop him from going on. 'Mac, we just had a little too much to drink.'

He grabbed my wrist. 'Don't blame this on booze, all right? Some things happen because it's time for them to happen.' I pulled my hand away.

'What do you want from me, Mac?'

'Everything. Nothing. Hell, I don't know, Barbara. To listen, maybe. To get to know me and give me a chance to know you.' A car drove by blaring heartbreak blues from a 40's saxophone. That's the trouble with real life, no background music.

'Mac, I'm married.'

'No shit.'

'And I don't fool around.'

'If I thought you did, Barbara, if I thought for one single second you did, I wouldn't have stopped coming to your house after Sophia left. It drove me crazy thinking of you alone all day in that house. I had to force myself to walk past.'

'Mac –'

'Look, I always made it a point to stay away from married women. But that was before I had this one-on-one with death. Before I met you. I figure I'm being given a chance at something, here. And to tell the truth, Barbara, I don't think you're as happily married as Cameron thinks you are.' He paused, leaving plenty of room for a reply if I were so inclined. I wasn't. 'I need you to know how I feel. If you tell me to back off I will.'

'Yes,' I whispered. 'Please.'

Mac swayed unsteadily, then turned and walked away.

And then I was crying, big huge gut-wrenching sobs, because I thought I might be losing something precious.

The train ride home was interminable. How could I have thought I was ready to reenter the real world? I'd been gone too long. Lost all my coping skills. The day had ripped me in half. Too many emotions, too many decisions. I couldn't live that fast.

Mac's face floated up in the train window. Something he'd said about his ex-wife haunted me. She thought he'd been out with another woman. But he wasn't. He'd been caught up in his work with a passion and dedication she hadn't understood. Is that what I was doing to Franklin? Silently accusing him of things that never happened?

I owed it to seventeen years of marriage, to our two children, to fight to keep our home and family together. If it was humanly possible, I would try and create the same excitement in my marriage that I'd felt in that dark booth at Riccardo's. Oh, God, it felt good to be wanted like that. What *would* have happened if Mac had come to my home when I was alone?

The desire I felt for Mac – so unexpected, so explosive – scared the hell out of me. More than that, it made me realize how very very far away love had gone from my life.

JUNE

157–165

TEN

'That's the most ridiculous thing I ever heard!' I puffed alongside Kathlyn as we neared the old lighthouse, the halfway mark in our walk to Nautilus.

'It's true,' she said. 'People don't seem to take me as seriously as when I was heavier.'

'Like who?'

'My children, my employees, Pete.'

'Kathlyn, it's all in your head. As a matter of fact, people don't take me as seriously now that I'm heavier.' 'People' being Franklin and the children. 'How do you explain that?'

'I'm not picking a fight, Barbara.' Angry red splotches erupted on her ivory cheeks. 'I'm telling you that as soon as I dropped below 200 pounds, people began treating me like a ball of fluff.'

We reached the lighthouse, touched the bricks, and turned west toward town center. 'Do you want me to agree with you so you have an excuse to put the weight back?'

'You're a real source of comfort this morning. All I'm saying is my views don't carry the weight they used to.'

'Ho-ho.' I wiped sweat off my face with the back of my sleeve. The sight of me in sweats was only slightly less nauseating than the sight of me in leotard and tights. The one thing that bolstered my morning courage was, next to Kathlyn, I looked thin. 'Maybe we should exchange homes. People in my house are beginning to talk around me, over me, through me. Rikki doesn't ask my advice, Jason forgot to invite me to his eighth grade Open House, Franklin invents reasons to keep me away from campaign headquarters.'

'My, my, don't we sound paranoid.'

'I swear to you, the heavier I get, the less they see me. I'm becoming invisible. The opinions of a fat person don't matter.' It was safe to say 'fat' around Kathlyn. She never considered anyone under 250 as anything but 'plump'. In my own mind I grudgingly admitted to 'heavy'. But it was a temporary condition. And I hid it so well. Thanks to Nautilus, I was firm. How some women let themselves become sloppy fat was beyond me. By keeping in shape I'd avoid stretch marks and flabby skin when I took the weight off.

'You promise you're going to keep your appointment with Dr Chen this time?' Kathlyn asked.

'Next Tuesday. Ten-thirty. And, for God's sake, don't tell anyone.'

'You are a very strange person, Barbara Avers.' Sweat stained her headband and dotted her upper lip. She pumped her massive arms back and forth Olympic style, picking up the pace for the last ten minutes. 'You'll talk to anyone and everyone about going to Weight Watchers, Nutri-Systems, and the Diet Center but you're embarrassed about seeing a hypnotist.'

'It's nothing I'm particularly proud of.' I had to jog to keep up with her. 'It's like admitting I can't lose weight like a normal person. That I can't overcome this little problem without extraordinary help.'

'Weight is no little problem and there's nothing extraordinary about hypnotism. Incantations, maybe. Swinging dead cats in graveyards at midnight, yes. But hypnosis is perfectly legit.' A group of julienned joggers ran toward us and we instinctively crossed the street. 'It's not your fault you can't be in the kitchen preparing food without eating. And you can't help it if prepackaged diet foods give you world-class gas.' Kathlyn had a way with imagery. Actually, she talked as compulsively as she did everything else, telling everyone her life story the first three minutes she was with them. I seemed drawn to the type, comforted by their patter, content to listen for hours to detailed descriptions of the minutiae of their lives. Sarajane had been a talker. And Mac. One dead. One in Phoenix. Both missed, although I was relieved Mac hadn't hung around to see how fat I'd become.

'Just this once, Kathlyn, I'd appreciate your not broadcasting my plans to the world, I don't want people thinking I'm out of control.'

'Barbara, it doesn't take a crystal ball.' She raised an eyebrow at my body which strained the seams of one of Franklin's old sweat suits. Why hadn't I married a Large? 'If you fight Dr Chen, you're going to have trouble being hypnotized. Of course,' she mimicked my voice, 'if you want an excuse not to take all that weight off . . .'

We chugged in silence through the quiet morning streets. The advantage of getting to Nautilus by 6:30 a.m. was that, except for a few lakefront joggers, none of the neighborhood women I knew were out that early. My contemporaries, most of whom had sought to find themselves through careers, had become disenchanted with the long hours, unreliable help, and stranglehold of retail. Dumping unsympathetic husbands and opening boutiques with the alimony payments wasn't the fun it was cracked up to be.

Sarajane and I had felt vindicated in our decision to stay home, puff puff, as we watched the romance of going to work killed by the reality of working, puff puff. Having an interesting answer to the dinner party question 'And what do *you* do?' no longer outweighed the boredom of work routines that were more grind than glamour. What our acquaintances wanted was to own a business, hire a fabulous manager who was great with help/customers/bookkeeping (and who wouldn't steal them blind), work enough hours to have fun while still leaving time for tennis and multiple vacations, and net $80,000 a year.

Chanting the mantra of motherhood, the same women returned home to rediscover their children (grown fond of their un-mothered freedom), cooking (my blue corn tortilla's more authentic than your blue corn tortilla), breakfast with the women (formerly lunch with the 'girls'), and work out at the gym (the hell with toning, let's build muscle). Best of all, they once again slept past morning rush hour which meant I was safely home and out of sight before they rolled out for their first cup of freshly ground decaffeinated espresso.

There was one major disadvantage of getting up at sunrise to dress, make the kid's lunches, and put on coffee for Franklin before I left to meet Kathlyn for our Diet Center weigh-in and morning exercise. I had to fight to stay awake past 9:30 at night. I thought Franklin would be miffed, finding me asleep over an open book when he came to bed, but he encouraged me to go to Nautilus and 'keep up the good work'. At first I assumed he was supportive because he was hopeful Nautilus would help. Gradually, I developed an uneasy feeling he was relieved I conked out before the evening news. The night before, I'd tried seducing him after dinner. Franklin, nervous, jittery, limp, pleaded uneasiness because the kids were in the house. In all fairness, Franklin had always preferred sex as a night-cap. With his schedule as tight as it was, it probably seemed counterproductive having sex too long before he planned to go to sleep. Most nights he wasn't home before I passed out.

A few times these past months I awoke in the middle of the night to find him sleeping downstairs on the sofa. 'I wanted to read,' he'd say, 'but I didn't want to disturb you.' Other times he was gone from the house. 'Couldn't sleep,' he'd explain, 'so I went to campaign headquarters to do some catch-up work.' On those nights I'd consider the detective's name hidden in my nightstand and, almost immediately, suffer paralyzing guilt.

'I've been thinking of going to Nautilus later in the day so I could sleep later,' I said, trying the idea out on Kathlyn.

'Never happen,' she said, slowing her pace for our two-block warm-down. 'If you didn't have me to drag you out of the house, you'd stop exercising.'

'There are worse things.'

'Like?'

'Like not being awake for Franklin when he needs me. It's been three weeks.'

Her eyes widened in mock surprise. 'Three whole weeks?'

'Don't start. Franklin has – had – a strong sex drive. The last time we missed three weeks was ten years ago when he had his gallbladder out. This being healthy is ruining our sex life.'

'If it bothers you so much, have him wake you when he's ready for bed.'

'I suggested that but Franklin says it wouldn't be considerate of him. That I have as much right to my schedule as he has to his.'

'Sounds like gift-wrapped bullshit.' I'd thought so, too.

'What about you?' I asked. 'Don't you get tired?'

'Exhausted. Every day at three o'clock I feel like I've walked straight into a brick wall, so I go into my office and take a one-hour nap. My staff has instructions not to interrupt me during that hour – no calls, clients, whatever – under penalty of death.'

'I've never been able to nap in the middle of the day. I tried a couple of times when I was pregnant but it made me feel guilty.'

'Guilt's ruining your sex life, kid.'

'My weight's ruining my sex life.'

'Your guilt about your weight's ruining your sex life. Obesity never stopped me from being one hell of a sexy lover. In fact, most of my obese friends go out of their way to be creative.' She laughed the wind chime sound I had grown to love. 'Although, Pete says if I lose much more he's going to have to go out and find a "real woman". He's always liked his women big.'

'Don't you feel threatened?'

'Why should I? I figure if he loved me fat he can love me thin. When he talks like that I just ignore him and keep banging his brains out.' Kathlyn was as sexually aggressive as I was reserved, constantly buying books and 'marital aids' to spice up her sex life. 'Let me take you to my favorite sex shop. I think I need to educate you to the possibilities.'

'Kathlyn, I couldn't!'

'Doesn't hurt to look.'

'Franklin's not the type.'

'All men are the type.' I hadn't met Pete, but I suspected he was in a perpetual state of blissful exhaustion.

'If I bring home stuff from a sex shop, Franklin will think I'm up to something.'

'You are. Besides, aren't you the least little bit curious about what one of those places is like?'

'Yes, I mean, who isn't.'

'Wouldn't your readers be curious?'

'I hardly think Cameron would like a column on sex shops.'

'You never know. Come with me and you might find one of those story angles you're always talking about.'

I puffed along, trying to keep her pace. A vice tightened on my chest. I couldn't draw a full breath. The tops of my feet hurt. My shins were about to splinter. 'Maybe I'll go with you, on the chance there's a column in it,' I said, 'but I'll have to figure out something else to help my marriage. I think I'm not trying hard enough. Or maybe not the right way.'

She slowed for a moment and I sensed she was about to drop one of her bombs. 'You can feel as guilty as you want about your sex life, Barbara Anne Avers, and you can blame your husband's disinterest in you on your weight if you want to, but do you know what I think?'

I held my breath.

'I think . . .'

'Did I ask?'

'. . . Franklin's got himself a lady.'

'That's ridiculous. You've never met Franklin. You don't even know him.'

'Barbara, I was married to a Franklin named George. You can learn a lot from a cheating spouse.' She leaned against the elm outside Nautilus to stretch out her calf muscles. I stretched opposite her. 'And my ex gave me one hell of an education.'

'Franklin is nothing like your first husband.' Why had I said anything to her? That would teach me to keep my thoughts to myself. 'Our only problem is, between Franklin's campaign duties and my new schedule, our timing's been thrown off. As soon as the kids leave for camp, Franklin and I will have the whole house to ourselves for eight glorious weeks. I can attack him anywhere any time. You'll see. I'll lose this weight, make romantic picnic dinners at the beach, learn the art of erotic massage. I am going to bring back the old magic.'

'Sometimes, dear heart, even Houdini gave up.'

I flipped her an impeccably manicured finger and burst through the doors of Mr Nautilus's torture chamber. The phrase 'Franklin's got himself a lady' wouldn't leave me. It was the first time I'd heard the words spoken and they had the sound of truth.

I made it through my Nautilus workout in twenty minutes, ending with sit-ups on the slant board next to Kathlyn. The young staff kept WXRT turned to glass-shattering decibels, making talking impossible. I signaled Kathlyn that I was going to the bathroom before we headed home. She signaled back that she'd begin a second set until I came out. For a woman who hated exercise, Kathlyn had been showing increasingly unusual behavior.

I loathed the way my thighs looked when I sat on the toilet. Most of my new weight had settled between my waist and knees. A problem area even when I was thin, my thighs now spread out like two massive yeasty loaves of dough. Despite my workouts and sit-ups, my seated navel floated on a roll of flesh. A recent development were the soft folds of skin hanging over my knee caps when I stood, as if my thighs were trying to slide down to my ankles.

Quickly washing my hands, I avoided looking in the locker-room mirror with its harsh fluorescent overhead light. The week before I'd caught a glimpse of a soft second chin in a three-way mirror. I'd turned away quickly, telling myself it had been an unfortunate trick of lighting or strange tilt of my head. I didn't look back to double-check. Maybe I could do an article on the importance of lighting, how to be kind to your guests over thirty. I could contact a few lighting designers, learn about the psychology of lighting. I'd add that to my new IDEAS file.

A half-dressed scarecrow of a woman sat at the small dressing table next to me applying makeup to her haggard face. Her eyes caught mine and widened uncertainly.

'Barbara?' Her speech was sluggish.

'Yes?' I yanked a paper towel from the holder and roughly wiped my hands, unsettled at being recognized while wearing sweats. I couldn't place her.

'Joelle. Joelle Turner.' Her expectant eyes were too wide, her smile crooked. The Joelle Turner I knew from years of PTAs and Open Houses was a soft round woman, quiet, shy.

'Joelle! I'd never recognize you. You look . . .' like shit, like hell, like you are a thousand years old and aging fast, like something sucked the sweet life out of your face and left molted skin '. . . different.'

She laughed crazily and I glanced around, embarrassed for her. 'Isn't it *fabulous!* I've lost sixty-two and one quarter pounds as of this morning! How d'ya like *that?*' Could she be drunk so early in the morning?

'That's just great, Joelle. Believe me, I know how hard it is.'

For the first time, her dark eyes really focused on me. Her face clouded, the corners of her tight little mouth drooped sadly. 'Awww, Barb. You were always so *thin!*' She gripped my arm, pulling me conspiratorily toward her. Furtively looking around, she reached into her makeup bag and pulled out a vial of pills. 'Here,' she pressed them into my hand and folded my fingers over them, 'take these, three times a day half hour before meals.'

I tried to hand them back. 'Thanks, Joelle, but I tried diet pills. They made me jittery.'

'That over-the-counter shit?' The Joelle I knew didn't say 'shit'. Her fingernails dug into my flesh. 'They don't do diddly. I tried. This stuff works. Just look at me.' She released me, leaving little crescent tracks up my arm. Standing, she twirled girlishly, her little lacy bikini panties pathetic over the sag of melting skin. Her ribbed tank top flattened her small breasts like old water balloons, pushing the nipples low and outside. Strike two. The room began swimming.

'Great,' I said, swallowing back the bile in my throat. I'd accept the pills and flush them later, before I became tempted, before I became Joelle. 'Thanks.'

'Oh, and take this.' She pulled a folded sheet of paper from the case. 'It works!'

I glanced at the sheet titled THE MIAMI HEART INSTITUTE DIET. 'Thanks,' I said again, backing out of the room, away from the grotesque thing that used to be Joelle Turner, away from the caricature of what I was trying so hard to become. I picked up Kathlyn who was finishing reps on the pull-over.

'Are you going to call or should I?' asked Kathlyn as we speed-walked home.

'You don't think this is legit?'

'Read it to me again.'

We jogged in place near the train tracks while I opened the sheet and read the list of 'diet' foods which included hot dogs, ice cream, and saltine crackers.

'That's dumber than that bogus Mayo Clinic egg diet.'

I refolded it and put it in my pocket. Kathlyn could be wrong. The diet pills were in the pocket. I pulled them out and showed them to her. She snickered.

'Those little beauties will put you in la-la land.'

'At least I'll be thin,' I said, surprised to learn I didn't really intend to flush them. I was desperate enough to try anything. Besides, there was no danger of my becoming as grotesque as Joelle Turner. I was only a hundred fifty-seven. She'd been much heavier.

Kathlyn's left eyebrow arched, an early warning sign of her considerable temper. 'You actually thinking of taking this garbage?'

'Kathlyn, you of all people should understand –'

She whacked the pills out of my hand. The vial shattered, spilling the pills into the gutter. 'When you're three hundred and forty-two goddamned pounds,' she shouted, 'you can talk to me about desperate.'

'You had no right to do that!' I stood shaking on the

edge of the curb, staring at the pills. 'They can't be all that bad. Thousands of people take them. Joelle and I go to the same doctor and he wouldn't prescribe something that would hurt her.'

'That stuff's poison.'

'You're not my keeper.'

'No, you idiot. I'm your friend!'

I gazed longingly at the pills. I could still gather them and wipe them off. Kathlyn heard me thinking, stepped off the curb, and crushed the pills with her Nikes.

'You . . . you . . .' I stepped toward her, tears choking me. I dug my nails into my palms to keep from hitting her.

'Good,' she smiled, dancing around me like a fighter, motioning me to take a punch, 'that's a start. Why'd you stop? Why the hell don't you let go, Barb? What's the worst that can happen?'

'Just leave me alone,' I snapped, walking away.

She danced after me, taking fake jabs, her fat bouncing as she bobbed up and down. 'I mean the worst. I'll get mad? So what? I'll yell back?' I started jogging. Her voice followed me. 'Big fat deal.'

'Stuff it!' I shouted.

'Better! I like it! Keep it up!'

'Leave me alone!'

'What's the worst, Barbara?' She was shrieking now. 'Try fighting at home, kid. The worst is that he'll leave you? Is that the worst? Might not be so bad.'

'Get out of my life!' I screamed, ignoring the surge of gym-shoed commuters dashing for the oncoming train. I started running, under the lowered barricade, over the tracks, out of the business district, across the park, back toward the safety of my home.

'DOES THIS MEAN,' she boomed, crossing the tracks just ahead of the train, chasing me through the park, 'WE'RE NOT GOING TO THE PROM?'

The life went out of my legs as if someone had kneed them from behind. I fell to the ground, hunched over on all fours, laughing and crying, not giving a damn what people thought as Kathlyn gathered me in her big soft arms and rocked me for a long long time.

I found the slip of paper I'd torn from Sarajane's envelope and dialed the number.

'Hello. Halsey Investigations. How may I help you?'

'My name is Barbara Marlow. I'm doing a series of columns for the *Globe* and I would like to set up an interview with Mr Halsey.'

'He's out of town until the seventeenth. Would you like to schedule something now or call back?'

'Now,' I said, before I lost my nerve. 'I'll reconfirm when he's back.'

We set a tentative date and I marked it down. Maybe by the time I went to see him, I really would be interested in doing a column. The idea of siccing a detective on Franklin nauseated me. I didn't know, when the time came, if I could do it. But by forcing myself to make an appointment I had taken my first stroke out of a stagnant pond.

ELEVEN

I made my tenth and final run through all the rooms in the house checking in drawers, under beds, inside closets to be sure Jason and Rikki weren't leaving anything behind they'd need during the next eight weeks. They'd forgotten a couple of little items, like Jason's toothbrush and Rikki's retainer. Seven-thirty in the morning and I was drowning in sweat.

'That's it, then,' I said, huffing into the kitchen. Franklin was hugging Rikki and Jason tightly.

'Ohhhhhhhh, I'm gonna miss you guys.' He looked at me over the tops of their heads. 'You give them money?'

'No. The camp said not to send –'

'The camp said,' he mimicked, dramatically pulling out his wallet, flipping it open, peeling off two crisp twenties and pressing them into the children's hands. 'A person's gotta have some walking-around money,' he said. 'Now, let's get these duffles in the car.' The pain in my back teeth reminded me to unclench them. I wiggled my lower jaw. I wasn't about to pick a fight the morning the children were leaving. But it was exactly this sort of thing Franklin

171

and I were going to have to work out in the next two months.

Rikki and Jason lugged one khaki duffle out the back door toward the car. Franklin, whose gym-toned body was at peak strength, swung the other duffle onto his shoulder. 'Bring the sleeping bags,' he ordered as he banged out the door.

'Yasssir, boss!' I said, doing a little shuffle off to Buffalo. How did that go? Step shuffle step step. Felt wrong. Maybe it was . . .

'Barbara!' bellowed Franklin. 'Let's go!'

I slung my purse and the two carry-on bags over my shoulder and grabbed the sleeping bags, catching a whiff of my sweaty self as I locked the door behind me. No matter. I'd linger in a hot bubble bath the moment I returned. Do my finger and toenails. Weed my eyebrows. Oh, frapturous joy! Two months of serious pampering coming up. Look out, Franklin! It's gonna be a new me.

He was kneeling in the driveway kissing the children. It had the look of good-bye.

'Aren't you coming to send them off?' I asked.

'Don't try and make me feel guilty, Barb.'

'Guilty? What are you talking about? I wasn't trying –'

'Dad has a meeting,' said Rikki, as if I should have known.

'For the campaign,' said Jason, chief FIT TO LEAD button passer-outer.

'You might have told me, Franklin,' I said, stomach knotting, heart pounding, not at all sure what difference his telling me would have made. Except it would have shown some care, some concern, and it sure as hell would have explained why Franklin's usual grubby Sunday look had been replaced by a *Gentlemen's Quarterly* casual elegance.

Franklin stood, smoothing invisible wrinkles out of his slacks. No eye contact. 'Didn't I tell you? Sorry.'

'Couldn't you have made the meeting one hour later?' Starring Barbara Avers in her new role as nagging wife. 'After all, the kids will be gone two months.'

'We don't mind,' Rikki said quickly, stowing her carry-on and sleeping bag in the back of the wagon. 'Dad's real busy right now.'

'Yeah,' said Jason. 'Anyway, Dad's coming up visiting day.'

So was I. But we all knew it wasn't the same.

The kids and I climbed into the wagon, accompanied by the ear-piercing creak of rusty doors. Usually, Rikki and Jason fought to ride shotgun. This time they sat in the back seat staring out their respective windows. Rikki hadn't asked to drive. Were they suffering separation trauma? Were they feeling the tension between Franklin and me? I kept silent during the ride, not wanting them to think they had the option of not going to camp. I needed two months alone with Franklin. I had a marriage to mend and I could do it better without the kids around. We entered the massive mall parking lot.

'You don't have to wait for us,' said Rikki. So much for separation trauma.

'Of course I'll wait.'

'That's for babies,' said Jason. 'None of the other mothers wait.'

I hit the brakes and turned around. 'What the hell's going on here?' Neither of them looked at me.

'Nothing,' said Rikki. 'You just don't have to treat us like we were little kids, that's all. I mean, we've been going away for years. You can drop us off, then do whatever you have to do.'

My heart melted. 'Do? What do I have to do that's more important than this? Visiting day is a whole four weeks away.' The poor kids. They must have been thinking that if their father didn't care enough to see them off, did their mother really want to? Just because I was furious with Franklin for not coming, I couldn't let the kids go to camp thinking badly of him. 'Don't be angry that Dad isn't here. You know he loves you and he'd –'

'Of course he loooooooves us.' Rikki oozed sarcasm. 'That's not it at all.'

'Then, would you mind telling me what it is?'

'Forget it! Just forget we said anything. We try and do something nice for you, save you from a boring wait – I mean, you're always complaining about having to wait at the doctor's, wait at the dentist's, wait at swim lessons, wait at the grocery.' Franklin's voice poured out of her.

I turned away and drove through the nearly deserted lot to where the first cars had gathered to wait for the buses. The millisecond the car stopped, the kids jumped out, pulled down the wagon's back door, and hauled out their camp gear. Slamming the door, they began dragging their duffles, bags, rackets, to the front check-in table. I watched, still reeling from Rikki's attack. All right, if they wanted to be independent, who the hell was I to get in their way? I'd stay in the car until the buses took them away.

I checked my reflection in the rear-view. Two world-class pimples, one on my chin, the other on the bridge of my nose, were forcing their swollen red way to the skin's surface. The morning had been too hectic to allow time for makeup. Actually, I had left myself plenty of time to get Rikki, Jason, and myself ready but at the last moment Franklin needed his pants pressed. 'Now?' I'd asked. He offered to set up the ironing board and iron if I could just get out the big wrinkles. Hell, if he was willing to do all that, how could I refuse? I decided pressing his pants would be my first step toward patching our marriage. At that time I still thought he was dressing up to send the kids off to camp. Silly moi.

I dug around in my purse frantically looking for the cover stick I kept in my makeup bag. 'Oh, no,' I groaned, suddenly picturing the small floral bag sitting on the kitchen table. Rikki had taken it out, borrowed a lipstick, then left the bag a few inches from my purse. Some quirk of nature kept her from returning a thing exactly where she'd found it. In my rush, I'd forgotten it.

The lot filled with cars and faces familiar from years of car pools, school functions, social events, parties. Divorced couples arrived separately, united momentarily in the sending off of their children lest either parent appear unloving. Some cars held new boyfriends, girlfriends, new spouses complete with *their* children. These outsiders waited in the cars, willing to put up with the one hour's inconvenience that would buy them eight weeks of freedom. Funny. It was the still-married people who dared to be absent, going to play golf, shoot skeet, have campaign meetings.

I combed my hair with my fingers. A hair caught in a broken nail and tore it halfway through. I ripped off the rest. The harsh sun hit the windshield like a spotlight, detailing facial lines, wrinkles, pimples, unplucked eyebrows, pre-menstrual puffiness. That *was* pre-menstrual puffiness, wasn't it? I swung the rearview away and gripped the key in the ignition. There was no way I could take my face out in public. Why shouldn't I leave? The kids wanted me to. I pinched my fingers on the metal but couldn't force myself to turn the key. I hadn't kissed them good-bye, which meant four weeks of feeling guilty about not kissing them good-bye. I had to have my kisses no matter how bitchy Rikki was behaving.

Rolling the car window down, I tried waving. I didn't want to draw attention to myself by honking and God knows I didn't want to get out of the car. I ran my tongue over my teeth. Unbrushed. I *always* brushed. How could I have left the house looking like this? Of course, I'd thought Franklin would be with me and, somehow, that had let me shift attention away from myself to getting the kids ready. Where had my mind been? Did I think I'd be able to hide in his shadow?

Waving at the kids wasn't working. Rikki, deep in a

crowd of girls who looked dishearteningly alike, shrieked at each newly arriving friend. Jason compared cassette tapes with a group of boys. Some of the boys had hit pubescent growth spurts and Jason looked like a little kid next to them. My little boy. Leaving unhugged for four weeks. I had to get out of the car. I smoothed the wrinkles of the gauzy cotton sundress I'd liberated in desperation from Sarajane's section of my cedar closet. None of my old clothing fit me anymore. Even my oversized blouses weren't oversized enough. I was so sure I'd lose the weight before summer that, except for two 'downtown' dresses, I hadn't invested in the next size.

Why hadn't I taken Sarajane's wide-brimmed hat from the closet? Why had I left my sunglasses at home? Desperate for cover, I dug around under the seat, found three linty licorice jelly beans and popped them into my mouth. How much could three jelly beans hurt? The lint was definitely low-calorie. Still looking, my hand landed on an old pair of John Lennon sunglasses. Hooking the one remaining stem over my left ear, I checked the small round lenses in the rearview. I looked like the blind begger who used to work the corner of Michigan and Oak. By sliding the glasses down the bridge of my nose, I was able to partially cover the emerging pimple.

The crowd of adults chatted, idly measuring themselves against new arrivals. These were my people and I couldn't face them looking like this. My hand gripped the door handle, waiting. Timing was critical. I needed a diversion, something to occupy the crowd's attention long enough for me to run up to my children, kiss them, and take off. Where was a flying saucer when you needed one? On cue, four huge buses turned into the parking lot, horns blaring as they wound their way to the piles of duffles. Ask and ye shall receive. Campers jumped up and down, parents cheered, and everyone turned east.

I lunged out of the car, racing toward Rikki and Jason before I could chicken out. Grabbing Jason from behind, I spun him around. 'Have a great time!' I said, kissing and hugging him quickly. 'I'll miss you.' He wriggled away, embarrassed in front of his friends. He'd have to live with it.

I was making my way toward Rikki's group when she spotted me. The horror on her face stopped me like a slap. We stood, our eyes locked. For the first time I understood, really understood. I embarrassed her. That's why she'd wanted to be dropped off, so her friends wouldn't see me. I tried to remember the last time she'd brought any of these friends home, friends who used to live at our house, who loved to tell Rikki how beautiful her mother was. I lifted my pimpled chin, threw back my hunched shoulders, and walked slowly and defiantly toward her. She darted out of the crowd, signaling me toward the mall's tree-lined courtyard.

'What is it?' she asked with forced brightness, her voice shaking.

'I wanted to kiss you good-bye. I won't see you –'

'Bye,' she said, kissing me quickly on the cheek. 'Have a great summer. Gotta go.' She started toward the buses.

'I'll walk with you,' I said, feeling the need to hurt her the way she was hurting me. 'I haven't seen your friends in such a long time.'

She turned on me, angrily. 'I wish you'd stop treating me like a baby.'

'And I wish you'd start treating me like a human being.'

She startled like a deer in headlights, surprised at having been found out. When she stomped off I didn't have the heart to follow.

I hugged myself, biting down on my lips so I wouldn't cry. I had gotten to a point where I could go several hours without wanting a cigarette. Not now. Now I wanted a whole pack. All at once. Rikki strode across the parking lot, Franklin's taut body in miniature, softened by the curves of young womanhood. She pushed her way to the front of the crowd boarding the first bus and disappeared behind the black windows. I sniffed and sobbed, the taste of blood in my mouth.

'It's hard to let go.' Oh, God, someone overheard us. I braced myself and turned around. No one. 'Although,' continued a familiar voice from behind a hedge of lilacs, 'it's not always easy to tell who is letting go.' I inched toward the bush. Mac's unpatched eye peered back through the branches at me.

'Mac?'

'You know someone else who looks like this?'

'Oh, it's not . . . I didn't mean . . .' Stop babbling, Barbara. I took a deep breath, pushed the sunglasses up over the nose pimple to cover my teary eyes, and walked around the bushes into the shadowy garden. He sat on a bench, his bad leg propped up. I swallowed and prayed my sunglasses hid more of my face than I knew they did. 'W-what are you doing here?'

'Cameron promised to buy me a bagel if I helped get Michelle off to camp.'

'No, I mean why are you here, in Chicago?'

He gripped his leg with both hands and lifted it off the bench. 'Would you mind sitting down? It hurts my neck to look up at you.'

I sat next to him, arranging Sarajane's dress gracefully around me, trying not to think of how I looked. Maybe this was just as well. There was no way he could want me after seeing me like this. I cupped my hand to my chin, casually covering the pimple and the second chin.

'That's better,' he said. 'Thanks.'

'So?'

'Cameron offered me a job at the *Globe* –'

'He never said –'

'– and I'm taking it.' Your secret wish has been granted, Mrs Avers. Now what?

'Mac, that's wonderful.'

'I don't know about that. Talk to me in the middle of a blizzard. I may change my mind.'

A counselor called stragglers through a megaphone.

'Is your daughter going away for the summer?' he asked.

'Both children.' I had the feeling the news pleased him.

'Well, then,' he unhooked his cane from the back of the bench, and pushed himself up, 'why don't we go wave good-bye before the buses leave.'

'I already –'

'May I borrow your arm?'

'Yes, yes of course.' I stood, my heart thudding like a schoolgirl's. The scar down his face had faded against his deep tan. He looked more fit than I remembered. 'You seem to be walking much better,' I said, bending my left arm, extending the elbow toward him.

'I don't always use the cane anymore,' he said. 'But it's good to have around in crowds.' He reached up slowly, sliding callused fingers around my naked elbow. I shivered at the raw voltage of his touch. Damn. I'd almost convinced myself that the desire I'd felt for Mac had been a combination of the dark booth in Riccardo's and the liquor.

'You're cold?' he asked, trailing his fingertips over my goosebumps.

'A little bit.'

'Let's get you into the sunshine.'

He led me toward the parking lot with its crush of departing campers and parents and I could think of no way out. We walked slowly, his hand gripping my arm. I thought of forcing small conversation but could think of none. Sweat stains grew on the underarms of his khaki shirt. Walking was still a chore for him. I slid my free hand comfortingly over his and we inched along like refugees from a Tim Conway sketch. Mac was taller than I'd remembered, perhaps because he was not so bent over his cane. My head filled with his scent, an exotic blend of unfamiliar toiletries, sweat, and something animal.

In the distance Cameron's gangly body towered over a convivial gathering of neighbors. Shirley Cohen, who believed all men would leave their wives instantly if she but nodded her twice-lifted face, gripped Cameron's arm possessively, pressing it to her breast implants. Her platinum ponytail bobbed as she uttered the Marilyn Monroe squeal Franklin found charming. Harold Cohen, whom Sarajane swore was embalmed, watched comatose. It wasn't like Shirley to come on to a husband whose wife was around.

'Where's Myrna?' I asked Mac.

'Sisterhood board meeting.' His black curls glistened with sweat which ran freely down his temples.

'You are going to sit down.' I led him to a bench shaded by a small Russian Olive. Cameron seemed relieved when he spotted us. He unpeeled Shirley from his arm and came over.

'Mac tell you the news?' he asked, beaming. 'I've been after him for years.' Oh really? 'Quite a coup for the *Globe*.'

Michelle bounced up behind him to say good-bye. 'Hi, Mrs Avers,' she said brightly. I forced a smile. Michelle, always a slender girl, was nearly skeletal. 'Good-bye, Uncle Mac,' she said, kissing his forehead, eyepatch, nose.

'You call me if any of those boys get fresh,' said Mac.

'Are you kidding? I'll call you if they *don't!* Come

on, Daddy,' she gripped Cameron's hand, pulling him away, 'I've got to get on that second bus or I'll have to ride with the junior high kids.'

'Can't let that happen. Don't go away,' he called to Mac. 'I'll put the car around in a minute.' In her little halter top, Michelle's back was all spinal column and jutting back bones. Tall and lanky like her father, her arms looked like two sticks of wood joined at elbow and wrist by knob connectors.

I turned questioningly to Mac. He was staring at me, his eye so intent on my face it felt like a caress. 'Yes?' he said.

'I was wondering about Michelle. I haven't seen her in quite a while. I mean, does she seem a little thin to you?'

He rounded his soft lips into a pucker which did such strange things to my system. 'A little thin?'

'Well, I know Cameron said she was thin, but I hadn't realized . . .'

'A little thin.' He closed his eye and leaned his head back. Sunlight filtering through leaves of the Russian Olive danced small shadows on his face. I clasped my hands together in my lap, still uncertain how to occupy them without a cigarette. After a very long while, Mac brought his head back down and opened his eye at me. 'Barbara, why don't you ever say what's on your mind?'

'What do you mean?' and how did this conversation come around to me?

'You ask if I don't think Michelle is a "little thin". Yes, the way Niagara Falls is a trickle and World War

II was a dispute. Michelle is not a little thin. Michelle is terrifyingly emaciated. I call her my Biafran Beauty. And why are you so afraid to say what you're thinking?'

I bristled. 'Naturally, I'm curious, but I don't want to be rude.'

'Being direct isn't being rude, it is simply being direct. It is also the shortest distance between a question and answer.' He stretched his arm along the bench behind me. The proximity of his skin to mine stood my neck hairs on end.

'All right, then, is Michelle anorexic?'

'Bravo! Much better. Yes.'

'Is she getting help?'

'Yes, finally. She'd been losing weight all winter, hiding the loss under bulky winter clothing. I noticed it immediately the last time I was in.'

'That doesn't make sense. I thought anorexia happened when families were out of balance, not in homes with loving parents like Cameron and Myrna.'

'Being loving isn't always enough. Evidently Michelle felt she'd lost control of her life. Her father's high expectations made demands on her.'

'Cameron adores Michelle.'

'And she adores him, which is why she feared being less than perfect for him. If he was Republican, she was Republican. If he admired straight A's, then she'd bring homes straight A's. Hell, he always introduced her as his perfect daughter.'

'He was joking.'

'Kids don't always understand our jokes, Barbara.

And maybe we aren't really joking after all.'

This is my daughter, Rikki. Looks just like her father. Jason takes after my side of the family. Did Rikki interpret that to mean I was denying her as my daughter? That I favored Jason in some way? Was she pushing me away because I pushed her away first? I never paid attention to how I introduced my children. Was I creating demands? Expectations? Associations?

'What about Myrna?' I asked. 'She's so warm and caring. I can't believe she didn't notice what was happening to Michelle.'

'Myrna's not happy unless she's busy twenty-five hours a day. Problem is, she scheduled Michelle's life, too, with classes, clubs, lessons, volunteer work. That doesn't leave much time for a kid to be a kid. It got to a point where Michelle felt the only thing in her life she could control completely was how much she did or didn't eat.'

The buses pulled out, horns blaring, parents cheering. I waved because I was embarrassed not to, though I doubted my children were looking for me. They would have been if Franklin were here. I sank back on the bench. Mac's thumb trailed the curve of my shoulder and I looked away.

'I think I'd better go.' I didn't move. No part of me wanted to leave, yet every part was terrified to stay.

'Why not join us for breakfast?'

'Oh, no, I've got tons of stuff to do.' Like not eat in front of you. 'Franklin may be needing me down at headquarters today.' Ho ho.

'Our loss,' he said, kissing me softly on the cheek as Cameron came to collect him. They drove off and I walked the long way around to my car to avoid seeing people I knew. I had not felt ugly with Mac and Cameron. They didn't seem to see my pimples, my lack of makeup, my fat. For a short while I had stopped hurting.

I stopped at a deli to buy a dozen bagels, half-pound of belly lox, and a pint of chive cream cheese. Sort of a last hurrah before my appointment with Dr Cheng. Might as well give the hypnotist something substantial to work with. The salty salmon would blow me up but my pre-menstrual taste buds craved salt and spice. On the way home, unable to resist the intoxicating aroma of fresh baked bagels, I slipped one out of its bag and took a huge bite, holding the soft warm dough in my mouth. It tasted like Sunday on Astor Street when hungover newsmen sat stubble-faced and thick-lidded around the dining room table, eating bagels and playing poker. Franklin didn't like bagels. He was a white-bread man. Even now, when his well-publicized FIT TO LEAD diet specified whole grain wheat, I think he secretly longed for the non-taste of white bread. I swallowed the first bite and took another. No one started a diet on Sunday. Monday was the day for beginnings.

A man stood on my stoop ringing the bell. I took my foot off the gas and rolled toward my house, checking his hands for *Watchtowers*, vacuum cleaners, or long white bars of charity candy. Looked safe enough. He turned at the sound of my car pulling into the driveway. Old man. Tall. Shoulders hunched. White shirt and shiny suit too roomy for the thin body inside. He looked overpackaged. I held the warm bagel bag to my breast.

'May I help you?' I asked.

'Mrs Avers?' He clutched a hat in his hands, worrying the brim with knobby fingers.

'Yes.'

'I'm George Payne.' It took a few seconds for the name to register. Old Payne-in-the-glass.

'Why, yes, Mr Payne. How nice to see you.' I didn't open the door and invite him in. My universe quivered in anticipation of a bagel, lox, and cheese orgy. It was something best done in private, away from talky old men with dying wives. 'What can I do for you?'

'I thought Mr Avers might be home.'

'No, I'm sorry. He's at a meeting just now.' I took out my house key. 'And I'm afraid I'm in a bit of a rush myself. Is there some message you'd like to leave for him?'

He reached inside his jacket and took out a check. 'I wanted to give this to him, sort of in person, to thank him for his patience. I wish I could pay back the whole loan but things are still tight.'

His rheumy eyes were getting to me. Give this man a bagel. Set his world back on track. No, not now. I vant to eat alone. Just me and the Sunday papers. I love a *Parade*.

'I'm sorry your wife is so ill,' I said. I was. 'I know

Franklin is doing everything within his power to settle your case.' I didn't. 'I'm sure this terrible time will be over soon.' I wasn't.

'Thank you, Mrs Avers,' he said, pressing the check into my hand. I glanced at the amount. Ten dollars. About half the cost of my bag full of goodies.

'You know, Mr Payne. I'm sure it would be all right with Mr Avers, if you wait to pay back the loan until your case is settled. He could deduct the amount from the settlement.' I tried to hand back the check but George shook his head and backed down the stairs.

'I don't like owing,' he said. 'We're prideful people. Never owed nobody nothin' until Lucinda took so sick. Not a good feeling, owing people for things.' He put on his hat and adjusted the brim. 'Give my best to Mr Avers. Nice to have met you.'

A warm breeze flapped his clothes around his frail body. I watched him walk away until the aroma rising from the bag of bagels drove me inside.

TWELVE

I gripped the wobbly banister, hauling my body up three flights of rickety wood stairs and down a dingy corridor to Dr Cheng's office. A gnomelike man eased open the door, peeking out suspiciously, wiping dirty crooked hands on a filthy white coat before beckoning me inside. The scenario, with countless permutations, woke me repeatedly during the night. Franklin's gentle snoring next to me bolstered my resolve. The bonding between us was slipping and I couldn't seem to get a new grip.

Sex, when it happened at all over the last few months, had been waiting until: I was awake, Franklin was home, the children were asleep, and our ascending sun had a descending moon in the seventh house of Usher. Even then sex was fast and detached, bodies in by ten-thirty, out by ten-thirty-five. Guaranteed. The rare times Franklin was home, I sensed him doing me a favor wedging me between the end of the news and 'Nightline'. Have you hugged your hippo today?

Okay, I broke it, I'd fix it. I'd invade Kathlyn's favorite sex shop, stock up on oils, lotions and

189

whatever the hell else they sold. I'd check *The Reader* for courses in erotic massage and belly dancing. Best of all, most of all, all of all, I'd lose weight. And if that meant allowing an occult Occidental to fine tune my psyche, so be it.

I didn't realize I'd been staring at Franklin until his eyes fluttered open.

'Morning,' I said, softly.

'Time zit?'

'Seven-thirty,' I walked my fingers across the sheets toward him. No kids around. No need to be quiet. We could make love any old time we wanted.

'Seven-thirty?' He bounded out of bed and flew into the bathroom. 'How the hell'd I oversleep?'

'Oversleep? You always wake up at seven-thirty.' I rolled out of bed, fluttering after him in one of Sarajane's silk caftans.

'I'm going to have to get out earlier now. Until the campaign's over.'

'When are you going to sleep? You run out early, come in late.'

'There's too much to do, Barb.' He rummaged under the sink. 'Where the hell are the razors?'

'There should be a bag of Bics in back.' I liked the sound of it. 'Bag of Bics in back. Bag of Bics in back. Try saying *that* three times very fast.' Franklin wasn't playing.

'You look,' he said, standing aside, arms crossed. I did. No razors.

'Not a bloody bag of Bics in back,' I said. He glowered. Well, some of us thought it was funny. 'Sorry,

Franklin. I didn't notice we were low.'

'That new job of yours seems to be taking up all your time.'

'That's not fair.'

He stepped into the shower stall and turned on the water. Conversation closed. I went to his closet to get his sterling silver Elsa Peretti. The dop kit wasn't there. I checked all the shelves. Nothing.

'Where's your dop kit?' I asked, handing him a towel.

'My dop kit?' His drying off seemed more vigorous than usual.

'It's not in your closet.'

'What do you want my dop kit for?'

'It has a razor in it you could use to shave.'

'Oh.' He toweled off the top layer of skin. 'Oh, yes. I brought it downtown to campaign headquarters so I could freshen up between work and evening meetings and dinners.'

'Aren't you afraid someone will take it? I mean, a hundred-fifty-dollar razor can be pretty tempting.'

'You know, Barb,' he said, draping the towel over his shoulders, 'there's not much point owning nice things if you don't use them.'

First the leather jacket, now the Elsa Peretti. I turned and left the room. Franklin's got himself a lady. Franklin's got himself a lady. 'Shut up, Kathlyn,' I said.

'You say something?' called Franklin.

'Yes.' What did I say? 'I said it might not be a bad idea for us to rent a small apartment in the city for the two months the kids are gone. You wouldn't have an hour's ride to and from the house and we'd have more time together.' Quick thinking, Barb old girl.

He emerged from the bathroom and began dressing. 'Actually, I'd given that idea some thought.' Long socks left foot first, pants left leg first, take a freshly laundered shirt off its hanger. His rhythms were a part of my life. 'Not really an apartment per se, maybe just a studio, a place to crash the nights my work runs late.'

'Oh, yes,' I said. 'I bet it would be fun for a couple of months. Like when we were first married.'

'Barb,' button the shirt from the bottom up, 'I wasn't thinking of an apartment for *us*.' My world froze. Here it comes, ladies and gents. Night shot: Music up: Da-dum, da-dum. Long shot of shark fin in water. Da-dum. Innocent slightly overweight girl enters water. Da-dum, da-dum. Mid-shot, dorsal fin circling. Up tempo music, Da-dum. Girl out further. Too far. Cut!

Franklin glanced up and caught the expression on my face. It must have looked as horrible as it felt. He busied himself with his buttons. 'What I mean is, with the campaign expenses eating away at everything, I don't think we can afford a real apartment. Just a room.' I exhaled. He struggled with the top button. It popped off and flew across the room. 'Damn!' He ripped off the shirt, threw it on the bed, and took out another. 'Never mind,' he said. 'The last thing we need are any additional expenses. I can put up a cot at headquarters if I need to.'

He switched on the morning news and I sat on the edge of the bed waiting for my world to return to normal. I'd been reprieved. Half a minute ago I thought my marriage was over but I'd been given another chance. Oh Franklin, I'm sorry for the way I look. I hate the fat as much as you do. Please, please don't give up on me. I'm going to do something about this. Yes I am. This very day. I would tell you about Dr Cheng but I couldn't stand the pain if I told you I was going to lose weight and I didn't. I'd made that mistake with Weight Watchers and Nutri-Systems and Diet Center.

'Want to meet downtown for dinner?' I asked.

'Can't. Have two fundraising dinners. Polish American Club and,' he laughed, 'can't even remember what the second one is. It'll be a miracle if my stomach makes it through this. I'll probably be late. Don't wait up.' His kiss glanced off my widow's peak and he was gone. I started making the bed, bending and reaching to burn up extra calories.

It was probably just as well that we weren't eating out. I had no idea what Dr Cheng's diet would be like and there was no point going to a restaurant if I couldn't eat anything on the menu. I had tried eating out with Nutri-Systems, ordering a baked potato, a pot of hot water and a large bowl so I could mix my prepackaged food while the rest of the family ate from the menu. Rikki was mortified, Jason slipped under the table, and Franklin overtipped. The only ones who didn't seem to mind were the waitresses. We stopped going to restaurants.

* * *

Dr Cheng occupied the nineteenth-floor corner office of a new glass building half a block east of the Mercantile Exchange. Kathlyn had selected him from a myriad of mesmers because of his proximity to her office. She could squeeze in her daily session without disrupting her schedule. Kathlyn assured me most of Dr Cheng's patients had weekly appointments which shifted to monthly when they began the maintenance diet. But she felt the need of daily reinforcement. She was doing so well, she said, it would be a shame to mess up.

I rang the bell at the nurse's station bracing myself as the glass window slid open. A beautiful young nurse smiled warmly at me. 'Yes?'

Leaning into the opening, I whispered, 'Mrs Avers to see Dr Cheng. I have a ten-thirty appointment.'

Three slender nurses bustled in and out of the room behind her as she checked her appointment sheet. 'Ah, yes, Mrs Avers,' she blared into the waiting room, 'please fill these out.' She handed me a four-page form and slid the window shut.

The small reception area was packed with medium, large, and extra large women. Each week this time slot was set aside for new patients like myself. There were many more of us than I had expected. Settling into the last empty chair, I covertly measured myself against the others. Like the alcoholic reassured by the intake of heavier drinkers, I was relieved to be on the light end of the other women's considerable weight range. Somewhere, I reckoned, there was an eight-hundred-pound person taking solace in the photo of the thousand-pound man in the *Guinness Book of World Records*. Was he the end of the line, the king of the food chain, the crème de la heavy crème? O.K. guys, the one who dies fattest, wins.

I breezed through the first two pages of standard medical history questions. I had always been healthy, a major disappointment during my youth when I longed for the drama of a mysterious and lingering illness. Nothing deadly, simply severe enough to force my grandmother to give up a few of her organizations and meetings and taper off her weekly round of Maj Jong, Bridge, and Poker. I longed to have her home after school, to shower me with attention and sympathy, to brag to her friends about my quiet noble bravery.

The closest I ever came to chronic illness was severe menstrual cramps. Two months before my first period I'd awakened screaming during the night, fire tearing through my belly, my back, raging into my thighs. Certain my appendix had burst, my father bundled me into the car and raced through the deserted streets. No one at the hospital could figure out what was wrong with me and, as a consequence, they were afraid to administer a painkiller. After three hours, the pain passed, I was diagnosed as having had probable kidney stones, and was sent home, exhausted. I was desolate. I'd finally had my father's undivided attention and had been too sick to enjoy it.

The second bout came nearly a month to the night after the first. This time my grandmother poured a

shot of cognac down my throat, followed by four aspi-
rin and hot tea. She had me curl up in bed with her, my
belly against her rump, a heating pad against my back.
Years later, I realized she must have had an idea of
what was the matter, but she never said a word to me.
She considered the body a convenient vessel for trans-
porting the brain and discussed my body with me as
seldom as possible. My grandmother had never suffered menstrual pain. Until I came along, she'd firmly
believed it was a mass delusion of weak-willed women.
Because my pain surfaced before I began menstrua-
tion, she grudgingly acknowledged it was real. I don't
think she ever entirely forgave me.

I flipped the questionnaire to the second two pages
which delved into my lifestyle. Was I married or
unmarried, with or without children, did I work outside the home, what were my hobbies? The list wove
through my habits: Did I smoke, drink, gamble? Once
I started could I stop? Did I consider myself carefree,
troubled, happy, unhappy? Was I quick to anger? Did
I keep my feelings locked inside or let them out? The
final question proved the most difficult: Three things I
have never done that I would like to do are – . I stared
at that question, unable to think of anything that fit the
whole question. I had never jumped out of an airplane,
or eaten magic mushrooms, or had an affair. But
would I like to? Hardly the sort of response the good
doctor was looking for. Come on, Barbara. Think. I
shifted in my chair, uncrossed and recrossed my legs,
clicked my pen, sighed heavily.

'This is worse than applying for a job,' said the size

twenty next to me, flipping her questionnaire closed. Her boldly printed caftan was unmistakably Léonard. Sarajane had owned several and said they were worth every penny. She believed people 'of a certain size' looked grotesque in normal clothing and, once Sarajane escaped her mother's home, she never owned an article of clothing with a waistline. I glanced at the birthdate on the woman's medical form. It said she was nineteen but she looked ten years older.

'I can't think of anything for this last question,' I said.

'That? I had too many. I finally settled for hang glide, play a musical instrument, and be thin.'

'You've never been thin?'

'Nope. I weighed eleven pounds at birth and just kept going from there.' She laughed, casually brushing back an imaginary wisp of hair, flashing the huge pear-shaped diamond ring she'd wedged onto a pudgy perfectly manicured finger. I knew the gesture. Sarajane used it when meeting strangers, flashing her ten-carat cabochon like a cross in front of vampires as if dazzling jewels would ward off unkind thoughts. The fatter she became, the more obsessive she was about her makeup, hair, fingernails, jewelry, clothing, anything that might magically distract the eye and mind from her weight. The girl reached into her bag for a lace handkerchief. 'No one else in my family is heavy so we can't imagine how I happened,' she said. 'Oh, a few times I got down to one-sixty but I just couldn't keep it off. How about you?'

'I was thin my whole life. Then I stopped smoking and started eating.'

'You don't look so heavy to me.'

How could I tell *her* I felt obese? 'I thought I'd try and get back to my normal weight before I got much bigger.'

She nodded approval. 'It must be hard, seeing your body go from thin to heavy. I know it's creepy seeing mine wither away to one-sixty. Scares me, as a matter of fact. I get this weird feeling if I don't stop dieting, I'll disappear altogether.'

'But, you're going to try it again?'

'My parents have offered to send me to Europe if I take off seventy-five pounds.'

'That's quite an offer.'

'Yes.' She sighed, dotting her damp upper lip with the hanky. 'It works out pretty well. That's how I got my car and my apartment.' Her name was called and she pushed herself up out of the chair. 'Good luck,' she said. I stared after her, not sure I'd heard what I'd heard. She was using her weight as a tool to manipulate her parents. Did they bribe their fat daughter because they loved her or because she was an embarrassment?

'Fuck it,' I muttered. Weight created insanity within insanity, variations on a theme of fat. Weight confused and angered me. I had never had to think about weight my whole life, and now it occupied my every waking moment, shaped my days, channeled my life. I'd failed at my first attempts, but, dammit, this time I'd get the weight off. I was ready to be thin again.

The first half hour of my appointment was directed

by the nurses. They took my vital signs, blood samples, urine, had me strip down, weighed me. One sixty-three and a quarter. Like most doctor's scales, this one weighed heavy and, naturally, I'd eaten breakfast. The nurse took me to a large machine and handed me a hollow plastic tube the size of my middle finger. One end fit over a projection on the machine and she told me to take a deep breath, then blow into the tube. I did. Digital numbers flashed on a small screen, moving up from zero to twenty-five.

'What's this for?' I asked.

'It tells us if you're being a good girl,' she said, jotting the numbers onto my file.

'What do you mean?'

'When you lose weight, your body eats its fat stores. We can measure the process – ketosis – with this machine. Next week, if you're really doing what you should be, these numbers will go quite high.'

'Doesn't my weight tell you I'm dieting?'

'Oh, some of our naughty patients take diuretics or enemas before coming in to fool us into thinking they're losing weight. The scale can lie, but this little machine never does.'

She put me in an examination room, told me to dress, and left. When I was ready, I opened the door, hoping to overhear something from one of the other rooms. Kathlyn wouldn't describe the hypnosis procedure to me, afraid I'd build up a resistance to the process before I began. I thumbed through the stack of magazines on the end table. *Better Homes and Gardens, Redbook, Glamour*, the doctor stocked a wide variety of women's magazines, every one of which listed a new diet on the cover. Inside, the slick pages were crammed with recipes, advertisements, tips, hints, most of them pertaining to food. My mouth watered over the four-color photos of chocolate chip cookies, meringue pies, cheese and fruit, appetizers, main courses, desserts, snacks. I glanced at my watch. Eleven-thirty. I'd been in the office over an hour and I was famished.

'Ah, Mrs Avers.' Dr Cheng forged into the room, his large frame crushing the withered old man of my fantasy. He extended a beefy hand.

'Dr Cheng?' His grip was strong, direct.

'Let's see here . . .' He sat at his desk, flipping his glasses down from their resting place atop his head, losing himself in my file. His gently slanted eyes were outlined by thick black lashes. His smooth light brown skin had tiny crinklings around his eyes and mouth. 'So, you're a friend of Kathlyn's.' He swiveled his chair around and leaned back, lacing his fingers over his chest.

'Yes.'

'She's quite a character.'

'You noticed?'

He assessed me closely, lifting his glasses back up onto his head. 'You're concerned about your weight?'

'That's why I'm here.'

'Were you interested in hypnosis?'

'Beg your pardon?'

'Hypnosis. Kathlyn has preferred to use that as part

of her weight-loss program but I also do straight weight-loss counseling. Not everyone is crazy about the idea of being hypnotized.'

I wasn't alone. 'Oh, really. I wonder why?'

He shrugged, wiping his eyes wearily with forefinger and thumb. 'Fear of losing control, perhaps.'

'We've already lost control, haven't we? I mean, isn't that why we come to you?'

'Is that how you feel, Mrs Avers, that you're out of control?'

'My weight certainly is.'

He flipped my questionnaire open, scanning it quickly. 'You make weight gain sound like a generic problem,' he said, not looking up. 'Lose Control – Gain Weight. Has a nice ring to it. It would certainly make my job easier since I could devise a generic solution. But I assure you my patients have a wide range of reasons for being overweight. I have quite a few patients who like themselves just the way they are. But their doctors want them to reduce because of heart problems or joints which can't bear the weight, that sort of thing. Not everyone wants to be thin. Not by any means. Then again, for some of my patients, excessive weight *is* their control.' I thought of the young girl in the reception area. 'Whether a patient is anorexic or obese often depends on which will be most offensive to the controlling person in her life.'

'Her, Doctor?'

His sparkling dark eyes lifted off the page and

looked unwaveringly into mine. I wondered if this was the beginning of the hypnosis. I shifted my gaze to the wall over his left ear. 'My patients usually are "her", Mrs Avers.'

'Why?'

He laughed heartily. 'That would take more time than either of us has right now. But I can tell you that ninety percent of my weight clients are women and the few men I get are usually dragged in by wives or referred by physicians. Now, what did you decide about hypnosis?'

'Why not? Although, I'm not sure I can be hypnotized.'

'No one's ever tried?'

'Once. When I was eleven. My dentist had me stick my thumb out in front of me, stare at it, and count backward from ten.'

'And?'

'We both sat there staring at my thumb. All I could think was how ugly my thumb looked. I bit my nails so far down they were bloody half the time, and that day the thumb was infected on the side, all green and white and swollen. I pretended I was hypnotized so I could stop holding my thumb up.' I winced, remembering the pain of the drill.

He looked at my hands. 'You stopped biting your nails.'

'The minute I started smoking.'

'And now you're replacing cigarettes with food.'

'Yes.' I was actually wringing my hands. I pressed them into my lap, forcing them to be still. 'One of the problems of playing musical neurosis is I wonder what's going to be next. It's scary to toss one crutch away before lining up the next one. With my history, if I give up eating I'll probably take up drinking.'

'I'll tell you a little secret,' he said, 'there's no law that says you have to play the game. This may be the time in your life you find the strength to get up and walk away and leave all those crutches behind once and for all.'

The earth lurched. He didn't seem to notice.

'Do you think I can be hypnotized?'

'There's one good way to find out.' He turned on a soft corner light and shut off the overhead. 'Rest both feet on the floor. Good. Now rest your arms on the arms of the chair. Fine. I want you to look at that shadow on the wall and relax. Listen to my voice,' it was low and soothing, 'and relax. Good. As I count to ten, you will feel your eyelids grow heavy. Very heavy. It is becoming an effort to hold them open.' My eyelids grew heavy. I melted into the darkness. He began counting. My eyelids closed when he hit '10'.

I can open my eyes any time I want but I'm more comfortable this way at the moment and I think I'll follow his deep rumbling voice down a loooooong escalator deeper deeper down and down and during this coming week I will have no desire for candy bread potato chips pizza cake pie or any other food I know is not good for me when I feel hungry I will take a deep breath and the feeling will pass when I am sorely tempted I will think of the way I *want* to look and the hunger will vanish no matter how much food is left on

my plate I will eat only until I am no longer hungry
then I will stop eating I would like to stay in this dark
place listening to the hum of his voice telling me how
beautiful I am and how much more beautiful I am
going to be and I wish he wouldn't count backward
'10 . . . 9 . . . 8 . . .' no stop I'm not ready to come
back but my eyelids feel lighter my body floating up
and up '3 . . . 2 . . . 1'. My eyes opened and I was
back.

'I . . . I don't know if I was hypnotized or not,' I
said.

'It's certainly not easy to tell.' He flipped my file
closed.

'Couldn't you have run a match under my palm or
something?'

'I think our best gauge will be how well you do this
week.' He pulled a sheet of paper out of his desk
drawer. 'This is the diet you're to follow. It's 800
calories a day so it's critical that you take the vitamin
supplements the nurse will give you. And you must
drink six to eight glasses of water a day to wash the
ketones out of your system. Questions?'

I couldn't think of any. We shook hands and he
disappeared into the next room. The nurse came in
with my supply of multi-vitamin pills, vitamin B complex pills, and calcium pills. I made an appointment
for the following week, paid my $150 first-time fee
which included my medical work-up, and strode
determinedly into the noon sun.

I dreaded meeting Kathlyn for lunch. She would
ask if I'd been hypnotized and I didn't know the

answer. On my way to her office I passed a Caramel Corn store, its syrupy smell coating the air. It was a magic smell that transformed expensively suited financiers into little boys who needed to stop for small bags of maple, or chocolate, or caramel covered popcorn. Taking a deep breath, I passed the store without a glance. I'd *never* been able to pass a Caramel Corn store, even when I was thin. That meant I had been hypnotized, after all! With the vigor and determination of a born again dieter, I threw back my soon-to-be-thin shoulders and walked briskly to Kathlyn's office.

THIRTEEN

Early morning had the rich loamy smell of fresh-turned dirt. Why hadn't I noticed it before? Losing weight was a mind expanding drug, a half-pound down on the morning scale gave me the ultimate high. I power-walked to our halfway-between meeting spot marveling at the glint of dew on blades of grass. The little things. 'For in the dew of little things, the heart finds its morning and is refreshed', a line memorized years ago from my mother's volume of *The Prophet*. I'd read it, wondering if my fingers gripped the red leather in the exact same place hers had, if my eyes were reading from the exact same distance. She'd margined 'Wonderful' and 'so true' in a childish scrawl, years later running a line through and rewriting 'Trite' and 'Saccharin' in her flowery college script. There was nothing written later. She'd had no 'later'.

Kathlyn was late. I jogged in place a few seconds before going to her house. The extra quarter mile felt good. Maybe I'd start doing it every day, keep up the big mo. I'd lost seven pounds in less than two weeks. Franklin's good-bye when he left for Springfield the night before felt a few degrees warmer. I was on a roll. Kaiser. Poppyseed. Cinnamon with raisins. I took a Dr Cheng deep breath and the hunger passed.

A lawn full of ancient oaks and drooping willows shielded Kathlyn's trim Tudor from Sheridan Road traffic. The trees absorbed the sounds of the street. They also muffled the house sounds which is why I didn't hear dishes crashing and Kathlyn screaming until I was nearly at the back door.

'Of all the small [crash] minded, loathsome [crash] sick men in this world [crash] I had to pick the king of the crappy crop [crash]!'

I eased open the door and peeked in. 'Kathlyn?'

She whirled around, black hair flying, eyes wild. 'Pete's left me.' She heaved a dish at his photo which she'd mounted on the refrigerator with Oreo magnets. The fake cookies fired up my taste buds and I deep breathed against a doubled-stuff desire. 'Ingrate. [Crash] Idiot.' Her son and daughter peeked in from the next room and I waved them away. 'Couldn't even face me,' she screamed at the photo. 'Had to leave a note. Coward.'

'Kathlyn –'

'Don't stop me! I'm not done with him yet. That mutant son of a dyspeptic camel.'

I crossed the room and pulled a stool into the sheltered alcove between the stove and wall. Every cabinet door had been thrown open and Kathlyn was emptying the shelves row by row. Methodical madness. I'd missed the wine-glass warm-up act but was in time for the dinner-dish show.

'Not fat enough for you? [Crash] Did I ever, one time, complain about your receding hairline? [Crash] Your beer gas. [Crash] That annoying way you cleared your throat in the morning. [Crash] Your relentlessly beige clothes? [Crash Crash] I did not. I did not. I loved you . . . you goddamned ingrate [Crash].'

By the time she reached the back-of-the-cabinet coffee saucers, chipped creamers, party platters, her Nautilus-toned arm slowed like a wound-down toy. She tried throwing with the other hand but missed the refrigerator completely. I waited until she stood still a full half minute, an unthrown sugar bowl poised and ready. Crunching up behind her, I eased the bowl out of her hand.

'Awrrrr, matey,' I said, gripping her shoulder tightly and leading her into the den, 'there's some wot say it were the soup bowls done her in.' I helped her into the large pit and poured a half glass of bourbon.

She shook her head. 'Too many calories. That stuff turns to pure sugar in your system.'

'Give it a rest, will you?' I pressed the glass into her hands and directed it to her lips. She drank. The kids tiptoed into the room. 'Not now,' I told them.

'That's all right.' Kathlyn held out her arms and her children clamored into the pit, cuddling up to her. 'Hey guys,' she nuzzled their heads, 'we always hated those old dishes anyway.' They giggled with relief. The dishes were gone but mommy had survived intact. She kissed their cheeks. 'Did I scare you?' They nodded. 'Didn't mean to. Honest. It's just, oh hell, life isn't always the way we want it to be, is it?' She hugged them mightily, and my gut knotted with the need to hold my own children. To comfort them. To have them comfort me. 'I'm sorry Pete left. I'm gonna miss him.'

'Us too,' said her son.

'I'm not gonna tell Dad,' said her daughter. 'He'll say, "I told you so".'

'Hey,' Kathlyn stroked her daughter's hair, 'there's nothing to be ashamed of here. I wish Pete had stayed and I'm sad that he left. But it got to where we needed two different things out of life. Now, is that anything to be ashamed of? No ma'am. And if your daddy can't handle that, it's his problem, not yours. But we don't keep secrets around here. That's for spineless jellyfish. Okay?'

' 'Kay.'

I left them alone, returning to the kitchen to sweep the shards into a pile. Two more weeks until camp visiting day. I'd be fifteen pounds down. Maybe more. I hadn't written the kids anything about it. Let them be surprised. Let them be proud of me again. Please God.

Kathlyn made throwing things look like fun although I couldn't imagine I'd ever have the nerve to try. She was the type that could carry off having a live-in boyfriend, or letting her children see her lose control. Where does a person get that kind of courage? I tripled the thick plastic garbage bags but that didn't stop sharp points and edges from poking through. The breakage made three loads. I unrolled sheets of paper towels, wet them, and slid them across the floor with my shoe, picking up those invisible bits of glass that love bare feet. When I finished, I went back to the den. The kids had gone upstairs to get ready for their day camp and Kathlyn was draped like a rag doll, shoulders hunched, legs stretched apart in front of her, arms and drink resting on a scrap book lying open on her lap. I climbed into the pit and put my arm around her.

'Feeling a little better?'

'This was me when I met Pete,' she said, tapping her finger on a mountain in the photo. She looked at least fifty pounds heavier than when I'd met her at Weight Watchers. 'I was near my top weight.'

'Which was?'

She shrugged. 'My scale only goes up to 350. I don't know if I broke 400, but it took me a long time to get back to 350 when I started dieting.'

We leafed through the album, through the life of a Kathlyn I never knew. Several pages were filled with photos of her looking like the Goodyear blimp in drag; chiffon gowns, sequins, ruffles, the stuff of little girl's dreams. She looked free in the photos, twirling and spinning, bending over to let the camera peek down her low-cut gown.

'When were these taken?'

'About ten years ago. I was living in New York and someone told me about – how did she put it? – oh yes, "a group of people like me". Thin people don't say "fat" to our faces. Anyway, I went to a party this group gave and saw women who made *me* look thin, dressed up just like normal people. It was wall-to-wall tits and ass and cleavage that didn't quit. Blew me away. My whole life I'd hidden my body under tents of fabric, and then Kabang! I was free to be my sexual self without feeling self-conscious. I begged my husband to go there with me. I'd been about sixty pounds overweight when we married and gained another hundred after our second baby was born.'

'Do you have a picture of him?'

She flipped to the front of the book. They were a formidable couple. She might have been a large woman, but her husband dwarfed her.

'Big Irishman,' she said. 'Big appetites. Cigar smoking, whiskey drinking, card playing son-of-a-bitch. A hell of a lover when he was sober. He didn't like little women, was afraid he'd break them. He didn't mind me large, but he couldn't love me fat.' She turned back to a photo of her and Pete at a party and touched a finger to his face. 'I was celebrating my divorce the night this photo was taken. It was a good time. It was the first night Pete and I slept together.'

'Where'd you meet Pete?'

'He belonged to that fat club, too.'

'But, Pete's thin. Did he used to be fat?'

'Never. He just likes large women.'

'Can I introduce him to Franklin?'

She smiled. The bourbon was working its magic. 'When you think about it, desiring a fat woman is no weirder than desiring a thin woman. A matter of taste and conditioning. Our society thinks there's something defective or kinky about men who like their women big or vice versa. Fat-admirers – that's what we call our non-fat friends – have a hard time finding the freedom to be with the people they're attracted to.'

'Pete was a fat-admirer?'

She nodded and swigged the rest of the drink. 'Remember when I dropped below two-fifty? Pete got concerned. He'd never been interested in women much lighter than that. When I hit two hundred, he panicked. I tried everything I could think of to keep him interested. Erotic movies, exotic oils, nude massages, lacy do-das, leather wot-nots, everything.'

'Except gain the weight back?'

'Except gain the weight back. It was the one thing I couldn't do. And it's the one thing he can't live without.'

'Come on,' I said. 'Let's play hookey. We'll hit the road. Invade Great America. Go antiquing in Richmond. You name it. My treat.'

She rolled her head toward me and tried to focus her watery eyes. Tears formed at the corners. 'Barbara, you're a real friend.' My skin goose-bumped. 'Honest to God.'

'Kathlyn, if you get sentimental on me I'm leaving.'

She sniffed and dug shreds of damp Kleenex out of her pocket. 'I've never had a friend. Not a real one. Not one who wasn't another fatty looking for someone who would like them for their real self. The girl I was closest to in high school befriended me because she looked thin standing next to me.'

'Oh, c'mon.'

'Swear. Found out senior year when she shed a hundred pounds and me, in that order. Jesus. Can't believe it still hurts to think about.'

'Oh, Kath.' We hugged and cried for a good long time, until the children came down and piled on top of us. Kathlyn rolled over onto her knees and crawled out of the pit. 'I'm going to get these two bandits off to camp, then I'm going to work.'

'No hookey?' I pouted.

'If I don't go to work I'll start eating. Right now I don't think I could stop.'

'I know the feeling. I'll give your love to the torture machines. Oh,' I said, remembering, 'do you want to cancel our – um – outing tonight.'

'Outing?'

I nodded my head at the children. 'You know, the *outing*. You were going to show me your – ah – shop?'

'Sexpressions!' She laughed. 'I forgot. No reason to cancel. By tonight I'll probably be needing a pick-me-up. I've got a sitter lined up but after what's happened I'd like to get these two characters tucked into bed before we go. Why don't I pick you up at nine.'

'If you change your mind,' I half hoped she would, 'just call. I'll be home chained to the computer.'

'Sounds kinky.'

Long tongues of morning sun flicked across Lake Michigan and zapped the last droplets of dew. The day was going to be a scorcher. I figured by the time I finished working out at Nautilus and walked home the air would be as heavy as my mother-in-law's rum cake. A la homemade mode. Dollop of fresh whipped cream on top. Chocolate almond coffee. Deep breath in. Exhale nice and slow.

I strode full out, arms swinging, legs pumping. I was going to work out all by myself. For the first time. Big girl now. In control. Didn't need someone pushing, pulling, holding my callused iron-pumping hand. This was a new Barbara Avers, independent and determined. Of course, if Kathlyn didn't work out today, she'd go tomorrow. And, since our trainer said using the machines two days in a row did something yucky to the muscles, I wouldn't be able to work out with her. On the other hand, if I skipped today and joined her tomorrow, we'd be right back on track.

I veered to the left, tacking toward home. I could work out by myself any time I wanted. It was just that, today, I didn't want. 'I can stop drinking any time.' Echoes of my father reassuring my grandmother. He didn't want, either. I broke into a slow trot trying to outrun the childhood memory. That had been happening to me a lot lately, memories bubbling up unexpectedly, as if my visit to the *Globe* had uncorked the past.

FOURTEEN

The intersection of Belmont and Broadway looked like a Fellini cattle call. Panama-hatted pimps and semi-nude hookers strutted their early evening stuff alongside deck-shoed yachtsmen and Lake Shore Drive matrons. Workdays over, boats bedded in Belmont harbor, the day-timers finished decaf and dinner at Ricki's and headed home. Saabs and Mercedes pulled out, gold-trimmed Caddys and Chevys pulled in. Good-bye swans, hello peacocks. It was the changing of the guard in New Town and I was coming in on the wrong shift.

Kathlyn watched everything but the road. Unfortunately she was driving. We'd spent twenty minutes circling a four-block area where illegally parked cars were hemmed in by double parkers. There'd be champagne and caviar on the tow trucks tonight. We approached the sex shop for the fifth time.

'Geez, will you look at her!'

'*Someone* in this car should watch traffic,' I said, sneaking a peek at the neon leathered platinum blonde wobbling down Broadway on five-inch mules.

'She's got to be eighty years old.'

'It's these yellow street lights. They add fifty years and sixty pounds to everyone. Why, I'll bet they even make me look heavy. Kathlyn!' She jammed the brake to the floor barely missing a Chevy peeling out from the curb.

'A space!' she whooped, swinging in nose first. 'It's a sign. An omen. This trip was meant to be. It's going to save your marriage.' She scraped one of two motorcycles parked in the space behind. A covey of large men of the black leather persuasion turned toward the sound.

'Maybe we should go,' I said as Goliath walked toward the bike. 'He doesn't look user-friendly.'

'Nonsense.' Kathlyn tossed her keys into her purse and checked her makeup in the rearview mirror. 'Lock up when you get out,' she called, walking straight back to the motorcycle, squatting down to inspect the spot she'd hit. The action-starved street crowd caught the scent of Something About to Happen and moved in for a look. By the time I pushed through, the giant, arms akimbo, stood glowering down at her. Kathlyn ran her hand admiringly along the bike.

'This is one hell of a knucklehead,' she said. His snarl curved to a smile. 'Have you stroked the motor?' He knelt next to her and began pointing things out. I didn't know what the hell Kathlyn was talking about but she was charming the silver spikes right off the biker. After a few minutes the two of them exchanged business cards and, accompanied by boos and hisses from the crowd, parted with a friendly handshake.

'What's with the Wild Bunch?' I asked, while she put his card in her purse.

'I used to date a biker, back in the dark ages. That's one beautifully rebuilt old bike I ran into. Luckily, I just scratched the primary cover. I offered but he wouldn't take any money.' We walked toward Sexpressions. 'Turns out he's a printer who likes to travel and I'm a travel agent who needs some printing. Helps to keep your options open. Never know when opportunity's going to knock.'

'For a moment there, I thought you were making a date.'

'It could happen. Although, from what I know about the dress codes around here, I don't think he's interested in women.'

The window of Sexpressions was tastefully decorated, probably in deference to the public grammar school on the next block. Sexual deviants can be good neighbors too. I studied the assorted bottles of oils and frilly underpants, postponing the moment I would have to go inside. Two mini-skirted hookers leaned against the Sexpressions window exchanging stir-fry recipes. What was I doing here? How had I let Kathlyn talk me into this? There couldn't possibly be a column in a sex shop.

'Sarajane and I used to pass one of these places on our way to school,' I said, stalling.

'Ever go inside?'

'Once, on a dare. We ran in, circled the place, and ran back out. What a filthy, foul-smelling hole-in-the-wall that was. Cans of films were stacked under hand-printed signs saying Hot, Very Hot, Sizzling, Sex-Rated. One wall was covered with magazines of naked women who were all squeezing forty-two-inch breasts at the camera. Later, a boy in our school told us the shop had a back room where men watched dirty movies and whacked off in little booths. Sarajane and I nodded even though we didn't have a clue what whacking off meant.'

'I see,' said Kathlyn. 'And that was your last sex shop?'

'Yep.'

'I guess if you've seen one you've seen them all. This one's about the same. But, as long as we're here, we might as well go in.' There was no way out of this. 'Oh, try and stay away from men in raincoats. And it's perfectly all right to knee someone who tries to feel you up.'

'Great, I'd hate to break protocol.'

'I'll stay close. There's safety in numbers.'

I felt a modicum of relief as a mid-sixtyish conservatively dressed couple passed us on their way out of the shop. I'd been terrified I'd look so out of place everyone would turn and laugh. The couple walked arm in arm, chatting amiably. Grandmama would have approved. Appearances, appearances. Ever so important. Everything, really. Of course daddy's not drunk, just resting after a hard day. Of course Franklin's not unfaithful, just overworked. Whips and chains might be rattling away inside the couple's little yellow Sexpressions bag, but that was hunky dorey as long as they looked normal.

'Ready?' asked Kathlyn, her hand on the door.

'Yes.' No. 'Of course I am.' Not. 'You're making such a big thing out of this.'

'All right. Just remember, I'm here if you need me.'

The shop was beautiful; muted decor, well-placed lighting, unobtrusive music, enticing fragrance. Sexpressions might have been any hi-tech trendy shop. There were no racks of dog-eared paperbacks, no wall of x-rated videos, no slobbering sex fiends or cigar-chomping manager. The manager, in fact, was a squeaky clean young man who ran the shop from behind a center island of glass display cases. Sexpression's subdued clientele milled around inspecting the contents of the cases and the elaborate wall displays that ringed the room. I'd seen more pulsing sexuality in the country club kiddy pool. I punched Kathlyn in the arm.

'I'm going to kill you,' I whispered, punching her again, 'extremely slowly and exceedingly painfully.' She giggled, then burst out laughing, grabbing me in a huge hug.

'Had you going for a minute, didn't I? Boy I wish –' she went off into peels of laughter. A few people turned, smiling. It was that kind of laugh. 'I wish you . . . could have seen your f . . . face. You were s . . . cared.' As pissed as I was, her hysteria got to me and we stood laughing like a couple of idiots.

'You're a shit,' I said.

'Tsk, tsk, tsk. What language from a Lady. Come on, I think we better start you at the shallow end.'

Glass shelves filled with merchandise lined the

thirty-foot wall that ran from the door to the back wall. We joined the steady line of people who moved cafeteria style past the dozens of small items, laughing and joking, filling little shopping baskets.

I felt I had stepped into a Dali painting where everything was neat and clean-lined and beautifully presented. All so familiar, really, until you looked at the *subject* of the painting. Until you focused in on those pleasing shapes which were really melting watches, or breasts or penises.

The section's most popular item was a matchbook-sized white packet with black code lines. The small print read: Generic condoms for cheap fuckers.

'They put the non-threatening stuff here near the door,' explained Kathlyn. 'The gag gifts you'd buy for a surprise fiftieth birthday party.' She wound up a duck-footed plastic penis and sent it waddling along the shelf. 'I wonder if I'll still be doing it when I'm fifty.'

'Winding up plastic penises?'

'Winding up any penises. Since Pete left, I've been seriously considering celibacy.'

'He's only been gone one day.'

'And so far I've been celibate. Oh, look at this!'

She held up candy panties, put them down to squeeze the Blue Ball drink coasters, left them to open a box containing a pull-toy bed with a couple in the missionary position under the sheets. Kathlyn set the bed down and pulled it along the floor. The faster she walked, the more frantically the couple humped. She made the rounds of the shop, laughing and joking with people who turned to look.

'This is almost as good a way to meet people as walking a dog,' she said, folding the toy back into the box. 'Better. No trips to the vet, pooper scoops, doggy breath.'

'Yes, but think of the kind of people you'll attract.'

'Right. I'd better take two.' She tossed the toys into her basket and began decimating the second shelf of goodies.

In all my nervous agonizing over this little outing, in all my worst-case scenarios, the one reaction I never even marginally considered was having fun. This was serious business, after all. Franklin and I had not made love in weeks. The handful of occasions we were both in bed awake at the same time I played encore after encore of my previously successful, albeit limited repertoire. I stroked, tickled, fondled, licked, blew, sucked, bit, warmed, oiled. The man wouldn't rise to the occasion. Nothing. Nada. Niente. A few mutterings of being tired, an air kiss smacked in my general direction and it was goodnight Barbara.

Kathlyn convinced me Sexpressions could save my marriage *if it was saveable*, by providing tools to jump start my dead sex life. I'd relented with the grim inevitability of a sick child taking medicine. I'd come braced for a Wagnerian opera and found the curtain rising on the Marx Brothers. Walk this way. The banter of people around me sure did lighten things up. It was time to get my tootsies wet.

I picked up a box the size of a J&B bottle. 'How much does your lay weigh?' Inside was the statue of Justice holding her scales. One was shaped like a sling to hold a penis. The other accommodated weights supplied with the box. The weights were imprinted with sayings like: 'Close, but no cigar.' 'Weigh it again, Sam.' 'I love a quarter pounder.' Justice, the naughty girl, peeked out from under her blindfold.

'Interesting,' said Kathlyn, weighing her middle finger. 'I could keep a comparison weight chart.'

'So much for celibacy. Where do people *get* the ideas for these things?'

'Socrates, Shakespeare, Woody Woodpecker. Where do any of society's truly great ideas come from? This store is a tribute to moments of deep meditation, brilliant insight –'

'And a shipment of tainted joints.'

'Oh, wow, look at that.' Kathlyn whisked off to a display of gingham-covered jars labeled Pickled Penises.

I turned at the sound of a plinking bump and grind. The silver-sideburned CEO next to me was cranking a Penis in the Box. Mesmerized, I held my breath, waiting. The music stopped and I jumped as the lid flew open. A huge penis flew out. He looked at me, laughing.

'Surprised you too?' I nodded, averting my eyes as he palmed the tip of the penis, pushing it back into the box. 'I wonder why that happens.'

'You turned the handle.'

'No, I mean why we jump. After all, it's not like we didn't know it was going to pop.'

'I'm not much for surprises,' I said. 'I've hated those boxes since I was a kid, not knowing when the damned clown would jump out at me.'

'Sounds like some of the dates I've had,' he said, winking. I did a quick wedding ring check. He wasn't wearing one. Not all men did. Still . . . I casually rubbed my eyebrow with my left hand. Didn't want him to waste prime pick-up time on a married lady. We inched forward with the line but I felt his focus had shifted from the shelves to me. Needed to get him back on track.

'Shopping for a gag gift?' I asked.

'Not really.' His eyes, which had stayed so nicely fixed on mine, drifted downward then drifted back up. If fat bothered him, it didn't show. He smiled, a tiny dot of spittle in the corner of his mouth. 'I'm on what you might call a foray.'

'Oh, I see.' I didn't, but it wasn't a line of conversation I intended to pursue. Avoiding breast and penis items, I grabbed a pack of cocktail napkins, examining their assorted dirty jokes as if deciphering hieroglyphics.

'I figure,' he said, his body intimately closer without having actually moved, 'a lot of people go to bars to meet people who like to drink. Or grocery stores to meet people who like to eat. Me? I come here. If you get my drift.' Not so much drift as avalanche.

'Uh-huh,' I said. 'That must be a real time-saver. Oh, my friend's calling. Well, good luck to you.' I jumped the line, joining Kathlyn as she added three Pickled Penis jars to her basket.

'Cocktail napkins?' she reached into my basket. 'I bring you to the best sex shop in the city and you buy cocktail napkins?' She took them out and tossed them on the shelf. 'Come on, let's get to the good stuff.'

Vibrators dominated the far end of the wall. I had seen them advertised for years in mail-order catalogues. Usually, a demure young model held the vibrator against her cheek and looked blissfully off into the distance. The copy always ran something like 'Massage those hard-to-reach places'. Lately I'd seen a few boxes hidden behind the drug-store counter. At Sexpressions people pulled vibrators out of boxes, tossed them to each other, held them up, turned them around, compared surfaces, colors, sizes.

'This is like having to buy one of those lipsticks in those hermetically sealed tubes,' complained Kathlyn, grasping one vibrator after another. 'You just don't know how you'll like it until you get home. What kind do you use?'

'Revlon. Maybelline.' She was not amused.

'You mean to tell me you don't own a vibrator?' The man behind her turned to listen.

'You want to take out an ad?'

'Everyone has a vibrator.'

'Don't be stupid, Kathlyn.'

'Aha!'

'What "Aha"?'

'You always attack me when you know I'm right.'

'You're not even close to being right. Less than one half of one percent of the entire American population outside New York and California has ever even seen a real vibrator let alone touched one.' I was excellent at creating convincing statistics.

'You are so damned provincial,' she said, jabbing

me with a ribbed polka-dotted model. 'You can buy these things at the grocery store, for god's sake.'

'Right next to the cucumbers.' Her nostrils flared. 'I can also get snails and chocolate-covered bees at the grocery store but just how many shopping carts do you think those go into?'

Kathlyn gripped my arm and pulled me back between the racks of crotchless panties and see-through teddies.

'Listen to me, Barbara Marlow Avers. I've got your number. You're trying to pick a fight with me. You want me to blow up so you can do your quiet rage routine and stalk out of here. But you're staying and you're going to look around and learn a few things. And if it embarrasses you –'

'I'm not embarrassed.' I couldn't pull my arm away.

'And if it embarrasses you, you can slip into your girl reporter mode. Operate at that rarefied emotional level you love so much. Pretend you are information-gathering for the great reading public. Hell, we haven't even gotten to the display case of tit rings and peter pumps.'

'This place has nothing to do with Franklin and me.'

'You stay out of this, Barbara Avers. I'm talking to Barbara Marlow. I want her to see the wall displays of rubber and leather and love balls and . . .'

Kathlyn ran a list of items. She might as well have been speaking Swahili. What I did understand was if I didn't know what she was talking about, most of my readers wouldn't either. Her idea of my doing a column had been spewed out in anger, but it had merit.

The question was could I overcome my prejudices and sexual shyness, do a quick change in that old moral phone booth. The great middle America didn't get much middler than me.

'I doubt a column on sex shops would be a topic of interest to Cameron,' I said. Her grip eased. She knew she'd won.

'Maybe no one's written about them the right way.'

'I can't imagine an angle. He's pretty straight.'

'The pot calling the kettle. Listen, Barbara, you're the one who told me there's *always* an angle. People are curious. Be their eyes. Let them peek into places they've never been.'

'You're trying to get me fired.'

'I'm not naive. I know how hard it was for you to walk in here. We all fear the unknown. But there is nothing in this room to fear.'

'To laugh at, maybe . . .'

'But I also know something as silly as candy pants can help a marriage if it's at all helpable.'

'Helpable?'

'Stop editing and listen. Bringing home some of these items will show Franklin you are still trying.'

'Dropping thirty pounds will show I'm trying.'

'Screw that. If Franklin doesn't respond to some of this stuff, at least you've done everything possible.' She tilted her head back, shaking out her long hair. 'Now,' she said, 'are you ready?'

'Ready.'

'Good. Take one of these, and one of these –' She loaded my basket with black 'One Size really does fit all' crotchless panties. 'And if you rub on this oil and blow, it feels hot. Drove Pete crazy, that insensitive ya-hoo. And, you're going to need some of these and maybe this and, oh yes, let's introduce you to the man and the bear.' She kept tossing vibrators into my basket and I kept taking them out.

'Let me learn to crawl before I walk,' I said.

'Honeybuns, I want you to fly!'

We circled the store slowly, studying every counter display, every glass case. I was amazed how unself-conscious I had become in such a short time. The wall of leather fascinated me. I stood in front of the clothes, straps, and odd-shaped garments trying to figure out how they were worn. What was it about leather, rubber, and bondage that fascinated so many people? A pleasant looking soft-spoken man walked up and stood next to me, hands clasped behind his back, rocking back slightly on his heels.

'Are you looking for a love slave?' he asked. Do you know the time? Would you have change for a dollar? Could you lash me to the bedpost?

'Oh, no. Thank you. But no thank you.' He smiled pleasantly and stepped back, standing alongside the wall, waiting for the next person who might show an interest in leather. I wondered if Franklin would like being tied to the bed. Not a bad idea. Probably the only way to keep him there.

The manager, as it turned out, was a font waiting to be tapped. Social Studies teachers from local colleges brought classes in to demystify sex. A state agency responsible for counseling people on birth control brought the staff in every few months to learn the proper way to put on condoms. This after members of the staff were found to have given faulty information resulting in pregnancies. Bananas were fine for television demonstrations, but the state was into hands-on realism. Sexpressions was a different species from that shop Sarajane and I had run through all those years ago. The manager patiently told me what things were, how they were used, why they were used. I left an hour and fifty dollars later with goodies for Franklin and a column for Cameron.

My personal take was tame. I refused the vibrator. But I did buy assorted flavors of oils, crotchless panties, lovebeads, edible body paints, and a few other items. I'd start slow. I wanted to seduce Franklin, not terrify him. There was always plenty more where this came from. He'd be tired when he returned from Springfield. Those trips were physically and emotionally exhausting. But our anniversary was coming up and I'd made special plans for a special night. That's when my new purchases would make their debut.

Kathlyn dropped me off near midnight. The answering machine light was flashing. Franklin hadn't called. Mac had. He'd been calling pretty regularly since he came back. Setting up his new apartment was driving him crazy he said and he needed to know where to buy three million different household items. I kept our conversations light and he didn't push. But some nights – when Franklin wasn't home and my column wouldn't write and I felt so fat I lost all sense of my edges – on those nights Mac's calls reached out to me like a lifeline.

JULY

165–175

FIFTEEN

'Seven and a half pounds?' The nurse jiggled the scale weights.

'I've started jogging,' I said, 'to help speed things up.'

'Really?' She gave the word three syllables. I was stunned by the ice in her voice.

'Yes, reeee-al-ly. No laxatives, water pills, enemas, amputations. Just your basic blood, sweat, and starvation.'

'Let's try the scale in the next room,' she said. 'This one's been acting up.' In the next room I was down seven and three-quarters. 'Were you pre-menstrual at your last weigh-in?'

'Nope.'

'Very well,' she said, entering my weight on my chart, 'let's check your ketones.' I hummed happily as I followed her to the ketone room.

She waited, pen poised over my chart as I blew into the plastic tube. She frowned. She disconnected the tube, readjusted it, punched buttons on the machine and reset dials.

'Again,' she said. I blew again, watching the red

digital numbers race upward on the ketometer. 'Wait here,' she said. I heard her urgent whisper down the hall, 'Dr Cheng, can you come here a moment?'

The doctor watched as the nurse slipped a new plastic breath tube onto the machine. I placed my lips over it and exhaled. The numbers raced upward, stopping at 68.

'Quite remarkable,' said Dr Cheng, clasping my hand warmly. 'You are to be commended, Mrs Avers. I don't believe we've ever had a sixty-eight before. Thirty-four is average. You are burning your own body fat at a fantastic rate.'

'Mrs Peterson was a sixty-four,' said the nurse, reluctant to let me have my victory. 'It wasn't difficult for Dr Cheng to find out she was binging and purging.'

'How sad,' I said. 'Personally, vomiting makes me sick.'

The appointment took less than five minutes. The doctor asked questions as he checked my blood pressure.

'Any problems with the diet?'

'None.'

'Are you taking your vitamin supplements?'

'Yes.'

'Any dizziness?'

'During my morning jog I have trouble breathing sometimes and I feel dizzy but it passes.'

'I told you no taxing physical exercise while you're on 800 calories.'

'Dr Cheng, I promise you, the way Kathlyn and I jog is not taxing.'

'What do you eat for breakfast?'

'A banana.'

'Eat two bananas.' I nodded, not committing myself to another 80 daily calories if I could avoid them.

'There is one other small thing,' I said. 'I'm going off my diet tonight. *Just* tonight.'

'A special occasion?' He didn't seem upset.

'Yes. Very. My eighteenth wedding anniversary.'

'Mrs Avers,' he said, gently, 'you are a grown woman. It is up to you to decide when and what you will or will not eat.'

'Yes, but if I didn't announce to you I was going off the diet I'd feel like I was cheating. Now I can enjoy myself with a clear conscience.'

He slid his glasses up on his head and smiled. 'The fact that you're planning ahead for a deviation is a healthy sign. It's so simple to eat a little less before and after to adjust for the extra calories. The people I have difficulty helping are the ones who go off their diets and think they've blown their only chance to be thin.' He reached across the desk and patted my hand affectionately. 'Enjoy this evening, Mrs Avers. Happy anniversary.'

Instead of hypnotizing me personally, Dr Cheng put me into a dark quiet room where I sat in a comfortable chair and listened through earphones to his taped voice hypnotizing me to ENVISION A NEW YOU. Could I be hypnotized by tape? I went under immediately, floating down down down to where the words that would save my life waited to be spoken. I would be beautiful yes I would not be hungry yes I would not crave chocolate sweets potato chips pizza cheese anything I knew to be harmful and fattening yes I would eat only until I was full then stop yes if I went to eat something when I was not hungry I would take a deep breath and feel full and satisfied yes yes yes. '10 . . . 9 . . . 8 . . .' I did not want to surface if I could only stay in that calm dark place at peace with myself not hungry until all the weight was gone '3 . . . 2 . . . 1'. My eyes popped open and I felt as if I'd awakened from a deep nap.

Kathlyn had taken the appointment before mine and was waiting in the reception area. 'Well?'

I gave her my stats as I wrote out the check for the $25 appointment. Getting thin slenderized the wallet.

'Buy the tape,' she said. 'You can listen to it at night to reinforce the message.' The tape cost another twenty-five dollars. 'You're beginning to look thinner,' she said as we walked outside.

'I should. I just took off fifty dollars.'

She laughed, slipping her arm through mine, leading me through the downtown crowds. Noon breezes fluttered my full-skirted silk dress. I'd always loved the dress on Sarajane. Naturally, it swam on me, especially after my weight loss, and I'd had to belt in the excess. But none of my own summer clothes fit. I'd have to make do with Sarajane's wardrobe another twenty or thirty pounds longer. It would be insane to buy new clothes for a size I'd never be again.

To the rest of the world Kathlyn and I looked like two overweight women, that is, if the world cared to look, which it didn't. The unstricken avert their eyes as they pass the deformed, the crippled, the scarred, the fat, sneaking a 'there but for the grace of God' peek after we pass.

At 183 pounds, the striking black-maned Kathlyn drew many sidelong stares. I could almost hear people thinking, 'Such a pretty face. Why doesn't she lose weight?' To me, of course, Kathlyn looked positively svelte.

'Strangers have actually stopped me on the street to tell me how beautiful I'd be if only I were thinner,' she'd told me. 'It's as if they thought I hadn't noticed I was obese.' I thought of my catty little asides to Sarajane at the country club pool. Why hadn't any of those overweight women I was 'just trying to help' come over and punched me out? God, what an ass I'd been. Why hadn't Sarajane said anything to me?

So far, no strangers had offered me advice. Only family. Intellectually I knew that women my weight inhabited the 'matronly' purgatory bridging the heaven of thin and the hell of fat. Emotionally, I felt grotesquely fat, constantly embarrassed by my body. I wished I could wear a sign explaining the condition was only temporary. My stomach knotted whenever I left my house with the terror of running into someone I knew. I'd begun grocery shopping at ten-thirty at night 'to avoid those endless check-out lines', and I'd abandoned my posh local salon for one in Evanston where the young black owner genuinely understood my curly hair.

'Salad for lunch?' asked Kathlyn.

'No,' I said, 'I'd rather have a salad.'

'If you insist.' She took me to her favorite take-out salad bar which guaranteed no preservatives in the veggies. We filled huge plastic containers with lettuce, spinach, sprouts, cucumbers, bell peppers, bok choy, cauliflower, broccoli, and zucchini. Two heavy ladies in line ahead of us loaded their lettuce leaves with three bean salad, fruit, miniature ears of corn, cheeses, nuts, meats, olives, macaroni salad, tuna salad, potato salad – all verboten on our diet. Their salads had more calories than a cheese Whopper with fries. Hell, if you're going to have the calories you might as well have the fun. But then you can't tell your hubby/ children/doctor/therapist 'Well, I only had a salad for lunch. I can't imagine *why* I'm not losing weight'. Madness. Kathlyn and I strolled to the Daley Center Plaza and found two seats facing the sun. We settled in among the crowd of clerks, attorneys, office workers, and shoppers gathered for the noon show.

'Dressing?' asked Kathlyn, pulling a jar from her purse.

'Thanks, no,' I said, 'I brought my own.'

I took out my little jar of salad dressing made from two teaspoons of safflower oil which I'd blended with apple cider vinegar, Dijon mustard, and a dash of tarragon to taste. Shaking the dressing, drizzling it over my salad, I wondered if Rikki would be embarrassed by this, too. This wasn't quite as blatant as mixing Nutri-Systems packets at restaurant tables. I recapped the jar, twisting the lid tightly. I didn't think she'd mind my using my own salad dressing. Would she? My fingers squeezed the lid. I seemed to have lost a handle on what she would or wouldn't mind. Flesh of my flesh. I needed to patch whatever had gone wrong between us. For starters, when I visited her at camp I'd eat my salad sans dressing so as not to offend or upset her. Now that I was losing weight, she wouldn't be so embarrassed by me and I could begin making friends again with her. I didn't think I could bear living with the bitchiness she'd shown that day I'd sent her off to camp.

'I adore eating outside!' Kathlyn shook her head back, her shiny black hair brushing the edge of the seat. 'It exhilarates me. Like playing hookey.'

'I haven't eaten outside since last summer at Ravinia,' I said, salivating, remembering the contents of the wicker basket spread out on the lawn. 'Herb pâté, crisp French bread, creamy Camembert, seedless red grapes, white burgundy.' Kathlyn and I drew in deep breaths, letting them out slowly.

'Shut up and graze,' she said, forking a spinach leaf into her mouth. We chewed our salads violently.

Small children ran squealing up and down the base of Picasso's giant sculpture which, like Eiffel's tower, had been hated, ridiculed, tolerated, and finally loved, unofficially adopted as its city's symbol. The street sounds and faces recharged me with the raw current of the city. I'd begun daydreaming about moving back, wondering if I could talk Franklin into it.

'Is tonight the night?' asked Kathlyn.

'Yes.' I smiled at the small tingle of excitement in the pit of my stomach.

'Does he know, yet?'

'Not exactly. Not everything. I told him to keep tonight open. That I'd planned a surprise.'

A slow cat's smile played on her lips. 'Feeling pretty good about yourself, aren't you?'

'Yes.' I sighed. 'Finally.'

'Sexuality's in the psyche, Honeybuns, and don't you forget it.'

A hard-driving jazz beat boomed from four huge speakers and the Lynda Martha Dance Troupe leapt onto the stage. I felt a warm kinship with the slender dancers whose pastel leotards moved like a second skin over their protruding rib-cages and hip bones. Between my weight loss and Nautilus workouts, my body would be as fine-tuned and lithe as theirs. I would hit 105 fitter and healthier than ever. Maybe I'd even take a jazz dance class. Why the hell not? All things would be possible when I was thin. I nibbled my salad contentedly, swaying to the music, at peace with the world.

After the performance, Kathlyn and I snapped the lids on our unfinished salads and set them atop the large garbage cans for the street people who hovered like pigeons. I walked Kathlyn back to her office.

'You really think tonight is going to help?' Kathlyn's voice was tentative and held no hope.

'I know you don't think so,' I said. 'But it's exactly what Franklin and I need. We've each been going through a rough few months. Usually, when one of us is down, the other is up. I think both of us have felt neglected lately. Tonight will be like going back to square one and starting over. Without the hurt. Without the anger.'

We stopped outside Mom's Travel Agency which bustled with lunch-hour trade. A cauldron of beef-barley bubbled on the stove in Mom's tiny corner kitchen. The seductive smell was sucked onto the street via a strategically placed exhaust fan. A gingham-aproned grandmother cheerfully ladled the soup into white styrofoam containers and cut chunks of San Francisco sourdough into baskets. 'The Gray Shark' was Kathlyn's top salesperson. Customers contentedly sipped soup, slathered sweet butter over the bread, and ordered trips from the mounds of travel brochures overflowing the tables.

I didn't like the concerned look on Kathlyn's face. It smacked of sentimentality. 'Will you call if there's a problem?' she asked.

'Kathlyn, will you stop? Do you think I would have stayed with Franklin all these years if he was as horrible as you think he is?'

'*Me*? I've never even met the man. I've only seen him through your eyes!'

'Do I make him sound that bad?' I looked down guiltily. 'I haven't been feeling very good about myself and I've been taking it out on Franklin.' I put my arms around her and hugged her tightly. 'Won't you try and be happy for me? I promise you, tonight is going to make all the difference in my marriage.'

She hugged me back. 'These things don't always go the way you think they should. I don't want to see you hurt.'

'Don't worry about me,' I said. 'I'm fine. I really

and truly feel today is the first day of the rest of my life.'

'You're trying to make me puke.'

'Just seeing if you're paying attention.'

'All right, I'll stop nagging. Where will you be?'

'The honeymoon suite at the Ritz-Carlton.'

She whistled softly. 'Why the hell didn't you ask me? I could have gotten it for you wholesale.'

'Will you go sell a cruise to Beirut and leave me alone.'

'Got the stuff?'

'Yes, Kathlyn.' I opened my shopping bag and flashed the yellow Sexpressions bag.

'Something decadently sexy to wear?'

'I'm on my way to Neiman's.'

'Neiman's? What you want is something push-up topless, backless, sideless, and frontless from Frederick's.'

'Bye, Kathlyn.'

'Hold on a sec.' She dug around in her huge woven bag and brought out a present gift-wrapped in familiar yellow paper. 'This is a little something for you.'

'For me?' I asked, tearing the wrap.

'Some men like it too. Depends on how open they are to new experiences. Shit! I forgot to buy batteries.' As soon as I saw the words Deluxe Three-Speed Vibrator I rewrapped the box.

'Kathlyn –'

'Gotta go.' She laughed, diving through the lunch hour crowds, calling back 'Good luck tonight.'

SIXTEEN

'Richter, Hannah, Avers, and Love.' The receptionist's midwestern twang was unfamiliar.

'Mr Avers, please.'

'One moment, please.' A tinny Mantovani clicked onto my ornate French phone.

I flopped back, bracing myself against the rush of pain pulsing from blistered toes to cramped calves. Kicking off my high heels, I sank wearily into the Ritzy white satin quilt. Downtown meant dressing up meant high heels meant sit down a lot or suffer. It didn't help that my feet had to carry around a few extra pounds. The pain tapped teen memories of easing off high heels during movie dates and not being able to get the shoes back on. My toes curled remembering the feel of bare feet on popcorn pieces, drink-sodden carpeting, sharp candy box edges, chewed gum. I doubted Rikki owned a pair of high heels. Thank god I wouldn't have to put my shoes back on until morning. Wonder if room service served Adidas.

The receptionist returned mid-Mantovani. 'I'm sorry, Mr Avers is in conference. May I take a message?'

'Yes, this is Mrs Avers.'

'Mrs Avers?'

I feebled my voice. 'His mother.' Behave, Barbara. The bedside digital flipped to 4:05. 'Little Frankie's expecting my call.'

'Oh.' Uncertainty. Mau-mau that old Flak Catcher. 'Do you want me to get him out of the meeting?'

I stared up into the mirrored ceiling. The pain in my feet pinched my face. I could use a little get-ready time. 'No, don't bother. Just tell him tonight's coven is meeting at the Ritz-Carlton, room 1760, 5:30 sharp. B.Y.O.S.'

'B.Y.O.S.?'

'Bring Your Own Sacrifice.' I waited as she repeated the message, then hung up. There was work to do.

Padding painfully to the living room, I started unloading my bags of surprises. Into the refrigerator went the truffle pâté, assorted cheeses, and other delicacies. My thumbnail automatically pierced the plastic-wrapped Godivas before I came to my senses. INHALE . . . I am not hungry for this chocolate covered cherry . . . EXHALE . . . the sweet syrupy center . . . INHALE . . . the explosion of tangy juice into my mouth . . . EXHALE. I gritted my teeth, salivated, and waited until the need to eat passed.

'Lead me not into temptation,' I sang, tossing the chocolates into the small fridge and escaping to the bedroom with the rest of my purchases.

With reverence, I lifted the two-piece peignoir set

from the Neiman's box. 'Just you wait, 'Enry 'Iggins
. . .' Three hundred fifty dollars didn't seem too
much to invest in a marriage, especially once the
Neiman clerk showed me how the side seams of the
unstructured 16–18 could be tapered as I slimmed to a
6–8. I arranged the black satin robe and gown on the
bed, running the backs of my fingers along the sensu-
ous maribou edging. Layers of fat had deadened the
tinglings and wantings best sellers are made of. This
Seduction of Franklin was making me feel sexual
again. 'There'll be a hot time in the old town tonight.'
I unpacked the Sexpressions bag bedside. Oh, to see
the look on Franklin's face when I greeted him at the
door of the suite.

'And now, Messieurs-Dames, *la pièce de résist-
ance.*' I ceremoniously carried the last bag into the
spacious marble room dominated by a sunken pool.
Not big enough for laps, perhaps, but arena enough
for eight veddy veddy good friends or one frisky couple. A wall of floor-to-ceiling windows faced south
over Chicago, the view reflected opposite in a wall of
mirrors. By narrowing my eyes and blurring my sight,
the pool seemed afloat over the city.

'Drum roll, if you please.' I trilled my tongue and
twisted the crystal faucets, adjusting the forceful
stream of water to the cool side of scalding. One by
one, I lifted my little surprises from the bag, lining
them like soldiers along the tub's edge. Almond bath
beads, loofa, gardenia body oil.

Steam billowing from the half-filled tub clouded
the mirrored wall like a soft-focus lens. Sweeping my

hair up seductively, lifting my left eyebrow, pursing my lips, I tried for a misty Marilyn Monroe. I got a damp ZaZu Pitts. No matter, the scene would play better at night with the room lights dimmed and a bottle of bubbly under my newly narrowing belt.

The cool marble floor soothed my swollen feet as I walked to the windows. Chicago stretched below me, spreading out, reaching up. A low western sun ricocheted off blocks of buildings, shooting long shadows down narrow streets as Chicago wound down for the day. To the east, Lake Michigan pointed its blue-gray tip south toward Indiana. I paced, impatient for the city at night, for glitzy lights slashing the dark sky like neon paint on black velvet. Tonight, Franklin and I would lie candlelit in warm water gazing out over our city. We would feed grapes and wine to each other, slide wet oily bodies one against the other, share slick underwater kisses.

I shut off the faucets and undressed, not bothering to pull the drapes. What I called private, Franklin called prude. All right, adjust those binocs and telescopes, you peeping perverts, it's a new Barbara lookin' right back at you. I unbuckled the belt, flinging it into a corner. Franklin complained I was too fastidious. I could change. Slowly working open the tiny pearl buttons, I let the silk dress slide off my shoulders, down my body, into a heap on the floor. In the spirit of compromise, I turned my back to the windows as I slipped off my panty hose, slip, and bra.

The hot water burned my blisters, shooting spikes

of pain from toes to finger tips. I giggled. Franklin was going to have to carry me out to the car tomorrow morning. Good thing he lifted weights. Stop that. Fat thoughts are not sexy thoughts. If I couldn't walk tomorrow, what the hell, maybe we'd stay in the room an extra day. Ah, decadence. It took a few minutes, but I finally eased my entire aching body into the tub, floated back, and closed my eyes.

The phone rang. I opened one eye. No phone nearby. It rang again. For four hundred and fifty dollars a night was it asking too much for a tub-side extension? A third ring. Only one person the call could be for. I hauled my body out of the tub, grabbed a towel, and sloshed into the bedroom.

'Yesssssss?' I said, breathlessly. I could at least *sound* like Monroe.

'Barbara?'

'Yesssssss,' I said, batting my eyes, wiggling my bottom lip.

'Something wrong?' Franklin was practically shouting.

'No, you love-starved hunk. I'm being sexy.'

'Oh. It's all this noise, I can barely hear you.'

The bedside digital clicked to 5:05. 'Franklin, are you still at the office?'

'No. Headquarters.'

'Welllllll,' I whispered huskily, 'someone is waiting for you –'

'Barbara, I swear I can't hear you. Can you speak up? Wait. Hold on. Hold on.' The noise level around him dipped a few decibles. A television blared in the background. After a moment, Franklin was back. 'Barbara, haven't you heard the news?'

'No. I've been busy –'

'Well turn on seven, no, make that two, seven's already done it.' I dripped to the TV, braced for electrocution, and turned it on. I expected World War III, a nuclear reactor explosion, a cure for Aids. What I got was Warner Roth's shiny bald head nodding at the press corps.

'Warner Roth?'

'That son-of-a-bitch gave me his word he wouldn't run.' Unrestrained rancor. Abodanza of Anger. Franklin was pissed. I held the phone away from my ear as he shouted. 'Do you know what this means?'

'Yes,' my words were encased in ice, 'you're not coming.'

'Jeez.' He lowered his voice. 'I can't believe how selfish you can be sometimes.'

'Me?!' I sat heavily on the bed, rousing wisps of black boa. 'As I recall, we made this date a while ago. I don't see why your campaign can't wait until tomorrow.'

'You think I wanted Warner in this race? We're after the same voter, for crissakes. Now I have to design a strategy to make the voter see me as the only logical candidate.'

'Tonight?'

'My staff's here, now, Barb. Half of them can't make it tomorrow. You and I will reschedule. I promise. I don't know why the hell you wanted to celebrate our anniversary now. I knew we should have waited until after the election.'

'November?'

He was silent. The room behind him had grown still and I felt his staff eavesdropping. 'What do you want from me, Barbara?'

'What I want is for you to come here, now.' I wasn't sure that was true any more.

'That's what you want?'

'Yes.'

He sighed wearily. 'We'll be there in half an hour.'

'What do you mean –' The line went dead. I slammed the phone into the cradle, bashing my thumbnail.

It was an hour and a half. The glum group plodded into the suite, wrinkled jackets finger-hooked over their shoulders, ties loosened, shirts unbuttoned against the muggy Chicago evening. This melange of Chicago's movers and shakers smelled ripely of booze, smoke, and sweat. Some were new to me but a few of the faces dated back to the days I played bartender for my father's legendary all-night poker games. The old guard's shock at the new me showed before they could conceal it. And I'd been such a pretty little girl. I couldn't believe I'd been stupid enough to feel sexy just a little while ago. My rage swelled inside until I thought I would burst from the pain of it.

Franklin brought up the end of the line guiding a slender blonde by the elbow. She looked cooled from the inside out. Fine strands of ash-blond hair were pulled straight back from her high shiny forehead and gathered into a black chiffon bow at the base of her long nape. She had what my father called the Sak-sy look of the horsey set, the type that gave tone to society pages and polo matches. Her crisp peach linen skirt and white embroidered linen blouse were unmarked by the damp heat except for a few crotch wrinkles. I smoothed my hands over Sarajane's silk dress which hadn't taken kindly to being left in a heap on the steamy tub room floor.

'You must be Mrs Avers,' she stuck out a slender hand, shaking mine with surprising firmness.

'Yes, I must be,' I said. 'And you are . . .'

'Ashley Pembrooke. I'm the public relations coordinator.'

'How intriguing.'

'Oh yes, Mrs Avers,' she slid her arm through mine and led me into my suite, Franklin trailing behind, 'my work is very exciting. Of course,' she patted my arm, 'Franklin explained how disinterested you are in the political process, so I won't bore you with details. Could I trouble you for something cold to drink?'

'The kitchen's over there,' I said, patting her arm right back. 'Help yourself.'

'I'll get it, Ashley,' said Franklin.

'Hello, Franklin,' I said, as he sped past. He didn't seem to hear.

The group commandeered the living room. Open briefcases spewed papers, charts, legal pads, files. Franklin found the delicacies it had taken me three hours to buy and threw them to the ravenous pack which finished them off, killed the three bottles of champagne, and ordered room service.

Choked by the cloud of cigar and cigarette smoke – Just one lousy drag! Ain't no sech thing – I wandered into the bedroom. It looked different. I'd emptied and cleaned the tub, put away the oils and lotions, and hung my peignoir in the closet. The room looked the way it had when I'd arrived. The magic I'd created was gone. Is it magic if there's no audience? I'd leave the peignoir for the maid. A small token. I tucked the Sexpressions bag in my purse until I could decide what to do with the stuff.

My final problem was how to get from the bedroom to the front door without making a complete ass of myself. Winding strips of toilet paper around my blisters, I pulled on my panty hose and tried to cram my feet back into my shoes. They wouldn't fit. I found a serrated knife in the kitchen, sawed open the backs of the shoes, cut triangular pieces off the toes, and shoved my feet inside. Grabbing my purse, I forced myself to walk like a normal human being through the living room.

'I think I'll take in a movie downstairs,' I called over my shoulder.

'Good idea,' said Franklin, barely looking up. 'We may be here all night.'

'No problem,' I said cheerily. 'I'll just buy new batteries for my vibrator.' Exit. Curtain. Applause.

The movie theater's main door was seventy-five excruciating steps from the Ritz elevator. As soon as I hit the carpeted interior, I pulled off my shoes and stuck them in my purse. I had my pick of Sly Stallone, Bette Midler, and John Hughes. There were four more movies playing across the driveway in Water Tower Place but, given the condition of my feet, they might as well have been on Mars. I bought tickets for all three movies.

The girl at the candy counter was entrenched in a Harlequin romance. 'Mmmmmmmm,' I said, furrowing my brow, looking off into space as if trying to remember.

'Help you?' she asked.

'Yes, please. Let's see, Susi wants a small buttered popcorn.' The girl moved to action. 'And, oh, Linda wants a large Junior Mints. And I think Sharon . . .'

I sighed often. I sighed before, during, and after the popcorn, the Junior Mints, the Dots, the Milk Duds, the Diet Pepsi. They barely dented my anger. I sighed as I hit the counter again on my way to Hughes, and later, to Stallone. Deep breaths no longer affected my craving for food. I'd have to talk to Dr Cheng about the transference of sigh-cology.

Because, by the time the last satisfying bit of blood and guts spewed out over the closing credits, and I'd hailed a taxi home, and I'd liberated my throbbing feet, I was still perfectly able to eat. But I'd lost what little appetite, desire, or hope for reconciliation I'd had left for one Franklin Avers.

SEVENTEEN

Halsey Investigations was snapped like a Miës van der Rohe Lego piece into a sprawling one-story office complex. The glass and chrome construction smothered a tract of prime farmland a couple of minutes west of the mall. Convenient. Women could put away lunch and their spouses without killing an entire afternoon. I wondered if Sarajane selected Halsey because he appealed to her love of convenience. I cruised the building for number 1506 and found it tucked discreetly in back. Not my idea of a private eye. Where was the grime, the smarm, the creaking urine-soaked stairs? The Maltese Falcon couldn't get past Halsey's front door without being preened, pruned, and pedigreed. This section of the North Shore liked its jewels hung on the outside.

'Yes?' The pretty receptionist was not cracking gum. A mutant.

'Miss Marlow to see Mr Halsey.'

'One moment, please.' She pressed a phone button with a long red fingernail and announced my arrival. 'Please have a seat, Miss Marlow. Mr Halsey will be right with you.'

The office's masculine tones and massive furnishings inspired confidence. Secrets would be safe among the oak desks, brass tables, leather upholstery, plush carpeting. A future State Senator could be followed with the utmost discretion. I shuddered. That's not why I was here. Following Franklin may have sparked the idea for this article, but I had to pass beyond my interest into the bigger story.

I settled into a gray leather chair and flipped through my small spiral notebook, my journalist's tool, prop, security blanket. This notebook was labeled 'Detective' and bore the date of the day I called Halsey's office to set up the interview. I barely recognized the list of questions jotted across the first couple of pages. Some of the question fragments written two weeks before now made no sense. Others looked vaguely familiar. It was as if they had been written by someone else. In a way, they had.

The writing process always began like this, with the feeling of being outside looking in. I'd scribbled these questions in a frenzy of highly charged creative energy. It's a nice mind-set to visit but no sane person can live there. The problem now was to recapture and recreate that clarity of thought. It was a mystical and purifying process, like changing pond water to Perrier.

I forced myself to read and reread my notes, moving slowly out of Halsey's office and into the pages of the notebook. I felt a subtle shifting of psyche. Good-bye Barbara Avers. Hello Barbara Marlow. The hodgepodge of questions lined up neatly on the page. I renumbered them for the strongest order, took some out, added others. By the time Halsey's door opened I had set the interview questions in my mind, noted the description of his waiting room and listed a sampling of magazines fanned on the thick glass table: *Forbes, Money, Elle, The Smithsonian, Architectural Digest, Reader's Digest, People, Better Homes and Gardens*.

'Miss Marlow?'

'Yes.'

'Please, come in.'

I rose easily, gracefully, a full seventeen years lighter. My senses shifted to overdrive. The scent of freshly brewed coffee mixed with spicy perfume and, as Halsey approached, masculine aftershave. 5'11", forty-two, cop's eyes, basketball player's feet and hands. A few dark hairs sprouted from the large fingers he wrapped around mine in a gently firm grip. His were the flat knuckles of a good streetfighter.

'Thank you for seeing me,' I said, jotting 'handshake' as I walked into his office, a concrete detail I might use to show character. Not the painful squeezing handshake of the insecure or the dead fish half-hand of the unconcerned. 'You said your schedule is tight. How much time do we have?'

He checked his Rolex. 'Half an hour o.k.?'

'I'll try.' I went through my rap, repeating what I'd told him on the phone about doing a column for the *Globe*.

'Usually I have my angle before I start –'

'Angle?'

'Angle, slant, hook, the quirky twist that makes an old subject fresh. Everyone's interested in detectives because you're the guys who find out what's going on behind the curtains. But there's been a lot of stuff written about the profession. What I'm looking for is something no one's done before.'

'Wow, I don't know –'

'Don't you worry about it. Interesting things begin to happen when people start talking about their jobs.'

Halsey leaned back, answering preliminary questions quickly and simply. 'Former detective with the Chicago Police Department. Began own practice twelve years ago in small storefront. Built to a five-person office. Handle everything: spousal surveillance to corporate security.'

He was relaxed and informative but also guarded. I found out why when I paused between questions.

'I'm curious how you happened to come to me for this interview,' he said.

'You're one of several private investigators I've contacted. I've interviewed the others by phone but I wanted to walk into a detective agency to gather up the sights and sounds.'

'Yes, but who recommended me? I'm not in the phone book. Brings in the kooks.' It hadn't occurred to me to check.

'Ah, yes, well I happen to know – to have known – someone who used your services for a long time. Sarajane Quinlin?'

'You were a friend of Sarajane's?' He didn't move but I sensed a subtle softening.

'Best friends since fourth grade.'

'She told you about me?'

'Not exactly.' I hadn't intended to mention Sarajane. Now I knew I had to tell him the truth or I'd lose him. Cops, like newsmen, knew bullshit when they heard it. They also respected the truth. 'I cleaned out her closet after she died. Your reports were in there.'

He whistled softly through his front teeth. 'You mean she kept that stuff around? I told her if she wasn't going to use it to burn it. Not that it was my business what she did with it. I mean she paid for it. Still –'

There was a soft knock on the door. The secretary breezed in with a silver tray laden with a coffee service and plate of Ganache baked goods. I estimated fifteen pounds of silver and a pound and a half of pastry. She set the tray on Halsey's desk, smiled sweetly, and left. He watched me watching.

'The lady lifts weights,' he said, pouring out two cups of coffee. 'She was my chief operative in Sarajane's investigations.'

'Her? I thought she was your secretary.'

'Secretary's on vacation so the staff's taking turns filling in. I don't hire temps. Can't take a chance on strangers nosing through my files, using privileged information for cocktail conversation.' I jotted 'discreet' in my notebook, underlining it several times.

'I'm surprised Stanford didn't notice such a beautiful woman tailing him.' Would Franklin?

'She's a dog without makeup.' He laughed at my expression. 'Just kidding. Suki's great at disguises. Cleaning women, bag ladies, matrons. A real chameleon. And when she gets dolled up –' He kissed his fingers in tribute. 'She's brought in more insurance fraud convictions than all my other operatives put together. Dangle her in front of a man claiming to be disabled by an industrial accident and she'll have him dancing out of his wheelchair in an hour. Those chocolate things are great.' He slid the pastry plate to me. Accepting food and drink from an interviewee strengthens the bond. I took a bite.

'Mmmmmmmmm,' the rich chocolate coated my tongue. 'I'm in love.'

'They're really decadent.' Halsey helped himself to an eclair. He'd left the two bottom vest buttons open and the others were seriously straining. 'You know, Miss Marlow –'

'Barbara.'

'Barbara. I'm a little curious. Those reports of mine you found in Sarajane's closet. Did you leave them?'

'No. I took everything with me.'

'Uh-huh,' he said, nodding. 'Now, I had the impression Sarajane knew she was dying for quite a while.'

'She never came right out and said she knew. But, yes, I'm sure she did.'

'Yet, right up to the end she didn't tell you about me or the photos in her closet.'

'I . . . I don't think she ever intended me to see them.'

'Is it possible Sarajane left the evidence behind so her husband would find it?'

'Yes. That's exactly what I think she did.'

'Me too.' He stirred cream into his coffee, tapping the silver spoon against the thin china cup. 'Then why, may I ask, did you take them?'

I sipped the coffee. Talking about Sarajane after all this time was bringing back some of the pain. 'I was afraid Stanford would use the photos and information to make fun of her somehow. I mean, here she was knowing about all of his infidelities and not confronting him. It made her look weak. Pathetic, in a way.' Like someone we know, Barbara sweetie honey baby?

'Don't be too hard on her, Barbara. Sarajane wasn't unusual. I get a lot of people in here, mostly middle-aged women, who just want to know what's going on. They don't have any plans to divorce. Maybe divorce is against their religion. Maybe they have a nice life-style and don't want to wreck it. Whatever. But they want to know who their competition is. Younger or older? Fatter or thinner. Handsomer or prettier. Richer or poorer?'

I picked up my pencil casually, trying to keep it from shaking. 'Are people who suspect their spouses of playing around always right?'

'No, of course not. For some reason, women are right more than men.' My hand shook as I wrote.

'Why do you think that is?'

'Dunno.' He sipped his coffee thoughtfully. 'Maybe they read the signs better.'

'Signs?'

'You know, sudden changes. Maybe the husband starts dressing a new way, driving a flashy or expensive car, wearing a different cologne. Maybe he has a sudden weight loss or starts muscle building, or changes to a healthy diet, has cosmetic surgery.'

'Hair transplants?'

'Yeah, like that. Another common sign of a cheating spouse – let's say it's a husband – is he starts finding fault with everything the wife does. She's letting herself go, the house is a mess, the children are wild. She's too dull, she's too wild, too predictable, too spontaneous. She never wants to go out, or stay in, or whatever it is he wants to do.'

'Sounds like she can't win.'

'You got it. Sometimes guilt sets in and a cheating husband showers his wife with gifts, or a wife will come home from her lover and make her husband a seven-course meal. But these are exceptions. Most of my clients talk about a distance they feel between them and their spouses, as if their spouses don't see them, as if they've become invisible.'

The room heaved. A high-pitched ringing shot between my ears and out my eyes.

'I have a theory,' he said. I raised my eyebrows to indicate interest and hoped I didn't pass out while he was talking. 'I think people who fool around think everyone fools around. That's why so many husbands have their wives tailed. The husbands are getting a little on the side and can't believe their wives aren't. Some men want proof of their wives' infidelities to keep on hand as insurance in case the wives learn about the men's affairs.' I forced my pencil into lines and squiggles across the paper. 'When I was a cop,' Halsey said, 'we had a professional shoplifter give seminars to store owners on how to protect themselves from theft. This guy would always start by saying, ''Everyone's

lifted something sometime in his life.'' That bugged a
lot of people in the audience who never had. And what
about people who cheat on their income tax because
"everyone does it''. I mean, that's just not true. But
that's how a lot of people justify their behavior to
themselves.'

Struggling for control, I changed the subject from the
bedroom to the boardroom. Part of me listened, asked
questions, took notes. Most of me agonized over what
to do. I was here for an interview, yes. But I knew the real
reason I had come. Since the fiasco at the Ritz I was
desperate to have proof that Franklin had a lover. It was
like I knew, but I wanted to *know*. The idea of hiring a
private investigator was underhanded, sneaky, and
repulsive. Nearly as despicable as infidelity.

'. . . developers want to know why they are constantly being underbid by their competition. Companies want to trace goods disappearing from their
loading docks. Stores want names of salespeople
helping themselves to five-finger discounts.' My notes
sketched the portrait of a modern investigator.

Did I have the nerve to have Franklin followed? What
if he wasn't doing anything wrong? What if I was
blaming him for destroying the marriage when all the
time it was me? Did I want to know that? Was I strong
enough to cope with that?

'. . . premarital investigations.' The unfamiliar
phrase caught my attention and brought me back full
force to the interview.

'I never heard that term before,' I said, sensing a
story angle.

'It's the hottest new direction in interpersonal investigations. Not that people haven't had prospective husbands or wives investigated before, but never in the amount we're seeing now.'

'Why the increase?'

'Depends who you ask. More coffee?'

'Yes, thanks.' My hands were shaking. I set my cup on the desk and slid it over to him. After he filled mine, he poured himself a second cup. Halsey didn't seem in a hurry to end the interview. I relaxed.

'A buddy of mine in LA says the premarital started with a few women who contracted AIDS from husbands and lovers they didn't know were bisexual. But, that's LA. My premarital investigations are more financial than sexual. Clients are mostly women in their thirties, and mostly marrying for the first time. They've built up a nice career, have sound investments, a good financial situation, and they want to protect that. You'd be surprised how many guys out there misrepresent themselves. Drive expensive cars, dress well, eat at the best restaurants, talk up their income. But they're dragging a long trail of bad debts. Landing a rich wife is an easy way out for them.'

I spent the next ten minutes digging into this area. Like most cops I'd known, Halsey was a gifted storyteller. My father said it came from hours of drinking with their buddies after work. After the first few drinks, the audience couldn't follow intricate details. Cops learned to cut the fat from their stories if they didn't want to wind up talking to empty bar stools.

'And what if it were your son or daughter getting

married?' I asked Halsey. 'Would you suggest they investigate their intended?'

'Yes.'

'No hesitation? No doubt?'

He shrugged. 'I know the idea has all the romance of premarital contracts. But we've lost the good old days when we all grew up together in the same neighborhoods and knew each other from kindergarten.' He rocked his chair, absently twisting his wedding band. 'Maybe I've been around too long, seen too much. There are men and women who make their living traveling from one end of this country to the other, becoming intimate with people, then robbing them of everything that's not an attached body part. When my kids are ready to marry, I sure as hell expect to do a quick check to be sure their intended is who they say they are.'

'And if your kids didn't want you to?'

'I won't tell them. Unless I find something their intended didn't think was worth mentioning. Prison record, former spouse, children.'

'Isn't that breaking faith with them?'

'Truthfully, after the stories my kids have heard around our dinner table, I can't imagine them not wanting me to check out their fiancées.' He leaned forward on his desk, looking me square in the eye. 'People today aren't shy about using private investigators, Barbara. Since no-fault divorce, we're no longer associated with creeping around motel windows with high-power film and long-lensed cameras. The stigma's not entirely gone, but it's fading fast.

Look at this place. I'm a businessman. I work for large corporations and some of the biggest local celebrities. You'd be amazed how many people you know have used me or another investigator at one time or another. I would say the odds are most people have some area of their lives that could be made easier or clearer by hiring a good private investigator.'

'Most people?'

'Uh-huh. Most.'

I scanned my notes. 'And how, if someone hires you to follow a spouse, do you get the reports to them?'

'Some clients pick the information up here. Others have me mail it to their home in a plain manila envelope. Some use their office or a post office box. A few like reports by phone.'

I closed my notebook and put it into my purse. 'I want to thank you for the interview,' I said, pulling out a Kleenex. 'And now, if you have a moment, I'd like to hire you. I think, you see, I think my husband,' I wiped my eyes and blew my nose, 'oh God how many times have you heard this one?'

'Never from you.' He came around with a large box of tissues and I felt his large reassuring hand on my shoulder.

'I . . . I think my husband is seeing someone else. And I want to know for sure.'

I left his office with a wad of tissues, three chocolate cookies wrapped in a napkin, and the sense that I'd set some gigantic teetering rock into motion. Straight downhill.

AUGUST

175–190

EIGHTEEN

I pulled into our driveway, checked my mouth in the rearview for traces of powdered sugar, and tapped the horn. My foot brushed the package of Entemann's chocolate donuts under my seat and I nudged them back with my heel. Franklin slammed out of the house, hurled his briefcase into the back seat and strode around to the driver's side. I didn't slide over.

He hovered. I waited, hands clasped tightly in my lap, staring out the windshield at the house. Shards of red foundation brick flecked the ground. Ring around the hous-ey, all fall down. Why hadn't I noticed before? Have to call the tuck-pointer.

'Oh for crissake,' he said. 'Shit!' He slammed his hand on the car's roof. 'Shit,' he said again, kicking the front tire on his way around to the passenger side.

'Funny how ideas come to you,' I said, heading out of the driveway toward the tollway. Franklin reclined his seat and closed his eyes. 'I mean, there I was, running around like a crazy person at five-thirty this morning, loading the kids' Care packages into this car, rushing out to gas up, check the oil, test the pressure in the tires, fill the windshield solvent. All of which I could have done last night.' I glanced over and caught one eyeball semi-open. It snapped shut. 'Except you didn't bring this car home until after I'd gone to sleep.' Pause, two, three. 'And I guess it didn't occur to you to do any of the things that needed doing.' Sigh, two, three. 'I suppose I could have gassed up the wagon . . .'

'It's a lousy road car.'

'I agree. In fact, that's the idea I was talking about. It came to me somewhere between gassing up and cleaning the windows. I'm trading the wagon in on a new car.' His lips thinned and his nostrils flared. Tsk tsk. I'd made him angry. Oh, poo.

The more I thought about buying a new car, the more I liked the idea. I'd never, in my entire life, picked out a car. City born and bred, I didn't even drive until I had children and Franklin realized I'd need his sporty two-seater for car pools. He signed me up for driving classes and had a new station wagon waiting red-ribboned in our driveway the day I came home from the maternity ward with Rikki. A new one followed every three years. Car, not kid.

Research would be fun. What kind of car would I buy? Flashy? Practical? Elegant? Wild? What color? Size? I could hardly wait to road test. What a relief to try on something that would clear my hips.

Sunday morning traffic was light. An occasional trailered car towed a speedboat toward the lakes of Wisconsin. A line of motorcyclists roared down the center lane two abreast, leathered and studded against the wind. 'You know,' I said, 'I've never seen a woman motorcyclist driving with a man holding on in back.' Driving was masculine, holding was feminine. Business was masculine. House was feminine. Women's magazines and sit-coms could pay all the lip service they wanted to liberation, but motorcyclists and Franklin knew the TRUTH. And it shall set them free. From the kitchen. Hell, even Betty was saying she may have been wrong. Friedan, not Crocker.

The tires rumbled over the toll-booth speed bumps. I dug change out of the stash in the ashtray. 'In there for two points!' I yelled, tossing the coins into the yawning funnel. The yellow gate swung up and I peeled out, shouting 'With a hearty hi-ho silver, awaaayyyyy.' I lowered my voice, looking around in awe. 'Who was that masked woman?'

'You are becoming very strange, Barbara.'

'Thanks. Although, me lad, there's them what sez I be strange these last seventeen years. Them what knew me BF Hee-hee.' I sang, 'I was lost but now I'm found.' Amazing. Earth to Barbara. You're babbling. Shape it up. 'So, you see, there's no real point in my having a station wagon. I'm through with car pools and bowling alley birthday parties and you don't seem to need my help carting stuff around for your campaign. A car like this handles ever so much nicer.'

'Barbara,' both eyes opened, left eyebrow arched, voice carefully modulated, 'I couldn't begin to afford to buy you this kind of car. My campaign's strapped my finances to the limit. This car costs forty thousand dollars.'

'Yes.' Sweetness and light. 'I imagine that's why it handles so very well.'

'Is *that* why you're driving?' Now things made sense. 'To test the car?'

'Ah, there it is, out in the open.' I opened my window and shouted, 'Ladies and Gentlemen, why is this woman driving the car when there's a perfectly good person-of-the-male-persuasion in the seat next to her?'

'Could you close the window. It's cold.' I did.

'No, Franklin, I'm not driving to test the car.' Anger and nervousness burned deep in the roll of fat above my navel. I fought to keep my voice and face calm but the steering wheel was slick with sweat. 'What happened, Franklin, was, while I was racing around this morning getting everything ready for the trip, things I could have done last night had your car been parked in my garage – if you get my drift – it occurred to me that if I have to do all the shit work I should at least have some of the fun.'

Franklin snorted. 'Fun? This drive is hardly *fun*, Barbara. Jeez, I don't know what's with you, lately. You think I'm out there having *fun?* You think going to work every day is *fun?* You think running a campaign is *fun?* You think driving five hours up and back to Wisconsin is *fun?*'

Calm. Stay calm. Don't back down. Don't back down. Slow breath in through the nose, out through the mouth. 'I'll let you in on a little secret, Franklin. Driving for five hours sure beats the hell out of *watching* someone drive for five hours.'

He wrenched his body to the right, turning his back to me. If I reached under the seat for a donut, would he hear the cellophane crinkle? Why hadn't I taken the donuts out of the package? Why weren't they boxed in flannel? I jammed the plug of the Passport into the cigarette lighter hole, wincing until the piercing radar-detecting beep wound down. Picking up speed, I tried to catch some of the stragglers doing seventy.

Franklin's angry shoulders tightened against the thin cotton of his shirt, hand press, on hangers, medium starch collar and cuffs only. A light flashed in my head, a goddamned beacon. I was shlepping five miles a week to Wang Ho's 'the only person alive, Barbara, who knows how to do a proper shirt' so a cool blonde could slip perfectly laundered shirts off Franklin's perfectly willing body. The beacon flickered and died. I didn't have absolute proof of the affair. Not yet.

Halsey's investigative reports showed Franklin and Ashley together almost constantly at headquaters, meetings, meals. I said that wasn't especially incriminating considering she was working for his campaign. Detective Halsey, far less trusting, thought they were having sex in a small hotel room the campaign rented for visiting out-of-state contributors and guests. It was a room I hadn't mentioned to Halsey because I hadn't known about it. Halsey was suspicious of a couple of Franklin's downstate trips and said he expected to provide photos in the next couple of weeks.

Coffee. I needed coffee. Blast through that wad of donut dough stuck in my throat. If I pulled into the Oasis would Franklin take over the wheel? And, if he did, what would I do? Climb into the passenger seat? Refuse to get in? Stand and wave bye-bye as he took off for the camp? 'I'm sorry, children, your mother didn't come to see you. I can't imagine why. But I'm here. I love you.' Better not tempt fate. I clenched my teeth and passed the Oasis. As mile followed silent mile, my innards churned for the undrunk coffee and uneaten donuts.

The distant spires and rolling scaffolding of Great America broke the flat horizon. Rikki and Jason loved that place. Once a summer for ten years I'd taken them there. At first we'd sought out gentle rides; antique cars traveling on a fixed rail, cars shaped like animals which traveled round and round in a circle, the merry-go-round. Later there were faster rides, bumper cars, roller coasters, arcade games. Still later they'd bring along friends and I wasn't needed except to drive back and forth. Other children had mothers who worked, or who didn't have cars, or who wouldn't drive more children than their car had seatbelts, or who could drive to Great America but not back, or who didn't want to be responsible, or . . . If any of those 'modern' fathers I read about in those uplifting newspaper and magazine articles lived in our neighborhood, they'd never come forward and volunteered to drive. I'd bring a lawn chair and a book, settle into a shady corner, and enjoy the quiet time to read and smoke.

Franklin had come along once, shamed into taking us by a TV commercial. The actor-daddy surprised his family by giving up Sunday golf and televised sports to take everyone to Great America. Our children were too young to understand the myth of truth in advertising. Franklin felt sick after his first ride, told the children he was leaving in one hour with or without them, and stationed himself on a bench as we scurried to as many rides as possible before the hour was up. WELCOME TO GREAT AMERICA. Burnt out bulbs dotted the flashing sign. I sped past. Now that Rikki drove I'd never need to go there again. Pieces of my life were sloughing off like dead skin. How would I replace them? Was there new growth underneath?

A little tension in the trapezoids told me I was slouching under the weight of the silence. Head rolls left. Head rolls right. Chins up, chins down, fight fight fight. Needed a touch of sound in the car. It took me a moment to locate the energy source on Franklin's custom hi-tech radio/cassette player. I touched the ON button. Hard-driving rock blarred from all six speakers. Franklin's hand shot out, jamming down the volume and punching the tape eject button. He glared, as if I'd startled him deliberately, then turned away again.

'Why is everything my fault?' I asked his back. 'This isn't my car, my tape, or my volume.' I slid out the strange tape. Franklin always had me buy Jean-Paul Rampal, madrigals, Simon and Garfunkel. From where cameth 'Funky does Down and Dirty'? I hooked the thin brown tape under my incisor and pulled the cartridge away from me. The tape unraveled nicely and I dropped it to the floor, pushing it back with the donuts. Cellophane be damned. I grabbed a doughy lifesaver and chewed until my heart stopped pounding. After the donut was history I turned on the radio, hit the a.m. button, tuning to Dr Jean White who'd kept me company Sunday mornings while I car-pooled to religious school.

'Well, I've certainly never met a man who reads romances.' Jean was in her condescending mode.

'Oh, I expect you have,' said the sotto-voiced interviewee, 'you just don't know it. Quite a few of my fans tell me their husbands read my books.'

'Let's talk about sex.'

'I'd much rather talk about romance.'

'I'm sure my listeners would love to know the difference.'

'Sex is penis in the vagina. Masters and Johnson write about sex: genitalia, form and function . . .'

'Geeze,' said Franklin.

'. . . The physiology of sex is put under the microscope and studied in detail. Many of today's novelists seem to draw heavily from scientific books. Personally, I'm bored by detailed descriptions of who's doing what to whom with what.

'Romance, however, is the longing, the wanting, the dreaming, the hoping. It is the fire a woman feels when she meets HIM. And if she is denied him, if he is forbidden, she becomes consumed with passion. He is always on her mind. While she's washing dishes, driving the children to school. She can't help herself. This is romance, and my challenge is to create a tension between the heroine and hero that will keep the reader turning the pages all the way to the satisfying end.'

'What in hell are you listening to?' said Franklin.

'An interview.'

'That's not what I meant.'

'Then why don't you say what you mean?' Mac's words fit nicely into my mouth. Mac. A reflexive contraction of the vaginal walls. I say, is there life down there as we knew it?

'Can't you find some music?'

'I like talk shows.'

'Since when?'

'I've always liked talk shows.'

'Well, this is sure the first I've heard.'

'That's because I turn them off when you walk into the kitchen. I know you don't like them.'

'Then why don't you turn this one off?'

'I'm driving. And, as you've pointed out over the years, the person who drives gets to pick the radio station. Since you're the only one who ever drives when you're in a car, I've listened to your music, your football games, your baseball games, your stock reports, your news programs.'

'I didn't realize it was such a hardship.'

'Boring as hell. But I thought that was the way real families did things inside cars. And, since you're the one who set up the car rules, I don't see why you're having such a hard time accepting them.'

'It's important to understand,' the author continued, 'the majority of my readers seem to have sufficient sex in their lives. What's missing, what they read my books for, is romance. They understand the heroine's spark of wonder and excitement, her need to be loved, wanted, desired. Luckily for me my characters can be stronger than the heroines of, say, five years ago. I know many people still think of romance heroines as wimps at the mercy of the fates. But today's heroines are bright, interesting, independent –'

'Idiotic,' said Franklin. 'What shit.' He folded his arms across his chest, his mouth and eyes clamped shut in thin lines. The program lasted until I pulled into a gas station on the outskirts of Wanatobo to gas up and ask directions.

'It's cheaper if you pump your own,' muttered Franklin, making no move to get out and pump.

'Yes,' I said, 'but I don't want to hug the kids with my hands smelling of gasoline. I'm going in to get a map.'

His snarl followed me out of the car. 'You don't need directions, for crissakes. We've made this trip for years.'

'And we've gotten lost each time.'

I walked into the small station, visited the ladies room, bought a Snickers which I finished in four bites, and a cup of coffee to sustain me during the fifteen-minute ride to the camp. I also bought an oversized pair of white dice with black dots which I hooked over the rearview before taking off again. I needn't have worried about Franklin taking over the driving. He sat, his gold Cross pen clenched in his teeth, studying papers from his briefcase with a ferocious intensity. God forbid the teenager pumping our gas didn't understand Woman was driving the car because Man had important work to do. Since Franklin threw up when he read in a moving car, the charade lasted until our rear wheels left the gas station.

I slowed on the pitted dust road leading to Camp Omni and joined the long line of visiting-day cars.

'You're coming with me tomorrow afternoon?' I asked. Franklin bit the skin around his thumbnail and stared out his window.

'Can't.'

'You promised.'

He spun around. 'You forced me! I've told you I have too much to do right now. Why the fuck can't you understand that? I don't even know what I'm doing here today.'

'Visiting. Our. Children.' My anger was quieter but no less intense. 'If you don't keep our appointment with Dr Mays,' I said, evenly, 'I'll tell the children we're separating.'

'Separ – ?'

'Which is what will happen if you don't come with me to see her.'

He leaned toward me, sneering, his spittle spraying my face. 'What kind of mother are you?'

I leaned toward him, praying the coffee had washed away the chocolate on my breath. 'What kind of husband are you?'

'Good God, Barbara, what difference will another

few weeks make one way or the other? The kids are happy here. Why upset them? All of a sudden, you're hell-bent on turning our lives into turmoil.'

The donuts solidified into concrete. A counselor waved us into the parking area. 'You're good, Franklin. You really are. You break *your* word about seeing a marriage counselor and *I'm* the one who's supposed to feel guilty.' I swung the car into a space and stared out the windshield. 'Are you going with me tomorrow or do I tell the children?'

'I don't know you anymore, Barbara.'

'Maybe you never did. Maybe I stopped being me when I married you.'

'Oh? And just who have you been for the past seventeen years?'

'Who you wanted me to be. Who I thought I should be. The perfect wife. The perfect mother. I thought that's what married ladies did.'

'You thought right.' He jammed the papers back into his briefcase. 'I'm not saying being a housewife's not work, Barbara. I'm not insensitive to the demands in your life. But you chose your job. Being a wife and mother was all you ever talked about. Or have you forgotten?'

'No,' I said softly.

'So why are you blaming me for letting you do what you wanted?'

'You're turning this all around.' He opened his door. Rikki and Jason waved from the camper's hill at the end of the lot, straining at the rope they were not allowed to cross. 'Are you coming with me to Dr

Mays,' I asked, 'or do I tell the children we're separating?'

'I'll go,' he said. 'Maybe it's time someone talked some sense into you. I sure as hell can't any more.'

Franklin stormed out of the car toward the children. His clenched body unclenched as he walked. I swallowed back tears as the children ran from the waiting pack into his arms letting him swing them around and around.

NINETEEN

I pulled myself up the steps of the cornflower blue
Victorian. Five stupid steps and I was already out of
breath. Margaret Mead opened the screen door. 'Mr
and Mrs Avers?' She smiled warmly. 'I'm Dr Mays.
Please, come in, come in.'

Franklin, usually four paces ahead of me, lagged
behind as I followed the square little doctor through
the cluttered entry-way. I sidestepped the jumble of
footwear which included one laceless pink toe shoe, a
muddy pair of work boots, bent-eared rabbit slippers,
and cowboy boots whose pointy toes reached for the
sky. We passed through the spacious oak foyer. A
giraffe sculpted from chrome automobile bumpers
was seasoned with beach towels, sweaters, jackets,
hats, scarves. A Chicago Bears helmet hung off its left
ear, a tattered black top hat off the right. The house
smelled of baked bread and cloves, orange zest and
lemon furniture wax. It was the scent of my dream
house. Homes with happy mothers, fathers, and
children. Homes where everybody loved everybody
happily ever after. The pretend homes of a motherless
daughter.

Dr Mays waved us into a cozy bookcase-lined office. Shelves sagged under rows of well-used books. Excess books were crammed horizontally across the tops of the others. The one neat shelf, directly behind the doctor's desk, was labeled HIS – HERS – OURS.

'Kathlyn didn't mention you were a writer,' I said, which was strange since Kathlyn had given me everything but a D&B on the good doctor. 'And your husband writes, too?' Translation: Are you happily married, doctor? Are you qualified to find out what I'm doing wrong?

'Nothing mainstream, I'm afraid,' she said. 'Technical data. Rats in mazes. Corporate screenings. That sort of thing. Please, take any seat.'

Franklin walked to the far side of the room, jammed his fists into his pants pockets and slouched against a shelf of books. I eased into the kid leather chair facing the desk.

'May I offer you tea?' she asked.

'No, thank you,' I said.

'Mr Avers?'

'Can we get on with this?'

'Certainly,' she said, unruffled by his rudeness. 'Why don't you tell me a little bit about why you're here?'

'Me?' asked Franklin. 'I'm here because my wife threatened to tell our children we were separating if I didn't come. That's why I'm here.'

'I wouldn't have done it,' I said, as much to Franklin as to her. 'Not really. But I couldn't think of any other way to get him to come.'

'I see.' She scribbled a notation on a yellow legal pad. 'You must feel strongly about this meeting, Mrs Avers. Why is that?'

Why is that, why is that, why is that. My thoughts were wrapped tightly as a burrito. I searched frantically for the delicate edge that would begin the unfolding. 'Something is wrong in our marriage,' I said. The room was quiet as they waited for me to go on. I had nowhere to go.

'What makes you feel that way?' asked the doctor.

'I . . . I'm not sure. Lots of things.'

'Can you pick one out?'

I closed my eyes and saw the Wheel of Fortune spinning. I forced it to slow down. It landed on: 'I don't feel we're communicating.' Franklin snorted. He'd taken to doing that a lot. 'Franklin seems, oh I don't know, distant. Preoccupied.'

'Damned right,' he said. 'Damned right I'm preoccupied.' He walked to the doctor's desk, jabbing his forefinger into the padded leather top. 'Do you know where I should be right now? Campaign headquarters, that's where. I'm launching a major political campaign. My law firm's in the middle of a complicated trial. I don't know what I'm doing here.'

'I don't know what I'm doing here,' I said, completing the litany with him.

'You've heard this before?' Dr Mays asked me.

'Constantly over the last month and, of course, all day yesterday.'

'Yesterday?'

'We visited our children at camp. Franklin spent most of the time in the car working.'

'I was lucky I could get away at all! Jeeze!' He slapped the desk and walked to the bay window overlooking Lake Michigan.

'When Franklin did come out of the car,' I continued, 'to join us for lunch and watch five minutes of Jason's soccer game, he told everyone what a busy man he was and how he didn't really have time to be there.'

'Part of being a politician,' Franklin said to the window, 'is to let people know what you're up to. To let them know you're working even when it seems like you're just visiting your kids at camp.' He turned to the doctor. 'My wife is so caught up in her own world she doesn't have a clue about what's going on in mine.'

'Have you tried to tell her?'

'What the hell do you think I just did? I told her, and you -- if you'd pay attention – exactly what I'm up to. My life's an open book. I'm not hiding anything from anybody!'

'Has anyone suggested you are? You sound so angry.'

'Excuuuuuuuse me,' he said. I cringed. 'I tend to get excited when I'm being ganged up on. Barbara's the one who wanted this meeting. Why don't you help her out with her problems?'

'You seem to have such a clear idea of what her problems are . . .'

Franklin held up his left hand, using his right to jam

down his fingers as he roll-called my defects.

'Her best friend died' – this little piggy went to market – 'and Barbara can't get over it.

'She stopped smoking' – this little piggy stayed home – 'and became a bitch on wheels.

'She's put on a ton of weight' – this little piggy had roast beef, and candy and hot buttered rolls, and – 'and lost all regard for her appearance.

'She's stopped making a decent home for her family.' – And this little piggy had none.

'Are these all right for starters?' – And this little piggy went weeeeee, all the way . . . where?

'It gives us an idea of direction,' said the doctor. She turned to me and smiled. 'Mrs Avers?'

I tried to swallow the molten lump in my throat. 'I think that about covers it.'

'Not nearly,' said Franklin. He began pacing. I fixed my eyes over the good doctor's right shoulder, straining to make out the titles of her books. A grandfather's clock ticked my marriage away in the corner. When Franklin resumed, his voice shivered the back of my neck. 'All of a sudden, nothing I do is right. I work too much. I'm at the office too much. I have too many meetings. I'm sexist. I don't pull my weight in the family. And then she wonders why I'm not in a hurry to come home at night.'

I stared at the titles of the books behind her. If I could remember their titles in the exact order tomorrow, my marriage wouldn't fall apart. 'I'd like us,' I said, 'to talk to the doctor about our anniversary at the Ritz.'

'That again?' He stopped pacing. The clock sounded like a time bomb in the sudden silence. 'Barbara, I'm tired.' Tic. 'I don't need this shit.' Toc. 'You want to stay and talk, fine.' Tic. 'You have things to work out? Then do it.' Toc. 'I wish I could help you but I can't.' Tic. 'And I'm not going to stand here while you try to make your problems my problems. Dr Mays,' he nodded in her direction and strode out of the room. Tic, tic, toc, toc, Ka-blewy! The titles of the doctor's books bled together as Franklin's footsteps stomped across the foyer, the entrance hall, the front porch. I lost them on the cement stairs and couldn't find him again until the car roared to life and screeched out of the driveway.

'I guess that's that,' I said, pressing my head into my hands, swallowing against the tears.

'Here.' The doctor pushed a jumbo Kleenex box closer to me, not looking away as I cried. 'You must be feeling very disappointed just now.'

I laughed through deep jagged breaths. 'Kathlyn said you were given to understatement.'

She smiled. 'I suspect you had high hopes for this meeting. You were hoping for a beginning . . .'

'I should have left things alone,' I said. 'I know our relationship hasn't been great lately, but Franklin has been under a lot of pressure. He's not usually so abrasive.' Oh, isn't he, Ducks?

'You don't have to excuse Franklin's behavior, Mrs Avers. In fact, you can't. You're not responsible for it.'

'No? Take a good look at me, Doc.' I held my arms

out wide, the skin under my arms hanging like pulled taffy. 'We're talking cause and effect. I'm not defending him.' Like hell. 'It's just that, in all fairness, I want you to understand why he acted the way he did. He can be quite charming when he isn't under such stress.' Especially if you're a thin blonde on the firm side of thirty. I dug my car keys out of my purse before remembering Franklin had taken the car.

'We still have quite a bit of time, Mrs Avers,' said the doctor. 'There's no need for you to leave. It might be helpful to talk about how you're feeling.'

'I . . . I'm not feeling up to talking about this just now.'

'All right.' She tented her fingers against her lips and swiveled in her chair. 'Let's talk about where you bought your shoes.'

'My shoes?' I was so keyed up that her humor didn't register at first. I laughed, nodding. 'It's just that, with Franklin not here, it would be like talking behind his back.'

'Then how can you get help for yourself? Remember, he's the one who chose to leave.'

'Still . . .'

She regarded me kindly from behind round metal-rimmed glasses. I held my breath, wondering if she'd push me. Wondering if I wanted to be pushed. I could feel her thoughts re-routing, trying to find another way to lead me through the maze to where I needed to be.

'All right,' she said, 'perhaps there's something else

on your mind you can talk about. You mentioned the children's camp.'

I blew my nose and nodded.

'You have boys or girls?'

'One . . . one of each.'

'A coed camp? Interesting. And how was your visit?'

'Ah, well, that's another story altogether.' I reached for the pitcher on her desk, my shaking hand splashing water into a glass. I sipped, then sipped again. My camp visit was not the sort of thing I had planned to tell anyone. Ever. But I was running out of things *not* to discuss with the doctor.

'You have children?' I asked.

'Four.'

'Ever have things you've said to them come back to haunt you?'

'All the time.'

'Yesterday the words of Barbara the Thin came back to haunt Barbara the Fat.' I gripped the glass, reliving yesterday's pain. 'My voice, my intonation, my vitriol, my hate poured out of my daughter's mouth. It was like the scene in *The Exorcist* when the daughter opens her mouth and the devil's voice spews out. Rikki was too ashamed of the way I looked to come near me. She pulled me aside and accused me of being weak-willed, of lacking pride, of letting myself go.'

'And what did you say to your daughter?'

'Say? What could I say? She's right.'

'Your husband and daughter seem to share many of

the same strong feelings about you and your weight. So, may I say, do you. What about your son?'

'Jason? He, at least, seemed happy to see me. But I overheard,' oh, Lord, the pain, 'him tell his cabin-mates I was his aunt.'

'You didn't correct him?'

'Look at me, doctor. I'm a mess. I didn't want to embarrass him.'

'He embarrassed *you*. Do you always put the feelings of everyone in your family before your own?'

'Yes, of course.'

Upstairs, someone ran scales up and down a guitar. A cardinal the color of fresh blood settled on the catalpa branch shading the bay window. Lake Michigan's shoreline blazed with red, yellow, and orange wind-surf sails. I ran a Kleenex under my eyes, removing streaks of mascara. 'Yes,' I said again. 'I thought that's what mothers did.'

Her voice was barely a whisper. 'Has it ever, once, occurred to you that the problems you are blaming on your weight might have existed while you were still thin?'

'That's ridiculous. Everything was fine when I was thin. Franklin loved me, my children were proud of me. Hell, I was proud of myself.'

'And you and your husband communicated?'

'Yes, we . . . That is, we talked about things.'

'Personal things?'

'Business, of course. And some home things. Friends, children, you know.'

'What about feelings, problems, emotions?'

'No, no we didn't talk about things like that.'

'No? Why's that?'

'It's not the way he was raised. The way I was raised. My mother died when I was born. My father was a newsman. We discussed world affairs, politics, real topics.'

'Man talk.'

'Yes. He used to say everything else was fodder for the women's page.'

'Charming.'

'I didn't mind. It was his style. Anyway, I had Sarajane to talk to.'

'Sarajane?'

'My friend.' The pain of her death double-whammied with Franklin's leaving. 'This incredible mess I seem to have made of my life began the night she died and I gave up smoking and started putting on weight.'

'Did it?' The doctor studied me a while, then pushed up slowly from her desk. 'I am going to bring us some nice hot tea. When I come back I would like you to tell me a little about your friend, Sarajane.'

Her hand comforted my shoulder as she passed. With trembling fingers, I smoothed the skirt of Sarajane's dress, one of the few I could still squeeze into. A loose hem thread tickled the back of my calf. Upstairs, the guitarist hit a wrong note, paused, then continued on as if it hadn't mattered. I brought the dress hem to my teeth, biting off the dangling thread close to the fabric. With luck, perhaps I could keep from unraveling until I was home.

* * *

I assumed Franklin would have gone to his office but his car stood in the driveway, trunk open. A large suitcase took up most of the trunk. As I paid the cabbie, Franklin came banging out of the house, his arms laden with clothes on hangers. He didn't see me until he was almost at the car. Brought him up by the short hairs, it did.

'Going somewhere?' I asked.

He brushed past me, laying the clothes neatly on top of the suitcase. 'I think we need a little time apart from each other,' he said.

'Funny, I thought we needed time together. It's hard to try and work things out long distance. Unless, of course, we don't want to work things out.' The world started moving in slow motion. This was IT. The 'X' on the map. The 'You are here'. 'What shall I tell the children?'

He slammed the trunk shut. 'Why the hell do you have to tell the children anything?'

'They might wonder why mumsy and daddums have different zip codes.'

'You're overreacting, as usual. This is just a short break. I was going to Springfield tomorrow, anyways.'

'Anyway.'

'What?'

'The word is "anyway". I always cringe when you say anyways.'

'You never mentioned it before.'

'You never walked out on me before.'

His hands fisted on his hips. 'I think we need a couple of weeks apart, to think things over.'

'Oh. And what is it, exactly, I'm supposed to be thinking over?'

'You're being difficult.'

'I'm being abandoned!'

'Come on, Barbara, we've both known this was coming. It was just a question of when.'

'No, Franklin. You knew it was coming. I was *afraid* it was. I mean, what the hell do you think the Ritz was for? What did you suppose our appointment with the marriage counselor was all about? I am trying to keep this marriage together.'

'Why? We have nothing in common any more. I was hoping we could stay together until after the election –'

'After the election!' Every single second of the last few months snapped into focus. 'You son of a BITCH!' I hauled back my arm and slugged him as hard as I could. He was stunned. I hit him again. 'After the election!'

'Barbara –' He grabbed my arms and held them. I brought back my leg and kicked his shin. 'Yeow!' He jumped in a tight circle, rubbing the wound. My voice came out a scream.

'All the time I've been trying to make this marriage work, you've been biding your time until after the election?' I popped open the trunk, grabbed his clothes, and flung them into the street.

'Barbara!' He hopped to pick them up.

'You knew you were going to leave me?' I unzipped

his suitcase. 'You've been waiting because you're afraid divorce wouldn't look good to the voters?' I swooped my arms under his clothes, lifted them out, and threw them at him. 'Was that Ashley's idea? A little p.r. advice? Stay with your wife until after the election?'

His upper lip curled into a snarl. 'Don't you *mention* her name!'

I put my fists where my hips used to be. 'Ashley! Ashley! Ashley! Ashley!'

'She has nothing to do with this!' He grabbed his clothes from the ground and stuffed them into the trunk.

'Oh, yeah? You've been fucking her and fucking me at the same time, but sure as hell not the same way.' A woman coming up from the beach shepherded her two children across the street.

'Keep your voice down,' he said.

'Fuck you and the white horse you rode up on!'

He slammed the trunk. 'You don't know what you're talking about, Barbara. And you leave Ashley out of this.' He climbed into his car and slammed the door. 'You're the one who caused this. Look at yourself.'

'No, you look at yourself, Franklin.' I stood next to his window. 'If you loved me, you'd stand by me. When Sarajane died, I needed you. For the first time in our marriage *I* needed *you*, and you weren't there for me.'

'You're not the only one with needs, Barbara.' He started the engine and put the car in gear.

'Yes, but your needs were always tended to.'

'I took care of this family,' he said. 'I worked my ass off to take care of this family.'

'I'm not talking food and clothing here, Franklin.' He started pulling out. I grabbed hold of his shirt.

'Let go, Barbara.'

'I'm talking about love and caring.'

'Let go!' He ripped his shirt out of my hands and peeled out of the driveway.

TWENTY

I stormed through the house in long angry strides, banging doors open, slamming doors shut. Up the front stairs, through the hall, down the back stairs, through the house, up the front stairs, through the hall. Round and round and round she goes. The good Dr Mays' tea and fresh baked banana bread started coming up on the sixth go-round. I forced myself to keep swallowing it down until I reached Franklin's closet where I unleashed waves of vomit over his shoe shelves. With superb timing, I hit every pair, lingering over his running shoes and Italian imports. A few drops drizzled onto my dress and I wiped them off with one of his new silk suit jackets.

Dry heaves. My head tried to fall off and I had to hold it on as I started my rounds again. 'Son of a bitch,' I said. 'Son of a bitch.' Through the hall, down the stairs. Around. Needles poked the insides of my eyes. My thighs chafed. I had a hunch I wasn't acting rationally but couldn't fit any two thoughts together in a logical way. 'Son of a bitch. Son of a bitch.' On one pass through the kitchen I grabbed at the phone. It crashed to the floor but I had to keep moving. I didn't grab the receiver until the next time through. I stomped in place, punching Kathlyn's number.

Two rings. Three. 'Hi. If you're calling Kathlyn, Peter, or Laura, you have the right number at the wrong time.'

'Son of a bitch. Son of a bitch,' I was off and running again. Two rounds later I tried Kathlyn at work. She was out. I hurled the phone against the wall and kept moving.

Somewhere around my thirtieth trip, the white heat in my knees buckled my legs. I sank to all fours. Can't crawl in a dress, knees get all caught up inside. Cram the skirt into my white cotton underpants. Crawl up the front stairs, down the back. Press on. Nothing takes the place of persistence. Carpet needs cleaning. Vacuum's not hitting the dustballs in the corners. Wool carpet fibers stick to sweat. 'Son of a bitch.' Round and round and round she goes. Slower and slower. Where she stops . . . All body systems shut down on a pass through the dining room. I collapsed spread eagle on the Kirshan. The rug prickled. Dust coated my nose and throat and my tongue was thick with thirst. Summoning my last soupcon of energy, I lifted to my knees and crawled to the living room bar.

'There you are, you little Dickens,' I said, liberating a full bottle of Franklin's 25-year-old Napoleon Brandy. I leaned back against the sofa and took a long swig. It burned and warmed and cut a path through the dust. Another swig. And another. Quarter-way through the bottle my thoughts began to queue up. I smiled. The rage had been temporary, a coat of emotional armor shielding what I was really feeling. Relief. Reliefreliefreliefrelief. At least – at last, there was an end to it.

'Congratulations, I said, hoisting the bottle, 'you've just lost 168 pounds of ugly fat.' I swigged mightily. It was all so clear. There was no way I could have saved my marriage. I knew that now. Had known it but wouldn't see it. Franklin left me a long time ago. He just forgot to walk out. I'd denied it like hell. After all, how could the perfect husband leave the perfect wife and mother? Nice of me to put on eighty pounds, supply him with an excuse. Something we could both blame without having to dig deeper. 'Here's to the pounds of one hand clapping.' I drank a toast. If I'd lost the eighty pounds, hell, if I'd never gained them in the first place, it wouldn't have made any difference.

How far back did the end begin? I tried tracing the line of our relationship. No great ups or downs. Sort of a straight line, like death on the old electro-cardiogram of life. I curled up on the floor. The brandy's calories had gone directly to my eyelids. Made them too fat to keep open. Maybe I'd had enough brandy for a while. Somewhere around the two finger mark, I set the bottle down and let my eyelids close.

Blind! I'd gone blind! My eyes stared wide open and the world was black. The skin of my cheek prickled, flattened as it was against the fibers of the itchy oriental. Drool trickling from my mouth pooled on the rug. Why was I on the floor? I sat up quickly. A lance pierced my right eyeball and I went down.

Riiinnnnngggggg. The front doorbell. 'Go 'way,' I moaned. If I didn't breathe, and pushed my palm against my temple, the pain eased. *Riiinnnnnggggg*. 'I'm blind,' I said. 'Go 'way.' Silence. Footsteps shuffled along the front porch. My eyes adjusted to the night. Outside, the dim streetlamp backlighted my picture window. A ragged man skulked to the window and peered into the house. Franklin had sent someone to bump me off! I held my breath, remembering. Son of a bitch. The man clutched a bulky case. A magnum won't do 'er, boys. Bring on the bazooka. My assassin knocked on the window.

'Mrs Avers?' Old voice for a killer. 'Anybody home?' I knew that assassin.

'Mr Payne?'

'Oh,' relief, 'yes.'

I rolled upright, regretting it immediately. 'Mr Avers isn't home just now.' Something feathery had nested in my throat. I pressed palms to temples. His shadow didn't move. 'And I'm not feeling all that well.' The house was too dark for him to be able to see in, but I pulled my skirt out of my underpants and wiped the drool from my cheek. One does have one's pride.

'I . . . I don't mean to impose, Mrs Avers . . .' He didn't move.

Payne, Payne, go away. 'I'm really sick, Mr Payne. I wouldn't want you to catch anything.' My breath was delta force. I swigged some Napoleon and gargled. He was still there.

'My wife passed on last night,' he said.

Shit. 'I'll be right there.'

He looked like I felt. We settled in the kitchen. There was something about Mr Payne that made me want to feed him. I put out a plate of Matt's oatmeal and raisin cookies from my secret stash and poured us tea. The bazooka case turned out to be a photo album.

'It was really you I came to see,' he said, gliding his long bony fingers along the top of the album. 'I've been reading your newspaper column to Mrs Payne. You write good. Funny. Made her smile, you did, and that was a real blessing these last weeks.' A faucet flipped full-force. Tears streamed down his cheeks, his liver-spotted hands trembling as he pulled out a huge white handkerchief. I wasn't up to this.

'Now, now,' I said, reaching over, patting his shoulder. 'There, there.' Brilliant, Barbara. Luckily, he didn't need clever, just human. A soothing word, a comforting touch. I'd forgotten the raw power of one human being caring about another. He honked loudly, then folded the handkerchief back into his pocket.

'I'd never ask for myself, you understand.' He opened the album. I knew without looking it would start with their wedding picture. Isn't that how we all begin? The difference was he and his wife made it to the finish line. Not a whole hell of a lot of that going around these days.

'She was very beautiful,' I said.

'Doesn't begin to do her justice. The more you knew her, the prettier she got. Not a mean bone in her. Not an unkind word for anyone.' He led me through their lives. It had never been easy for them but they hadn't seemed to notice. The photos ended at the beginning of her illness. He closed the album and rested his hands on top. 'I know I have no right to ask,' he said, 'but I was wondering if it might be possible to have a little mention of her in your paper. A few words about who she was.'

I put my hands on his. 'I can't promise much,' I said, 'but I'll try.'

I asked a few questions, dates, and jotted down the information. He gathered his pictures and pushed up from the table.

'Funeral's tomorrow at two,' he said. 'I'd be pleased if you and Mr Avers . . .'

'Of course I'll come. I'd be honored. But I'm afraid Mr Avers is in Springfield on business.' Son of a bitch. I sent Payne home with his memories and the rest of the cookies.

Ballis was on night desk.

'I'd like to do something on her. A little human interest piece.'

'Who was she?' he asked.

'A sick old woman.'

'So?'

'So, can I have some space?'

'She do anything big?'

'Yeah, Ballis. The biggest. Kept the same man

crazy in love with her for forty some odd years.'

He whistled. 'Like to see that one on the front page. Bring in what you got, Marlow, and I'll leave a note for Mort to run what he can.'

'Thanks. I'll bring it in the morning.'

'Just hope it's a slow news day.'

I hung up the phone and tried to stand. Sitting down had been a mistake. It had given my joints time to weld shut. There was no way I could write anything feeling and smelling the way I did. I forced my body up the stairs to the shower.

Six separate sprays pulsed hot water from all sides. I lathered my hair, my body, scrubbed with a loofa, rinsed, scrubbed again until my skin burned and I felt cleaner than I had in months. Spreading my legs, I shot the hand-held spray up between my legs. Mmmmm, might become a shower person. Or buy batteries for Kathlyn's three-speed gift. Or call Mac. No. *Globe* scuttlebut was he had a lady. Damn. Double damn. I switched the spray to pulse. Still buzzed from the brandy, I started humming a faintly familiar operetta. The song's lyrics came flowing out. 'Old Payne in the glass/won't be a pain in the ass/ aaa-neeeee-mooooooore.' Where the hell had that come from? Franklin's song. Franklin's words echoing off the shower stall walls. No. It couldn't be.

I shut off the water, pressing my forehead against the tiles, trying to remember *exactly* what he had sung. The same words came out. I remember the morning he'd sung it. Jason and Rikki stood in the hall outside the bathroom, laughing at Franklin's

lyrics. It had been a few months ago. The Payne case
had been settled! Couldn't have. Wouldn't Mr Payne
have the settlement money? How long does it take an
insurance company to issue a check?

I toweled off. If the case had been settled, why
hadn't Franklin told Payne? It didn't make any sense.
Even if insurance money wasn't paid out immediately, it would have eased the Paynes' lives to know a
check was on its way.

I threw on a pair of sweats, went to the kitchen, and
put up a pot of coffee. It was possible Franklin didn't
want to raise Mr Payne's hopes until the money came
in. He thought Payne was already a nuisance, maybe
Franklin was afraid he'd hang around the office full-
time until the check came through. Much easier for
Franklin to reach into his own pocket, loaning Payne
small amounts of money to tide the Paynes over.
Maybe it was protocol for attorneys not to say anything until the matter was entirely closed. Hadn't
Franklin often talked about how antsy laymen
became when they had to wait months or years for the
courts to settle their cases?

Or perhaps Franklin – may he lose the election by a
landslide – had the money and simply forgot to mention it to Mr Payne. Cut it out, Barbara. Franklin
might be an ass, an egomaniac, a self-centered son of
a diseased yak, but he's no thief. You don't live with a
man for seventeen years and not know he's a thief.

I poured a mug of coffee and flicked on the computer. The black screen turned green and a cursor
flashed in the corner, waiting. Write. Write. Write.

Write. A cigarette would help. At least that hysterical craving had cooled to a mild wanting. Food, however, was somethin' else. Why the hell had I sent the cookies home with Payne? Nothing in the house to set those creative juices flowing. Sit down, Barbara. Swiga cuppa java. My fingers itched for the phone. I had some questions for Franklin. Springfield my ass. He was privately polling Ashley Pembrooke; a little blow-by-blow campaign advice. There was no way I was going to call her apartment and come off like a jealous wife. Frankly, Pemby dear, I don't give a damn.

I eased my sore bones into the computer chair and wrote LUCINDA PAYNE across the top. I'd write the piece tonight, drop it off in the morning, then stop by Franklin's office to tell his staff about Mrs Payne's death. And, ever so casually, I'd inquire as to the status of her case.

A little after one o'clock I dragged my weary body up to bed. Someone had definitely been jumping on my parts with cleats. *Son of a bitch, Franklin*. Turn, toss, toss, turn. I was back at the computer by one-thirty, getting a jump on next week's columns. Of the five of us Cameron had started on the column, three were left. Next week was my turn to do two. *Why didn't he tell Payne the case was settled*? At four, the words on the screen started dancing the tarantella. I shut off the computer and stared at the dark screen a long long time.

I'd always wondered how alcoholics knew when they'd 'hit bottom'. Years ago I'd done a story on female addiction, and every recovering alcoholic I interviewed could pinpoint the exact moment when she had nowhere to go but up. I didn't exactly doubt them, but I couldn't understand how something like that could be so clear. It was. Bring in the angels and trumpeteers, we are having a moment of revelation. My mother was dead and she wasn't coming back. Sarajane was gone and she wasn't coming back. Franklin was gone and he wasn't coming back. Barbara Avers was gone and she wasn't coming back. Not the way she was. Not anymore. It was time to bury the dead.

I pushed myself away from the desk, climbed to the attic, and began bringing Sarajane's clothes down to my bedroom. It took five trips and my legs were screaming, but I brought down every last thing of hers I had. Stripping off my sweats, I tried on her clothes until they littered the floor around me. My own clothes still filled my closet although it had been months since I could wear them. I had liberated Sarajane's clothes from the storage bags and hung them in the attic closet. But I couldn't stand the thought of them actually hanging in my closet as if they belonged there.

The first time I couldn't zip up one of her dresses, I'd panicked. Must have been one of the smaller garments she'd bought when she lost all that weight for our high school reunion. I had no idea what size I was. Sarajane had been cutting tell-tale labels out of her clothes since fifth grade when a girl peeked in her gym locker and blabbed her size all over school.

'If your size embarrasses you,' I'd asked, 'why don't you lose weight?'

'It doesn't embarrass me,' she said. 'I like the way I am. What I don't like is people making an issue of my weight and asking why I don't lose it.' I never mentioned her weight to her again. And now, some of her clothes were too tight on me.

For one hour, I tried on every single piece of clothing, forcing myself to look, *really* look at myself. Sarajane's flowery, flouncy clothing looked silly on me. Her colors – beige, peach, pale blue – washed me out. I'd worn them anyway. Why? Remembrance of friends past? Penance for being fat? I unzipped the last dress, a navy blue sailor outfit with square white collar, and threw it onto the floor.

Now it was just the mirror and me. All of me. 'Hello, Barbara,' I said. 'Are you still in there?' My arms hung down, hiding five or six inches of fleshy hip and thigh. I lifted my arms out to the sides. Take it from the top, and a one/and a two. Puffy eyes – could be the bottle of brandy and lack of sleep. Full cheeks dripping into double-and-a-half chins, hiding the area where my neck used to be. Rounded shoulders. Hanging upperarms. Tips of elbows not bad. Wrists heavy. (Maybe I'd become big-boned all of a sudden. It would give me another few pounds on the weight charts.) Fingers chubby.

My arms strained from being held out and I lowered them, turning sideways. Suck it in! I sucked. Nothing moved. Small breasts fuller but sagging on the sides.

Torso wide, stomach and hips huge. I looked like a snowwoman, built in tiers. Man, get a load a dem thighs! Gen-u-ine, industrial strength, pony express-sized saddlebags. Kneecaps a couple of indented dimples in the middle of my legs. Thick calves. Thick ankles. Fat feet. Chubby toes. Th-th-th-that's all, folks. C'mon, there's got to be something salvageable.

'You have great naturally curly hair,' I said. 'Breathtakingly beautiful eyes.' I batted the puffy lids. 'You have strong finger- and toenails and wonderfully delicate earlobes.' I pressed my nose against my reflection. 'You're bright, creative, and can type. It ain't much, kid, but it's a beginning.'

I shoved Sarajane's clothes into bags. I'd drop them at the homeless women's shelter on my way to the *Globe*. Next, I took all of my 'thin' clothes out of my closet and brought them to the attic. If they didn't fit in one year, I'd toss them, too. The three garments left in my closet were the caftans Kathlyn's dressmaker had made. Six o'clock. No time to jog this morning. Better call Kathlyn.

'Thank God,' she said when I told her about Franklin. 'You o.k.?' I assured her I was. Her day was booked so we made plans to meet for dinner the next night. I grabbed my piece on Mrs Payne, loaded Sarajane into my car, and headed out into the new day.

TWENTY-ONE

I held my breath while the features editor scanned my article. He smiled, not a pretty sight on his particular face. Mrs Payne's story 'A Small Miracle' was in.

'Thanks, Mort,' I said, meaning volumes more than thanks, practically floating out of his office.

'Yeah,' he said. It helped that love and marriage were back in vogue with the American reading public. As usual, my private life was going against the national grain. I'd remained faithful when it was chic to fool around. Stayed married when everyone divorced. And now I was breaking up the exact moment society was rediscovering marriage.

Mac wasn't at his desk. It was barely 9:30, a time most *Globe* staffers were still prying their eyes open with coffee and. I settled my oversized self into his oversized chair and called Franklin's travel agent. Yes, she'd booked Franklin on the 7:05 a.m. flight to Springfield. Wait, she'd check. Yes, he'd boarded and yes the flight left on time.

I'd been doodling happy faces on Mac's Post-it pad. What could I write that would be breathtakingly clever? 'Hi!,' I scrawled, and slapped the note on his computer screen. I'd worry about clever later. Right now, I had a lot to do in a little time.

Half an hour later I entered the lobby of Franklin's office building. The coffee shop was on the south end of the lobby. Franklin's secretary, Miss Mumford, had gone on her coffee break at 10:10, exactly, for the past twenty years. She returned at 10:30, exactly. Hopefully, those twenty minutes would be enough. I positioned myself at the lobby's north end, past the bank of elevators. Leaning against the cigarette stand, I peered over the edge of a *Vogue*. Miss Mumford wasn't a smoker, gum chewer, or magazine reader. I was betting she'd get off the elevator and head right into the coffee shop. At 10:12, that's exactly what she did, and I was on an elevator to the fifteenth floor before the coffee shop door swung closed behind her.

'Why, hello,' all sunshine and light, hand extended, smile genuine. 'I don't believe I know you. I'm Barbara Avers, Mr Avers' wife.'

'Oh,' the latest-in-a-long-line-of-receptionists slipped a limp hand into mine, 'how do you do.'

'And you are . . .?'

'Sally. Sally Grubman.'

'I'm so pleased to meet you, Sally.' I dropped her hand and headed back toward the offices. 'Just have to pick up a few things for Franklin.'

'Mrs Avers?' She came tearing after me. 'I – I don't know if you're supposed to, I mean could you wait –'

'Miss Mumford can help me, dear.'

'But, she's on break.'

'Oh?' Surprise, surprise. I kept walking, talking over my shoulder. 'No matter. I know exactly where everything is. I used to practically live here, you know. Who do you think broke Miss Mumford in?' The reception desk phone rang. She wavered, uncertainly. 'Run along, dear. I'll be just fine.' She ran along. For slave wages she wasn't about to mix it up with a boss's wife, especially one who so clearly outweighed her.

How long had it been since I'd visited Franklin's office? The few times I'd come downtown since Sarajane's death he'd met me at restaurants, the theater, the gym. With a shock I realized I hadn't been to the office in over a year.

Files for old cases were all stored in a single room. Floor-to-ceiling filing cabinets contained thousands of cases settled by the firm. It was the logical place to start since I was sure Lucinda Payne's case had been settled. But I needed proof. Franklin – may his hair transplants unplug – would be innocent until proven guilty. The files were crammed tightly into the 'Pa-Pz' drawer. Franklin's files were easy to spot. He was the only member of the firm who put little check marks on the tabs next to the clients' names to indicate the case was closed. The files went from William Paxton to Anne Pzyskowski. Lucinda wasn't in there.

I went back to the front of the drawer and flipped through the files again. Maybe Mrs Payne had been misfiled. She still wasn't there. This could mean the case was still open. Every instinct told me no. Damn. There had to be a way to check. Checks. The checks

Franklin gave me to open his campaign account at Highland Bank. Checks from insurance companies made out to his clients. I'd bet anything those checks were for cases Franklin had settled. Cases like Mrs Payne's. I pressed my eyes shut, trying to picture the names on those checks.

'Cadbury!' I said heading for the 'C's', remembering how I salivated over the chocolaty name. That was before Franklin took his books away from me and moved them to his campaign office. I thumbed through the Ca drawer, through histories of lives in upheaval, lives like mine. Which divorce attorney's office would I be filed in? I'm sure Franklin would love to recommend someone. There was no file between Cacheviki and Caden. My heart gave a little leap. If the Cadbury case had been settled and the file wasn't here, maybe it was keeping the Payne file company in a secret place. Where?

The hallway was clear and I dashed into Franklin's office suite. Active files were kept in Miss Mumford's cabinet. I slipped the key from under the begonia, thankful it had been the plant and not the hiding place that had changed over the years. There was no Payne or Cadbury. I relocked her cabinet and re-hid the key. That left the files in Franklin's office. The preferred clients. The millionaires and politicians, entertainers and sports figures. Files he didn't trust to the wandering eyes of filing clerks, some of whom had been known to exchange privileged information for money. I took out my key, unlocked his door, and entered the room of a stranger.

THE DIETER

The gray and burgundy decor I'd worked months to create had been recolored to melon shades. Fe-fi-fo-fum, I smell the touch of a blond wo-man. Funny. He'd never mentioned he'd redecorated his office. Just like he never mentioned the open house at campaign headquarters. Must have skipped his mind.

Gone was the tufted leather couch Franklin saw in *Architectural Digest* and had me chase all over the country to find. Gone, too, the matching wing-back chairs flanked by three-legged side tables. And his desk! How many weeks had I fought it out with the furniture maker who resisted Franklin's particular list of demands regarding drawer size, inserts, hidden compartments, etc. I'd spent months of my life furnishing the office in the Gospel according to Franklin. And now it was gone! All of it. In its place was a room straight out of the 1930s, full of round-edged furniture and art deco accessories. More boudoir than boardroom. Fe-fi.

The bookcase had also been redesigned, the contents moved around, and it took me a moment to locate the dictionary. As I took it out, my own face, in all its thin arrogance, smiled from the back of the book shelf. I reached in and pulled out the family portrait Franklin used to keep on his desk. Those Audrey Hepburn cheekbones, Bette Davis eyes, that Katharine Hepburn jaw! I hadn't seen that face for months. Saint Barbara the Perfect. Puff, puff. Perfect portrait of the perfect family. Puff, puff. Franklin – may he need extensive periodontal work and develop an allergy to novocaine – sat slightly apart from Rikki, Jason, and me. I threw the photo into the garbage, opened the dictionary to 'K', and removed the key to his private files.

Cadbury's file was there, a check mark next to the name followed by a +. I flipped to Payne. Lucinda was there, too. Another check +. Their files were bulging with papers and notes. There was no way I could begin reading them in the little amount of time I had left. But the two of them were somehow connected and I was going to find out what was going on. Grabbing a legal pad from Franklin's desk, I quickly jotted the information on the top tab: Cadbury's name, address, and phone number, the case file number, and a money amount. The same with Lucinda Payne. Then, flipping back to the A's, I looked for any file with the check + mark.

'Those are private files!' I spun around as Miss Mumford barreled through the doorway toward me.

'Miss Mumford,' all smiles and sunshine, 'how nice to see you.' Her brow furrowed more than usual and she peered over her half-glasses at me.

'Mrs Avers?'

I'd forgotten. She'd known Barbara the Thin. 'Oh, yes,' deep sigh. 'Of course you didn't recognize me. I'm afraid I've put on a good deal of weight since I last saw you. But with the operations and all . . .' She adored illness. It was her passion. Miss Mumford was one of those people hungry for details of other people's operations. The glimmer of interest was unmistakable but she was too much the proper lady to probe.

'I had no idea.' She waited, hoping. 'Of course, I wondered why we hadn't seen you around. I just assumed those little articles you wrote for the *Globe* were keeping you busy.' Little articles. I smiled through gritting teeth.

'It must have given you quite a start, coming in here, seeing some strange woman rummaging through Franklin's files.' How long could I stall? I turned back to the files, searching and writing as I talked. 'But Franklin left for Springfield without his notes and, well, you know how fussy he is. Had to have this immediately.'

Her long narrow nose bent way out of joint. 'He might have called me.'

'But, Miss Mumford,' so surprised you didn't know, 'that was the very first thing he did. He tried calling you last night, at your home. There was no answer.'

'I was home.'

Write faster, Barbara. Two more names, three. 'You know,' come to think of it, 'he was packing with one hand and calling you with the other.' Faster. 'I'll bet he misdialed. I'll bet that's exactly what happened. Anyway, I had to come down to drop off some of my little articles to the *Globe* so I volunteered to stop by.' Her nose bent back into place and we were friends again. But I was still invading her turf.

'Perhaps I can be of some help.'

'Nearly done. Just jotting a few names he needs.' I thanked God for my shorthand. 'But I could do with a cup of coffee.'

She left reluctantly. Six names, seven. Through the L's and the M's. 'Here's your coffee,' she said, setting a styrofoam cup on his desk.

'Did I say coffee?' Silly me. 'Talk about old habits dying hard. The doctors haven't let me have coffee for months. You know how caffeine can be. I meant to ask for tea. Herbal. If you don't mind.'

She raced out and I made it through the P's before she returned. Franklin's phone rang. She picked it up. 'Mr Avers' office.' Nothing in Q and R. One in S. The pencil point broke. I grabbed another off his desk. 'Why yes, Mr Avers. I'll do that immediately.' Franklin! 'Do you wish to speak with Mrs Avers?' I heard his shout halfway across the room. 'Wh-why, yes, she's right here.' Pause. Write faster. 'Getting that information you wanted from your private files.' One name in T. Write faster, faster. I heard the phone slam on the desk a second before I felt the file drawer slam on my fingers.

'Owwwwww!' The pain was sharp.

'Mrs Avers, I must insist you leave, this instant!'

'Miss Mumford!' Outrage. Indignation. I eased my fingers out of the drawer. They were skinned and dented. 'Whatever is the matter with you?'

'You have no right to be here. Mr Avers said –'

'Franklin? Now, what has that naughty boy been telling you?' I marched to the phone. 'Franklin?'

'Barbara, what the hell are you doing in –'

'That wasn't a nice trick you played on Miss Mumford.'

' – my office!?'

'Yes, well, she didn't know you were kidding.' I laughed, trying to engage Miss Mumford in the playfulness of it all. 'She actually thought you were serious and she slammed my poor little fingers in the drawer.'

'You're in my file drawers? You get out of that office, Barbara. Now!' I blew on my skinned fingers. A few knuckles reddened with blood and held Miss Mumford's attention.

'No, I don't.' I laughed, covering the receiver with one hand. 'Franklin wants to know if I need a good P.I. attorney.' She blanched and pantomimed that she'd get the first-aid kit from her desk. As soon as she left I cradled the phone to my ear and went back to the files. I couldn't concentrate on Franklin and writing at the same time so I ignored him. Nothing in U, V, or W. Only two more, one in Y and one in Z. Franklin's voice in my left ear soared way past middle C. Miss Mumford returned.

'I love you too,' I smiled at the phone, and made kissing sounds. 'Hope your fundraising goes well. Hurry back. Bye.'

'I'm sooo very sorry, Mrs Avers.' She was coming at me with the iodine. 'But he's never teased me like that before.' She was blushing furiously. 'He sounded so very sincere.'

'Franklin's quite the actor when he wants to be.' I said, trying to get the two last names, not looking forward to the sting of iodine. 'Why don't we wait just one second with that. I'm nearly through.'

The phone again. I knew it was Franklin. As she

answered, I tore the two last files out of the cabinet and ran toward his office bathroom. Miss Mumford really came at me this time, her Naturalizers outdistancing my high heels two steps to one. 'You stop!' she shouted. 'Give me those files.' She grabbed them and I yanked them out of her hands, fumbling behind me for the bathroom doorknob.

Her eyes were wild. My back was against the bathroom door and, as she hurtled toward me, my hand found the knob. The instant before impact, I stepped to one side and threw the door open. She flew inside and I yanked the door shut.

'Let me out!' She pulled on the knob and banged on the door. I leaned my weight back, holding the door shut with the file-holding hand, writing with the other. I figured I outweighed her by a good fifty pounds, enough to let me get the last names copied down. By the time I finished, she'd stopped banging and shouting. She was talking to someone. The bathroom phone! I raced to the cabinet, put the files back, and ran out of the room. The receptionist was coming at me, blocking my way.

I pushed her aside, lunged out of the office and down the hall, ducking into the large law firm whose offices faced the elevators. The receptionist looked up inquiringly.

'Can you tell me where the ladies room is?' I asked.

She directed me and I thanked her, then stood at the door, propping it open with my toe to give me a view of the elevators, fumbling in my purse for some imagined item. Moments later, one of the elevators opened and two security guards flew out, clubs drawn, racing down the hall toward Franklin's office. Dashing from the office into the elevator, I didn't dare breathe until the doors slid shut.

Kathlyn spotted me the second I walked into Mom's, and came tearing through the crowd, grabbing me tightly, hugging me for a good long time. 'I'm so glad that lousy relationship's over,' she said, laughing and crying and slapping my back. I think she would have swung me around if it weren't for the crush of people trying to balance travel brochures and cups of soup, and the fact that I probably outweighed her. I hugged back.

'You okay?' she asked.

'Better every minute.' Someone called to her and she motioned them to wait. 'Look,' I said, 'I didn't come to bother you. We'll talk at dinner tomorrow. Right now, I need to borrow your office.'

'It's yours.'

I closed the door to the quiet cubicle and slumped into her chair. The scene in Franklin's office came crashing down around me. I couldn't believe what I'd done! Breaking and entering. Or, was it entering and breaking? Criminal trespass. Assault with intent to take shorthand. Miss Mumford probably had an APB out on me. I'd go to jail. Wonder if I'd lose weight. Bread and water's so starchy. The sight of the prim secretary lunging at me, her pinched face contorted! I smiled. The *sound* of her whooshing past me into the office bathroom! I chuckled. Franklin's telephone voice hitting notes Yma Sumac would envy. I guffawed. When had I had so much fun? Not quite as dramatic as Kathlyn's dish-smashing, but it sure as hell held my interest.

The 'Gray Shark' came in with a styrofoam cup of gazpacho topped with croutons, cucumber bits, and diced onion. 'From the boss,' she said, setting it on the desk. 'Said to tell you it's lo-cal and healthy, but you should eat it anyway.'

'A bunch of comedians,' I grumbled. She waited, arms folded over her apron until I took a small sip of the cold soup, then closed the door behind her. The last solid food I'd had was the good Doctor's banana bread, which was probably crusting on the shoes in Franklin's closet. Maybe it was the bottle of brandy or the all-night coffee or the lack of sleep, but I hadn't thought about food until the gazpacho was set in front of me. Even then, I wasn't all that hungry and put the soup to one side, setting out the list of names I'd copied at Franklin's office. I called Mac.

'Didn't know you were an artist,' he said. It took me a moment to remember the smiley face I'd stuck on his computer.

'I'm a woman of many talents. How did you know that was mine?'

'Mort told me you'd been in. Showed me your piece on Mrs Payne. Made me jealous as hell.'

'Because I write so incredibly well?' He laughed and I could see the crinkle of lines around his eye, the slight crookedness of his smile, the jaunty tilt of his eyepatch.

'Your writing's passable –'

'Passable!'

' – but I was talking about your "miracle", two people living together forty years and loving each other as much as they did.'

'Oh, that,' I said.

'Yeah, that. So?'

'What?' I yawned mightily.

'I don't mean to bore you, but it's your nickel.'

'Sorry. Not much sleep last night.' Like none. 'I need to know how I find out if a legal case has been settled.'

'What kind of case?'

'Personal injury.'

'Local?'

'Yes.'

'Go over to the Daley Center and . . .' I copied the instructions. 'What's up?'

'Just curious about something. Does it take long to get the files?'

'Depends. It can take a week or so,' my heart sank, 'if it's an old case and they have to dig around in the warehouse.'

'Recent.'

'Should get it right away, although the clerk can get pretty backed up sometimes. Tell you what. I'm going to be in the building anyway and the clerks know me. If you give me the name and an idea of what you're looking for, I'll check it out for you.'

It was almost eleven-thirty. The funeral was at two and I had to stop at the bank first. I didn't have time to go to the courthouse but I was dying to know if Franklin was stealing from his clients. The problem was whether I wanted to wave my suspicions under the nose of an old bloodhound like Mac. He'd be sure to ask questions if I gave him the long list of names I'd stolen from Franklin's office. Maybe I could throw Mac off the scent by checking just one name.

'All right,' I said. 'I may be doing a follow-up piece on Mr Payne and I wanted some of the figures on his wife's case. How long they had to wait while the case was pending. The date and amount of settlement.'

'The amount of settlement might not be in the file.' I bet those were the figures I'd copied off the file tabs.

'Oh. Well, any of the action in the case would be good. It seems crass to bring that up with a man whose wife just died. I thought I'd get the information myself. Don't know if I'll use it but I'd like it in my file.'

'No problem. I'm going over there now. Have it for you by lunch. Want to meet?'

'Can't. I'm going to Mrs Payne's funeral and I have errands before that. I'll call you later. And Mac, thanks.' I looked down at my notepad. In the middle of the Gregg squiggles and lines, I'd penciled MAC in large letters formed by chains of little hearts.

Highland Bank was on my way to the cemetery. Franklin always advised his newly widowed clients that, before they cried, they should visit the safe deposit box. I wasn't widowed, which was just as well since I didn't intend to cry.

By 12:30, I'd opened a safe deposit box in my name and taken out the one I shared with Franklin. Setting both boxes on the table in the private room, I filled mine with all the items held in joint tenancy: stock certificates, bonds, insurance policies, and our wills. The wills. I'd been furious when Franklin explained, ever so patiently, the tax reasons for setting up an estate plan. We wouldn't want the mean old government taking all of Franklin's hard-earned money, now would we, Poopsy? Even in death, Franklin intended to retain control over me and the children. His estate would have an administrator who would dole out the money.

'Barbara, I've seen women duped out of their inheritances by religious groups, gigolos, bad business investments –'

'I am not those women.'

'What about your friend Karen Blackstone who refused to share Melvin's money with their children?'

'Their *children* are thirty-eight and forty-two. The daughter hasn't called Karen in five years and the son's only gainful employment is umping softball games. We're talking a three-month season. Melvin kept those kids dependent on him. Karen is cutting them free. And when have I ever failed to put our children's concerns ahead of mine?'

He'd gone ahead with the estate plan and named a hard-nosed, tight-ass, humorless partner as trustee. Luckily I still smoked then. Puff, puff. It got me through my anger. Puff, puff.

The one good thing the trustee did was suggest Franklin make a detailed list of all his assets including stocks, building investments, every source of money.

How thoughtful. It was a satisfyingly long list. I'm sure my divorce attorney would find it most helpful. I folded it neatly into my box and weighted it down with the five silver bars and rare coins in small plastic boxes. I'd been hoping for cash. Franklin had always kept cash in the box, a few hundred, a few thousand. It fluctuated over the years but some emergency money had always been there. Now there was nothing. I had a feeling the campaign was draining him faster than he'd expected. Lady Ashley had some fancy ideas about television time and full-page newspaper ads. Probably hard for Franklin to say no to a woman who was saying yes to him. The last items I transferred were the velvet boxes of my mother's jewelry.

'Hi, Mom,' I said. 'My life is a little complicated right now.' I stroked the velvet tenderly. 'Was your life ever complicated? Grandma and Daddy made you seem so untouched by the rest of the world. I always pictured you as a white-robed angel floating above the problems and emotions of real people. But you weren't, were you?' Old Mrs Whittiker's footsteps creaked outside the door. Who *was* I talking to?

'I don't blame them. They felt sad for their little motherless girl. They thought I needed you to be special, somehow better than real people. But what I really needed, what I need now, is to believe you were a living, breathing, human being, with warts and scars and unclean thoughts and that sometimes living this life got to you, and that you and Daddy had problems just like everybody else, and I'm sorry it took me all these years to know that about you, about myself because it must have been hard for you to be worshipped when all you wanted was to be loved.' I set the boxes inside and flipped the lid down. 'I do love you,' I said. 'And, Mom, keep your eyes open for Lucinda Payne. She's a special lady, too.'

Upstairs, I stopped at a personal banker.

'Somehow we let our checks run out without reordering,' I said. Oh, silly me. 'We need about twenty-five emergency checks until the new ones come in.' I gave her the FIT TO LEAD account number and waited while she checked my signature against the signature of the person who had opened the account. Ten minutes later I was on the way to the funeral, twenty-five blank checks tucked safely in my wallet. Whether I used them or not depended on what I found – or didn't find – in the courthouse records.

TWENTY-TWO

The miniature Arc de Triomphe stood at the hub of the old cemetery. Spokes of roads radiated from the square stone building, dividing the grounds into wedge-shaped sections which had become segregated over the years by religion. In the end, the rich and poor, black and white coexisted for eternity in the one section they knew to be closest to God.

I was first to arrive and waited in my car until the heat became oppressive. Maybe the others were inside but hadn't driven. I walked into the building. It was empty except for Lucinda's closed casket which perched atop a gurney-like contraption with wheels and metal cross braces. It wouldn't have killed the cemetery people to drape a piece of fabric over the sub-structure. I walked toward her, my steps echoing off the marble floor and walls. Two huge candles in six-foot gold holders flanked the head of the casket.

'I'm sorry I never got to meet you,' I said softly. The casket had the blue marbleized finish of a ten-pound bowling ball. I touched it expecting cool marble and got warm plastic. A car pulled up and four women joined me. Neighbors, they said. Others wanted to come but everyone worked, you see. A round-cheeked minister bustled in followed after a moment by Mr Payne. His sagging face shifted upward when he saw me. We embraced, taking comfort in each other. He greeted each of the other women by name, thanking them for coming. Behind us, the minister began sighing and rustling the pages of his bible with the impatience of a parent whose children are dawdling. I took Mr Payne's arm and approached the casket.

'He's not our regular minister,' whispered Mr Payne. 'Ours is ministering in Peru for a year. Nice man. He'll be sad to hear about Lucinda. Don't know where the congregation found this fella. He hasn't been a whole lot of comfort.'

The minister began immediately. He hadn't known Mrs Payne and hadn't bothered to learn anything about her. He droned vague platitudes about women, none of which bore any resemblance to any woman I'd known and certainly not to Lucinda Payne. This was followed by monotoned prayers read from a book. My eyes fixed on the tiny vest buttons straining over the reverend's round belly. A man of impure sexual habits, picked his nose in the illusionary privacy of his car, told sexist and ethnic jokes in his restricted club, cheated on his tax return and wife with equal indifference. I was relieved when his voice stopped.

'We can go now,' he said, extending an arm to shoo us out.

'I'd like to see her into the ground,' said Mr Payne. I squeezed his arm.

'That can take a while,' said the minister, his kindly tone slipping a notch.

'I have time,' said Mr Payne. 'And I'm paying for yours.' *That* was the Mr Payne Franklin used to complain about, the man who knew his rights and kept after them, the pain in Franklin's ass. He led me out of the cool chamber into the furnace of the August afternoon.

'I'll bet Lucinda loved you at least as much as you loved her,' I said.

'She sure made it feel that way.' The minister hurried past us, diagonaling across the Jewish section into the Catholic section, waving down the grounds crew. Mr Payne and I waited at the grave site lost in our own thoughts. My last funeral had been Sarajane's. Hundreds of people crammed into her church for the service, the priest cried openly and couldn't finish, the family read favorite poems, shared precious moments. I later heard Stanford telling a cute young thing of the under-twenty persuasion, 'Oh, yes,' sigh, sigh, wipe the eye, 'we had seventy-five cars in the cortege.' Sarajane's funeral, and he'd been counting cars.

The grounds crew arrived and removed the astroturf carpet covering the gaping hole that would receive Mrs Payne's earthly remains. It took a while for them to get the gurney in position over the grave. While we waited, a taxi pulled up and Mac got out. From the depth of his sweat stains I reckoned the ride had not been air-conditioned.

'Glad I caught you,' he said, shaking hands with

Mr Payne. He introduced himself and pulled a clipping out of his pocket. 'I thought you might like an advance copy of Barbara's article on your wife.' Mr Payne took it and tried to read but the small print defeated his teary eyes and trembling hands.

'Would you?' he asked, handing it to me.

'I'd be honored.' As her casket was lowered, I read aloud the story of one woman's life and love and the speck of the universe she had shaped into a haven for herself and her husband. The words had been agonizingly hard to write and I was finding them nearly impossible to read. My voice cracked often, punctuated by pauses caused by my trying not to cry.

When I finished, there were no sounds. Even the grounds keepers had stopped to listen. I didn't flatter myself that it was my words that held them, but the recounting of the beauty of her life. They lowered her gently, then stepped back as we finished.

Mr Payne took the article from me, stepped to the edge of the grave, and fluttered the paper on top of the casket. 'Now everybody in Chicago's going to know you,' he said. 'They'll get to meet you and love you.' His eyes met the minister's. 'And I hope you were paying close attention, Reverend, because what you just listened to was the sound of a proper eulogy.' He picked up a handful of dirt and tossed it on the casket. Mac and I did the same. We walked Mr Payne to his wreck of a car, said our good-byes, and watched him leave. The car backfired loudly, shooting black clouds from the tail pipe.

'Not a fancy man,' said Mac, resting his arm on my

shoulder. Without thinking, I reached up and slipped my hand in his. He squeezed it and I squeezed back.

'Thanks for coming,' I said. 'That article made all the difference.'

'I thought it might make today a little easier for him. According to the court file, he and his wife sure as hell went through a lot these past couple of years.'

'You saw the file?' The enthusiasm escaped before I could stop it. Overdone for a little background information. It didn't get by Mac.

'Got copies right here.' He patted his jacket pocket.

'May I have them?'

'Oh, no you don't,' he said, 'I don't come that cheap. You want information you pay. It's going to cost you one ride home.'

'Get in,' I said, sweating from more than the heat. 'You can read while I drive.'

Forty minutes later I turned off the outer drive at Lincoln Park. I gave up trying to find one single way in which the evidence Mac brought did *not* prove Franklin a thief. The file showed the case had been going on for two years. The amount of the suit was for five million dollars. There was a note indicating the case had been settled four months before although a dollar amount was not on file. I felt Mac watching me as he doled out the information. I shifted my face into neutral. This didn't make sense. No one threw away an almost sure-bet jury award. No one but an attorney running for political office who needed instant cash. Son of a bitch.

Traffic crawled along Fullerton as gapers ogled young girls walking to the lake. There was enough fabric in my caftan to make a hundred of their bikinis, complete with matching beach bags. I turned left, past Ambria, Un Grand Cafe, the street of favorite restaurants Franklin and I frequented when we were still two of the beautiful people. Puff, puff. And I dined on an appetizer, salad, and dessert. Puff, puff. With just a glass or two of the driest white wine splashed with soda. Puff.

'This is it,' Mac said. I pulled up to an old apartment building overlooking the formal garden between the Conservatory and Lincoln Park Zoo. 'You've been awfully quiet.' He didn't make a move to get out of the car.

'It's been a rough couple of days.'

'Want to talk about it?'

I shook my head. Had to have time to think. I would confront Franklin with what I'd found and give him one last chance to try and explain why he'd done what he had. What I thought he had. Maybe I was missing something. There might be a perfectly logical explanation sitting right in front of me. I could be overreacting.

'There you go again,' said Mac. My eyes snapped into focus. I'd been staring through him. 'Come on up a second. Let me show off my new apartment.'

'Can't. I have to get home.'

'Five minutes. Humor me.'

'Mac, there hasn't been a parking space in this neighborhood since the Chicago fire.' On cue, a family crossed the street in front of my car, the children carrying zoo balloons, the parents walking hand in hand. They climbed into the car parked in front of us and drove away. I looked at Mac and he shrugged.

'It's all done with mirrors,' he said.

He set his cane aside the moment we entered the apartment. 'It's mostly for show, now, the old sympathy ploy.'

'And you don't want my sympathy?'

'Of all the many things I want from you, Barbara, that doesn't make the top hundred.'

I escaped into the living room. 'It looks like you've always lived here,' I said, walking around the large soft furniture, glancing at the full-wall display of mineral specimens, Indian pottery, Kochina dolls. He stood at the door, watching me pretend to examine the shelves of books enclosed by leaded glass doors. I shouldn't be here. I wasn't ready for this.

'Like it?' I jumped.

'What's not to like?'

'Come on, I'll show you the rest of the place.' It was an old Pullman apartment which began at the living room and traveled via shiny pine planking down the long hall to the kitchen. The first room off the hall was a lapidary complete with tumbler, buffing and sanding belts, and a table of well-used tools. Boxes of stones lined the wall shelves; opal, quartz, many I didn't recognize. Large crates along the floor brimmed with large uncut specimens. There were boxes of jewelry findings, metal rods and a small acetylene torch.

Mac's bedroom was inviting. He'd built a platform for the king-sized bed with shelves behind it to hold his books and reading lamp. I looked for tell-tale signs of a live-in girlfriend but didn't see any. His reading tastes were eclectic; mysteries by Kaminsky and Craig, biographies of criminals and athletes, stacks of *Sports Illustrated*, the Sunset series of How To books, Philosophy. A summer quilt lay folded at the foot of the bed. Four large pillows were plumped at the head. Nearly two days since I'd slept. The bed beckoned like Nirvana and I wanted to curl up on the cool sheets and sleep forever.

I forced myself out of the room. We skipped the bathroom and checked out the last room, a home office with desk, computer, reference books.

'I missed lunch,' he said, guiding me into the kitchen, piling items from the refrigerator onto the butcher block in the center of the room. I pulled up a high-backed stool and watched. He uncorked a burgundy and poured out two glasses.

'To my first house guest,' he said, clinking his glass to mine.

'First?' I asked. 'I heard you had a lady.' He laughed.

'My rumor, to hold off a nice woman at work without hurting her feelings.'

'Then I'm honored,' I said. 'Here's to your new home.'

'Here's to good friends.' We locked arms and downed our wine, his cool lips brushing mine as I lowered my glass.

'Mac.'

'Friends,' he said, innocently, in motion again, cutting, dicing, grating. The wine glasses refilled and emptied and he had me open another bottle to let it breathe. He was sautéeing onions and garlic when the wine, unimpeded by food in my stomach, went directly to my head.

'If you'll excuse me . . .' I said, trying to walk normally out of the room. I intended to go to the bathroom and splash cold water on my face, neck, and wrists. But my feet knew better and walked me straight to the bedroom where my last conscious act was to try and hit the bed as I fell straight forward, rather like a large tree cut down at the base.

Coffee. Chicory. Toast. Mmmmmm. Smells to wake up to. Grandma must be up early, getting Daddy off to work. Strange smell on the pillow. Not mine. Room sounds all wrong. Air conditioner hum, distant music. Someone singing. I opened my eyes. Bright sun streamed through crystals dangling in front of the windows. Rainbows danced around the room. I put a pillow over my face.

'Good, you're up.'

'Not.'

Mac tugged the pillow off my face, studied me closely, then put it back. 'You're right,' he said. 'Some things are better left covered.'

'Thanks.'

'You have exactly five minutes to do whatever it is you do in the bathroom in the morning.'

'What happens then?'

'Breakfast will be served in the living room.' He walked out and I waited until his uneven steps faded before making a dash for the bathroom.

The old bevel-edged medicine cabinet mirror was cloudy with age. But even my soft-focus image couldn't mask the reality of raccoon eyes caused by sleep-smeared mascara and a face puffy from god knew how many hours of sleep. I searched the cabinet for repair materials.

He knocked on the door. 'Finding everything okay?'

'I don't suppose you have mascara remover.'

'Fresh out.' He limped away to finish whatever it was he was doing. I leaned forward on the sink and tilted my head at myself.

'You may not look great, Barbara, but you are who you are. And, take it from an old friend, it's all right.' I smiled at me, then made a grotesque face. 'And if you buy that one, Honeycakes, I've got this bridge in Brooklyn you're gonna love.'

Globs of Vaseline finally softened the mascara. I washed my face, smoothing on a thin coat of vaseline as moisturizer. The only comb I could find had thin compact teeth which broke on their adventure through my tangle of curls. I found an unopened toothbrush under the sink and was scrubbing my teeth when Mac knocked on the door again.

'You have ten seconds,' he said. I rinsed and spat. 'And I think I have a new toothbrush under the sink.'

'Too late,' I said, 'I already used yours.'

He growled as he walked away.

Breakfast was fabulous. Fresh strawberries, yogurt, warm bran muffins, and lots and lots of hot coffee. We sat on the living room floor around a low table. It was six in the morning. I'd slept fifteen hours.

'You're great for a guy's ego,' Mac said.

'You should be flattered I feel so comfortable around you. I mean, I don't pass out at just anyone's house.'

'You missed a great linguini in clam sauce. I wasn't sure if I should wake you.' He was staring into his coffee mug. 'I thought Franklin might be worried about where you were.'

'He's out of town,' I said, too loud and too quick.

'Fundraising downstate. Yes, I know. I thought if he tried to call you and you weren't home . . .'

'But you didn't wake me.'

'No.' He reached out and curled a strand of my hair around his finger. Every nerve ending in my body jumped to attention. 'I sat on the edge of the bed a long, long time watching you, thinking I should wake you.' He traced his thumb down my cheek and across my lips. I kissed it. I don't know who was more surprised. 'But if I woke you, you might leave.' He took my face in his hands. 'And I wanted you to stay.' He kissed my left eye. 'I wanted to wake up to you.' He kissed my right eye. 'Have you wake up to me.' His lips were warm and oh so soft on mine as he eased me down to the rug. I pulled him to me, closing my eyes, feeling the wonder of his rough-skinned hand gliding up my leg, under my dress, caressing my skin, touching, stroking. I sing the body electric, yessir, I surely do. I moved freely in the full caftan. Mac seemed to sense I wasn't ready to be naked in front of him, and made no move to take it off.

He was a great toucher. I held my breath at first, terrified he'd be repulsed by my body, stop suddenly and remember he had to go somewhere. Like to the dentist. But his touch kept on and on and on and I fell into it, letting it work its magic on me.

There was a muted tearing sound and I opened my eyes as Mac ripped a condom package with his teeth. I'd been on the pill since I was nineteen and had never seen a man use a condom. I watched, a part of me fascinated by the process, a part of me unable to believe I was about to do what I was about to do. Mac caught me watching and winked.

'Wanna help?'

'Yes.' How could people complain about condoms taking away the enjoyment of sex? Mac knelt beside me as I stroked the condom down over him. It was one of the most singularly erotic moments of my life.

'You're sure about this, Barbara?'

'I keep waiting for the feeling that this is wrong,' I said. 'And it's not coming. My only regret right now – I mean this is my *only* regret – is that we didn't do this when I was thin.'

He laughed and kissed me and slid his body over mine. We made love with hungry urgency. The hell with foreplay. That could come later. Right now I needed him deep inside me and he needed to be there. Oh, the wonder of feeling him in me, filling me, making me whole. The same body Franklin found impossible to navigate sailed effortlessly with Mac. I lost myself in the feel of him, the smells and sounds and wanting of him until, his whole body shuddering, he cried out with the joy of coming. We held each other, laughing, kissing, and I couldn't get enough of holding him in my arms. After a while, he fell asleep, his head on my breast. Sunbeams crawled across the floor, shining on the soft hairs of his legs, the beads of sweat on his body. I kissed his forehead, his hair, hugging him tightly until I fell asleep.

The phone woke us. It was on the table near my head. I fumbled for the receiver and handed it to Mac. 'When?' He sat up, motioning for the pencil and pad. I handed them over. 'Right. Right. Got it. Be there in twenty minutes.' He tossed me the receiver and kissed my nose.

'Frankie Lorenzo's body just turned up in a car trunk at O'Hare.' He rebuttoned shirt, rezipped pants. 'Passersby smelled something rotten.'

'Ugh!' I pulled a pillow over my face. He eased it back, kissing me, his eye so full of love it made me ache. I couldn't remember anyone looking at me that way. Not ever. No matter how many eyes they had.

'Will you wait here for me?' he asked.

'You kidding? I have people to go, places to see.'

He laughed. 'Is that a yes?'

'No. That's a no. And don't give me that look.'

'You're mad because I'm leaving.'

'Don't confuse me with your ex-wife. I know all about crime reporters. Nothing I have can compete with the allure of a bullet-riddled body decaying in a car trunk.'

'He was stabbed.'

'Whatever. But you're not the only one around here with work to do. Besides, you still owe me a dinner and I mean to collect.'

'Tonight,' he said. 'Wait a minute.' He opened a desk drawer and tossed me a key. 'I'll be back by six. If something comes up, I'll call.' Another kiss and he left.

If Mac had an iron, it was well hidden. I couldn't afford to kill two hours driving to my house for fresh clothes, then all the way back downtown to the Court House. The steam from my shower smoothed most of the wrinkles out of the caftan-turned-nightgown. I bathed slowly, soaping every part of my body with a giant sponge as textured as Mac's hands.

By eight forty-five I stood at the bus stop with the rest of the commuters. I'm in love with a wonderful man, I thought smiling, and he's in love with me. How delicious it felt to have a secret. Leaving my car parked in front of Mac's bordered on a commitment. Even if I came to my senses during the day, which was a real possibility, I would have to return for my car. And I'd go up to the apartment to leave the key. And once I was in his apartment . . . Sometimes I had to force myself to do what my instincts told me was in my best interests. Mac was. I was still shocked how easy it had all been. How right making love had seemed. Who woulda thunk it?

Passengers crowded the aisles of the La Salle Street

bus and the driver talked them back until all of us squeezed on. I would reach the Daley Center by the time the Clerk's office opened. There was no way to tell how long it would take to research the names I'd stolen from Franklin's private files. I had a sense time was running out. Now that Franklin knew I'd been after something in his office, he'd be trying to figure out what I was up to. Once he did, he'd begin working on a way to stop me.

TWENTY-THREE

The Daley Center's windows reflected a happy lady with an idiotic grin on her un-made-up face. Daddy always said I was a lousy poker player. It wasn't until I was riding the elevator to the eighth floor that it occurred to me I might not be allowed access to the records. Mac said they were available to the public but he'd spent so many years digging through places like this, slipping a buck here, a buck there, he probably used tricks he didn't know he knew.

Following Mac's instructions, I turned right, passed a long counter, computers, and metal baskets. Picking up a piece of white paper, I wrote down the case numbers I had copied from Franklin's files and walked back to the counter.

The clerk in Records picked up on my mood, smiling and joking as, one by one, he pulled the files. I was itching to open them but he kept them behind the counter until he had them all. I followed him down to the end where he handed the files to a woman at a computer.

'Your attorney number?' she asked, entering the case number on her screen. Mac hadn't said anything about my needing a number.

'I . . . I don't have one. That is, I'm not an attorney. You see –'

'Files cannot be taken from the room,' she said, not interested in my life history. 'You can go sit at one of those tables if you want to look through the files then return them here when you're done.'

'Thank you.' I picked up the files and settled in for a long read.

All twelve cases had been filed in the last few years. Most had been settled in the last few months. The folders were filled with legal histories. One of the most interesting documents listed pre-trial demands made by Franklin on behalf of his clients. Lucinda Payne's pre-trial demand was for five million dollars. I checked the information I had copied off her file in Franklin's office. Franklin had written two hundred thousand next to his little check mark. If I was reading that right, he had sold Lucinda for a fraction of what her case was worth and had never given her a penny of the money.

The rest of the cases were for comparatively small amounts, ranging from fifteen to thirty thousand, each settled for far less than the original suit. Maybe Franklin selected these cases so as not to draw his partners' attention. A missing few thousand could be hidden in a personal injury firm that handled millions of dollars in suits each year. The date on Lucinda Payne's folder indicated her case had been settled first. That would have given Franklin start-up money for his campaign. The smaller cases may have been settled as he needed money, a need which seemed to have escalated recently – three cases settled last month – thanks in large part to Ashley's expensive p.r. ideas. She was out to make a career and Franklin was out to make her. It all worked out rather neatly. The more I uncovered, the more I felt emotions quaking inside me, building up, wanting to explode. By noon I'd recorded information on all twelve cases and returned the files. I left the Daley Center and stepped off the edge of the Earth.

You marry a man with force and power and drive and energy because that's what your father had and that's what turned you on more than any other thing in this world and you grab onto this man's coattails and hang on for dear life because he's in a terrible hurry to be great or famous or powerful or more probably all three and there aren't a hell of a lot of men out there generating electricity the kind of elec- tricity that makes things go and happen and you run double-time through your life doing the things wives of great men are supposed to do the things your mother would have done trying to keep up with him and create the perfect home so he'll have a haven to come home to at night a place where he's loved and he's king and all of us tell him he's wonderful isn't Daddy wonderful and wise and he believes us which magically makes it all true and lets it be possible for him to go out into the world and be the best he can be which you know is great indeed and all this time you've devoted your life to him you're so grateful to be a part of his success which is your success and aren't we the envy of everyone we know the beautiful successful popular Avers what a perfect couple they are even though they have been having a few teensy weensy problems lately but who doesn't and isn't it a shame or haven't you heard that he steals from poor people so he won't have to disturb his lovely lifestyle which is comfortable and looks so awfully good on him.

I don't remember boarding the bus or getting off, buying the bag of peanuts or sitting on the zoo bench. It's possible during that time I killed a family of seven or defecated on a public street. If arrested I would have no defense.

'Sorry, your honor. I entered a blackness so total, so complete, so absolute it erased time. Nothing exists for me between my leaving the Daley Center and being accosted by the bag lady.'

'You were in a state of shock?'

'State of shock? What an insipid, puny, inadequate little phrase. How can you use it to describe an extraordinary, gigantic, absolutely altered state of being. Or non-being. I wasn't in any state of shock. I was in . . . No. I wasn't in anything. I wasn't. All of me was sucked back through my life leaving no one where I should have been. My life didn't fall apart, it disappeared. I was not here those two or three hours in question, your honor. Didn't exist. I'd still be there –'

'Where?'

'Nowhere, if the bag lady hadn't punched me into being again.'

'You were very rough on her.'

'Yes, well, she caught me at a bad time.'

'Lady?' Someone pounding my shoulder. 'Lady?' Pound, pound. City dump breath. Shoulder in severe pain. Must have been hit for a long time. 'Lady, you home?' A black curtain lifted on blinding daylight. My eyes, wide-open, were transfixed by something in front of me. My hand. Straight out in front of me, in the most rigored of mortis, holding a peanut. Why the hell was I holding a peanut? Elephants swayed across the way. The zoo. I was at the zoo, holding a peanut out to the elephants. 'Lady.' Pound, pound.

'Stop that!' I screamed, swinging my peanut-holding arm around, whacking my tormentor off the bench. 'Leave me alone!'

She cowered on the ground, layered in exotic mixtures of clothing, trembling. I rubbed my sore arm. A counselor ushered his campers away from us.

'What the hell are you hitting me for?'

'You wasn't eating your nuts.'

'What's it to you?'

'You ain't eaten 'em. The animals ain't eatin' 'em. I figured maybe I could have 'em. I coulda stole 'em and you'd never known. You was gone.'

'Yeah.' How'd she know? 'Well, I'm back.'

'So?'

'So?'

'What about them nuts?'

I looked down. A full bag of peanuts rested on my lap.

'Yeah, sure.' I handed her the bag. 'Can't miss

what I never knew I had. Like Franklin's clients.
Right? Who's hurt? You're right, you could have
stolen them. But you,' I helped her up onto the bench,
'you have integrity. Character. Morality.'

'Damn right.' She cracked a nut with her back
teeth. The ones in front were missing.

I took a twenty out of my purse and tucked it into
her pocket. 'That's for honesty,' I said. 'It should
be rewarded. And dishonesty, dishonesty should be
punished.'

'Damn right.'

I stopped at the neighborhood grocery on the way
to Mac's dreaming of pâté, brie, a spinach crepe from
Nicole's bakery, and crisp French bread. I hadn't
eaten since six in the morning and my knees were
watery. My shopping cart shifted to automatic, heading straight for the cookies but I hit the brakes at the
yogurt. A small Dannon's plain should hold me until
Mac came home. It would be a shame to ruin my
appetite for the dinner he was making. I grabbed a
couple of diet pops, not knowing if there'd be any at
his house. It was strange not to know what he did or
didn't like. So much to learn. Did I have the energy to
begin all over again? Maybe it wouldn't be so exhausting if the other person helped make it work. Moving
up the steep hill of a relationship had to be easier on
tandem than unicycle, especially if the other person
wasn't peddling in the opposite direction.

Mac hadn't come back. I cleared the living room
table of the breakfast dishes. There were a few strawberries left from the morning and I sliced them into

the yogurt, stirring it around. Settling into a large chair in the living room, I stared out across the park. Now what? What does a person do when she finds out her husband and the father of her children is a crook? How about confronting him, Barbara? Isn't he allowed his day in court?

I called Franklin's campaign headquarters to get his speaking schedule. It was possible that after I broke into his office Franklin had warned his staff not to speak to me. But a young enthusiastic volunteer answered and nearly fell all over herself trying to get Mr Avers' wife the information she wanted. He was, she said, having lunch with a farmers' group and he was scheduled for a major fundraising dinner this evening. She gave me the name of his hotel complete with telephone and room number.

'Oh,' I said, by the by, 'I have that information Ashley wanted on the Governor's wine preference.' Mumbo-jumbo will voodoo you. 'Would you be a dear and give me her room number?' She did. Now, how did I guess Ashley would be with him? In an adjoining suite. Smug son of a bitch. Didn't even book rooms on separate floors.

I rested my hand on the phone. A battery operated clock, the antique hands set into the face of a polished piece of stone, clicked the seconds. Around and around. I pictured Franklin in his suite, closet filled with hand-tailored suits and Italian leather shoes. A man with expensive tastes and access to all the money he needed to live the good life. It wasn't right. Something had to be done, and I had to do it. But, besides

Franklin and me and the people he had robbed there were Rikki and Jason to consider. This would take some thinking. Another half hour passed before the idea came, an idea so clear and so right that I immediately picked up the phone and dialed Franklin's room. I took a huge spoonful of lukewarm yogurt while I waited.

'Franklin Avers here.' I swallowed the wrong way and started choking, coughing into the phone. 'Hello? Hello?'

'It's me,' I gasped, more air than voice. 'Wait.'

'Barbara? Is that you? Goddamnit, answer me!'

The coughing wouldn't stop. 'Went down my windpipe,' I gasped, rasping like the Godfather.

'Where the hell are you? I've been calling since yesterday.'

'Mrs Payne died.'

'What the hell were you doing in my office? You had no business going through my files. I want the key to my office back. Do you hear me?!'

'Just a minute.' I set the phone down, strolled to the kitchen, opened a can of pop, put some ice in a glass, and passed two other phones on my way back to the living room. 'Need a drink,' I said, slowly pouring the pop into the glass, taking a couple of sips. 'Now, as I was saying, Mrs Payne died.'

'What the fuck does that have to do with you breaking into my office and assaulting Miss Mumford and the receptionist?'

'She had this blue phony marble casket. I think she was the kind of woman who would have loved to be buried in a hand-crafted pine coffin. But, as you know, blue plastic was about all Mr Payne could afford.'

Franklin grew quiet. 'You went to her funeral?'

'It was the least I could do. Mr Payne came to our house two nights ago.'

'What the hell did he want?'

'Said he came over to tell you about Mrs Payne's death. But he really needed company.' Silence. 'Anyway, it seems Mrs Payne liked my writing so Mr Payne thought maybe I could write one of my "little articles" about her.'

'Barbara, tell me what you were doing in my office.'

'You know exactly what I was doing in your office, Franklin. I was trying to find out why money from a case you'd closed a few months ago had somehow not made its way into Mr Payne's pocket.'

'You don't know the first thing about this,' he said. 'This is a complex legal case. There are many legal matters still to be settled.'

'Oh, Franklin, I was expecting more from you. If not honesty, at least more creative excuses.' I took out my list of names and opened them on the table. 'All right, then what about the Cadbury case, or the . . .' I read them all, running them like a lighted fuse into the long silence on the other end. Somewhere over the phone a door opened and a woman called to him. I heard her ask him what was wrong. He must have waved her away because the door reclosed.

'Barbara, you have no idea what this is all about.' I

knew the tone of voice, it was the exasperated one he used while rubbing his eyes with thumb and forefinger, the one he used to buy time while he was regrouping for a new attack.

'Ooooo, goody! I *wov* when Papa Fwanklin expwains big business to wittle Bawbwa.'

'Christ, I'll never understand how I stayed with you as long as I did. Don't you understand? Nothing has been taken from those people.'

'I wonder if they'd agree.'

'Their cases could have dragged on for *years*, and even then they'd have no guarantee of settlement.' The front door opened and Mac walked in. He came over, planted a huge kiss square on my lips, then left me to the privacy of my phone call. Franklin kept talking. 'They don't expect their money yet. A third of it is mine, anyway. I'm just using the other temporarily until my campaign chest fills up. It's done all the time. Each client will be paid back, with interest. I can't believe you think any of this is wrong.'

That was it, then. No excuses, no reasons. He'd stolen the money, pure and simple. My soon-to-be ex-husband robbed from the poor and gave to himself. 'You're right about one thing, Franklin. I'll never understand how you stayed with me as long as you did, either. But right now, I'm grateful as hell you left.'

'You aren't going to do anything stupid?'

'Like go to the police? I'd have been there in two seconds if it weren't for the kids. I'm afraid we've done enough to them already. No, Franklin, I'm not off to the cops. I've thought of something much better.'

'Don't be stupid. You've liked your life well enough all these years – living in a fancy house, wearing fancy clothes, going fancy places. It's your fault I had to borrow for my campaign.'

'This too, Brutus?'

'You're pissed because I'm leaving you. You want to get even.'

'God, I love the way your mind works. The shortest distance between two convoluted points is a guilt trip through me.'

'Don't do a thing until I come home!'

'When are you coming home?'

'A week from Sunday.'

'Perfect. I'll be home. And I hope to have a wonderful surprise waiting.'

'Barbara! My future is at stake here.'

'And mine. And the kids. Who's on first, Franklin? Why is it always you?'

'I'm warning you –'

I hung up, shaking.

'You all right?' Mac came in with a couple of drinks and handed one to me.

'Thanks,' I said. 'That was Franklin. We had a little disagreement.' Mac tilted his head. 'All right, all right, we had a major blow-out.'

'Better.' He punched a stereo button and Vivaldi joined us. I closed my eyes, letting the madrigal take me over. Mac pulled up a chair next to me, trailing his finger tips along my arm. We were quiet for a very long time. 'What's this?' he asked. I opened my eyes. He'd been reading the list of clients' names and settlement amounts I'd left on the table. I grabbed it away.

'Nothing,' I said, flustered. Mac was always catching me off-guard. 'Lucinda Payne's name is on that list, Barbara.' I stuffed the list in my purse. 'Something about that whole business doesn't feel right to me.'

'What whole business?'

'There was a stipulation to dismiss in that file I copied for you. That means Lucinda Payne's case was settled. I don't know the amount of the settlement, but, judging by her casket, his clothing, and his car I don't think the Paynes ever saw any of that money.'

Mac was making the connections I was afraid he would. I wasn't going to lie to him, but I wasn't going to help him either. I sipped my drink trying to decide what to do.

'Barbara, word on the street is Franklin's having trouble funding his campaign.' Bingo!

'I thought you were the one who believed in coming right out and saying what you're thinking.'

'All right,' said Mac, 'I think Franklin's risking his ticket to become Congressman Avers.'

'Risking his ticket?'

'His license to practice law. I think Franklin is bleeding his accounts to foot the bill for his campaign.'

'I've got to go.' I searched the room for my shoes. 'Where are my shoes?'

'And I think you found out what he's doing and for some dumb reason, you're covering for him.'

'If Franklin were stealing, do you think I'd be dumb enough to put you onto the case?' I tore up the cushions, looked under the sofa. 'What did you do with my shoes?'

'Maybe you asked me to look up the Payne file because you wanted him to be found out.'

'Maybe you don't know what the hell you're talking about.'

'Why are you defending him? He's gone. He's out of your life. He's an arrogant, egocentric, pompous ass. And your shoes are over there under the desk where you left them.' I put them on while standing up which meant I was hopping around the room on one foot. I've had more dignified moments. 'I don't know why the hell you're helping him get away with this.'

'You don't know anything. You're so used to living with bad guys that you think everyone in a three-piece suit is a crook.'

'I'm going to follow up on this, Barb. I want you to know that. I can't walk away from something like this.'

The air went out of the room.

I could feel a line of energy connecting Mac and me. I stood there wanting him to hold me and make my world all better. And I knew he wanted that, too.

'That's exactly what I'm asking you to do, Mac.'

'He's hurting innocent people, Barb.'

I nodded and crossed the room to pick up my purse.

I didn't know I was crying until Mac reached up and wiped tears off my cheek.

'This isn't how I want things to go between us, Barbara.'

'No. Me neither.' I covered his hand with mine and pressed it against my face.

'Stay here.'

'I can't. This isn't about me or Franklin. You don't have children so maybe I can't explain this to you. But Rikki and Jason are a part of me the way nothing ever has been in my life. And I am not going to let Franklin or you or anyone else do something stupid that will ruin their young lives. Having a father go to jail can do that.'

'Maybe your kids are stronger than you think they are.'

'Maybe there are other ways to solve this.'

'You know I can't back away from this.'

'Don't hurt my children, Mac. I could never forgive you if you did.'

I drove west to the Edens, then due north for five hours until I reached the hotel nearest the kids' camp. In the morning I would take them out, away from their friends and activities, and tell them Franklin and I had separated. I didn't want them hearing it from friends. I didn't want them getting some gift-wrapped lie from Franklin. I would tell them Daddy didn't live home anymore. That I was sorry the marriage had broken up but that our lives would go on. All our lives. Most of all I would hug them and tell them I loved them, would always love them, and it was their choice whether they wanted to stay at camp or come home. I thought they would want to stay with their friends, but it was up to them.

And then I would drive back home to make preparations for Franklin's homecoming.

TWENTY-FOUR

Somewhere between the second and third case of champagne the party which had begun with the polite formality of a Sunday church meeting kicked off its shoes and loosened its tie. I'd invited Franklin's clients to bring their family and friends for a brunch celebration and by three o'clock the same people who had timidly approached the house at noon rollicked like a gathering of millionaire lottery winners.

It had been ages since I'd entertained. I fluttered around playing hostess, chatting, laughing, seeing the platters were kept filled by the catering staff. Every now and then I'd lean against the doorjamb, smiling at the happy noisy people swarming like locusts across platters of deli, whole smoked Lake Michigan coho salmons, omelets made to order at the buffet table by two chefs in tall white hats, a cornucopia of fresh fruit, cheese and fruit blintzes, baskets of toasted New York bagels and bialys, and bottomless pots of hot coffee. I was too excited to be hungry although I did sample thin slices of honeydew when I felt a twinge. I'd lost seven pounds the last few days, starting the night I tossed my cookies in Franklin's closet. I hadn't gone back in there to check things out. I reckoned his closet wasn't my problem any more.

Nothing warms a room as wonderfully as laughter and conversation and I was high on the sounds of people enjoying themselves. I'd had the caterer set up round tables in the living room so people wouldn't have to juggle dishes on their laps. Franklin *hated* eating off his lap so I figured he wouldn't mind the few hundred extra dollars it cost to have his clients comfortably seated. The floral centerpieces were inspired! Threaded among the baby orchids were travel brochures of Bora Bora, Tahiti, Maui, the Amazon, New Zealand, Australia. The stuff of dreams, these places could become a reality for my guests, especially with the five-thousand-dollar travel gift certificates to Mom's Travel Agency I'd enclosed with their settlement checks. I figured Franklin owed them at least that.

There wasn't enough money in his campaign account to cover all their checks although the large downstate donations he'd deposited during the week helped considerably. The rest of the money came from the sale of stocks, real estate investments, our home, artwork, possessions. The money was there in one form or another. It was amazing how quickly I'd been able to turn most of our assets into cash and arrange for the conversion of the rest. Franklin had me signing family papers for so many years that it was no problem to provide his 'signature' on all the necessary documents. He couldn't say anything without risking disclosure which would lead to disbarment which would lead to disaster. Not that he didn't deserve it – may sex give him itchy hives in unscratchable places – but the children didn't. Rikki, Jason, and I would have to start over. I was going to be their mother the way it felt natural to be their mother. Not the way I thought my mother would have done it. Not the way Franklin might or might not have approved of it. There was no percentage in perfection. I didn't know what my gut way of mothering would be but, good or bad, it would be all mine. I hoped it would be good and I prayed it wasn't too late.

I'd been in the kitchen checking on the dessert trays when I heard the applause begin. I raced to the doorway in time to catch the look on Franklin's face. The underlying horror of walking into a house full of his clients – *this* house full of *these* clients – wasn't quite masked by his attempt at a smile. He turned a peculiar shade of green.

'For he's a jolly good fellow . . .' I began, marching from the kitchen through the tables toward Franklin. The others picked up the tune, clapping in time, cheering loudly at the end. Ashley stood statue-still behind him in the doorway. He must have brought her along for strength. He always did like an audience. I threaded my arm through Franklin's, smiled my sweetest smile at Ashley while mouthing 'Thank you', then turned to the guests.

'Take a good look,' I said to them, 'you've actually made a politician speechless.' They laughed. I was on a roll. Franklin's arm felt rigid as an iron bar but he dared not yank it away from me in front of this adoring crowd. He couldn't risk them wondering why he wasn't as happy as they were.

'Franklin was so excited that the recent reorganization of court calls helped settle all your cases in such a short period of time,' total bull double-speak but only Franklin knew that, 'that he couldn't think of a nicer way to celebrate.' I picked up the packet of envelopes off the credenza and waved them in the air. 'And now, Ladies and Gentlemen, the envelopes please.'

I passed them one at a time to Franklin. The group cheered as he called each client's name, handing them their envelope and shaking their hand like a dean at graduation.

'Speech! Speech! Speech!' they chanted until Franklin was forced to say something. Anything.

'Um,' he cleared his throat. 'I'm delighted to see you all here. Um . . . I'm afraid I'm exhausted from my week in Springfield so, if you'll excuse me, I'll just have a few words with Mrs Avers, and we'll be back to join you.'

I signaled to the waiters to begin dessert service then let Franklin lead me through the tables and down the hall to the den. Once we got there, I yanked my arm out of his hand. His fingers left angry red imprints on my skin.

'I could kill you,' he said.

'You shouldn't really say that in front of witnesses.' He spun around. Ashley had followed us into the den and was closing the door behind her.

'Afraid we were necking?' I asked her.

She smirked and slithered to Franklin's side. Her smirk was a lot like Franklin's smirk. I suspected they found many of the same things funny: plague, pestilence, famine. I could picture them in bed, two iron-hard bodies clashing and smirking. Made me chortle, it did.

'Barbara,' he said, 'do you have any idea what you've done?'

'What *I've* done? You really don't see what *you've* done, do you, Franklin? I was wondering how you were going to turn this one around. You steal money from people who have suffered terrible tragedies and then have the *nerve* to tell me it's my fault my life's been torn to shreds.'

Franklin shoved his hands in his pants pockets, I suspected to keep from hitting me. He paced the small room.

'You never have understood power, Barbara. Your father could have told you that the same rules don't apply to the powerful.'

'Don't you dare mention my father.'

'This is the way elections are run and won and if we thought you were more interested and sympathetic, we would have tried to explain that to you.'

'We?'

'Oh, don't play dumb, Barbara. It doesn't suit you.'

'Ashley, dear,' I said, 'what if Franklin loses?'

She laughed, ever so amused. 'Franklin is a winner, Mrs Avers.'

I sat in the large chair at Franklin's desk and

swiveled thoughtfully. 'You didn't answer. What if Franklin loses?'

'The only way he'll lose is if you bring this little matter to light.'

'This "little matter" of him stealing money from clients for campaign funds? If he's such a shoo-in, why couldn't he raise money legitimately?'

'Have you thought about your children?' she asked. 'Worse than Franklin will suffer, your children will suffer.'

'Noooo,' I cleaned my fingernails with his letter opener, 'I never thought about the kids.'

Franklin picked up right on cue. 'That's right, Barbara, I did this for them. To give them a father they can be proud of. Senator Avers.' His truth is marching on. Wave them ol' stars and stripes, that's it, that's it good, good. What turned my stomach was he believed it. I handed him the folder marked Halsey Investigations.

'Did you do this for the children, too?' I asked. He opened the envelope. Franklin and Ashley were big on hand-holding and snuggling in intimate booths over candlelit dinners. Especially in Kansas City where they liked to jet for a night or two when they were supposed to be in Springfield. 'Did you do *this* to make the children proud, Franklin?'

'You can't understand, can you?' He threw the photos on the desk. 'Are you so fucking stupid?'

'Not any more. How come no one in this room will answer my question? What if you lose? Does Imelda here still want you punching her old voting hole?'

He leaned over the desktop at me. 'Don't be crude.'

'Right. Although, I do think it's an issue you two might consider. I don't think she's the type to hang around a loser, Franklin. Not like some of us who signed on for better or for worse.'

'You think you're going to keep me, Barbara.'

'I find the idea nauseating.'

'Although,' said Ashley, 'it would be better for the campaign if you two stayed together until after Franklin was elected.'

I leaned back and put my feet up on the desk top. 'And would the children live with you?'

'Of course they'd be welcome to visit any time,' she said, not realizing the question had been intended for Franklin.

'Oh, no, Ashley,' I said, 'I think they'll be ever so much happier with you. They don't seem to want me around any more. Franklin's helped them see what a ridiculous figure of a woman I am. What a large ridiculous figure of a woman I am. I'll take them holidays and summers, of course. But they'll be happier with their senator of a father and his thin new wife.' Ashley turned ashen.

Franklin was missing this entirely, hearing only what he needed to hear.

'Are you saying you won't take this matter to the press?'

'That's what I'm saying, Franklin. I think you're right about the children. Growing up is tough enough without having a crook for a father.'

'I'm glad you're being sensible.'

'Oh, Franklin, I'm nothing if not sensible.' I swung my legs down and took my ledger out of his desk drawer. 'You might want to look at these figures before you go back out to your adoring clients.' I opened the page to the impressive numbers. 'This, you see, is the amount you have paid out to each of them.' He came around the desk and I gave him his chair. He was going to need it. 'I gave them each the full settlement amount, *including* your third. So awfully nice of you to have waived your fee. Then, too, there is the matter of the little travel gifts from you. You really should try and control your generous nature,' I said. 'The house sold almost immediately and I had our broker sell all our stocks and . . . well it's all there for you to see. Now I should get back to our guests. I trust you'll find your own way out.'

He shook his head over the page of numbers. 'I can't believe you did this to me. This is the end of everything.'

'Now that,' I said, doing a Loretta Young out the door, 'depends entirely on one's point of view.'

FEBRUARY

150–?

TWENTY-FIVE

Frigid air whipped our faces as we abandoned the warm church for Michigan Avenue. I threw my arms around Rikki and Jason, leaning into the gusting winds, struggling toward the corner. It was hard to take a breath, but I swallowed little gulps of air to rid my nose and mouth of the cloying sweetness of Stanford's aftershave/cologne/hair gel. I'd touched cheeks with him after the memorial service, nodding politely at the lady affixed to his arm. Not the size four after all but more near a 9/10. It was obvious she adored Stanford. Took all kinds. Perhaps he would be happier in this marriage. The post office had forwarded Franklin's invitation to me by mistake and I sent it on to him. He'd had the good sense not to come.

I glanced at Rikki and Jason as we gripped hands and raced across Michigan Avenue to Water Tower Place. 'Button up,' I thought, and 'put on your gloves, your hat, your earmuffs,' but the thoughts went unspoken. The children had sat me down one evening and explained that if *I* felt cold, I was free to do what I needed to do to become warm. They were old enough to be given the same right. I'd told them it was hard to break a seventeen-year pattern of mothering and I wanted them to be understanding if I slipped up now and then. In a way, it was a relief not to be held responsible for every little detail of every one else's life. 'They'll get sick,' warned the old Barbara. But so far there'd been no colds, frostbite, chilblains, pneumonia, flu. When I'd forget and begin a sentence 'Why don't you . . .', as in 'Why don't you read where there's more light?', 'Why don't you put on your slippers?', they'd make a face to remind me.

In turn, they stopped trying to lay guilt trips on me about meals not made or laundry not done. I taught them how to use the stove and washing machine and we set up a rotating work schedule. When they complained, I told them they couldn't be treated like adults when it suited them and as children when they didn't want household responsibility. 'It's either/or,' I said. 'And it's your choice.' They picked adulthood.

It took us a few months to begin living together as three people who respected and loved each other. We had some tough old demons to exorcise. The kids helped me apartment hunt and we settled on a cozy six-room flat on Armitage near Lincoln. The apartment hadn't been renovated yet, which was why I could afford it, and it meant ferocious drafts when the wind blew in from the northwest. But the place was convenient to the kids' new schools, the city, and especially the bus lines. Stranded without a car for the first time in their lives, Rikki and Jason quickly learned their way around CTA schedules.

Saturday visitors mobbed the Water Tower escalators and the three of us crowded together for the ride up into the mall.

'All right,' I said, 'where should we eat lunch?'

'Mikey D's!' said Jason.

'It's all breaded, fried, and fattening,' said Rikki.

'They have salads.'

'There's nothing there I want to eat.'

I smoothed back an errant strand of Jason's hair. Was he nearly as tall as I was? 'Tell you what, Jase, what if I take Rikki to the Eaternity? When you finish your hamburger, come on down and have dessert with us.'

Rikki got in line at the order counter while I staked out a window table whose occupants were finishing their second after-lunch cigarettes. One of them gave me that 'Where do I know you from?' look I'd been seeing since the *Globe* began using my photo. My column ran four times a week now and a few papers across the country had picked it up which brought in a few extra dollars. For some reason, probably desperation or a low speakers' budget, local groups had begun inviting me to speak. I was awful at first, rushing through a half hour's material in ten minutes, but I became better each time and the money bought us little extras like shoes, sheets, and lunch at a Water Tower cafeteria. We weren't rich, but I was able to pay our rent and put food on the table. It helped me understand another part of Franklin. He was right that being the provider was a heavy responsibility. But what he never mentioned was the feeling of self-sufficiency and freedom built into each paycheck.

The smokers got up to leave as Rikki came with our tray.

'You all right?' she asked, sliding into the booth, unloading the tray onto the table.

'Sure. Why?'

She shrugged. 'Oh, I thought, you know, maybe hearing a sermon about Sarajane and all might have been hard on you.'

I reached across the table and took her hands in mine. My mother's sapphire and diamond ring sparkled on her finger. Rikki had stopped biting her fingernails in its honor. A few of the pieces the kids and I didn't like were sold to help us get started in our new life.

'No, Rikki, today wasn't hard on me. I learned to live with Sarajane's death a long time ago. Today was a time for people who loved her to get together and honor her memory. It was bittersweet, but not painful.' I squeezed her hands. 'And thanks,' I said.

'For what?'

'For thinking to ask about my feelings. It helps when people you love care about you.'

'Aren't you mad Daddy didn't come?'

'He didn't love Sarajane, honey. He didn't even like her. Besides, what he does or doesn't do doesn't affect me anymore.'

We nibbled our salads.

'I had a fight with Daddy last weekend.' I swirled my lettuce around and kept quiet. Didn't want to be the nosy ex-wife pumping the kids for information. Tell me, tell me. 'He took us to a sushi bar, and you *know* how Jason loves sushi.'

'Especially if it's made by McDonalds.' We laughed.

'Right. But Miss you-know-who just loooooves sushi. Anyway, Jase and I were loading up on rice, which is about all we could find to eat, and Daddy told me that if I didn't watch what I ate I'd grow up looking like you.'

'Shit,' I said under my breath.

'So I told him I thought you were beautiful.' I smiled, loving those words from that particular mouth. 'And he got this dumb look on his face and pointed to Miss you-know-who and said, "Now, that's beautiful." He makes me so mad. Dragging her along like she's part of our family. Like he can't stand being alone with Jason and me. I mean, he never talks to us when she's around except to tell us what not to do. So I said, and I know it probably wasn't right, but I said, "Well, she's not as beautiful as some of your other lovers." '

My world went on hold. I stared at my daughter's mouth and forced myself to focus on the words. Tell me, tell me.

'And Daddy turned all red and grabbed my wrist and twisted it until I yelled and told me I had quite a mouth on me. And I told him *that* part I'd gotten from him. And I think he was almost going to hit me but there were all those people around so he threw some money on the table and stormed out with Miss you-know-who running after him.'

Rikki looked at me with those huge brown doe eyes. This was not easy for her. 'Daddy had lovers before

Miss . . . before Ashley,' she said, quietly. 'Way before. Lizbeth Raleigh's mother saw him downtown with a friend of hers. When I asked him, he said it was business. But then Lizbeth told me other things about him and that woman. This time I gave him the names of places he'd been seen and I told him I knew what he was doing. I really hoped he would tell me I was wrong, that he wasn't fooling around at all. But he decided to take me into his confidence. Told me the trouble the two of you were having.'

'How . . . how long ago was this?'

'I'd just turned fourteen. I remember he said Juliet married at fourteen so he felt I was old enough to understand adult problems. And to keep an adult secret. I mean, he made me feel so grown up.'

Three years ago? We weren't having problems three years ago. Oh, weren't we, ducks? Puff, puff. 'And you've been carrying this around with you all this time? Oh, Rikki. How could he have done that to you?'

Fat tears rolled slowly down her cheeks. 'He made it sound so logical. You didn't give him the love he needed. You were so busy with Sarajane, and organizations, and us that you didn't have time for him. That's why he spent so much time away from home.'

'I think he had that the wrong way around. I was trying to fill the hours he was away.'

'I know that now. But I didn't then. And when you started putting on all that weight I thought well here's the proof of what he's been saying all along. You just didn't care about him.' She sobbed quietly and I moved around to her side, hugging her, rocking her. 'I . . . I'm sorry. I p . . . probably shouldn't h . . . have told you.'

'Shhhh. It's all right. Shhhh. Oh, honey, I'm so glad you got that heavy secret off your chest.'

What a miracle it was to hold onto this child I feared I had lost, to stroke her hair and comfort her. We'd declared an uneasy truce when she returned from camp. Both of us promised to start fresh. At first she talked about going to live with Franklin and as much as it tore me up inside I told her it was her choice. I also told her I loved her and would miss her if she left. She waited, perhaps feeling his indifference. Through the months, we learned to trust each other and care, and love. She stayed.

'I – I just didn't want you to believe what he'd said about him having an affair because you gained weight.'

'Thanks, sweetheart. I think I probably knew that.'

Jason slid in across from us, sneaking a bag of fries out of his jacket. He wasn't supposed to bring food into the restaurant but I kept quiet. If they threw him out we'd meet him later. It was nice living with people who accepted responsibility for their actions. Rikki tooted her nose loudly into a napkin.

'What's with her?' he asked.

'Girl talk,' I said.

He rolled his eyes. 'Can I have money for dessert?'

'Where do you put all the stuff you eat?' He trotted

off for a sprinkle-covered donut and I kissed Rikki's forehead. 'I love you,' I said.

'Enough to take me shopping?'

'Don't press your luck.'

'Oh, Lord, smell that garlic bread.' Kathlyn bounded into the tiny kitchen, her arms laden with bakery boxes. 'I do believe I've died and gone straight to Italian heaven.'

'I told you not to bring anything. Where am I going to store all that stuff?'

'Store it? Honey, you live with two teenagers. It won't last the night.' She was already in motion, putting down the boxes, wiping bread crumbs off the counter, cleaning out the sink strainer. 'Gregory? Gregory? Come on in here and meet my friend.' A man in his late twenties, with biceps the size of Kathlyn's waist, walked into the room. 'Gregory, this is Barbara. Barbara, Gregory.' I wiped my wet hands on my apron and we shook. I think I felt something break.

Jason and one of his new friends came barreling into the kitchen clutching hockey sticks and pucks, asking Gregory to autograph them. It appeared Gregory was some sort of hockey star. I shooed the three of them out of the kitchen. Jason's popularity at school would rise a few notches on Monday.

'So, who's coming for dinner?' asked Kathlyn, tearing apart lettuce leaves, tossing them into the bowl.

'Oh, you and Gregory. Jason and his friend. Rikki and her friend. And me and my friend.'

I picked up the garlic bread and brought it out to the

table. She was waiting for me, knife in hand, when I returned.

'All right, all right,' I said. 'Mac's coming.'

'Well, it's about time. I've had just about all I could take of your platonic relationship.'

'I didn't say it was anything more than that.'

'Don't have to. Your face is redder than this pimento.'

'It's not like I don't see him every day at work.'

'It's not the days that count, Honeybuns, it's the nights. I'll finish the salad, you go smear on some lipstick.'

'Yes, Mom.'

The dinner was fabulous. Even Kathlyn sampled a bit of everything. She'd decided she liked herself at a hundred twenty and was maintaining it by never letting herself gain more than two pounds. 'Two pounds are possible, five pounds are a problem.'

I'd stopped 'dieting' and started eating only what I needed each day to keep me from feeling hungry. I didn't eat out often but when I did I ordered what I wanted and cut the portion in half, taking the other half home. If it was something that wouldn't keep well, I left it. I learned to overcome feeling obligated to uneaten food. At home, I microwaved Weight Watchers dinners and used up some Nutri-Systems pre-packaged meals I still had around. I cut the Diet Center's 'apple a day' into paper-thin slices as my evening treat while I read. And each day I drank eight glasses of water and took my multi and B complex vitamins. Lately I'd added calcium. I doubt any of the weight-loss programs would have approved my methods, but they suited me for now.

The *Globe* was a two-mile walk each way and I did it in just over half an hour. Pounds came off slowly but steadily. I no longer allowed the upward or downward movement of the scale's needle to determine my mood each day. I expected my weight to bob up after my once a month treat of brunch at Cricket's or pasta at Pronto, but then it would start back down again. I didn't know where my weight would finally settle. I did know I'd never be 105 again. The strange thing was I couldn't remember, really, why it had ever mattered as much as it had. My need for cigarettes, too, had all but disappeared. I was able to go one, maybe two days straight without thinking about smoking and probably could go longer except for the smokers around me at work. The craving would pop up at odd times – after a meal, while talking on the phone – then disappear just as quickly.

Jason set the table, decorating the tablecloth with rock specimens he'd cut and polished at Mac's. Rikki assembled a huge antipasta with circles of pimentos, proscuitto, olives, artichoke hearts, and forty other delicacies that set our food budget back two decades. It was almost too beautiful to eat but we'd manage. Mac arrived bearing bottles of Italian red, a long stem rose and an enticingly erotic kiss. Kathlyn whisked him away to meet her friend.

I still shuddered when I thought how close I had come to losing Mac. He did follow up on the Payne case. Luckily it was after my little party and Mr Payne told Mac he'd received his settlement. Mac called to tell me he was letting the matter drop but made it clear he wouldn't have if Franklin hadn't dropped out of the election. Mac still thought I should have turned Franklin in. But he understood I didn't see I had a choice in the matter. Once we made peace with each other, Mac began spending time at our place, getting to know Rikki and Jason. And me. It had taken us a few months but we'd finally reached a time when it felt right to move on.

I sat at the head of the table, watching my family and friends enjoying the food, wine, each other. I was more at home in this drafty little apartment than I had ever been anywhere in my life. Mac reached over and squeezed my hand. It was time.

In a little while, Kathlyn would leave, dropping Jason and Rikki at Franklin's for the weekend. The way things went, Franklin usually managed to bring them back by Saturday. The first couple of times he'd stayed home with them. Then he started leaving them alone while he went out on a date which he always insisted was business. His apartment was in an unfamiliar neighborhood and the kids would call me and beg to come back home. Now, to everyone's relief, Franklin just brought them back and spared us all any excuse.

It would be nice to have a weekend alone with Mac, but we would do the best we could with one night. And, if that night went well, we could try another. And another. But, for now, we had tonight and for now it would be enough.

A selection of bestsellers from Headline

FICTION

TALENT	Nigel Rees	£3.99 ☐
A BLOODY FIELD BY SHREWSBURY	Edith Pargeter	£3.99 ☐
GUESTS OF THE EMPEROR	Janice Young Brooks	£3.99 ☐
THE LAND IS BRIGHT	Elizabeth Murphy	£3.99 ☐
THE FACE OF FEAR	Dean R Koontz	£3.50 ☐

NON-FICTION

CHILD STAR	Shirley Temple Black	£4.99 ☐
BLIND IN ONE EAR	Patrick Macnee and Marie Cameron	£3.99 ☐
TWICE LUCKY	John Francome	£4.99 ☐
HEARTS AND SHOWERS	Su Pollard	£2.99 ☐

SCIENCE FICTION AND FANTASY

WITH FATE CONSPIRE The Destiny Makers 1	Mike Shupp	£3.99 ☐
A DISAGREEMENT WITH DEATH	Craig Shaw Gardner	£2.99 ☐
SWORD & SORCERESS 4	Marion Zimmer Bradley	£3.50 ☐

All Headline books are available at your local bookshop or newsagent, or can be ordered direct from the publisher. Just tick the titles you want and fill in the form below. Prices and availability subject to change without notice.

Headline Book Publishing PLC, Cash Sales Department, PO Box 11, Falmouth, Cornwall TR10 9EN, England.

Please enclose a cheque or postal order to the value of the cover price and allow the following for postage and packing:
UK: 60p for the first book, 25p for the second book and 15p for each additional book ordered up to a maximum charge of £1.90
BFPO: 60p for the first book, 25p for the second book and 15p per copy for the next seven books, thereafter 9p per book
OVERSEAS & EIRE: £1.25 for the first book, 75p for the second book and 28p for each subsequent book.

Name ....

Address ....

....

....